THE CHRIST-HAUNTED LANDSCAPE
Faith and Doubt in Southern Fiction

THE
CHRIST-HAUNTED
LANDSCAPE

Faith and Doubt in Southern Fiction

BY

Susan Ketchin

University Press of Mississippi
JACKSON

97 96 95 94   4 3 2

The paper in this book meets the guidelines for permanence and durability of
the Committee on Production Guidelines for Book Longevity of the Council on
Library Resources.

Library of Congress Cataloging-in-Publication data on page 408
British Library Cataloging-in-Publication data available

To

CLYDE

Contents

Acknowledgments

The making of a book, like the raising of a child, is by its very nature a collaborative venture. The contributions of many people over time—scholars and storytellers, editors and independent bookstore owners, lovers of fiction, friends and family—are manifest in this book. I am deeply grateful to all who have given of themselves during the research and writing of this manuscript, a process which began over four years ago.

I am especially grateful to:

Kelly Atkins and Paula Penick, for their enthusiasm and tireless help early on, when the book was little more than a dream; and to Hannah Byrum for her inspired editorial assistance with all aspects of the manuscript in the critical months before the book went to press;

To my editor, JoAnne Prichard, for her steadfast commitment and her true stories that would invariably assure me in uncertain times that all would turn out just fine; to Anne Stascavage and Ginger Tucker for their editorial and organizational help, and to Carol Cox for her careful copyediting of the manuscript; her letter of encouragement in the final stages of labor was that of a poet;

To Louis Rubin, for his musical prose, his faith in generations of fiction writers, his faith in me;

To Sally Fitzgerald for her steadfast and brilliant work in bringing Flannery O'Connor to me and to the world, for her generous spirit and eloquent reminiscences;

To Elizabeth Kirk and the Ninth Coolidge Research Colloquium, Cambridge, MA for providing a congenial balance of companionship, solitude, and intellectual challenge that enabled creative work on this book to flourish;

To the Friday Lunch Bunch, for their lively, if irreverent theology, wit, and knowledge of things hoped for;

To Susan Roth, without whose faith and help this book would not have been written;

To Bill Brettmann who knows the value of naming things; to John Justice, Frances O'Roark, Nancy Olson, Scott Byrd, Joe and Ann Mann, Ray Person, Bill Coolidge, Gary Hawkins, and Rolf and Ronnie Lynton, for their insightful readings of parts of the manuscript, for encouraging me in my desire to seek truth in the world of the passionate imagination;

To Iris Hill, Alex Harris, and the Center for Documentary Studies for their loving attention to the transformative power of word, image, and music; especially to Bill Butler and Darnelle Arnoult, true artists and "real professionals";

To Nanci Kincaid and Tim and Katie McLaurin for their quiet heroism;

To Jan Tedder and Jim Henderson and Tom and Laurie Scheft for their stories;

To Eric Bates and *Southern Exposure* Magazine for enabling me to read good fiction by many talented southern writers and get paid for it;

To my students over the years; what they taught me laid the groundwork for this book;

To Catherine Houghton, and all the community of women and men at St. Bartholomew's Church who have felt a longing for God in memory, story, and song;

To Melba Brandes, whose stories of her childhood in Mississippi inspired delight and sadness, and hope, amidst loss, for things unseen, the basis for this book;

To all the authors in this book who gave so generously of their time, their genius, and their hearts;

Most of all, I am grateful to my family, to Susan Truma, Lila, Oma, my brother, Bo, my daughter, Catherine, and my husband, whose continuing love and support, wit, and patience have sustained me and given me life.

Introduction

A little more than a generation ago, Flannery O'Connor made an astute observation about herself and her fellow southerners: "By and large," she said, "people in the South still conceive of humanity in theological terms. While the South is hardly Christ-centered, it is most certainly Christ-haunted. The Southerner who isn't convinced of it is very much afraid that he may have been formed in the image and likeness of God." Still earlier in this century, H. L. Mencken had written, more vituperatively, that the South consists of a "cesspool of Baptists, a miasma of Methodists, snake charmers, phony real estate operators, and syphilitic evangelists." Although it might be argued that O'Connor and Mencken were exaggerating a bit, there is much evidence to suggest that they were then—and are still today—on to something.

Ninety percent of southerners identified themselves as Protestant as against sixty percent of those from other regions, according to a recent survey by sociologist John Shelton Reed. In that same study, cited in Robert R. Moore's "Literature and Religion," in the *Encyclopedia of Southern Culture*, Reed also noted that there is more agreement in belief and practice among southern Protestants than among non-southern Protestants or Catholics.

That old-time religion, evangelical Protestantism, has always been a dominant and distinctive force in southern history and culture. As Alfred Kazin has pointed out, for generations of Southerners, religion constituted a way of life; it was "the most traditional and lasting form of southern community." The power of southern religion had its origins in the South's unique history of close ties to the land, of slavery, and of defeat in war. For southerners, the "loss of the Civil War was a religious crisis," Kazin maintains. Southerners have remained "obsessed with the elements of blood, pain, and sacrifice in the Christian story," he argues, because they "never quite got over a sense of guilt—this not about the injustice of slavery, but about the uncertain personal transgressions, whatever these could have been, that alone explained why the devout and God-fearing Confederacy could have gone down in defeat."

The distinguishing features of this religious tradition are its strict adherence to biblical teachings and private morality, the notion of a real and active presence of God and Satan in the world, the belief in a factual existence of heaven and hell, and an emphasis on preaching the gospel and saving souls. Strong Calvinistic doctrines such as the absolute sovereignty of God and the depravity of human beings, the soul's salvation by grace alone, and the infathomability of Divine Will constitute a significant underpinning of southern evangelicalism. But Charles Reagan Wilson writes, as compelling as these doctrines are, they all rest upon the conviction that the individual's personal experience of and relationship to God is of ultimate importance. In addition, this religion also stresses individual free will: the doctrine that the individual is terrifyingly free to choose to do good or evil. Thus, to be born again, to be purified through the individual's acceptance of the action of God's grace, is often characterized as the central and defining religious experience of one's life. For many southerners, the experience of failure and disgrace after the Civil War as well as the unshakable conviction of being misjudged became interwoven with these Calvinist doctrines of Divine Will operating in all things.

Historically, southern children were immersed in this intense tradition, hearing from the cradle onward ancient tales of bliss, sin, guilt, and redemption from the Old and New Testaments, with their many layers of historical and psychological meaning and rich use of symbol and archetype. In earlier days, much of this saturation might have taken place in tent revivals, camp meetings, hell-fire preachings and revivals, at snake-handling rituals, or more likely then as now, in a church or Sunday school, in vacation Bible school, or in prayer meetings. What was most significant to the development of the southerner's imagination, whether he or she attended church or not, was that Bible stories were woven into everyday experience, told as part of daily life, weekdays and Sundays. They informed the worldview of all, believers and nonbelievers alike. Doris Betts writes, "Most southern writers would agree with William Faulkner, who said his childhood occurred against such a strong religious background that he absorbed Christianity as if by osmosis. As Faulkner said in the *Paris Review*, "My life was passed, my childhood, in a very small Mississippi town and that was part of my background. I grew up with that. I assimilated that, took that in without even knowing it. It's just there. It has nothing to do with how much of it I might believe or disbelieve—it's just there."

Along with this immersion in an intense religious culture, most people who have grown up in the South are heirs to the rich storytelling tradition common in agrarian, rural cultures. Many southerners have heard countless stories about the people they know and those they are connected to, past and present; these stories form the invisible sinews that hold family, community and land together over generations.

Imaginative southerners throughout the region's history have attempted in some significant way to deal with this potent cultural heritage. The task was not an easy one, for it was a heritage fraught with painful contradictions: on the one hand, it provided for the writer a sustaining sense of kinship, identity, community, and continuity; on the other, the region's legacies of violence, slavery, poverty, and defeat engendered an undeniable sense of tragedy and alienation. As a result, the southern novelist has been concerned with nothing less than the soul's salvation or loss to eternity. William Faulkner, Richard Wright, Allen Tate, and many other notable writers in the first half of this century were haunted by this sense of paradox. Of Faulkner, Kazin writes, "William Faulkner accepted the South as fevered and complex. . . . His vision is as unrelenting a vision as anything can be. . . . [It] conveys a sense of being trapped, in direct trouble, forever on the very edge of existence. Yet, what is never doubted in his fiction is humankind's consuming yearning for God." Robert Brinkmeyer has argued in *Three Catholic Writers of the Modern South*, that Allen Tate, Caroline Gordon, Walker Percy and others derived meaning and purpose from their traditional southern upbringing, and many began to explore in their art the means to reinvigorate their lives with this knowledge.

In the fifties and early sixties, the modern South, along with the rest of the country, became an increasingly secularized and scientific society, with the resulting threat that cherished values of family, community, and place would be eroded. Yet writers such as Robert Penn Warren, Katherine Anne Porter, William Styron and Ernest Gaines continued to concern themselves with these values and to explore the tragic sense and high drama of their own and their culture's religion.

As Brinkmeyer has pointed out, much of the great fiction we've come to associate with the southern literary landscape of the early to middle part of the century can be understood to have resulted from the interplay, the pressure and resistance, between dichotomies in the southern writer's changing culture and self. It is from such tension that great art often arises. Brinkmeyer stresses, for example, that it was the tension between Walker Percy's secular consciousness, which was firmly rooted in the twentieth-century southern landscape and traditional stoic ideals, and his desire to restore "myth, meaning, and mystery to what he saw as a morally irresponsible world" that led him to turn to the Catholic church. In describing her own struggle between her identities as a southerner and a Catholic, Flannery O'Connor wrote, "The writer must wrestle with it like Jacob with the angel until he has extracted a blessing."

The legacy left by William Faulkner, Flannery O'Connor, Walker Percy and others, then, is complex and provocative, one of high literary achievement wrought out of a profound engagement and intense quarrel with their particular history and region, a uniquely rich and contradictory culture that had at once both defined and tormented them. The power of these writers' fiction for us lies in no small measure in their struggles with important issues of identity and meaning within the larger context of their religion.

Today, the region that has produced such great literature is undergoing dramatic change. With the far-reaching social and political upheaval of the 1960s, the increasing urbanization and industrialization of recent years, and the election of two white southerners to the White House with strong backing from black southerners, many southerners have wondered if, for better or worse, the South is losing its distinctiveness and identity. Is the South becoming the no-South? Although it is impossible to tell the implications of such a cultural transformation as it is taking place, I am inclined to agree with historian George Tyndall and literary scholar Louis Rubin when they point out that throughout the area's history, "the end of the line" has often been predicted, but "the South has long had a habit of incorporating seeming disruptive change within itself and continuing to be the South." Today, though individual southerners' circumstances may differ greatly, the similarities among them are still striking. The region still exerts a strong influence on its inhabitants and commands their loyalties, for as Rubin observes, "Genuine human communities, as contrasted with mere economic and social combinations, are hard to come by in this world, and that is what the South has been." Thus Mary Ward Brown can still describe the southern community she sees today as "the southern Bible Belt, where people talk about God the way they talk about the weather, about His will and His blessings, about why He lets things happen."

Although southern identity has remained distinctive, the political and social changes of the 1960s created a watershed in southern thought. After the 1960s, old assumptions of the defeated, tragic South were seriously challenged. What, Fred Hobson asks, was the writer of the seventies and eighties to do with a suddenly "Superior South"—optimistic, forward-looking, more virtuous, now threatening to become more prosperous and politically powerful? "Success" would require new voices, and less reliance on—or obsession with—the past. Hobson notes that today, the southern writer, like other contemporary American writers, must grapple with age-old human yearnings in a rapidly changing, postmodern world, a world in which issues of order, structure, and meaning are constantly being raised, and all the old assumptions about the world and humankind are being called into question.

As I pondered the significance of all this, the idea for this book was born. As a fifth-generation southerner of Scots-Irish ancestry who was raised until adolescence in an austere, "hell-fire and brimstone" church, I am a "recovering Calvinist." I am also a passionate reader of fiction, and I have found along with many others that the mythic visions of writers such as Faulkner, O'Connor, Porter, and Percy have provided profound insights into and provocative questions about my own life, serving as both balm and torment to my southern soul. As I read them and struggled with these questions, I wondered to what extent, if any, today's writers who were born and raised and are now living and working in the South are engaged in those same questions and are feeling the same tensions that so shaped the fiction of the great southern writers of the past. What role has religious faith or religious seeking played in the fiction I read and in the lives of today's writers? How, I wondered, has religion as it was taught and practiced here distorted, enhanced, shaped the artist's imagination and vision? Are there writers living and working in the South today who are struggling with issues of identity and meaning in their lives and in their art? Do the Bible's stories, symbols, and language still have influence? What tensions between culture, particularly religious culture, and artistic vision face the writer today? What, in Flannery O'Connor's words, "spurs" the writer to tell stories? Does the writing—or the reading—of fiction have the power within itself to be redemptive? Some of these questions were asked to writers of a generation or two ago; some new ones have arisen: Has our secular world in this late part of the twentieth century made obsolete the validity of any religious concerns in (or out of) fiction?

I decided to go directly to the source. I would interview the writers themselves about their faith and their fiction, their religious culture and their art. I would seek out writers whose work, in my opinion and in the general critical opinion of others, had great literary merit and distinctive, interesting voices, who seemed to grapple with religious issues consistently throughout the body of their work, and who do so primarily in works of fiction, rather than in nonfiction or poetry. Though focusing on writers whose religious concerns seemed to have arisen from the predominant tradition of Protestantism, I would also include Catholicism since it had been so influential in the fiction of many of the South's most noted writers. (I decided to save other religious perspectives, which have been less salient in this region, for another book. The works of Steven Stern and others writing fiction from a southern Jewish perspective, for example, are interesting and worth noting). With one exception, the writers I talked with were born and raised in what historically has been called the South (Sandra Hollin Flowers was born in the Southwest); all claim southern family and ancestry. Each has been living in the South for twenty years or more.

What such a selection process revealed was an almost overwhelming wealth of talent on the contemporary southern literary scene. Thus it is inevitable that many writers of outstanding literary achievement will be left out; these include Josephine Humphreys, William Styron, Ernest Gaines, Elizabeth Spencer, Eudora Welty, and Cormac McCarthy, among others. I hope the twelve authors in this collection are representative of the diversity, excellence, and vision of southern writing today.

I interviewed the writers at length but informally about their religious upbringings and beliefs, and about how these may have shaped or affected their artistic visions. We never managed to stay strictly on the subject, but instead ranged over many topics related to the South: fiction, religion, men, women, race, class, modernity, and of course, the Civil War. Along with each interview is a critical commentary on that writer and a representative piece of fiction. In the tradition of the *Paris Review*, a descriptive profile of the author in his or her milieu introduces each interview.

It turned out to be true that for all of these writers, their religious culture and the issues it presented to them personally and aesthetically were of crucial importance. For some, religion has served as a prism through which to interpret human experience, for others as a target for satire. In all cases, though, the fitting metaphor for their anguished struggle with issues of faith and doubt, of religious and aesthetic integrity, has been that of a crucible. Thus, though it may be said that the South is coming to resemble the rest of the country and that the old ways are changing, my conversations with these authors suggest that Flannery O'Connor's notion of the "Christ-haunted" South still holds true today. Like Hazel Motes in *Wise Blood*, we are pursued relentlessly by the wild, ragged figure of Christ moving from tree to tree in the back of our minds, motioning to us to turn around and come into the dark. Although contemporary writers are, like O'Connor, "very much concerned with matters of the Spirit," they are determined to keep their fiction from becoming polemical. As Larry Brown put it, the art must come above all.

The writers in this collection represent a broad spectrum of artistic sensibility and religious experience as southerners, from avowed belief to profound skepticism, from intense fascination to anguished struggle. For Reynolds Price, Doris Betts, and Mary Ward Brown, an essential purpose of writing fiction is to reveal and seek to understand the deepest mysteries of faith, to describe a world that is both concrete and metaphysical. Price writes because of his "bent" to write and because he would "understand what is mysterious—in the behavior of the visible world, the behavior of God, of my friends and enemies, strangers, and finally, of myself." Mary Ward Brown says, "Someone asked me one time why southerners always write about race and religion. I said I can't help it; I can't resist doing so. If I am called a 'religious writer,' it's because I write to the glory of God, and to celebrate the privilege of being alive. I want my stories to be as true as possible for this reason." Betts attempts to give subtle shape to her vision, which is rooted in the cold, rocky reaches of Scots-Irish Calvinism: "I prefer to whisper, the reliable attention-getting method of mothers of young children."

For others, like Sheila Bosworth, Will Campbell and Larry Brown, biblical stories and themes provide powerful structures and rich imagery. Born and raised a Catholic in New Orleans, Bosworth wrestles with basic tenets of her faith, yet she sees these very issues along with Catholicism's institutional structures and symbols as invaluably rich resources informing her fiction. Larry Brown, who uses an interplay of biblical images in "A Road-side Resurrection" to suggest several contradictory meanings, says, "I write about loss, about people proceeding out from calamity. These people are aware of their need for redemption. We all spend our time dealing with some kind of hurt and looking for love." In *Cecelia's Sin*, Will Campbell explores the origins of true belief, depicting radical and, compared to contemporary mainstream Baptist thought, even fanatical believers whose purity of vision and steeliness of conviction are evocative of Abraham's, his knife poised on Mount Moriah, a ram hidden in the thicket.

Some writers seek to express the ambiguities and tension between their religious culture and their imaginative vision by creating fresh ways of seeing entrenched symbols and institutions. Some must create new metaphors altogether. Randall Kenan draws on a potent blend of Calvinism, folk religion, a Baptist upbringing and his African-American cultural roots in rural Chinquapin, North Carolina, to create a veritable pantheon of spirits, palpable forces at work for good or ill, with literal visitations by angels and possessions by evil spirits taking place in the modern, everyday world. Sandra Hollin Flowers's protagonists find a true knowledge of the Spirit inescapable, though not through the power of argument, preaching, or pious churchgoing but from a more primal, less controllable source, music.

For some the tension is dealt with in part through humorous, ironic detachment and satire. Such irony is the result of these authors' caring deeply about the traditions that nurtured them and of their commitment to the truths that seem to be in direct conflict with those traditions. In "Tongues of Fire" Lee Smith depicts the confusing of religious passion with sexual awakening, revealing through the voice of thirteen-year-old Karen the essential truth that religious fervor and erotic passion, rooted as they are in the same psychic territory, can get tangled up with one another in comic and tragic ways. In the works of Clyde Edgerton, Allan Gurganus, and Harry Crews, the tension often results in finely wrought, incisive comic satire. These contemporary satirists take the spiritual truths embodied in Christianity seriously and find their misuse or abuse quite painful. Through their humor, sometimes taken to provocative extremes, they poke fun at human pretentiousness. Yet, for all their outrageousness or wit, they ask the same serious question that O'Connor's Misfit did: What would happen if we actually took to heart what the Bible tells us, such as the story of the Resurrection? How do you resume a normal life after a naked angel has fallen from heaven into your backyard, as it did in

Allan Gurganus's "It Had Wings"? *Would* Jesus Christ have a kitchen, living room, and bedroom today as Raney maintains? How might redemptive love find its genesis and grow in a house where a corpse is being prepared for cremation in the kitchen by a crackpot mother-in-law-to-be and a demonic Rastafarian, Harry Crews asks in *Scar Lover?*

These twelve writers speak openly about faith and doubt, about feelings of ambivalence toward religion and its institutions. Each has created excellent fiction from the supreme tension between his or her religious and artistic visions. Although they explore profoundly differing visions of the meaning of spirituality, all have lived lives of passionate love for the Word, whether as revealed in sacred scripture or coming from their own hearts, and for the mystical power of storytelling, their art. Their writing shows us that our deepest wisdom lies not in seeking to formulate answers for ourselves but in asking questions, in listening to the responses the most creative among us may offer, and through our own imaginations, letting the power of the story break through, allowing the Word to become flesh in mysterious and powerful ways in our own lives.

THE CHRIST-HAUNTED LANDSCAPE
Faith and Doubt in Southern Fiction

LEE SMITH

God Not Only Speaks But Sings

Lee Smith was born in Grundy, Virginia, and received a Bachelor of Arts degree in English at Hollins College in 1967. After a stint as a reporter and editor for the *Tuscaloosa News*, Smith taught English in secondary schools in Tennessee and North Carolina. Since 1981, she has taught creative writing at North Carolina State University. A visiting professor of English at Duke University in the spring of 1991, Smith currently serves as founding board member and Fellow at the Center for Documentary Studies at Duke. Smith's first novel, *The Last Day the Dogbushes Bloomed*, was published in 1967; her subsequent novels include *Something in the Wind* (1971), *Fancy Strut* (1973), *Black Mountain Breakdown* (1980), *Oral History* (1983), *Family Linen* (1985), *Fair and Tender Ladies* (1988), and *The Devil's Dream* (1992). A collection of short stories, *Me and My Baby View the Eclipse*, was published in 1990.

Having received widespread critical and popular acclaim, Smith counts among her numerous awards the Sir Walter Raleigh Award for Fiction (1983 and 1989), the North Carolina Award for Fiction (1984), the John Dos Passos Award for Literature (1989), a Lyndhurst Fellowship (1990), and the Robert Penn Warren Award for Fiction (1991) from the Fellowship of Southern Writers. She lives in Chapel Hill with her husband, Hal Crowther.

Smith writes of the people and life of her native Appalachia with clarity and depth, in a style that has been described as pure music. She has been compared to Faulkner and Welty, but, as literary historian Thulani Davis notes, she "writes with such joy and laughing sensuality about Virginia/ Kentucky hill people that she could also be said to have an Appalachian streak of Garcia Marquez." Her primary characters are women who are seeking both to understand and receive acknowledgment of their wholeness as strong, creative, sexual females during a time of radical dislocation and social change, in a culture that would attempt to deny all but the most childlike or maternal expressions of womanhood. Dorothy Hill writes, "The serious issues of female isolation and identity make up the core of her work. She elucidates the female psyche in landscapes and homes jarred by increasing complexity and change attended by bewilderment and pain, and her fiction is a struggle to find healing and reconciliation." In *Oral History, Fair and Tender Ladies,* and *The Devil's Dream,* Smith draws from the archetypes in ancient myths of journey and quest for elements of plot and structure. These motifs acquire additional power by their rootedness in a particular landscape, the hauntingly beautiful, yet economically ravaged Virginia mountains.

She writes, Smith says, because she must—as a way of reclaiming self, to release emotion, and to give expression to her feelings about creativity and religion: "I continue to feel deep conflicts," Smith says in our interview, "but the link for me between my own religious feelings and creativity is that with writing, you go out of yourself—but you know you can come back. You won't stay stuck in the craziness. To become caught up in a fictive world is a craziness that you can come back from."

Smith's religious passion threatened to become all-consuming, and as an adult, she pulled back from it: "I still believe in God; I've just never been able to find a way to act on that without it taking me over. It's something I struggle with all the time." Smith plays out the struggle significantly in her writing, particularly in the characters of Ivy Rowe in *Fair and Tender Ladies* and Karen in "Tongues of Fire." She said of "Tongues of Fire" that it is "in a way truly one of the most autobiographical stories I have ever written. The family is all made up, but the character of Karen is absolutely the way I was as a child, including the obsessive reading and the obsessive religion."

Lee Smith's fiction is a rich panoply of fully-lived life, vividly comic and darkly tragic, infused with sensual detail and a deeply spiritual appreciation of the natural world of the Appalachian mountains and hollers. †

Tongues of Fire

The year I was thirteen—1957—my father had a nervous break-down, my brother had a wreck, and I started speaking in tongues. The nervous breakdown had been going on for a long time before I knew anything about it. Then one day that fall, Mama took me downtown in the car to get some Baskin-Robbins ice cream, some-thing she never did, and while we were sitting on the curly chairs facing each other across the little white table, Mama took a deep breath, licked her red lipstick, leaned forward in a very significant way, and said, "Karen, you may have noticed that your father is *not himself* lately."

Not himself! Who was he, then? What did she mean? But I had that feeling you get in your stomach when something really impor-tant happens. I knew this was a big deal.

Mama looked all around, as if for spies. She waited until the ice cream man went through the swinging pink doors, into the back of his shop.

"Karen," she said, so low I could hardly hear her, "your father is having a nervous breakdown."

"He is?" I said stupidly.

The ice cream man came back.

"Sssh," Mama said. She caught my eye and nodded gravely, once. "Don't eat that ice cream so fast, honey," she said a minute later. "It'll give you a headache."

And this was the only time she ever mentioned my father's ner-vous breakdown out loud, in her whole life. The older kids already knew, it turned out. Everybody had wanted to keep it from me, the baby. But then the family doctor said Mama *ought* to tell me, so she did. But she did not elaborate, then or ever, and in retrospect I am really surprised that she ever told me at all. Mama grew up in

Birmingham, so she talked in a very southern voice and wore spectator heels and linen dresses that buttoned up the front and required a great deal of ironing by Missie, the maid. Mama's name was Dee Rose. She said that when she married Daddy and came up here to the wilds of north Alabama to live, it was like moving to Siberia. It was like moving to Outer Mongolia, she said. Mama's two specialties were Rising to the Occasion and Rising Above It All, whatever "it" happened to be. Mama believed that if you can't say something nice, say nothing at all. If you don't discuss something, it doesn't exist. This is the way our family handled all of its problems, such as my father's quarrel with my Uncle Dick or my sister's promiscuity or my brother's drinking.

Mama had long red fingernails and shiny yellow hair which she wore in a bubble cut. She looked like a movie star. Mama drank a lot of gin and tonics and sometimes she would start on them early, before five o'clock. She'd wink at Daddy and say, "Pour me one, honey, it's already dark underneath the house." Still, Mama had very rigid ideas, as I was to learn, about many things. Her ideas about nervous breakdowns were:

1. The husband *should not* have a nervous breakdown.
2. Nobody can mention the nervous breakdown. It is shameful.
3. The children must *behave* at all times during the nervous breakdown.
4. The family must keep up appearances at all costs. *Nobody should know.*

Mama and I finished our ice cream and she drove us home in the white Cadillac, and as soon as we got there I went up in my treehouse to think about Daddy's breakdown. I knew it was true. *So this is it,* I thought. This had been it all along. This explained the way my father's eye twitched and watered now, behind his gold-rimmed glasses. My father's eyes were deep-set and sort of mournful at best, even before the twitch. They were an odd, arresting shade of very pale blue which I have never seen since, except in my sister Ashley. Ashley was beautiful, and my father was considered to be very good-looking, I knew that, yet he had always been too slow-moving and thoughtful for me. I would have preferred a more military model, a snappy go-getter of a dad. My dad looked like a professor at the college, which he was not. Instead he ran a printing company with my Uncle Dick, until their quarrel. Now he ran it by himself—or rather his secretary, Mrs. Eunice Merriman, ran it mostly by herself during the time he had his nervous breakdown. Mrs. Eunice Merriman was a large, imposing woman with her pale blond hair swept up in a beehive hairdo as smooth and hard as a helmet. She wore glasses with harlequin frames. Mrs. Merriman reminded me of some warlike figure from Norse mythology. She was not truly fierce, however, except in her devotion to my father, who spent more and more time lying on the daybed upstairs in his study, holding books or magazines in his hands but not reading them, looking out the bay window, at the mountains across the river. What was he thinking about?

"Oh *honestly*, Karen!" my mother exploded when I asked her this question. My mother was much more interested, on the day I asked her, in the more immediate question of whether or not I had been invited to join the Sub-Deb Club. The answer was yes.

But there was no answer to the question of what my father might be thinking about. I knew that he had wanted to be a writer in his youth. I knew that he had been the protégé of some old poet or other down at the university in Tuscaloosa, that he had written a novel which was never published, that he had gone to the Pacific Theater in the War. I had always imagined the Pacific Theater as a literal theater, somewhat like the ornate Rialto in Birmingham with its organ that rose up and down mechanically from the orchestra pit, its gold-leaf balconies, its chandelier as big as a Chevrolet. In this theater, my father might have watched such movies as *Sands of Iwo Jima* or *To Hell and Back*. Now it occurred to me, for the first time, that he might have witnessed horrors. Horrors! Sara Nell Buie, at school, swore that *her* father had five Japanese ears in a cigar box from the Philippines. Perhaps my father had seen horrors too great to be borne. Perhaps he too had ears.

But this did not seem likely, to look at him. It seemed more like mononucleosis to me. He was just *lying on the daybed*. Now he'd gotten his days and nights turned around so that he had to take sleeping tablets; he went to the printing company for only an hour or two each day. He rallied briefly at gin-and-tonic time, but his conversation tended to lapse in the middle of itself during dinner, and frequently he left the table early. My mother rose above these occasions in the way she had been trained to do as a girl in Birmingham, in the way she was training Ashley and me to do: she talked incessantly, about anything that entered her head, to fill the void. This was another of Mama's rules:

A lady never lets a silence fall.

Perhaps the most exact analysis of my father's nervous breakdown was provided by Missie, one day when I was up in the treehouse and she was hanging out laundry on the line almost directly below me, talking to the Gardeners' maid from next door. "You mean Missa Graffenreid?" Missie said. "He have *lost his starch*, is all. He be getting it back directly."

In the meantime, Mama seemed to grow in her vivacity, in her busyness, taking up the slack. Luckily my sister Ashley was a senior at Lorton Hall that year, so this necessitated a lot of conferences and visits to colleges. The guidance counselor at Lorton Hall wanted Ashley to go to Bryn Mawr, up North, but after the visit to Bryn Mawr my mother returned with her lips pressed tight together in a little red bow. "Those girls were *not ladies*," she reported to us all, and Bryn Mawr was never mentioned again except by Ashley, later, in fits of anger at the way her life turned out. The choices narrowed to Converse College in Spartanburg, South Carolina; Meredith College in Raleigh, North Carolina; Sophie Newcomb in New Orleans; and Sweet Briar, in Virginia. My mama was dead set on Sweet Briar.

So Mama and Ashley were very busy with college visits and with all the other activities of Ashley's senior year at Lorton Hall. There were countless dresses to buy, parties to give and go to. I remember one Saturday that fall when Ashley had a Coke party in the back garden, for the senior girls and their mothers. Cokes and finger sandwiches were served. Missie had made the finger sandwiches the day before and put them on big silver trays, covered with damp tea towels. I watched the party from the window of my room upstairs, which gave me a terrific view of the back garden and the red and yellow fall leaves and flowers, and the girls and their mothers like chrysanthemums themselves. I watched them from my window— just as my father watched them, I suppose, from his.

My mother loved to shop, serve on committees, go to club meet-ings, and entertain. (Probably she should have been running Graffenreid Printing Co. all along—I see this now—but of course such an idea would not have entered anyone's head at the time.) Mama ran the Flower Guild of the Methodist church, which we attended every Sunday morning, minus my father. She was the recording secretary of the Ladies' Auxiliary, which literally *ran the town* as far as I could see; she was a staunch member of the Garden Club and the Bluebird Book Club.

Her bridge club met every Thursday at noon for lunch and bridge, rotating houses. This bridge club went on for years and years beyond my childhood, until its members began to die or move to Florida. It fascinated me. I loved those summer Thursdays when I was out of school and the bridge club came to our house—the fresh flowers, the silver, the pink cloths on the bridge tables which were set up for the occasion in the Florida room, the way Mama's dressing room smelled as she dressed, that wonderful mix-ture of loose powder (she used a big lavender puff) and cigarette smoke (Salems) and Chanel No. 5. The whole bridge club dressed to the hilt. They wore hats, patent-leather shoes, and dresses of silk shantung. The food my mama and Missie gave them was wonder-ful—is still, to this day, my very idea of elegance, even though it is not a menu I'd ever duplicate; and it was clear to me, even then, that the way these ladies were was a way I'd never be.

But on those Thursdays, I'd sit at the top of the stairs peering through the banisters into the Florida room, where they lunched in impossible elegance, and I got to eat everything they did, from my own plate which Missie had fixed specially for me: a pink molded salad that melted on the tongue, asparagus-cheese souffle, and something called Chicken Crunch that involved mushroom soup, chicken, Chinese noodles, pecans, and Lord knows what else. All of Mama's bridge-lunch recipes required gelatin or mushroom soup or pecans. This was Lady Food.

So—it was the year that Mama was lunching, Daddy was lying on the daybed, and Ashley was Being a Senior. My brother Paul had already gone away to college, to Washington and Lee up in Virginia. At that time in my life, I knew Paul only by sight. He was incredibly old. Nice, but very old and very busy, riding around in cars full of other boys, dashing off here and there when he was home, which was seldom. He used to tell me knock-knock jokes, and come up behind me and buckle my knees. I thought Paul's degree of bustle and zip was *promising,* though. I certainly hoped he would be more active than Daddy. But who could tell? I rarely saw him.

I rarely saw *anybody* in my family, or so I felt. I floated through it all like a dandelion puff on the air, like a wisp of smoke, a ghost. During the year of my father's nervous breakdown, I became invisible in my family. But I should admit that even before my invisibility I was scarcely noticeable, a thin girl, slight, brown-haired and brown-eyed, *undeveloped* (as Mrs. Black put it delicately in health class). There was no sign of a breast anyplace on my chest even though some other girls my age wore B and even C cups, I saw them in gym. I had gone down to Sears on the bus by myself the previous summer and bought myself two training bras, just so I'd have them, but my mother had never mentioned this subject to me at all, of course. And even after I got the training bras, I remained—I felt—still ugly, and still invisible in the midst of my gorgeous family.

Perhaps it is not surprising that I turned to God.

I had always been *interested* in religion, anyway. When I was a little girl, my favorite part of the summer was Vacation Bible School, with the red Kool-Aid in the little Dixie cups and the Lorna Doone cookies at break. I loved to color in the twelve disciples. I loved to make lanyards. I loved to sing "You Are My Sunshine" and "Red and Yellow, Black and White, They Are Precious in His Sight." I loved to hold hands with Alice Field, who was my best friend for years and years until her family moved to Little Rock, Arkansas. I loved Mrs. Treble Roach, the teacher of Vacation Bible School, a plump soft woman like a beanbag chair, who hugged us all the time. Mrs. Treble Roach gave us gold stars when we were good, and I was *very* good. I got hundreds of gold stars over the years and I believe I still have them upstairs someplace in a jewelry box, like ears.

I had always liked church too, although it was less fun. I associated church with my grandparents, since we sat with them every Sunday, third pew from the back on the left-hand side of the little stone Methodist church which my grandfather had attended all his life, which my grandmother had attended since their marriage fifty years before. Usually my mother went to church too; sometimes Ashley went to church, under duress ever since she became an atheist in tenth grade, influenced by an English teacher who was clearly *not a lady*; my father attended only on Easter. Frankly, I liked those Sundays when none of them made it, when Mama just dropped me off in front of the church and I went in all alone, clutching my quarter for the collection plate, to sit with my grandparents. Even though I was invisible in my own family, my grandparents noticed me plenty. I was their good, good little girl. . . certainly, I felt, their favorite. I did everything I could to ensure that this was true.

My grandmother had wispy blue hair and a whole lot of earrings and brooches that matched. She was the author of four books of poems which Daddy had printed up for her at the printing company. She suffered from colitis, and was ill a lot. One thing you never wanted to do with Grandmother was ask her how she felt—she'd *tell* you, gross details you didn't want to know. My mama, of course, was entirely above this kind of thing, never referring to her own or anybody else's body in any way. My grandfather wore navy-blue suits to church with red suspenders underneath. He was a boxy little man who ran the bus station and had a watch that could tell you the time in Paris, London, and Tokyo. I coveted this watch and had already asked Grandaddy to leave it to me when he died, a request that seemed to startle him.

After church, I'd walk up the street with my grandparents to their house on the corner across from the Baptist church and eat lunch, which frequently ended with lemon meringue pie, my favorite. I kept a close eye out the window for Baptists, whose service was dismissed half an hour later than ours. There were so many Baptists that it took them longer to do everything. In pretty weather, I sat out on the front porch so that I could see the Baptists more clearly. They wore loud suits, and made more noise in general than the quiet Methodists.

Our church had only forty-two members and about twenty of them, like my grandparents, were so old as to be almost dead already. I was not even looking forward to joining the MYF, which

I'd be eligible for next year, because it had only eight members, two of them definite nerds. All they did was collect food for the poor at Thanksgiving, and stuff like that. The BTU, on the other hand, did great stuff such as have progressive dinners, Sweetheart Banquets, and go on trips to Gulf Shores. The BTU was a much snappier outfit than the MYF, but I knew better than to ask to join it. My mother had already explained to me the social ranking of the churches: Methodist at the top, attended by doctors and lawyers and other "nice" families; Presbyterian slightly down the scale, attended by store owners; then the vigorous Baptists; then the Church of Christ, who thought they were the only real church in town and said so. They said everybody else in town was going to hell except for them. They had hundreds of members. And then, of course, at the *very bottom* of the church scale were those little churches out in the surrounding county, some of them recognizable denominations (Primitive Baptist) and some of them not (Church of the Nazarene, Tar River Holiness) where people were reputed to yell out, fall down in fits, and throw their babies. I didn't know what this *meant*, exactly, but I knew I'd love to see it, for it promised drama far beyond the dull responsive readings of the Methodists and their rote mumbling of the Nicene Creed.

Anyway, I had been sitting on my grandparents' front porch for years eating pie and envying the Baptists, waiting without much hope to be seized by God for His heavenly purpose, bent to His will, as in *God's Girl*, my favorite book—a biography of Joan of Arc.

So far, nothing doing.

But then, that fall of Daddy's nervous breakdown, the Methodist church was visited by an unusually charismatic young preacher named Johnny Rock Malone while Mr. Treble Roach, our own preacher, was down at Duke having a hernia operation. I was late to church that day and arrived all by myself, after the service had already started. The congregation was on its feet singing "I Come to the Garden Alone," one of my favorite hymns. One unfamiliar voice led all the rest. I slipped in next to Grandaddy, found the right page in the hymnal, and craned my neck around Miss Eulalie Butters's big black hat to see who was up there singing so nice. It looked like an angel to me—probably the angel Gabriel, because of his curly blond hair. And he was so *young*—just out of seminary, somebody said after the service. It was a warm fall Sunday, and rays of colored light shot through the stained-glass windows at the side of the church to glance off Johnny Rock Malone's pale face. "He *walks* with me, and He *talks* with me," we sang. My heart started beating double time. Johnny Rock Malone stretched out his long thin arms and spread his long white fingers. "Beloved," he said, curling his fingers, "let us pray." But I never closed my eyes that day, staring instead at the play of light on Johnny Rock Malone's fair face. It was almost like a kaleidoscope. Then the round rosy window behind him, behind the altar, began to *pulse* with light, to glow with light, now brighter now not, like a neon sign. I got the message. I was no dummy. In a way, I had been waiting all my life for this to happen.

The most notable thing about me as a child—before I got religious, I mean—was my obsessive reading. I had always been an inveterate reader of the sort who hides underneath the covers with a flashlight and reads *all night long.* But I did not read casually, or for mere entertainment, or for information. What I wanted was to feel all wild and trembly inside, an effect first produced by *The Secret Garden*, which I'd read maybe twenty times. And the Rev. Johnny Rock Malone looked exactly the way I had always pictured Colin! In fact, listening to him preach, I felt exactly the way I felt when I read *The Secret Garden*, just exactly.

Other books which had affected me strongly were *Little Women*, especially the part where Beth dies, and *Gone With the Wind*, especially the part where Melanie dies. I had long hoped for a wasting disease, such as leukemia, to test my mettle. I also loved *Marjorie Morningstar*, *A Tree Grows in Brooklyn*, *Heidi*, and books like *Dear and Glorious Physician*, *The Shoes of the Fisherman*, *Christy*, and anything at all about horses and saints. I had read all the Black Stallion books, of course, as well as all the Marguerite Henry books. But my all-time favorite was *God's Girl*, especially the frontispiece illustration picturing Joan as she knelt and "prayed without ceasing for guidance from God," whose face was depicted overhead, in a thunderstorm. Not only did I love Joan of Arc, I wanted to *be* her.

The only man I had ever loved more than Colin in *The Secret Garden*, to date, was Johnny Tremaine, from Esther Forbes's book of that title. I used to wish that it was *me*—not Johnny Tremaine—

who'd had the hot silver spilled on my hand. I would have suffered anything (everything) for Johnny Tremaine.

But on that fateful Sunday morning, Johnny Rock Malone eclipsed both Colin and Johnny Tremaine in my affections. It was a wipeout. I felt as fluttery and wild as could be. In fact I felt too crazy to pay attention to the sermon which Johnny Rock Malone was, by then, almost finished with. I tried to concentrate, but my mind was whirling. The colors from the windows seemed to deepen and swirl. And then, suddenly, I heard him loud and clear, reading from *Revelations:* "And I saw a great white throne, and Him that sat on it, from whose face the earth and heaven fled away; and there was found no place for them. And I saw the dead, small and great, stand before God, and the books were opened. . . and whosoever was not found written in the book of life was cast into the lake of fire."

I can't remember much about what happened after that. I got to shake hands with him as we left the church, and I was surprised to find that his hand was cool, not burning hot—and, though bony, somehow as soft as a girl's. I looked hard at Johnny Rock Malone as he stood in front of our pretty little church, shaking hands. He was on his way to someplace else, over in Mississippi. We would never see him again. *I* would never see him again. And yet somehow I felt exhilarated and *satisfied,* in a way. I can't explain it. Back at my grandparents' house, I couldn't even eat my lemon meringue pie. I felt shaky and hot, like I might be getting a virus. I went home early.

My father was upstairs in his study, door closed. Nobody else was home. I wandered the house. Then I sat in the Florida room for a while, staring out at the day. After a while, I picked up my mother's sewing basket from the coffee table, got a needle and threaded it with blue thread, and sewed all the fingers of my left hand together, through the cuticle. Then I held out my hand and admired it, wishing desperately for my best friend Alice Field, of Little Rock. I had no best friend now, nobody to show my amazing hand to. Weird little Edwin Lee lived right across the street, but it was inconceivable that I would show *him,* the nerd, such a hand as this. So I showed it to nobody. I left it sewed up until Mama's white Cadillac pulled in the driveway, and then I cut the thread between my fingers and pulled it all out.

It was about this time too that I began to pray a lot (*without ceasing* was my intention) and set little fires all around the neighborhood. These fires were nothing much. I'd usually take some shredded newspapers or some Kleenex, find a few sticks, and they'd burn themselves out in a matter of minutes. I made a fire in my treehouse, in our garage, in the sink, in the basement, on Mrs. Butters's back patio, on Mr. and Mrs. Harold Castle's front porch, and in little Charlotte Lee's playhouse. Here I went too far, singeing off the hair of her Barbie doll. She never could figure out how it happened.

I entertained visions of being a girl evangelist, of appearing with Billy Graham on television, of traveling throughout Mississippi with Johnny Rock Malone. I'd be followed everywhere I went by a little band of my faithful. I made a small fire in the bed of Ashley's new boyfriend's pickup truck while he and my sister were in the den petting and watching the Hit Parade. They didn't have any idea that I was outside in the night, watching them through the window, making a fire in the truck. They all thought I was in bed!

Although I was praying a lot, my prayers were usually specific, as opposed to *without ceasing.* For instance I'd tell one friend I'd go shopping with her, and then something I really wanted to do would come up, and I'd call back and say I couldn't come after all, that my grandmother had died, and then I would go to my room and fling myself to the floor and pray without ceasing that my lie would not be found out, and that my grandmother would not really die. I made big deals with God—*if* He would make sure I got away with it this time, I would talk to Edwin Lee for five minutes on the bus, three days in a row, or I would clean out my closet. He did His part; I did mine. I grew in power every day.

I remember so well that important Friday when I was supposed to spend the night with Margaret Applewhite. Now Margaret Applewhite was totally boring, in my opinion—my only rival in the annual spelling bee (she won in third, I won in fourth and fifth, she beat me out in sixth with *catarrh,* which still rankled). Margaret Applewhite wore a training bra too. Our mothers, who played bridge together, encouraged our friendship. I'd rather do just about *anything,* even watch Kate Smith on TV, than spend

time with boring Margaret Applewhite. Still, earlier that week
when she'd called and invited me, I couldn't for the life of me think
of any good reason to say no, so I'd said yes. Then that Friday right
before sixth period, Tammy Lester came up to my locker popping
her gum (against the rules: we were not allowed to chew gum in
school) and—wonder of wonders—asked me to come home with
her after school that very day and spend the night.

Tammy Lester! Shunned by Sub-Debs, sent to Detention, noticed
by older boys. I couldn't believe it. I admired Tammy Lester more
than any other girl in my entire class, I'd watched her from afar the
way I had watched the Baptists. Tammy Lester lived out in the
county someplace (in a trailer, it was rumored), she was driven in to
school each morning by one or the other of her wild older brothers
in a red pickup truck (these brothers slicked back their hair with
grease, they wore their cigarette packs rolled up in the sleeves of
their T-shirts), and best of all, she was missing a tooth right in
front, and nobody had taken her to the dentist yet to get it fixed.
The missing tooth gave Tammy a devilish, jaunty look. Also, as I
would learn later, she could whistle through this hole, and spit
twenty feet.

Her invitation was offhand. "You wanna come home with me
today?" she asked, in a manner that implied she didn't give a hoot
whether I did or not. "Buddy's got to come into town tomorrow
morning anyway, so he could bring you back."

"All right," I said, trying to sound casual.

"I'll meet you out front when the bell rings." Tammy flashed me
her quick dark grin. She popped her gum, and was gone.

I didn't hesitate for a minute. I stopped Margaret Applewhite on
her way to health class. "Listen," I said in a rush, "I'm so sorry I
can't come spend the night with you, but my mother is having an
emergency hysterectomy today, so I have to go straight home and
help out." I had just learned about hysterectomies, from a medical
book in the library.

Margaret's boring brown eyes widened. "Is she going to be all
right?"

I sucked in my breath dramatically and looked brave. "We hope
so," I said. "They think they can get it all."

Margaret walked into health. I sank back against the mustard-yellow tile walls as, suddenly, it hit me: Margaret's mother knew my mother! What if Margaret's mother called my mother, and Mama found out? She'd be furious, not only because of the lie but because of the nature of the lie—Mama would *die* before she'd ever mention something like a hysterectomy. Mama referred to everything below the belt as "down there," an area she dealt with darkly, indirectly, and only when necessary. "Trixie Vopel is in the hospital for tests," she might say. "She's been having trouble *down there.*" *Down there* was a foreign country, like Africa or Nicaragua.

What to do? I wrote myself an excuse from gym, signed my mother's name, turned it in and then went to the infirmary, where I lay down on a hard white cot and prayed without ceasing for upwards of an hour. I promised a lot: If Mama did not find out, I would sit with Lurice May at lunch on Monday (a dirty fat girl who kept her head wrapped up in a scarf and was rumored to have lice), I would be nice to Edwin Lee three times for fifteen minutes each, I would clean out under my bed, I would give back the perfume and the ankle bracelet I had stolen from Ashley, and I would put two dollars of my saved-up babysitting money in the collection plate at church on Sunday. It was the best I could do. Then I called my mother from the infirmary phone, and to my surprise, she said, "Oh, of course," in a distracted way when I asked if I could spend the night with Tammy Lester. She did not even ask what Tammy's father did.

Then "*Karen,*" she said in a pointed way that meant this was what she was *really* interested in, "do you have any idea where your sister is right now?"

"What?" I couldn't even remember *who* my sister was, right now.

"*Ashley,*" Mama said. "The school called and asked if she was sick. Apparently she just never showed up at school today."

"I'll bet they had some secret senior thing," I said.

"Oh." Mama sounded relieved. "Well, maybe so. Now who is it you're spending the night with?" she asked again, and I told her. "And what did you say her father does?"

"Lawyer," I said.

Spending the night with Tammy Lester was the high point of my whole life up to that time. She did *not* live in a trailer, as rumored, but in an old unpainted farmhouse with two boarded-up windows, settled unevenly onto cinder-block footings. A mangy dog lay up under the house. Chickens roamed the property. The porch sagged. Wispy ancient curtains blew out eerily at the upstairs windows. The whole yard was strewn with parts of things—cars, stoves, bed-springs, unimaginable machine parts rusting among the weeds. I loved it. Tammy led me everywhere and showed me everything: her secret place, a tent of willows, down by the creek; the grave of her favorite dog, Buster, and the collar he had worn; an old chicken house that her brothers had helped her make into a playhouse; a haunted shack down the road; the old Packard out back that you could get in and pretend you were taking a trip. "Now we're in Nevada," Tammy said, shifting gears. "Now we're in the Grand Canyon. Now we're in the middle of the desert. It's hot as hell out here, ain't it?"

I agreed.

At suppertime, Tammy and I sat on folding chairs pulled up to the slick oilcloth-covered table beneath a bare hanging light bulb. Her brothers had disappeared. Tammy seemed to be cooking our supper; she was heating up Dinty Moore stew straight out of the can.

"Where's your daddy?" I asked.

"Oh, he's out West on a pipeline," she said, vastly unconcerned.

"Where's your mama?" I said. I had seen her come in from work earlier that afternoon, a pudgy, pale redheaded woman who drove a light blue car that looked like it would soon join the others in the backyard.

"I reckon she's reading her Bible," Tammy said, as if this were a perfectly ordinary thing to be doing on a Friday night at gin-and-tonic time. "She'll eat after while."

Tammy put half of the Dinty Moore stew into a chipped red bowl and gave it to me. It was delicious, lots better than Lady Food. She ate hers right out of the saucepan. "Want to split a beer?" she said, and I said sure, and she got us one—a Pabst Blue Ribbon—out of the icebox. Of course I had never tasted beer before. But I thought it was great.

That night, I told Tammy about my father's nervous breakdown, and she told me that her oldest brother had gone to jail for stealing an outboard motor. She also told me about the lady down the road who had chopped off her husband's hands with an ax while he was "laying up drunk." I told her that I was pretty sure God had singled me out for a purpose which he had not yet revealed, and Tammy nodded and said her mother had been singled out too. I sat right up in bed. "What do you mean?" I asked.

"Well, she's real religious," Tammy said, "which is why she don't get along with Daddy too good." I nodded. I had already figured out that Daddy must be the dark handsome one that all the children took after. "And she was a preacher's daughter too, see, so she's been doing it all her life."

"Doing what?" I asked into the dark.

"Oh, talking in tongues of fire," Tammy said matter-of-factly, and a total thrill crept over me, the way I had always wanted to feel. I had hit pay dirt at last.

"I used to get embarrassed, but now I don't pay her much mind," Tammy said.

"Listen," I said sincerely. "I would give *anything* to have a mother like that."

Tammy whistled derisively through the hole in her teeth.

But eventually, because I was already so good at collective bargaining, we struck a deal: I would get to go to church with Tammy and her mother, the very next Sunday if possible, and in return, I would take Tammy to the country club. (I could take her when Mama wasn't there; I was allowed to sign for things.) Tammy and I stayed up talking nearly all night long. She was even more fascinating than I'd thought. She had breasts, she knew how to drive a car, and she was part Cherokee. Toward morning, we cut our fingers with a kitchen knife and swore to be best friends forever.

The next day, her brother Mike drove me into town at about one o'clock. He had to see a man about a car. He smoked cigarettes all the way, and scowled at everything. He didn't say a word to me. I thought he was wonderful.

I arrived home just in time to intercept the delivery boy from the florist's. "I'll take those in," I said, and pinched the card which said,

"For Dee Rose. Get well soon. Best wishes from Lydia and Lou Applewhite." I left the flowers on the doorstep, where they would create a little mystery later on, when Mama found them, and went upstairs to my room and prayed without ceasing, a prayer of thanks- giving for the special favors I felt He had granted me lately. Then before long I fell asleep, even as a huge argument raged all over the house, upstairs and down, between Mama and my sister Ashley who had *just come in,* having stayed out all day and all night long.

"If a girl loses her reputation, she has lost *everything,*" Mama said. "She has lost her Most Precious Possession."

"So what? So what?" Ashley screamed. "All you care about is appearances. Who cares what I do, in this screwed-up family? Who really cares?"

It went on and on, while I melted down and down into my pink piqué comforter, hearing them but not really hearing them, dreaming instead of the lumpy sour bed out at Tammy's farm, of the moon- light on the wispy graying curtains at her window, of a life so hard and flinty that it might erupt at any moment into tongues of fire.

Not only was the fight over with by Sunday morning, but it was so far over with as not to have happened at all. I came in the kitchen late, to find Mama and Ashley still in their bathrobes, eating sticky buns and reading the funnies. It looked like nobody would be avail- able to drive me to church. Clearly, both Ashley and Mama had Risen Above It All—Mama, to the extent that she was virtually levitating as the day wore on, hovering a few feet off the floor in her Sunday seersucker suit as she exhorted us all to hurry, hurry, hurry. Our reservations were for one o'clock. The whole family was going out for brunch at the country club.

Daddy was going too.

I still wonder what she said to him to get him up and dressed and out of there. I know it was the kind of thing that meant a lot to her—a public act, an event that meant *See, here is our whole happy family out together at the country club; see, we are a perfectly nor- mal family; see, there is nothing wrong with us at all.* And I know that Daddy loved her.

Our table overlooked the first tee of the golf course. Our waiter, Louis, had known Daddy ever since he was a child. Daddy ordered a martini. Mama ordered a gin and tonic. Ashley ordered a lemon Coke. I ordered lemonade. Mama was so vivacious that she almost gave off light. Her eyes sparkled, her hair shone, her red lipstick glistened. She and Ashley were discussing which schools her fellow seniors hoped to attend, and why. Ashley was very animated too. Watching them, I suddenly realized how much Ashley was like Mama. Ashley laughed and gestured with her pretty hands. I watched her carefully. I knew Mama thought Ashley had lost her most precious possession (things were different *down there*), yet she didn't look any different to me. She wore a hot-pink sheath dress and pearls. She looked terrific.

I turned my attention to Daddy, curiously, because I felt all of a sudden that I had not really seen him for years and years. He might as well have been off on a pipeline, as far as I was concerned. Our drinks arrived, and Daddy sipped at his martini. He perked up. He looked weird, though. His eyes were sunken in his head, like the limestone caves above the Tombigbee River. His skin was as white and dry as a piece of Mama's stationery. My father bought all his clothes in New York so they were always quite elegant, but now they hung on him like on a coat rack. How much weight had he lost? Twenty pounds? Thirty? We ordered lunch. Daddy ordered another martini.

Now he was getting entirely too perky, he moved his hands too much as he explained to Ashley the theory behind some battle in some war. He stopped talking only long enough to stand up and shake hands with friends who came by our table to speak to him, friends who had not seen him for months and months. He didn't touch his food. Underneath my navy-blue dress with the sailor collar, I was sweating, in spite of my mother's pronouncement:

Horses sweat, men perspire, and women glow.

I could feel it trickling down my sides. I wondered if, as I grew up, this would become an uncontrollable problem, whether I would have to wear dress shields. We all ordered baked Alaska, the chef's specialty, for dessert. My mother smiled and smiled. I was invisible. When the baked Alaska arrived, borne proudly to our table by Louis, nobody could put out the flames. Louis blew and blew. Other waiters ran over, beating at it with linen napkins. My mother laughed merrily. "For goodness' sakes!" she said. My daddy looked stricken. Finally they got it out and we all ate some, except for Daddy.

Gazing past my family to the golfers out on the grass beyond us, I had a sudden inspiration. I knew what to do. I emerged from invisibility long enough to say, "Hey, Daddy, let's go out and putt," and he put his napkin promptly on the table and stood right up. "Sure thing, honey," he said, sounding for all the world like my own daddy. He smiled at me. I took his hand, remembering then who I had been before the nervous breakdown: Daddy's little girl. We went down the stairs, past the snack bar, and out to the putting green at the side of the building.

My dad was a good golfer. I was not bad myself. We shared a putter from the Pro Shop. We started off and soon it was clear that we were having a great time, that this was a good idea. The country club loomed massively behind us. The emerald grass, clipped and even, stretched out on three sides in front of us, as far as we could see, ending finally in a stand of trees here, a rolling hill there. This expanse of grass, dotted with pastel golfers, was both comforting and exhilarating. It was a nine-hole putting green. On the seventh hole, we were tied, if you figured in the handicap that my father had given himself. I went first, overshooting on my second stroke, sinking it with a really long shot on my third. I looked back over at Daddy to make sure he had seen my putt, but clearly he had not. He was staring out over the grass toward the horizon, beyond the hill.

"Your turn!" I called out briskly, tossing him the putter.

What happened next was awful.

In one terrible second, my father turned to me, face slack, mouth agape, then fell to his knees on the putting green, cowering, hands over his face. The putter landed on the grass beside him. He was crying. I didn't know what to do. I just stood there, and then suddenly the putting green was full of people—the pro, Bob White, in his jacket with his name on it, helping Daddy to his feet; our dentist, Dr. Reap, holding him by the other elbow as they walked him to our white Cadillac which Mama had driven around to pick us up in. Ashley cried all the way home. So did Daddy.

It was not until that day that I realized that the nervous breakdown was real, that Daddy was really sick.

I ran upstairs and prayed without ceasing for a solid hour, by the clock, that Daddy would get well and that we would all be *all right*, for I had come to realize somehow, during the course of that afternoon, that we might *not* be. We might never be all right again.

At least I had a New Best Friend. I banished all memory of Alice Field, without remorse. Tammy Lester and I became, for the rest of that spring, inseparable. The first time I brought her to my house, I did it without asking. I didn't want to give Mama a chance to say no. And although we had not discussed it, Tammy showed up dressed more like a town girl than I had ever seen her—a plaid skirt, a white blouse, loafers, her dark hair pulled back and up into a cheerful ponytail. She could have been a cheerleader. She could have been a member of the Sub-Deb Club. No one could have ever guessed what she had in her pocket—a pack of Kents and a stolen kidney stone once removed from her neighbor, Mrs. Gillespie, who had kept it in a jar on her mantel. But even though Tammy looked so nice, Mama was giving her the third degree. "How many brothers and sisters did you say you had?" and "Where was your Mama *from?*"

This interrogation took place upstairs in Mama's dressing room. Suddenly, to everyone's surprise, Daddy lurched in to fill the doorway and say, "Leave those little girls alone, Dee Rose, you've got your hands full already," and oddly enough, Mama *did* leave us alone then. She didn't say another word about it at the time, turning back to her nails, or even later, as spring progressed and Ashley's increasing absences and moodiness became more of a problem. Before long, Daddy refused to join us even for dinner. Mama *did* have her hands full. If I could occupy myself, so much the better.

I will never forget the first time I was allowed to go to church with Tammy and her mother. I had spent the night out at the farm, and in the morning I was awake long before it was time to leave. I dressed carefully, in the yellow dress and jacket Mama had ordered for me only a couple of months before from Rich's in Atlanta. It was already getting too small. Tammy and her mother both looked at my outfit with some astonishment. They didn't have any particular church clothes, it turned out. At least, they didn't have any church clothes as fancy as these. Tammy wore a black dress which was much too old for her, clearly a hand-me-down from someplace, and her mother wore the same formless slacks and untucked shirt she always wore. I could never tell any of her clothes apart. For breakfast that morning, we had Hi-Ho cakes, which we ate directly from their cellophane wrappers, and Dr Peppers. Then we went out and got into their old blue car, which threatened not to start. *On no!* I found myself suddenly, terribly upset. I realized then how very much I was dying to hear Tammy's mother speak in tongues of fire, a notion that intrigued me more and more the better I got to know her, because usually she *didn't speak at all.* Never! Her pale gray eyes were fixed on distance, the way my daddy's had been that day at the golf course. The engine coughed and spluttered, died. Then finally Tammy's mother suggested that Tammy and I should push her down the muddy rutted driveway and she'd pop the clutch. I had never heard of such a thing. In my family, a man in a uniform, from a garage, came to start cars that wouldn't start. Still, we pushed it. It started. I got mud all over the bottom of my yellow dress.

Which didn't matter at all, I saw as soon as we got to the church. There were old men in overalls, younger men in coveralls with their names stitched on their pockets, girls in jeans, boys in jeans. The men stood around by their trucks in the parking lot, smoking cigarettes. The women went on in, carrying food. Tammy's mother had a big bag of Fritos. The church itself was a square cinder-block building painted white. It looked like a convenience store. Its windows were made of the kind of frosted glass you find in rest rooms. The only way you could tell it was a church was from the hand-lettered sign on the door, MARANATHA APOSTOLIC CHURCH ALL COME IN. I asked Tammy what "Maranatha" meant and she said she didn't know. Tammy would rather be at *my* house on Sundays, so she could look through Mama's jewelry, eat lemon meringue pie at my grandmother's, and stare at Baptists. She had made this plain. I'd rather be at her house, in general; she'd rather be at mine. We walked into her church.

"*This way.*" Tammy was pulling my arm. Men sat on the right-hand side of the church. Women sat on the left. There was no music, no Miss Eugenia Little at the organ. Men and women sat still, staring straight ahead, the children sprinkled among them like tiny grave adults. The pews were handmade, hard, like benches, with high, straight backs. There was no altar, only the huge wooden cross at the front of the church, dwarfing everything, and a curtain, like a shower curtain, pulled closed behind it. A huge Bible stood open on a lectern with a big jug (of what? water?) beside it. More people came in. My heart was beating a mile a minute. The light that came in through the frosted-glass windows produced a soft, diffuse glow throughout the church. Tammy popped her gum. Tammy's mother's eyes were already closed. Her pale eyelashes fluttered. Her mouth was moving and she swayed slightly, back and forth from the waist up. Nothing else was happening.

Then four women, all of them big and tough-looking, went forward and simply started singing "Rock of Ages," without any warning or any introduction at all. I almost jumped right out of my seat. Some of the congregation joined in, some did not. It seemed to be optional. Tammy's mother did not sing. She did not open her eyes either. The women's voices were high, mournful, seeming to linger in the air long after they were done. "Praise God!" "Yes, Jesus!" At the conclusion of the song, people throughout the church started shouting. I craned my neck around to see who was doing this, but the back of the pew was too high, blocking a lot of my view. They sang again. I had never heard any music like this music, music without any words at all, or maybe it was music without any music, it seemed to pierce my brain. I was sweating under my arms again.

The preacher, Mr. Looney, entered unobtrusively from the side during the singing. Initially, Mr. Looney was a disappointment. He was small and nondescript. He looked like George Gobel. Tammy had told me he was a security guard at the paper mill during the week. He spoke in a monotone with a hick accent. As he led us all in prayer—a prayer that seemed to go on forever, including everybody in the church by name—my mind wandered back to a time when I was little and our whole family had gone to Gulf Shores for a vacation, and Ashley and Paul were there too, and all of us worked and worked, covering Daddy up with sand, and Mama wore a sailor hat. By the end of the prayer, I was crying, and Mr. Looney had changed his delivery, his voice getting stronger and more rhythmical as he went into his message for the day. This message was pretty simple, one I had heard before. God's wrath is awful. Hell is real and lasts forever. It is not enough to have good intentions. The road to Hell is paved with those. It is not enough to do good works, such as taking care of the sick and giving to the poor. God will see right through you. The only way you can get to Heaven is by turning over your whole will and your whole mind to Jesus Christ, being baptized in the name of the Father, Son, and Holy Ghost, and born again in Glory.

"Does sprinkling count?" I whispered to Tammy. I had been sprinkled in the Methodist church.

"No," she whispered back.

Mr. Looney went on and on, falling into chant now, catching up his sentences with an "Ah!" at the end of each line. People were yelling out. And then came, finally, the invitational, "Just as I am, without one plea, but that Thy blood was shed for me, O Lamb of God, I come, I come!"

The stolid-looking young woman sitting two seats over from us surprised me by starting to mumble suddenly, then she screamed out, then she rushed forward, right into Mr. Looney's arms.

I twisted my head around to see what would happen next. Mr. Looney blessed her and said that she would "pass through to Jesus" by and by.

"What does he mean, 'pass through to Jesus'?" I was still whispering, but I might as well have been speaking aloud; there was so much commotion now that nobody else could have heard me.

Tammy jerked her head toward the front of the church. "Through them curtains, I reckon," she said.

"What's back there?" I asked, and Tammy said it was a swimming pool that people got baptized in.

And sure enough, it was not long before Mr. Looney pulled back the curtains to reveal a kind of big sliding glass door cut in the wall, with a large wading pool right beyond it, the kind I had seen in the Sears catalogue. Mr. Looney pulled the heavy young woman through the curtains and hauled her over the edge of the pool. The water reached up to about mid-thigh on both of them. I couldn't believe they would just walk into the water like that, wearing all their clothes, wearing their *shoes!* Mr. Looney pulled back the woman's long hair and grasped it firmly. Her face was as blank and solid as a potato. "In the name of the Father and the Son and the Holy Ghost!" Mr. Looney yelled, and dunked her all the way under, backwards. Although she held her nose, she came up sputtering.

Now people were jumping up all over the church, singing out and yelling, including Tammy's mother, who opened her mouth and screamed out in a language like none I had ever heard, yet a language which I felt I knew intimately, somehow, better than I knew English. It was *my language*, I was sure of it, and I think I might have passed out right then from the shock of sheer recognition except that Tammy grabbed my arm and yanked like crazy.

"Get ready!" she said.

"What?"

"She's fixing to fall," Tammy said just as her mother pitched backwards in a dead faint. We caught her and laid her out on the pew. She came to later, when church was over, and then we all had dinner on the ground out back of the church. Later I sneaked back into the fellowship hall on the pretext of going to the bathroom, so I could examine the pool in greater detail. It was in a little anteroom off the fellowship hall, right up against the double doors that led from the sanctuary, now closed. It was a plain old wading pool, just as I'd thought, covered now by a blue tarpaulin. I pulled back the tarp. The water was pretty cold. A red plastic barrette floated jauntily in the middle of the pool. I looked at it for a long time. I knew I would have to get in that water sooner or later. I would have to get saved.

I was so moved by the whole experience that I might have actually broken through my invisible shield to tell Daddy about it, or even Ashley, but Mama met me at the door that afternoon with an ashen face and, for once, no makeup.

"Where in the world have you all *been?*" she shrilled. "I've been trying to call you all afternoon."

"We ate lunch out at the church," I said. "They do that." Out of the corner of my eye, I watched Tammy and her mother pull away in the battered blue car and wished I were with them, anywhere but

here. I didn't want to know whatever Mama had to say next. In that
split second, several possibilities raced through my mind:

1. Grandmother really *has* died.
2. Ashley is pregnant.
3. Ashley has eloped.
4. Daddy has killed himself.

But I was completely surprised by what came next.

"Your brother has been in the most terrible wreck," Mama said,
"up in Virginia. He's in a coma, and they don't know if he'll make
it or not."

Paul had been drunk, of course. Drunk, or he might not have lived
at all, somebody said later, but I don't know whether that was true
or not. I think it is something people say after wrecks, whenever
there's been drinking. He had been driving back to W&L from
Randolph-Macon, where he was dating a girl. This girl wrote Mama
a long, emotional letter on pink stationery with a burgundy mono-
gram. Paul was taken by ambulance from the small hospital in
Lexington, Virginia, to the University of Virginia hospital in Charlottesville, one of the best hospitals in the world. This is what everybody told me. Mama went up there immediately. Her younger sister, my Aunt Liddie, came to stay with us while she was gone.

Aunt Liddie had always been referred to in our family as
"flighty." Aunt Liddie "went off on tangents," it was said. I wasn't
sure what this meant. Still, I was glad to see her when she arrived,
with five matching suitcases full of beautiful clothes and her
Pekingese named Chow Mein. Back in Birmingham she was a Kelly
girl, so it was easy for her to leave her job and come to us. The very
first night she arrived, Liddie got me to come out on the back steps
with her. She sat very close to me in the warm spring night and
squeezed both my hands. "I look on this as a wonderful opportunity for you and me to get to know each other better," Aunt Liddie
said. "I want you to tell me *everything*."

But I would tell her nothing, as things turned out. This was to be
our closest moment. The very next week, Liddie started dating Mr.
Hudson Bell, a young lawyer she met by chance in the bank.
Immediately, Liddie and Hudson Bell were *in love*, and Ashley and

I were free—within the bounds of reason—to come and go as we pleased. Aunt Liddie asked no questions. Missie cooked the meals.

This was just as well with me, for I had serious business to tend to.

I knew it was up to me to bring Paul out of that coma. I would pray without ceasing, and Tammy would help me. The first week, we prayed without ceasing only after school and on the weekend. Paul was no better, Mama reported from Charlottesville. The second week, I gave up sitting on soft chairs and eating chocolate. I paid so much attention to the unfortunate Lurice May that she began avoiding me. Paul had moved his foot, Mama said. I doubled my efforts, giving up also Cokes and sleeping in bed. (I had to sleep flat on the floor.) Also, I prayed without ceasing all during math class. I wouldn't even answer the teacher, Mrs. Lemon, when she called on me. She sent me to Guidance because of it. During this week, I began to suspect that perhaps Tammy was not praying as much as she was supposed to, not keeping up her end of the deal. Still, I was too busy to care. I gave up hot water; I had to take cold showers now.

The third weekend of Mama's absence and Paul's coma, I spent Saturday night with Tammy, and that Sunday morning, at Tammy's church, I got saved.

When Mr. Looney issued his plea, I felt that he was talking right to me. "With every head bowed and every eye closed," he said, "I want you to look into your hearts and minds this morning. Have you got problems, brother? Have you got problems, sister? Well, give them up! Give them over to the Lord Jesus Christ. If his shoulders are big enough to *bear the cross*, they are big enough to take on your little problems, beloved. Turn them over to him. He will help you now in this life, here in this vale of tears. And He will give you Heaven Everlasting as a door prize. Think about it, beloved. Do you want to burn in Hell forever, at the Devil's barbecue? Or do you want to lie in banks of flowers, listening to that heavenly choir?"

I felt a burning, stabbing sensation in my chest and stomach— something like heartburn, something like the hand of God. The idea of turning it all over to Him was certainly appealing at this point. Another week of prayer, and I'd flunk math for sure. The choir sang, "Softly and tenderly, Jesus is calling, calling for you and for me." Beside me, Tammy's mama was starting to mumble and moan.

Mr. Looney said, "Perhaps there is one among you who feels that his sin is too great to bear, but no sin is too black for the heavenly laundry of Jesus Christ, He will turn you as white as snow, as white as the driven snow, hallelujah!" Mr. Looney reached back and pulled the curtains open, so we could all see the pool. Tammy's mama leaped up and called out in her strangely familiar language. Mr. Looney went on, "Perhaps there is a child among you who hears our message this morning, who is ready now for Salvation. Why, a little child can go to Hell, the same as you and me! A little child can burn to a crisp. But it is also true that a little child can come to God—right now, right this minute, this very morning. God don't check your ID, children. God will check your souls." "Come home, come home," they sang.

Before I even knew it, I was up there, and we had passed through those curtains, and I was standing in the water with my full blue skirt floating out around me like a lily pad. Then he was saying the words, shouting them out, and whispering to me, "Hold your nose," which I did, and he pushed me under backwards, holding me tightly with his other hand so that I felt supported, secure, even at the very moment of immersion. It was like being dipped by the big boys at ballroom dancing, only not as scary. I came up wet and saved, and stood at the side of the pool where Mr. Looney baptized Eric Blankenship, a big gawky nineteen-year-old who came running and sobbing up the aisle just as Mr. Looney got finished with me. Eric Blankenship was confessing to all his sins, nonstop, throughout his baptism. His sins were a whole lot more interesting than mine, involving things he'd done with his girlfriend, and I strained to hear them as I stood there, but I could not, because of all the noise in the church.

And then it was over and everyone crowded forward to hug us, including Tammy. But even in that moment of hugging Tammy, who of course had been baptized for years and years, I saw something new in her eyes. Somehow, now, there was a difference between us, where before there had been none. But I was wet and freezing, busy accepting the congratulations of the faithful, so I didn't have time to think any more about it then. Tammy gave me her sweater and they drove me home, where Aunt Liddie looked at me in a very fishy way when I walked in the door.

"I just got baptized," I said, and she said, "Oh," and then she went out to lunch with Hudson Bell, who came up the front walk not a minute behind me, sparing me further explanations.

Aunt Liddie came back from that lunch engaged, with a huge square-cut diamond. Nobody mentioned my baptism.

But the very next night, right after supper, Mama called to say that Paul was fine. All of a sudden, he had turned to the night nurse and asked for a cheeseburger. There seemed to be no brain damage at all except that he had some trouble remembering things, which was to be expected. He would have to stay in the hospital for several more weeks, but he would recover completely. He would be just fine.

I burst into tears of joy. I knew I had done it all. And for the first time, I realized what an effort it had been. The first thing I did was go into the kitchen and fix myself a milk shake, with Hershey's syrup. And my bed felt so good that night, after the weeks on the floor. I intended to pray without ceasing that very night, a prayer of thanksgiving for Paul's delivery, but I fell asleep instantly.

When Mama came back, I hoped she would be so busy that my baptism would be overlooked completely, but this was not the case. Aunt Liddie told her, after all.

"Karen," was Mama's reaction, "I am *shocked!* We are not the kind of family that goes out in the county and immerses ourselves in water. I can't imagine what you were thinking of," Mama said.

I looked out the window at Mama's blooming roses. It was two weeks before the end of school, before Ashley's graduation.

"Well, *what?*" Mama asked. She was peering at me closely, more closely than she had looked at me in years.

"Why did you do it?" Mama asked. She lit a cigarette.

I didn't say a thing.

"Karen," Mama said. "I asked you a question." She blew a smoke ring.

I looked at the roses. "I wanted to be saved," I said.

Mama's lips went into that little red bow. "I see," she said.

So later, that next weekend when she refused to let me spend the night out at Tammy's, I did the only thing I could: I lied and said I was going to spend the night with Sara Ruth Johnson, and then prayed without ceasing that I would not be found out. Since it was senior prom weekend and Mama was to be in charge of the decorations and also a chaperone, I felt fairly certain I'd get away with it. But when the time came for the invitational that Sunday morning in the Maranatha Church, I simply could not resist. I pushed back Tammy's restraining hand, rushed forward, and rededicated my life.

"I don't think you're supposed to rededicate your life right after you just dedicated it," Tammy whispered to me later, but I didn't care. I was wet and holy. If I had committed some breach of heavenly etiquette, surely Mr. Looney would tell me. But he did not. We didn't stay for dinner on the ground that day either. As soon as Tammy's mother came to, they drove me straight home, and neither of them said much.

Mama's Cadillac was parked in the drive.

So I went around to the back of the house and tiptoed in through the laundry room door, carrying my shoes. But Mama was waiting for me. She stood by the ironing board, smoking a cigarette. She looked at me, narrowing her eyes.

"Don't drip on the kitchen floor, Missie just mopped it yesterday," she said.

I climbed up the back stairs to my room.

The next weekend, I had to go to Ashley's graduation and to the baccalaureate sermon on Sunday morning in the Confederate Chapel at Lorton Hall. I sat between my grandparents. My Aunt Liddie was there too, with her fiancé. My daddy did not come. I wore a dressy white dress with a little bolero jacket and patent-leather shoes with Cuban heels—my first high heels. I felt precarious and old, grown-up and somehow sinful, and longed for the high hard pews of the Maranatha Church and the piercing, keening voices of the women singers.

But I never attended the Maranatha Church again. As soon as my school was over, I was sent away to Camp Alleghany in West Virginia for two months—the maximum stay. I didn't want to go, even though this meant that I would finally have a chance to learn horseback riding, but I had no choice in the matter. Mama made this clear. It was to separate me from Tammy, whom Mama had labeled a Terrible Influence.

"And by the way," Mama said brightly, "Margaret Applewhite will be going to Camp Alleghany too!" Oh, I could see right through Mama. But I couldn't do anything about it. Camp started June 6, so I didn't have time to pray for a change in my fate. She sprang it on me. Instead, I cried without ceasing all that long day before they put me and my trunk, along with Margaret Applewhite and her trunk, on the train. I tried and tried to call Tammy to tell her good-bye, but a recorded message said that her line had been disconnected. (This had happened several times before, whenever her mama couldn't pay the bill.) My father would be going away too, to Shepherd Pratt Hospital in Baltimore, Maryland, and Ashley was going to Europe.

Sitting glumly by Mama at the train station, I tried to pray but could not. Instead, I remembered a game we used to play when I was real little, Statues. In Statues, one person grabs you by the hand and swings you around and around and then lets you go, and whatever position you land in, you have to freeze like that until everybody else is thrown. The person who lands in the best position wins. But what I remembered was that scary moment of being flung wildly out into the world screaming, to land however I hit, and I felt like this was happening to us all.

To my surprise, I loved camp. Camp Alleghany was an old camp, with rough-hewn wooden buildings that seemed to grow right out of the deep woods surrounding them. Girls had been carving their initials in the railings outside the dining hall for years and years. It was a tradition. I loved to run my fingers over these initials, imagining these girls—M.H., 1948; J.B., 1953; M.N., 1935. Some of the initials were very old. These girls were grown up by now. Some of them were probably dead. This gave me an enormous thrill, as did all the other traditions at Camp Alleghany. I loved the weekend campfire, as big as a tepee, ceremoniously lit by the Camp Spirit, whoever she happened to be that week. The Camp Spirit got to light the campfire with an enormous match, invoking the spirits with an ancient verse that only she was permitted to repeat. At the end of each weekly campfire, a new Camp Spirit was named, with lots of screaming, crying, and hugging. I was dying to be the Camp Spirit. In fact, after the very first campfire, I set this as my goal, cooperating like crazy with all the counselors so I would be picked. But it wasn't hard for me to cooperate.

I loved wearing a uniform, being a part of the group—I still have the photograph from that first session of camp, all of us wearing our navy shorts, white socks, and white camp shirts, our hair squeaky-clean, grinning into the sun. I loved all my activities—arts and crafts, where we made huge ashtrays for our parents out of little colored tiles; swimming, where I already excelled and soon became the acknowledged champion of the breaststroke in all competitions; and drama, where we were readying a presentation of *Spoon River*. My canoeing group took a long sunrise trip upstream to an island where we cooked our breakfast out over a fire: grits, sausage, eggs. Everything had a smoky, exotic taste, and the smoke from our breakfast campfire rose to mingle with the patchy mist still clinging to the trees, still rising from the river. I remember lying on my back and gazing up at how the sunshine looked, like light through a stained-glass window, emerald green and iridescent in the leafy tops of the tallest trees. The river was as smooth and shiny as a mirror. In fact it reminded me of a mirror, of Ashley's mirror-topped dressing table back home.

And the long trail rides—when we finally got to take them—were even better than the canoe trips. But first we had to go around and around the riding ring, learning to post, learning to canter. The truth was, I didn't like the horses nearly as much as I'd expected to. For one thing, they were a lot *bigger* than I had been led to believe by the illustrations in my horse books. They were as big as cars. For another thing they were not lovable either. They were smelly, and some of them were downright mean. One big old black horse named Martini was pointed out to us early on as a biter. Others kicked. On a trail ride, you didn't want to get behind one of these. Still, the trail rides were great. We lurched along through the forest, following the leader. I felt like I was in a western movie, striking out into the territory. On the longest trail ride, we took an overnight trip up to Pancake Mountain, where we ate s'mores (Hershey bars and melted marshmallows smashed into a sandwich between two graham crackers), told ghost stories, and went to sleep finally with the wheezing and stamping of the horses in our ears.

Actually, I liked the riding counselors better than I liked the horses. The regular counselors were sweet, pretty girls who went to school at places like Hollins and Sweet Briar, or else maternal, jolly older women who taught junior high school during the regular year, but the riding counselors were tough, tan, muscular young women who squinted into the sun and could post all day long if they had to. The riding counselors said "Shit" a lot, and smoked cigarettes in the barn. They did not speak of college.

My only male counselor was a frail, nervous young man named Jeffrey Long, reputed to be the nephew of the owner. He taught nature study, which I loved. I loved identifying the various trees (hickory, five leaves; ironwood, the satiny metallic trunk; maple, the little wings; blue-berried juniper; droopy willow). We made sassafras toothbrushes, and brushed our teeth in the river.

On Sundays, we had church in the big rustic assembly hall. It was an Episcopal service, which seemed pretty boring to me in comparison with the Maranatha Church. Yet I liked the Prayer Book, and I particularly liked one of the Episcopal hymns, which I had never heard before, "I Sing a Song of the Saints of God," with its martial, military tune. I imagined Joan of Arc striding briskly along in a satin uniform, to just that tune. I also liked the hymn "Jerusalem," especially the weird lines that went, "Bring me my staff of burnished gold, bring me my arrows of desire." I loved the "arrows of desire" part.

We all wore white shirts and white shorts to church. After church we had a special Sunday lunch, with fried chicken and ice cream. "I scream, you scream, we all scream for ice cream!" we'd shout, banging on the tables before they brought it out. (In order to have any, you had to turn in an Ice Cream Letter—to your parents—as you came in the door.)

On Sunday nights, we all climbed the hill behind the dining hall for vespers. We sat on our ponchos looking down on the camp as the sun set, and sang "Day Is Done." We bowed our heads in silent prayer. Then, after about ten minutes of this, one of the junior counselors played "Taps" on the bugle. She played it every night at lights out too. I much admired the bugler's jaunty, boyish stance. I had already resolved to take up the bugle, first thing, when I got back home.

And speaking of home, I'd barely thought of it since arriving at Camp Alleghany. I was entirely too busy. I guess that was the idea. Still, every now and then in a quiet moment—during silent prayer at vespers, for instance; or rest hour right after lunch, when we usually played Go Fish or some other card game, but sometimes, *sometimes* I just lay on my cot and thought about things; or at night, after "Taps," when I'd lie looking up at the rafters before I fell asleep—in those quiet moments, I did think of home, and of my salvation. I didn't have as much time as I needed, there at camp, to pray without ceasing. Besides, I was often too tired to do it. Other times, I was having too much fun to do it. Sometimes I just forgot. To pray without ceasing requires either a solitary life or a life of invisibility such as I had led within my family for the past year.

What about my family, anyway? Did I miss them? Not a bit. I could scarcely recall what they looked like. Mama wrote that Paul was back home already and had a job at the snack bar at the country club. Ashley was in France. Daddy was still in Baltimore, where he would probably stay for six more months. Mama was very busy helping Aunt Liddie plan her wedding, which I would be in. I would wear an aqua dress and dyed-to-match heels. I read Mama's letter curiously, several times. I felt like I had to translate it, like it was written in a foreign language. I folded this letter up and placed it in the top tray of my trunk, where I would find it years later. Right then, I didn't have time to think about my family. I was too busy doing everything I was supposed to, so that I might be picked as Camp Spirit. (Everybody agreed that the current Camp Spirit, Jeannie Darling from Florida, was a stuck-up bitch who didn't deserve it at all.) At the last campfire of First Session, I had high hopes that I might replace her. We started out by singing all the camp songs, first the funny ones such as "I came on the train and arrived in the rain, my trunk came a week later on." Each "old" counselor had a song composed in her honor, and we sang them all. It took forever. As we finally sang the Camp Spirit song, my heart started beating like crazy.

But it was not to be. No, it was Jeanette Peterson, a skinny boring redhead from Margaret Applewhite's cabin. I started crying but nobody knew why, because by then everybody else was crying too, and we all continued to cry as we sang all the sad camp songs about loyalty and friendships and candle flames. This last campfire was also Friendship Night. We had made little birchbark boats that afternoon, and traded them with our best friends. At the end of the campfire, the counselors passed out short white candles which we lit and carried down to the river in a solemn procession. Then we placed the candles in our little boats and set them in the water, singing our hearts out as the flotilla of candles entered the current and moved slowly down the dark river and out of sight around the bend. I clung to my New Best Friend and cried. This was Shelley Long from Leesburg, Virginia, with a freckled, heart-shaped face and a pixie haircut, who talked a mile a minute all the time. It was even possible that Shelley Long had read more books than I had, unlike my Old Best Friend Tammy back at home in Alabama, who had not read any books at all, and did not intend to. Plus, Shelley Long owned a pony and a pony cart. She had shown me a picture of herself at home in Leesburg, driving her pony cart. Her house, in the background, looked like Mount Vernon. I was heartbroken when she left, the morning after Friendship Night.

It rained that morning, a cold drizzle that continued without letup for the next two days. About three-quarters of the campers left after First Session, including everybody I liked. Margaret Applewhite stayed. My last vision of the departing campers was a rainy blur of waving hands as the big yellow buses pulled out, headed for the train station and the airport. All the girls were singing at the top of their lungs, and their voices seemed to linger in the air long after they were gone. Then came a day and a half of waiting around for the Second Session campers to arrive, a day and a half in which nobody talked to me much, and the counselors were busy doing things like counting the rifle shells. So I became invisible again, free to wander about in the rain, free to pray without ceasing.

Finally the new campers arrived, and I brightened somewhat at the chance to be an Old Girl, to show the others the ropes and teach them the words to the songs. My New Best Friend was Anne Roper, from Lexington, Kentucky. She wasn't as good as Shelley, but she was the best I could do, I felt, considering what I had to pick from. Anne Roper was okay.

But my new counselor was very weird. She read aloud to us each day at rest hour from a big book named *The Fountainhead*, by Ayn Rand. Without asking our parents, she pierced all our ears. Even this ear-piercing did not bring my spirits up to the level of First

Session, however. For one thing, it never stopped raining. It rained and rained and rained. First, we couldn't go swimming—the river was too high, too cold, too fast. We couldn't go canoeing either. The tennis courts looked like lakes. The horses, along with the riding counselors, stayed in their barn. About all we could do was arts and crafts and Skits, which got old fast. Lots of girls got homesick. They cried during "Taps."

I cried then and at other odd times too, such as when I walked up to breakfast through the constant mist that came up now from the river, or at church. I was widely thought to be homesick. To cheer me up, my weird counselor gave me a special pair of her own earrings, little silver hoops with turquoise chips in them, made by Navajos.

Then I got bronchitis. I developed a deep, thousand-year-old Little Match Girl cough that started way down in my knees. Because of this cough, I was allowed to call my mother, and to my surprise, I found myself asking to come home. But Mama said no. She said,

We always finish what we start, Karen.

So that was that. I was taken into town for a penicillin shot, and started getting better. The sun came out too.

But because I still had such a bad cough, I did not have to participate in the all-camp Game Day held during the third week of Second Session. I was free to lounge in my upper bunk and read the rest of *The Fountainhead*, which I did. By then I had read way ahead of my counselor. I could hear the screams and yells of the girls out on the playing fields, but vaguely, far away. Then I heard them all singing, from farther up the hill, and I knew they had gone into Assembly to give out the awards. I knew I was probably expected to show up at Assembly too, but somehow I just couldn't summon up the energy. I didn't care who got the awards. I didn't care which team won—the Green or the Gold, it was all the same to me—or which cabin won the ongoing competition among cabins. I didn't even care who was Camp Spirit. Instead I lolled on my upper bunk and looked at the turning dust in a ray of light that came in through a chink in the cabin. I coughed. I felt that I would die soon.

This is when it happened.

This is when it always happens, I imagine—when you least expect it, when you are least prepared.

Suddenly, as I stared at the ray of sunshine, it intensified, growing brighter and brighter until the whole cabin was a blaze of light. I sat right up, as straight as I could. I crossed my legs. I knew I was waiting for something. I knew something was going to happen. I could barely breathe. My heart pounded so hard I feared it might jump right out of my chest and land on the cabin floor. I don't know how long I sat there like that, waiting.

"Karen," He said.

His voice filled the cabin.

I knew immediately who it was. No question. For one thing, there were no men at Camp Alleghany except for Mr. Grizzard, who cleaned out the barn, and Jeffrey Long, who had a high, reedy voice.

This voice was deep, resonant, full of power.

"Yes, Lord?" I said.

He did not speak again. But as I sat there on my upper bunk I was filled with His presence, and I knew what I must do.

I jumped down from my bunk, washed my face and brushed my teeth at the sink in the corner, tucked in my shirt, and ran up the hill to the assembly hall. I did not cough. I burst right in through the big double doors at the front and elbowed old Mrs. Beemer aside as she read out the results of the archery meet to the rows of girls in their folding chairs.

Mrs. Beemer took one look at me and shut her mouth.

I opened my mouth, closed my eyes, and started speaking in Tongues of Fire.

I came to in the infirmary, surrounded by the camp nurse, the doctor from town, the old lady who owned the camp, the Episcopal chaplain, my own counselor, and several other people I didn't even know. I smiled at them all. I felt great, but they made me stay in the infirmary for two more days to make sure I had gotten over it. During this time I was given red Jell-O and Cokes, and the nurse took my temperature every four hours. The chaplain talked to me for a long time. He was a tall, quiet man with wispy white hair that stood out all around his head. I got to talk to my mother on the telephone again, and this time she promised me a kitten if I would stay until the end of camp. I had always, always wanted a kitten, but I had never been allowed to have one because it would get hair on the upholstery and also because Ashley was allergic to cats.

"What about Ashley?" I asked.

"Never you mind," Mama said.

So it was decided. I would stay until the end of camp, and Mama would buy me a kitten.

I got out of the infirmary the next day and went back to my cabin, where everybody treated me with a lot of deference and respect for the rest of Second Session, choosing me first for softball, letting me star in Skits. And at the next-to-last campfire, I was named Camp Spirit. I got to run forward, scream and cry, but it was not as good as it would have been if it had happened First Session. It was an anticlimax. Still, I did get to light the very last campfire, the Friendship Night campfire, with my special giant match and say ceremoniously:

> Kneel always when you light a fire,
> Kneel reverently,
> And thankful be
> For God's unfailing majesty.

Then everybody sang the Camp Spirit song. By now, I was getting *really tired of singing.* Then Anne Roper and I sailed each other's little birchbark boats off into the night, our candles guttering wildly as they rounded the bend.

All the way home on the train the next day, I pretended to be asleep while I prayed without ceasing that nobody back home would find out I had spoken in tongues of fire. For now it seemed to me an exalted and private and scary thing, and somehow I knew it was not over yet. I felt quite sure that I had been singled out for some terrible, holy mission. Perhaps I would even have to *die,* like Joan of Arc. As the train rolled south through Virginia on that beautiful August day, I felt myself moving inexorably toward my Destiny, toward some last act of my own Skit which was yet to be played out.

The minute I walked onto the concrete at the country club pool, I knew that Margaret Applewhite (who had flown home) had told everybody. Dennis Jones took one look at me, threw back his head, and began to gurgle wildly, clutching at his stomach. Tommy Martin ran out on the low board, screamed in gibberish, and then flung himself into the water. Even I had to laugh at him. But Paul and his friends teased me in a more sophisticated manner. "Hey, Karen," one of them might say, clutching his arm, "I've got a real bad tennis elbow here, do you think you can heal it for me?"

I was famous all over town. I sort of enjoyed it. I began to feel popular and cute, like the girls on *American Bandstand.*

But the kitten was a disaster. Mama drove me out in the county one afternoon in her white Cadillac to pick it out of a litter that the laundry lady's cat had had. The kittens were all so tiny that it was hard to pick—little mewling, squirming things, still blind. Drying sheets billowed all around them, on rows of clotheslines. "I want *that* one," I said, picking the smallest, a teeny little orange ball. I named him Sandy. I got to keep Sandy in a shoe box in my room, then in a basket in my room. But as time passed (Ashley came home from Europe, Paul went back to W&L) it became clear to me that there was something terribly wrong with Sandy. Sandy *mewed too much,* not a sweet mewing, but a little howl like a lost soul. He never purred. He wouldn't grow right either, even though I fed him half-and-half. He stayed little and jerky. He didn't act like a cat. One time I asked my mother, "Are you *sure* Sandy is a regular cat?" and she frowned at me and said, "Well, of *course* he is, what's the matter with you, Karen?" but I was not so sure. Sandy startled too easily. Sometimes he would leap straight up in the air, land on all four feet, and just stand there quivering, for no good reason at all. While I was watching him do this one day, it came to me.

Sandy was a Holy Cat. He was possessed by the spirit, as I had been. I put his basket in the laundry room. I was fitted for my aqua semiformal dress, and wore it in Aunt Liddie's wedding. Everybody said I looked grown-up and beautiful. I got to wear a corsage. I got to drink champagne. We had a preschool meeting of the Sub-Deb Club, and I was elected secretary. I kept trying to call Tammy, from pay phones downtown and the phone out at the country club, so

Mama wouldn't know, but her number was still out of order. Tammy never called me.

Then Ashley invited me to go to the drive-in movie with her and her friends, just before she left for Sweet Briar. The movie was *All That Heaven Allows*, which I found incredibly moving, but Ashley and her friends smoked cigarettes and giggled through the whole thing. They couldn't be serious for five minutes. But they were being real nice to me, so I volunteered to go to the snack bar for them the second or third time they wanted more popcorn. On the way back from the snack bar, in the window of a red Thunderbird with yellow flames painted on its hood, I saw Tammy's face.

I didn't hesitate for a minute. I was *so* glad to see her! "Tammy!" I screamed. The position of My Best Friend was, of course, vacant. I ran right over to the Thunderbird, shifted all the popcorn boxes over to my left hand, and flung open the door. And sure enough, there was Tammy, *with the whole top of her sundress down*. It all happened in an instant. I saw a boy's dark hair, but not his face—his head was in her lap.

Tammy's breasts loomed up out of the darkness at me. They were perfectly round and white, like tennis balls. But it seemed to me that they were too high up to look good. They were too close to her chin.

Clearly, Tammy was Petting. And in a flash I remembered what Mama had told me about Petting, that

> a nice girl does not Pet. It is cruel to the boy to allow him to Pet, because he has no control over himself. He is just a boy. It is all up to the girl. If she allows the boy to Pet her, then he will become excited, and if he cannot find relief, then the poison will all back up into his organs, causing pain and sometimes death.

I slammed the car door. I fled back to Ashley and her friends, spilling popcorn everyplace as I went.

On the screen, Rock Hudson had been Petting too. Now we got a close-up of his rugged cleft chin. "Give me one of those cigarettes," I said to Ashley, and without batting an eye, she did. After three tries, I got it lit. It tasted good.

The next day, Ashley left for Sweet Briar, and soon after that, my school started too. Whenever I passed Tammy in the hall, we said hello, but did not linger in conversation. I was put in the Gifted and Talented group for English and French. I decided to go out for JV cheerleader. I practiced and practiced and practiced. Then, one day in early September, my cat Sandy—after screaming out and leaping straight up in the air—ran out into the street in front of our house and was immediately hit by a Merita bread truck.

I knew it was suicide.

I buried him in the backyard, in a box from Rich's department store, along with Ashley's scarab bracelet which I had stolen sometime earlier. She wondered for years whatever happened to that bracelet. It was her favorite.

I remember how relieved I felt when I had smoothed the final shovelful of dirt over Sandy's grave. Somehow, I knew, the last of my holiness, of my chosenness, went with him. Now I wouldn't have to die. Now my daddy would get well, and I would make cheerleader, and go to college. Now I could grow up, get breasts, and have babies. Since then, all these things have happened. But there are moments yet, moments when in the midst of life a silence falls, and in those moments I catch myself still listening for that voice. *"Karen,"* He will say, and I'll say, "Yes, Lord. Yes." †

Interview

When Lee Smith was a little girl, she gave God a tea party. Perhaps remembering that, she told me she was relieved when she learned that I would be interviewing Harry Crews; until then, she said, she'd been concerned that her interview would be the most "heathen" one in the book. Such good-humored worry about piety and heathenism is emblematic of Lee Smith's utterly engaging personality, how she greets and is greeted by the world. Of medium height and build, with blond hair and light blue eyes, a radiant smile, and Scots-Irish fair skin, Smith is noted for her generosity of spirit, quick wit, and completely unaffected, easy manner. A native of the small mining town of Grundy, Virginia, she speaks in a clear, mountain accent, telling stories with an ironic twist, a self-deprecating joke, or a pinprick at pretentiousness. In describing her genuine struggles with religious belief and morality, she says, "I'm so much *not* New Age."

An extraordinary number of friends from every part of the country and from all periods of her life still come to see her. On vacation at a friend's summer house in Maine, she sits at the kitchen table, looking out over the lake and mountains beyond, and writes funny post cards (one card that pictures a moose grazing in the foreground, a little apart from the herd, gets the caption: "Married moose dreaming of the single life").

Recently, Lee Smith teamed up with the Tarwater Band (a folk trio who named themselves after the backwoods prophet in Flannery O'Connor's *The Violent Bear It Away*) for a combined reading/concert in which she read from her latest novel, *The Devil's Dream*, and the band sang original and traditional mountain tunes from the book, such as "The Riddle Song" and "Shady Grove." Introducing a passage, she confessed, "I always wanted to write a story in which God speaks; in this one, He not only speaks, but sings."

Lee Smith claims that she cannot sing (or even keep rhythm), but all who know her know that she sings beautifully through her work and her life, with a feeling, a clarity—and a wallop—that is as extraordinary and as comforting as corn whiskey and wild honey. Throughout my interview with her, she talked with a lively sense of humor about her life and work. A keen listener, observer, and storyteller, Smith spoke openly and poignantly about her impassioned religious sensibility as a child, how in her beloved mountains God and nature were one, so that her "whole childhood was really full of God and wonders."

On a warm June day we sat drinking coffee on a chintz sofa in Lee's downstairs den. Bookshelves lined the entirety of one long wall; her writing desk sat in a corner between the bookshelves and the gray brick fireplace on the wall opposite us. Sliding glass doors provided a pleasant view out over thickly wooded land. The day was balmy, clear, and breezy, like many June days in these parts; the tulip poplars and oak trees were budding with new green leaves, providing rest for our eyes as we talked.

Let me begin by asking you about your religious sensibility and its origins. Flannery O'Connor once wrote that she always admired believers who came to the faith as adults because she would find it difficult to believe in some of the more mystical tenets of her faith without having been "brung up to it." How were you "brung up" to your religion as a child in Grundy? Do these experiences show up in any of your fiction? One way to approach this might be to talk about Karen, in "Tongues of Fire."

"Tongues of Fire" in a way is truly one of the most autobiographical stories I have ever written. The family is all made up, but the character of Karen is absolutely the way I was as a child, including the obsessive reading, and the obsessive religion. I was raised in a little church, the Grundy Methodist Church, that was very straight-laced, but I had a friend whose mother spoke in tongues. I was just wild for this family. I would have gone to live with them if they'd let me. My parents were older, and they were so overprotective. I just loved the "letting go" that happened when I would go to church with my friend.

And then later, I got a boyfriend who was a member of another church. This was a *wild* church. And I would go to the revival with him and be saved—constantly. So religion and sex—you know, excitement, passion—were all together. I couldn't differentiate between sexual passion and religious passion. This was what we all did on dates, was go to the revival. It was a turn-on.

Things were done very literally. One thing they did at that church that I'll never forget, was that they had a big ply-board thing, in the front of the church, full of light bulbs. This was at regular church. If you were present, you and your family, you'd go up and screw in your light bulb. And it would turn on. And over the top of the whole thing, it said, "Let Your Little Light Shine." And if you weren't there, it would be so obvious to everyone else in the congregation because your little light would not be shining. Something about that, I don't know—it was the only thing that was happening for me in terms of excitement.

You were saved several times?

Yes, I was just given to rededicating my life and being saved. All this was an embarrassment to my mother. I was a Methodist, and I had been sprinkled as a baby. I was perfectly saved as far as she was concerned and she wished I would quit going to these other churches and "acting up." You know, it was a "low-class" thing to do, in my mother's eyes. But even in the Methodist Church, which I went to, and MYF, and church camp every summer, and retreats, I was—more so even than Karen in the story—a very religious child. A *very* religious child. I was such a religious child that I used to think that I heard God speaking to me. In fact, I still think I may have. I mean I'm not putting that down. Because I was an only child, and I was by myself a lot of the time, and I did a whole lot of nonstop praying, reading the Bible, thinking, and so on. I loved Joan of Arc, and I loved these inspirational stories like Karen does.

Nature particularly inspired me. For instance when I was at camp, several times I was absolutely sure that I heard God, or saw a vision, or whatever. I'm sure there could be a psychiatric word for the kind of little child I was.

I was also given to rituals. Like before I went to bed at night, I had about twelve things I had to do. The door had to be cracked a certain way because there was a witch in the closet. The light had to be a certain way, this and that. I was always prone to imaginings.

Did this passion last throughout your girlhood?

Yes, up through high school—all the time I lived in Grundy. I would go to youth revivals. I would speak at youth revivals—up until the time I went away to school to St. Catherine's [a preparatory school for girls in Richmond]. St. Catherine's was Episcopal. I'm telling you, all that stuff, that institutionalized ritual, just knocked it out of me. It deadened all the passion. Somehow, in the town I grew up in, I associated religion with a kind of a life force. Then all of a sudden at St. Catherine's, since it was an Episcopal school and it had all these rules, I began to associate religion with a death force. I guess it's fair to say I outgrew it; I got interested in other things. It was one of those things of childhood.

Do you feel sometimes that you miss it? Or was it somehow a relief to go beyond it?

I was sort of glad to outgrow it because it was wearing me out. It was becoming clear to me that I was getting to be at an age that I would have to do a lot more with it, or just give it up. Because with me, I've always been, unfortunately, an all-or-nothing kind of person. I still feel that way now. I feel like, okay, if I want to start really going to church again, I'm going to have to really go.

I've heard you mention that before—that you'd have to be involved completely if you should ever think about becoming involved again. It is as if there aren't any restraining forces, that you must go whole hog.

Yes, anything I'm in, I get completely into, and for that reason, I think I have held back. I think it is because I was that kind of a child. I was so completely wrapped up in it. You know, I associated it with nature, and I was a real tom-boy. We played in the mountains, all the time. And it was like the whole world of my childhood was really full of God and wonders. But as you get older that sort of thing scares you because there are not any boundaries. It was terrifying. So I think in a funny way, I was glad to hit St. Catherine's, and all those rules, and all that mumbo-jumbo.

The ritual did seem to kill any joy; it's a "kill-joy." Though you felt that need for ritual in your daily emotional life as a child, the institution managed to overdo it. Was it a matter of overkill?

It was for me in terms of religion. After that I pulled back. I still have the sense of it, and probably some day I will have to find that

again. I have a feeling that it's out there. I associate it with the
mountains. At some point I'll have to move back to the mountains,
I think. At some point I'll have to throw myself into it all again.

*Have you ever been to any black church services? The times I've
been able to throw myself into things and even be transported have
been at black revivals.*

Yes, as a matter of fact I just heard Jesse Jackson in Atlanta, last
Saturday. Just the way the crowd is! Yes, being transported is
something that I have always both desired and feared. More than
anything else. It's what used to happen to me as a child, but it's
what's scariest to happen as an adult, because as an adult, you have
to be responsible. You know, I can't be transported. I have to go to
the grocery store.

Yes, and I have to be back by three to pick up the kids.

I can't have a religious experience; I have to be back by three. All
these people are depending on me. I did feel a sense of being lifted
up at Jesse Jackson's sermon; everybody was holding hands, swaying. That was a wonderful time.

*You know, I think it's significant that your sense of being carried
away as a child was so sensuous, so concrete. You felt closest to the
spiritual in the mountains, in nature. Everything was all of one
piece rather than the spiritual being divorced from the physical and
confined to an institution, a church, a separate place. In the usual
idea of what it means to be religious, church is where you go and
are asked to renounce the physical world as being the source of
temptation and sin. You're asked to separate the physical from the
spiritual, at least the sensual from the spiritual.*

I surely did have that sense at the Episcopal Church. I did associate that renunciation with all the rules at St. Catherine's. When I
went there, we had so many, many social rules.

*It's as if some churches fear the physical so much that they feel
they have to build a containment vessel for it, like they do for a
nuclear reactor.*

And strangely enough, I married somebody who had a similar
experience. Jim Seay had been the most religious boy in the world,
in Mississippi. In fact, he had gone to a Bible college, Mercer
College, and even when he was as old as twenty-one, he was going
to be a youth minister, and he went to Ridgecrest every summer.

But he had stopped all that by the time he got to Ole Miss, fairly late, in his twenties. When I married him, he, too, was threatened by the consuming power of his religion, didn't want to fall back into it. He did not go to church, did not want to go to church, did not want anybody else to go to church. Maybe if I'd married somebody who was a church-goer, I would have learned how to maintain a balance. Or seen how I could be religious and not have it take over my life. But as it was, for a long time, I didn't have anything to do with the church.

Yet, oddly enough, I was writing about it all the time. Except in my work, I didn't want anything to do with it. [Laughter] But I was always thinking about it.

Except in one of the most important areas in your life, your creative work.

Right, exactly. But I mean in my daily life, I just shied away from it.

I understand that so well. I had a similar experience growing up. And here I thought I was the only one. Have you ever read The Spiritual Life of Children *by Robert Coles?*

No, I have not. But I want to.

It presents with such respect accounts of the spiritual lives of these youngsters who talk quite openly and lucidly about their own spiritual lives and what we've been talking about. It's very moving to read.

And it's all real.

I think one reason it's so real is because for these children, religion involves their whole body, along with the whole mind and spirit. They do not have the capacity or the desire to compartmentalize the experience. And, as you said, you still feel a mixture of desire and fear, you still feel you have to "contain" yourself. Ironically, this only demonstrates that you are an intensely spiritual person.

Well, I have never gotten away from this ideal, this notion—I take it seriously. I'm always worried about what's the right thing to do. It's so hard to figure out in the real world what is the right thing to do. What is good? I struggle with it all the time. I spend a lot of time thinking about it. It's just old-fashioned morality, I guess.

It's making a genuine effort to know, to understand, to do what's right.

Yeah, I think we all have to make the effort.

There are some people who don't do that.

Yes, they just don't think it's anything to worry about. And you know, my whole notion of morality runs counter to the "Do your own thing, follow your bliss" idea. I'm so much *not* New Age.

What do you think of Joseph Campbell?

I love Joseph Campbell's ideas on religion and culture. I love to think in terms of comparative religions. I think Joseph Campbell is very much a moralist. But a casual reading or a casual interpretation of his theories does lead to a very hedonistic, New Age kind of thinking that a lot of people are following that I don't think he ever intended.

Some people might find a way to make any statement self-serving and hedonistic, in any case.

What they're looking for is more of a justification of what they're going to do anyway.

This intensity, and passion, and your need to achieve a balance —

Yes! I'm still working on it. I believe in God, I've just never been able to find a way to act on that without having it take me over. I'm scared I'll be taken over. I need to find a church somewhere, some way to be able to act on it more without feeling I'll be engulfed.

Caught up in the whirlwind.

Yes, I see it as a whirlwind, I really do. Also, as I get older, more and more, I see the importance of the church in the community. I was against the institution of the church for two reasons for a while—the Episcopal church was so deadening with its rituals, and the primitive church that had turned me on so much as a girl, well, they put down women. Therefore, as an adult, I still need to find a church that doesn't put down or stamp out things that I believe are basically good. It's something I struggle with all the time. Maybe I'll just die struggling with it and never get it reconciled. But it's real important to me.

It's a very painful thing, isn't it?

It's very real.

You mentioned something about it being something you've needed to pull away from, except in your writing. How do you think this struggle is played out in your writing?

I don't know. I'm not very articulate in talking about my writing. I'll say one thing, I'm one of those kinds of writers who writes a lot. I have written a lot ever since I was a girl. I write fiction the way a lot of people write in their journals. It's only several years later that you go back, read through your journal, and see what's going on. I go back and read my fiction, and see what's going on. *Fair and Tender Ladies* is so much about the struggle we've been talking about. And Ivy is like me; she is unable to find a religion that suits her—an organized religion. She makes up her own. Writing for her is sort of like it has been for me—a sort of a saving thing. Almost a religion of its own.

Writing is a kind of salvation?

Yes, as a way to get in touch with that intensity, a way of getting in touch with and staying true to me. I do feel, when I'm writing at a fever pitch, that intensity that you feel when you get saved. There's nothing else that makes you feel like that. There's getting saved, sex, and writing. Those are the only things I know of. [Laughter]

That pretty much says it all. Except, of course, chocolate pecan pie, which some people say is better than sex.

It might be! But anyway, Ivy struggles with those things, with the only religion she is exposed to, her mountain church, in the same way that I struggle. And she dies without finding God in the traditional sense. And I might too.

For Ivy's people, her community, religion is a serious matter. It evokes extreme behaviors. From early childhood, it was a norm for you to think about good and evil, and when you'll be saved, will you go to heaven or hell. That is one reason I loved Karen, and Tammy's mother in "Tongues of Fire." The book I'm doing is a book about southern religion as it's treated in southern fiction. There may be some fascinating connection between being southern and being compelled to come to terms with religion.

You do have to, if you grew up in a southern community. You can't evade it. Now you can grow up in some place like Chapel Hill, as my own children have, unfortunately, and not really be exposed to religion and not be called into account for not knowing anything. There are plenty of children who are not regular churchgoers, these days, whose families are not, and it's no social stigma, or anything. But in Grundy where I grew up, when some family was mentioned, somebody'd say, well, they're Methodist, or they're Presbyterian, or they go to So-and-So's church, or whatever. In the South, if you grew up at the time when we did in a small community, you were exposed to it intensely as a part of daily life. It is still true in small towns; it's only not true in university towns, and in towns as big as Atlanta and Charlotte.

You know, when Karen got saved, over at Tammy's church, as she was standing there dripping wet, Tammy suddenly looked at her differently, as if a wall had gone up between them. What was that all about?

I think that Tammy herself didn't take all that "religion stuff" as seriously as Karen. It was just a part of the way her mother was to Tammy. Tammy could take it or leave it; but for Karen, it was a big deal. Karen was on a spiritual quest. Tammy wasn't. To Tammy, it was just something that embarrassed her.

When Karen was spending the night with Tammy, she saw Tammy's mother reading her Bible at five o'clock in the afternoon, during "gin-and-tonic time," as Karen says. This was a striking difference between the two families and cultures that she had never thought about before. That contrast in turn came to be a wall between the two girls. When I read the story, it struck me how very sad this story is. It is a story about loneliness and difference, the alienation, of many of the characters. It's one of the saddest stories I've ever read.

It's a real sad story. It's really sad what's happening to the father there. It's dealt with in a sort of ironic tone, but it's just terribly sad, what's happening.

Here we've got a brother well on his way to alcoholism, in a coma, almost dead, a mother who has no earthly notion of how to handle anything, yet she's "got her hands full," a father who is slowly having a nervous breakdown, a sister who is promiscuous, and thirteen-year-old Karen whose wonderful gifts and seriousness about life are going by unseen.

She's invisible, as she says.

Like the "Camp Spirit." Did you become invisible in your family?

I didn't because I was an only child and I couldn't. I think I wanted to. I was entirely *too* visible. Which was why I was glad to leave home. So the story wasn't autobiographical in that sense. Everything I did when I was growing up was remarked upon.

Every breath you drew. Especially in a small town, I bet.

Oh yes.

Who are some other characters in your fiction who are trying to work out their religious ambivalences?

I think Crystal in *Black Mountain Breakdown* is. And in *Oral History,* what Richard Burlage goes to the mountains for is to become less "Episcopalian," to loosen up. To listen. In a way he's sort of an autobiographical character. It's the notion that if you loosen up too much, if you become too spiritual, you go nuts.

You said that writing has enabled you to make some kind of resolution of your own ambivalences?

I continue to feel deep conflicts. But the link for me between my own religious feelings and creativity is that with writing, you go out of yourself—but you know you can come back. You won't stay stuck in the craziness.

Several writers I've interviewed have talked about a deep conflict between their own creativity and the church, both its norms and teachings.

Yes, for me there is a great conflict between the church and my own creativity, all the time. I knew from the beginning I couldn't write about sex or violence, not and expect to go back home. For instance, when the play *Fair and Tender Ladies* was performed in my hometown at the high school auditorium, people came up to Barbara Smith [the actress playing Ivy Rowe] afterwards and talked to her as if there were no difference between the character she played and herself, the real person. And for them, there isn't. There is no difference between the characters and the writer who created them, either. Some church-going people were upset with the sex in the play. You shouldn't write about it, you shouldn't act it out.

But I must be honest when I write, or else why write? So, I've got to write about *some* sex, *some* violence. And about religion. I mean, Jesus has actually spoken to me. It happened to me. When I was young, about thirteen. I heard a voice and it said, "Lee." I think that's why I must write about it, we all must write about it.

Do you think that will remain true for writers and artists here in the South as it becomes, in Walker Percy's phrase, more "Los Angeles-ized"?

Oh yes, more so. I think religion is not dying out, but becoming more influential. You see more and more churches, more little churches everywhere. As a teacher, I see it more in my students.

Doris Betts describes herself as someone who consciously deals with Christian themes and images in her fiction. She says she tries not to hit you over the head with her beliefs, but instead to speak in a whisper, as one does in trying to get the attention of small children. Reynolds Price, too, has spoken openly about this dimension of his life and his writing.

Yes, and Doris and Reynolds Price are both great writers that way. I don't consciously think about those things. I do consciously go through rituals when I'm getting ready to write my novels. I read the Bible all the way through when I was writing *Fair and Tender Ladies.* Ivy did that, too. She hates a good part of the Bible. But she loves Ecclesiastes, where there is the passage about a time for everything. And, in fact, Ecclesiastes became the structure of the last chapter of that novel, and of the whole thing. I mean Ivy thinks the Bible has some "pretty good stories." But Ivy can't accept religion as being available to her—religion as it was taught to her in her mountain church was so anti-women. Also, those early primitive churches in the mountains taught salvation by grace alone—and that's a problem for me. It just seems like another way of justifying frontier hedonism—for men only, that is, not for women. It seems like much of that kind of religion was instituted by men and conspired to hamper women.

You deal with some of that in The Devil's Dream, *don't you?*

Yes, very much so. There was always this split in the mentality of the culture, in its members. In the early days, some bands I write about even had two names, the gospel name for Sunday mornings and the honky-tonk name for Saturday nights. There was always a pull between the honky-tonk life and the church and home life. There were these huge polarities. One big conflict was how to be a star and keep Jesus. Often in these early days, when you got saved, you were given your "gift song," the song you sang when you accepted Jesus as your saviour and renounced your old life. All your music had to then be sacred music, dedicated to God from then on.

There is an old story I read about in the Southern Historical Collection [at the University of North Carolina], and I wrote about it in the new book. It's about a mountain girl who sang and played a fiddle. One day her father forbade her to sing any longer, saying it was "of the Devil." Grief-stricken, she goes mad and plays the fiddle on her front porch until she dies. It's a true story. †

2

REYNOLDS PRICE

Saintly Outlaws

For over three decades, the works of Reynolds Price have explored problems of the wounded and wounding human spirit in relation to the palpable world and to the Divine. In novels, short stories, essays, plays, memoirs, poems, and biblical translations, Price says that he has sought to "understand what is mysterious—in the behavior of the visible world, the behavior of God, of my friends and enemies, strangers, and finally of myself." In his book *A Palpable God,* Price writes that in seeking to probe the mysteries of the unseen world, he finds the concrete world of the everyday South infused with an "almost blindingly lucid meaning."

Born in Macon, North Carolina, in 1933, Price received his Bachelor of Arts degree from Duke University. As a Rhodes Scholar, he studied at Merton College, Oxford. In 1958 he returned to Duke, where he is now the James B. Duke Professor of English. His novel, *A Long and Happy Life,* published in 1962, received the William Faulkner Award for a notable first novel. A collection of short stories, *The Names and Faces of Heroes,* appeared in 1963. Since that time, his publications have included the novels *A Generous Man* (1966), *Love and Work* (1968), *The Surface of Earth* (1975), *The Source of Light* (1981), *Kate Vaiden* (1986), which won the 1986 National Book Critics Circle Award, *Good Hearts* (1988), *Tongues of Angels* (1990), and *Blue Calhoun* (1992); the poetry collections *The Laws of Ice* (1985) and *The Use of Fire* (1990); a book of stories, *Permanent Errors* (1970); two books of essays, *Things Themselves: Essays and Scenes*

(1972) and *A Common Room: Essays, 1954–1987*; a play, *Early Dark* (1977); Biblical translations, *A Palpable God: Translations from the Bible with an Essay on the Origins and Life of Narrative* and the autobiographical work *Clear Pictures: First Loves, First Guides* (1989). His *Collected Stories* appeared in 1993.

Of his moral vision, Price says, "If I have a moral purpose for writing, it is to elicit understanding of and mercy toward as much of creation as I can present, and you the reader, can manage." He sees the origins of this vision and its expression in fiction as being rooted in the rich soil of rural Warren County, North Carolina, where he was born and raised—a place, Price maintains, where religion, race, family, and love of stories were powerfully influential.

It has often been noted that the most profound means of transmitting religious and social culture in the South is through stories about family and community history and about the whole of creation. Indeed, Price sees narrative as absolutely necessary for survival of the human race as human, saying that the need to tell stories is primal and may even be our ultimate salvation. "I've said in an essay [the introduction to *A Palpable God*] that the need to tell and hear stories is the second most important need after food. People are going to tell stories."

Seeing the Bible as the primary source for narrative, Price draws on its language and resonance in both his style and vision. Many of the most compelling characters in his works are essentially good-hearted people whose lives are bound up in ultimate matters of guilt and redemption. They live, on the surface, rather ordinary lives: eighteen-year-old Rosacoke, in *A Long and Happy Life,* is a country girl in love with young Wesley, the father of her unborn child; Blue Calhoun, a recovering alcoholic, works in a music store in Raleigh, North Carolina. Yet because of inchoate passions and devastating psychic wounds, each must tell a morally complicated tale of guilt, sorrow, and the search for the kind of forgiveness that can arise not from society's judgment, but only from a deepened understanding and a sense of shared burden. At the same time, people like Rosacoke Mustian, Wesley Beavers, and Kate Vaiden carry with them a sense that they don't belong in the world, that they are sojourners who live their lives on the margins of society.

As Price says in my interview with him, "I think that I've become aware in the last five or six years of something that seems to be going on forever in my work (which I wasn't especially conscious of before) and that is the degree to which my work has dealt with what I might call 'Christian outlaws,' or 'believing outlaws,' the 'virtuous or saintly outlaw'. From the very beginning, I think my work is witness to the fact that there are an awful lot of good people in the world, many of whom are the kinds of people who would not be approved by the official judgmental bodies of our culture." †

Full Day

Early afternoon in the midst of fall; but the sun was behind him, raw-egg streaks of speedy light from a ball-sized furnace in a white sky. Buck even skewed his rearview mirror to dodge the hot glare that would only be natural three hours from now. *Am I nodding off?* He thought he should maybe pull to the shoulder and rest for ten minutes. No, he'd yet to eat; his breakfast biscuit was thinning out. One more call; then he'd push on home, be there by dark. But he took the next sharp bend in the road; and damn, the light was still pouring at him, redder now.

Buck shrugged in his mind and thought of a favorite fact of his boyhood—how he'd searched old papers and books of his father's for any word on the great Krakatoa volcanic eruption in 1883. He'd heard about it years later in school—how an entire island went up that August in the grandest blast yet known to man. The sea for miles was coated with powdered rock so thick that ships couldn't move. And for more than a year, sunsets everywhere on Earth were reddened by millions of tons of airborne dust. Buck's mother would tell him, each time he asked, that the night before her wedding in 1884, the sunset scared her worse than his father did.

Like boys in general, he'd consumed disasters of all shapes and sizes but only from books and the silent movies of his childhood. Otherwise he often thought of himself as an average tame fish, safe in his tank. He'd missed the First War by only a month and was several years too old at Pearl Harbor; so even now, at fifty-three, he'd never witnessed anything worse than a simple crossroads collision, one death with very little blood. He suddenly saw how the light this afternoon was similar to that, though hadn't he watched the wreck in springtime? Early April maybe—surely dogwood was blooming.

Buck had sat at the Stop sign in what felt like a globe of silence and watched, slow-motion, as an old man plowed his toy Model A broadside into a gasoline truck, which failed to explode. Buck had got out and joined the young truckdriver in trying to ease the trapped old man (a country doctor, named Burton Vass, crushed by the steering wheel). Awful looking as he was, pinned into the seat, Dr. Vass wouldn't hear of their trying to move him till an ambulance came. But a good ten minutes before it appeared, the doctor actually grinned at their eyes. Then he said "I'm leaving" and left for good. So yes, Buck was maybe a fish in a tank. *Whose tank?* he wondered. But since he mostly thought about God in his prayers at night, he dropped the question now. God knew, he spent his life in a tank, this Chrysler gunboat, working to bring electric ease to country wives—stoves, steam irons, washers, freezers, fans.

He turned the mirror down again and tried the sun. It was now even stranger; and the leaves, that had only begun to die, were individually pelted by light till they shivered and flashed. Buck slowed and pulled to the narrow shoulder by a tall pine woods. He'd pushed too far but, on the back seat, he had a wedge of rat cheese, a few saltines and a hot bottled drink. That would calm his head.

The next thing he knew a voice was speaking from a great distance, toward his left ear. *It's nothing but your name. You're dreaming; dream on.* But the voice was only saying *Sir?* Eventually a second voice, young and hectic, echoed the word—*Sir? Please wake up.* Something in the pitch of the *please* helped him rouse. But he didn't reflect that the tone of the voice was much like the younger of his two sons at home.

It was almost night; he thought that first. But then he realized his eyes had cleared. It was dimmer, yes; the sun was tamer. He glanced at the clock—a quarter past four.

Then from as far off as in his sleep, the older voice came at him again, "Are you all right?"

He looked to his left and was startled to see a woman and a child. Young woman, boy child—maybe thirty and ten. They were two steps back from his side of the car; but at once their faces made him want them closer, though both were tense with doubt and fear. He lowered the window. "Good afternoon."

The woman was the one who retreated a step.

Fearless, the boy came on to the car.

Buck could have touched him. But he settled for touching the brim of his hat, a worn World War II bomber's cap. "Was I snoring too loud?"

The boy said, "I'm Gid Abernathy. No sir, I just thought you were dead."

It struck Buck cold. He actually put a hand out before him and flexed his fingers; then he worked them quickly one by one as if at a keyboard, running scales. He smiled at the boy. "Thanks, Gid, but not yet."

Gid's worry wasn't spent. "The schoolbus sets me down right here. Ten minutes ago, when I got out, I saw you slumped at the wheel and all; so I knocked on your glass and you didn't budge. I even tried to open your door—"

Buck noticed that oddly he'd locked it on stopping, a first time surely. It didn't strike him as brave or risky that a child tried to help so trustingly. This time and place—1953 in the coastal plain of North Carolina—were slow and safe; everybody knew it and moved accordingly. Gid was curious and very likely kind, not heroic. Still Buck thanked him and started explaining how tired he'd got from skipping lunch. He should have known not to mention hunger in a woman's presence, not in those times. Maybe in fact he did know it and, half-aware, brought down the rest of the day on himself.

The woman was wearing a clean house dress with short sleeves that showed her strong, but not plump, arms. Her face was an open country face; surely she also had never met with harm or deceit. While Buck thought that, she stepped up slowly through his thoughts and rested a long hand on Gid's bony shoulder. "I'm Gid's mother, Nell Abernathy. He always eats an after-school sandwich. I'll fix you and him one together, if you like." It seemed as natural, and she seemed as ready, as if they were in a cool kitchen now and she were slicing homemade bread and spreading butter that her own hands had churned.

Buck fixed on the best of her homely features. She had an amazing abundance of hair, not the new rust-red you saw so often now since the war but the deep auburn you imagine on women in daguerreotypes, the hair that looks as if each strand bears a vein that pipes blood through it. He'd never seen the like in his time; and he wanted to say so but thought it would sound too forward, too fast. He felt he was smiling anyhow and that now was the moment to say his own name, open the door and stand up at least. But while his eyes had cleared in the nap, he suddenly wondered if his legs would obey. They felt long gone, not asleep exactly but not all there. He tried it though.

A half-hour later he'd drunk buttermilk, eaten a thick tomato sandwich on store-bought bread and said what he thought would be goodbye to Gid. Gid said he was due at a touch-football game a mile due north in the woods from here. As he shook Buck's hand, the boy made his plan sound natural as any town child's game. Only when his thin short gallant frame had shut the porch door and run down the steps did Buck recall his own country boyhood. *Whoever played football in the woods?* But he quickly imagined a clearing big enough for two pygmy teams. And for the first time, he thought of a father, *Who's the man around here? Is he dead, run-off or still at work?* But it didn't seem urgent to ask for him yet.

So he looked to Gid's mother, here at the sink four steps away. Her back was to him, and he knew on sight that now she'd literally forgot he was here. Plain as she was, she was that good to see, that empty of wishes for him to perform. All his life he'd tried to show women the boundless thanks he felt for their being. From his long-dead mother on the day he was born, to Lib his wife just yesterday morning, Buck tried to tell each woman who helped him the strongest fact he knew in life, *You're reason enough to stay on here.* He honestly felt it and toward most women. To be sure, he knew there were bad women somewhere; he'd never met one. So he always meant the praise he gave them, mostly selfless praise with no hopes of any dramatic answer. And here past fifty, still he fell in love several times a month, with a face in a diner or crossing the street ahead of his bumper or dark on his back in a hot hotel room, staring at nothing better to see than a ceiling fan and old piss stains from the room above. He knew, and still could cherish, the fact of love-on-sight whenever his mind saw a winning girl; it would gently lie back on itself and tell him, *Buck, rest here for good.*

Not that he had. When he was twenty-seven he married Lib and had touched no other woman since, not with a purpose warmer than courtesy. That never stopped the joy or his ceaseless thanks. Hell, women had not only made him but named him—*Will* from his mother, *Buckeye* in childhood from his favorite sister. Now he fished out his pocket watch—quarter to five, Lib would be starting supper. He'd be half an hour late, no major crime. He folded the paper napkin with a care due Irish linen, and he said "I'm going to be late for supper." But his legs didn't move to stand and leave.

Buck's guess had been right; Nell jerked at the sudden sound of his voice and looked around, wild-eyed for an instant. But calm again, she said "You sure?"

"Of what?" Now his legs were trying to stand.

"That you can make it home?"

"Do I look that bad?"

She took the question seriously enough to move a step toward him and study his face. "You look all right. I just meant, you being dizzy on the road and sleeping so deep in the car when Gid found you—"

He was upright now but his head was light. "I could drive this last stretch, bound and blindfolded."

She looked again and said, "You may have to."

Buck meant for his grin to force one from Nell. But no, it didn't work; she was solemn as church, though better to see. Could he look that bad? He tried to remember where his car was parked. Had he driven on here from where he pulled off? Had he left it there and walked here with them? And where was here? He looked all round him—a normal kitchen in a well-worn house, maybe sixty years old, a high dim ceiling, heart-pine floor, white walls smoked to an even gray. He said "Did we leave my car by the road?"

Nell seemed to nod.

So he looked to the door that Gid had walked through and aimed for that. At first he thought he crossed half the distance, but the final half then doubled on him and kept on multiplying the space till each further step was harder to take; and he thought his feet were sinking through the floor, then his calves and knees, his waist and chest, till even his mouth had sunk and was mute before he could call on Nell or God or the air itself for strength or rescue.

It felt like a healing year of nights, endless dark with heart-easing dreams. But when his eyes opened, it looked to Buck no darker than when he had tried to leave the woman's kitchen. He heard a clock tick, it was near his face, it said five forty—a black Big Ben, with the bone-rattling bell that he used to wake up early to beat. His mother solemnly gave him one, the day he left home for his first real job. But surely he'd told Lib to chuck it, years back. Or was he doing the thing he'd done so often lately—dreaming he was young, in his first big boarding house, strong as a boy, with the body to prove it in daylight and dark?

He was lying on his stomach on some kind of bed, under light cover. With both dry hands, he felt down his length from the top of his butt to nearly the knees. All that skin was bare; and upward, the sides of his chest and shoulders were warm but naked too. And when he felt beneath himself, his dick and balls were warm and soft. Still what surprised Buck was the calm soul in him—no fear, no regret in a mind as fearful as any not locked in a state institution. He shut both eyes and gradually searched the sheet beneath him, as far as he could reach. His right hand soon met a block that was big but soft. His fingers stopped against it.

A woman's voice said "You know you're safe."

Buck's eyes were still shut. In the hope of knowing whether this was a dream, he thought *In three seconds I'll open my eyes, I'll look straight ahead, then shut them again.* He counted to three, looked, saw the same clock—five forty-two—and shut them again. It proved he was alive, awake and sane, though apparently stripped in a woman's bed. *Nell,* he finally thought of the name; then the memory of her face. He firmly believed he still hadn't touched her. *Two things may have happened. I fainted, somehow Nell got me in here, but why am I stripped? Or I've been here days, maybe years, and am sick.*

He had not been prone to wild thoughts, not in his life till now at least; and he halfway liked it. He suspected he smiled. *But Gid—oh*

Christ. Is Gid on hand? Buck tried to see if his hand could lift off the pillow—yes. He held it up and listened to the house. No sounds at all, not even from Nell. He settled back, brought his right hand to his face and felt for beard—the normal stubble of late afternoon. So he told her, "It feels very safe. Thanks, Nell. But did I collapse? Am I someway sick?"

She had seemed to sit on the edge of the bed, facing out from him toward the door—Buck saw the open door and a blank hall beyond it. And now she gave no sign of moving, surely not toward him. She said "You had a little sinking spell. You may have blanked out, but you didn't fall hard. I helped you in here. You slept half an hour."

"With you here beside me?"

"I just got back," she said.

"From where?"

"The phone. I called your wife."

"How do you know her?"

Her voice was smiling. "You'll have to excuse me, but I searched your pocket and found her number. I didn't know what—"

Buck said "Don't worry. But what did you say?"

"That you stopped by here, just feeling weak. That I thought you'd be back on the road soon, but did she know anything I ought to know?"

Buck almost laughed. "Such as, am I a killer?"

Her voice stayed pleasant. "Such as, do you have seizures? Are you diabetic?"

"What did Lib say?"

"Is Lib your wife? She said you were normal, far as she knew, just maybe exhausted."

Buck smiled but, on its own, his mind thought *Exactly. Nobody but Lib's allowed to be sick.* Lib was having what she herself called "the longest menopause on human record." Good-hearted as she was till five years ago, in the midst of that winter—with no word of warning—she suddenly balled up tight as wax till, for weeks on end, Buck could hardly see her, much less touch and warm her. Next she seemed to grow in-turned eyes, set all down her body, to watch herself—her own long stock of pains and self-pity, when he'd been the famous complainer so long.

By now they could sometimes laugh about it; and everywhere else in her life with others—their sons, her friends—Lib seemed to be waking from a long hard dream. She'd yet to welcome him truly back. And even if she did, the harm was done now and might never heal. She'd turned from his care and need so often that Buck was permanently lonesome in ways he hadn't felt since boyhood, roaming the deep woods north of his house and pressing his lips to dry tree-bark, just for something to lean his body against, some living thing to know that young Buck was clean and warm and could be touched with pleasure.

His right hand had stayed where it found Nell's hip. Three layers of cover kept them apart; he'd never probed or tried to stroke her, and she'd never pressed back into his fingers. As he went on waking, he began to like their balked contact. It gave him a trace of the friendly warmth of his sister Lulie, who was less than one year older than he and with whom he'd slept till his sixth birthday—pups in a box, warm and moving like a single heart.

He thought the next question and asked it clearly, "Whose room is this?" Before Nell could speak, he thought of the several answers he dreaded—her husband's and hers, even young Gid's. Not that he feared their linen and blankets, he just hoped to be in an open space, one he could rest in from here on out. He felt that happy and it sprang up through him in a peaceful flow.

Nell said "My father built this bed, oh sixty years ago. He and Mother used it, all their life together. She died and he came here to live with me, brought nothing much but his clothes and this bed. He helped us a lot till he went, last winter."

"He died?"

"Pneumonia."

"No, it's you and the boy, on your own now?"

"Seems like," she said. She gave a little chuckle as if she sat alone on the moon and watched her distant amazing life.

"How do you live?"

She laughed out brightly. "Like squirrels in the trees! No, I sew for people. Gid works in the summer, on the next farm over. My dad left us a small piece of money. We do all right, nothing grand but enough."

Then the lack of a husband and father was sure. *I'll ask to stay.* Buck understood that the thought should have shocked him. It didn't. The calm poured on through his chest, and for several minutes he napped again. When he came to, his right hand was back by his side; and he spoke without looking, "Why am I naked?"

She said "Remember? It was your idea. You had a little accident, when you blacked out."

"Oh God, I'm sorry."

Nell said "Forget it. It was just in the front, a spot the size of a baby's head."

"Did I wet my shirt too?"

"Not a bit," she said. "That was your idea; I tried to stop you."

Then I have to stay.

She said "I've got you some clean clothes out."

"You're a lightning seamstress." But then he thought *Her husband's clothes.*

"My dad's," she said. "You're his same size."

"I couldn't accept them."

"Oh he'd be thrilled. He couldn't bear to waste a half-inch of string. And Gid'll be way too tall when he's grown."

"You good at predicting the future?" Buck said.

She laughed again. "Height runs in his family, most of the men—"

Buck rushed to stop her before she clouded the good air between them with a useless name, "I'll be much obliged then, for one pair of pants.

Nell said "They're laid out here on the chair, khakis as clean as cloth ever gets and a clean pair of step-ins. I'm bound to go now and start our supper. You think you feel like trying to stand?" She seemed unhurried but as bent on leaving as if a walk to the dark heart of Africa faced her now.

Never, no ma'am, I'll lie right here. But he tried to move both legs and they worked. And his eyes were clear. All that refused was his mind, *Stay here. You're actually needed here. Not so, she and Gid are doing all right. Ask her though; just see what she says.* Buck heard his voice say the reckless thing, "Nell, what if I said 'Please let me stay'?"

He expected she'd wait to think that through. And at once she rose from the edge of the bed and took three steps on the bare wood

floor. Then she said "We had this time, here now. Your own supper's cooking, up the road, this minute."

As her low voice moved, Buck knew she was right. She seemed to
know much more than he remembered; whatever had happened, if
anything new, it hadn't changed the tone of her voice. So at least he
could trust that he hadn't been cruel or made a promise that he
couldn't keep. Then he saw his course clearly. The decent thing was
to try standing up, getting dressed, saying thank you and heading
on home. So he turned to his side and threw off the cover. He saw
his bare body; then said *"I'm* sorry" and reached again for the sheet
at least, to hide his lap. For the first time, that he remembered here,
he looked toward Nell.

She stood by a tall mahogany wardrobe and was half-turned
away, lifting a bathrobe from the high-backed chair. She was naked
as he and had been naked all that time she was near him. Before she
could cover herself, Buck rushed to print her body deep in his mind.
She was still young everywhere, with firm pale skin and no visible
scars (Lib's side was pocked by the cavernous scar of a ruptured
appendix). And the hair of her crotch was the same high color of
life and health that she showed the world on her striking head.
Then she was hid in the faded robe; and with no further look or
word, she brushed on past him and left the room.

Buck went to the same chair, found his pants in a clean ragged
towel, his shirt on a hanger—Nell had managed to iron it   a pair
of blue boxer shorts and the khakis she mentioned. He put on his
socks first, the shirt, then the pants. They were stiff with starch and
two inches short. He thought of his mother's old comic greeting for
outgrown pants, "Son, I see you're expecting high water" (they
lived twenty miles from the Roanoke River, a famous flooder).

Was this time-out, here under this roof, some high-water mark
in all his life? With the tender mind and heart he got from his
mother at birth, Buck had wanted an unadventurous life. And
except for Lib's three awful labors (two live boys and one dead girl),
he'd virtually got it. His chief adventures had come in his head.
Alone on the road, he sometimes lived through active nights with
imaginary women. But mostly he still enacted each possible threat
to life and limb, any time his family stepped out of sight. And his
own body, strong till now, had always seemed a rickety bridge over

too deep a gorge for a confident life in some place hard as the present world.

So sure, whatever had happened here—if nothing but what Nell owned up to, a fainting spell and a half-hour rest—was like a splendid volunteer, the giant flower that suddenly blooms at the edge of the yard, where you least expect, from a secret hybrid in last year's seed that has bided its time. When he'd tied his shoes, he stepped to the dark old mirror and smoothed his tangled hair. *Nothing visibly changed, not to my eyes—and who knows me better? Well, Lib but she won't see this time, whatever happened here. And if anything did, it was gentle and finished.* He could hear Nell drawing water in the kitchen. In less than an hour, if fate agreed, he'd be in his own house, among his first duties. He bent again to the peeling mirror and awarded his face a final grin. Then he went out to thank Nell Abernathy for one happy day.

In four months Buck will die from a growth that reached decisive weight in his body this full afternoon and threw him down.

His elder son has made this unreal gift for his father on the eighty-ninth passing of Buck's birthday, though he died these thirty-five years ago. †

Interview

On a cold January afternoon, I interviewed Reynolds Price at his brick and timber home in the countryside, a rolling, wooded land of oak and beech trees north of Durham, North Carolina. The house is situated at the end of a winding gravel driveway at the top of a rise overlooking a pond. The woods beyond are thick with bare hardwoods and pines; the slanting rays of afternoon sun through the trees were piercingly bright but not warm. On the telephone, Price had asked me to come around to the back patio and through the glass doors, where he was waiting for me in the den.

Taking my chilly hands in his, Price greeted me with a cordial smile and offered hot coffee or tea. I sat down in a dark wicker armchair and set the small recorder between us on the polished floor. Throughout the room on every available space on the walls and tables were paintings (by Price himself and others), religious icons, ceremonial masks, etchings, and artifacts from the Holy Land, precious mementos that Price has collected in the course of his travels abroad and that he has received as gifts from admiring friends. He talked to me for almost three hours, answering with candor, and sometimes sardonic humor, questions put to him that must have seemed at times only obliquely relevant to the subject at hand. At the outset, the usual distractions of late afternoon business threatened to impinge, but thanks to a telephone answering machine and Price's assistant, our conversation remained uninterrupted. Responding with generous good spirits to queries on and off the record, Price seemed to be drawing on a boundless energy that both springs from and fuels a passionate commitment to his subject, the craft and art of writing, as it reveals the awesome mystery of the Creator's relationship to His creatures.

I'd like to begin by exploring the relationship, as you see it, between your fiction and the mysticism that you have written about in Clear Pictures *and elsewhere.*

I've always spoken of mysticism, but I think I've come to realize that it can confuse people, so I should probably define my terms first. I don't use mysticism in any sense that implies the occult, or anything especially spooky or weird. I think I use mysticism in a more or less classical theological sense. That is, I'm attempting to describe a kind of religious experience which is primarily an experience directly between a given creature and what he perceives to be the Creator. It's been a very long time in my life since I have felt at home in a church, or felt any great desire to be a member of an organized body of fellow creatures or fellow believers. So, I mean mysticism in the sense of basically a one-to-one relationship between me and whatever I perceive to be the source that I'm in touch with, or that's getting in touch with me.

You do see these experiences as existing as a pattern or at least in a relationship rather than as idiosyncratic events?

Oh, yes. It's been a relationship for all of my life that I can remember. I'd say that I've been very conscious of it as an essential relationship ever since I was five or six years old.

You write about a memorable encounter with nature at about that age in Clear Pictures.

Yes. Of course, we all rewrite our pasts more or less constantly. But that's the first time that I have a conscious memory of feeling a special, personal contact with anything that I would call God. Before that time I went to Sunday school with my parents and was aware that they were people who went to church (though not terribly regularly). They were unquestioning recipients of their own religious training. In my father's case, he grew up and was baptized in the Baptist church; my mother was raised in the Methodist church. But I think that experience when I was about five, living in Asheboro, was the first real time that I began to have a sense of—and some special relationship in my own life with God. I don't think it's at all accidental that this time coincided with our having bought land in the country outside of town and that I was spending a great deal of time alone. As a child, because I had no sibling yet, I spent a lot of time just wandering in the woods and playing in the creek. Also a lot of these experiences that I felt were unique to me at the time, I've since realized are common to sensitive children alone in nature. As I've continued to read, I've run across various accounts in which people describe similar experiences in their child-hoods, and the experiences almost always coincide with a situation in which they are alone in nature (not in a city, or in the company of other human beings).

Alone as a child in nature—that was the circumstance in which you first felt that interpenetration and an interconnection that might be called a mystical experience?

Yes. But it was certainly nothing in which I or you, had you been present or had a movie camera and a tape recorder, would have seen anything unusual. I remember it as having occurred at a time when I had stuck a knife into a pine tree (I was in a great Tarzan phase of my solitary games), and I had this hunting knife with which I was always cutting things. It was not a sense that I hurt or damaged a tree but a sense that I had somehow thereby got in touch with another living thing, and then I rather rapidly had this sense that everything was alive and that it was all very intricately geared together. That was my first direct religious experience; that is to say, this experience did not come through either of my parents.

Have you read Josephine Humphreys's essay on the Book of Titus in Incarnation?

Yes.

Something she says in that essay seems to fit in here. She writes, "It may always be difficult for me to profess a Christian faith. The other day I read in the Episcopalian newsletter a description and a condemnation of Pantheism, an old heresy. Like a hypochondriac reading up on the symptoms of disease, I recognized the tell-tale signs. I had it without question. I've got others as well, heresies whose names I don't even know, and my personal spiritual life may well be forever plagued with them. I don't think a church will ever want me.

"But fiction doesn't require the writer to profess. In it I am free to work from the most inchoate of creeds following what leads turn up, secure in the knowledge that most exploration leads some-where. When I begin a book, I don't know what's in store. I trust in discovery. It usually comes. Fiction speaks indirectly, does not lay down laws. Sometimes I think of Crete when I'm writing, because I do try to love the material world, so thoroughly so that I may not escape a spiritual vision. But I think also of parables, Christ's

fiction, in which nothing is spelled out. I think of a God who does not lie."

I respond very much to what Josephine Humphreys says about feeling the necessity to love the physical world. And loving anything in a good sense means watching it extremely closely.

Like Mark Twain's eggs in the basket: Put all your eggs in one basket and watch the basket.

Exactly. As I was describing my experience in the woods to you, I was thinking of Alfred Corn, the Georgia poet, who edited that book. In his own essay in *Incarnation*, he talks about a mystical experience he had as a grown man. And I think he describes it as being in a park in New York City. One afternoon he suddenly got this very intense sense of the world, the nature of creation, of everything that is, as some kind of enormously intricate and totally interdependent organism.

Another thing I particularly respond to in that excerpt from Jo's essay is very much the sense that no church would want me. I would phrase it another way. All the churches I've been a member of want too much of me. They want too much of what seems to be entirely superficial and superficially exhausting. The moment I go to church, it seems the first thing they say is, "Will you give a poetry reading next Wednesday night? Will you coach the soccer team?" And you think, I just wanted to have a religious experience. Carl Jung says that wonderful thing: Organized religion is an excuse for not having a religious experience. I completely agree. I definitely don't judge anybody who has an intense social, even mystical, relationship with a community. I often regret that temperamentally I've never been able to be a church member, not since I was in high school or in the early years of college at least.

I've written, again in *Clear Pictures*, I think, about the two things that I felt made the situation of an organized worship service inimical to me. One of them certainly was my growing sense as a young man, in North Carolina, in the forties and fifties, of the immensely wicked implication of Protestantism in the whole racial situation— a situation which I don't feel has dramatically altered in the past few years, I'm sorry to say. The racial dilemmas are just bigger now because they include more groups of people, and more kinds of people than were around when I was a child and adolescent, when it was strictly black-white. There really is this sense that Christianity in all forms known to me, and as I observed it, in synagogue Judaism, in which churches seem to be perilously close to being social clubs, especially in the sense of what's expected of a given member. It is a really a frenetic kind of social commitment of a sort that I don't want. If I have social time, I want to spend it with people that I care deeply about; I don't want to be making brownies for the church picnic.

Members of contemporary churches sometimes refer to the "church family," and its role is often perceived to be more along the lines of a therapy or support group than a place of worship.

And that's fine, I'm just solitary enough and cantankerous enough to want to run a mile the moment anybody says that sort of thing to me. Or sees me as a "resource person" for the young people who want me talk to them about writing.

You're a "role model."

Ah, get away. So I wish them the best in the world. I think an enormous amount of practical good is done by organized churches, synagogues, mosques; but they turn out not to be the way through which I can conduct my relations with my neighbors and the Creator.

That's one of the pitfalls that may arise as I research my book. As I interview writers, I hope to straighten out from the beginning that this is not a book about church or an expression of what the church is, past and present, nor is it an exploration of a writer's special piety or social commitment. I want to focus on the interplay between the writer's creative vision, and its expression in the work. The other important dimension of my subject is that it is about writers who were born and raised in the South and who still live here most of the time. Many are still wrestling with that complex, contradictory reality of "The South."

I think what I would want out of a church is basically the sacraments: Baptism, communion, burying me when I'm dead. But when I was very ill in 1984 and '85 with the cancer surgery and radiation, I very much wanted to take communion. I was staying with a cousin in Goldsboro, and I just asked her if she could get her Methodist minister to come to the house and bring me communion, which he did on a couple of occasions that were important to me. To this day I have a very dear friend, an Episcopal priest, who brings me communion to the house on certain important days of the year for me. So I've got probably more of a profound respect for the organized churches than an awful lot of believing writers I know. But in practice somehow it doesn't seem to work out for me when I go. I think what I want out of a church is a situation where I could simply do as travelling Roman Catholics do. If you're a Roman Catholic and you travel to Secaucus, New Jersey, you wake up in your motel room on Sunday morning and you find out where the nearest Catholic church is, you go, and you bow your head, and you do or do not take communion at the end of Mass and you leave. It seems to me the complaint that a church member would make against my version would be: What you really want is cheap Christianity. You want all the goodies, the sense of warmth, the aesthetic beauty, the sacraments, the comfort; but you don't want to have to pay in the sense of having a continuous giving relationship with another group of believers. But, I do think my teaching and my writing are that. And they take up every kilowatt of remaining energy that I've got to spend. So I would fairly fiercely defend the kind of relationship that I would have dearly liked to have had with the church. I would have joined the Catholic church, which I seriously thought about doing in my adolescence, if I felt I could accept the whole dogmatic structure, including the infallibility of the pope and all that follows from that. I still probably am much more nearly "crypto-Catholic" than anything else. And I've always felt tremendously at home with Flannery O'Connor and Walker Percy for that reason among many others.

What are the flashpoints? As both O'Connor and Percy did, at what points do you begin to see conflict (if any) inherent within trying to treat your fiction as art, seriously, as you do, and your spirituality as you were brought up to it, and as you genuinely experience it now?

Let me start from the back side of that, which is where the conflict usually arises, as far I've heard or read about from fellow writers. That is, the conflict usually arises when an author feels that his or her own spiritual convictions require him to evangelize, to proselytize to win fellow adherents to the faith. I am many quarts low on evangelism. I really don't see that one of my main functions in the world is to be in the direct business of signing people up for a particular belief system. It seems to me that one of the great duties that arises out of my being literally talented (in the sense of Jesus's parable of the talents, in the sense of my being endowed with a certain kind of gold that a lot of other people don't have) is to invest that gold publicly in ways that will provide benefit for anyone who chooses to spend any time reading the work. And that is a must—writing as truthfully and as lovingly about the whole of the world as I can.

I said somewhere in an essay years ago that it's really no accident that the novel is not an ancient form. It's got relations to ancient forms like tragedy and epic, but the novel itself is a fairly new form. I think the novel is in many ways a Christian form, a Judeo-Christian form, and therefore relatively new. I think it's Judeo-Christian in the sense of its being a form of loving attention with absolutely no purposes of judging anything. We novelists try to just look at the world and say what we see there. I do think there are certain kinds of wonderful novelists who occasionally wind up feeling like policemen as you read their works. I always think that in E. M. Forster, and to some extent in Flannery O'Connor, you get the sense of this round-up of all the evil people who get sent off to hell at the end. And hell in Forster always means having to marry the wrong girl, the unimaginative, plain woman. Hell in O'Connor means being one of those people in Georgia who has to sit down and listen to your mother talk to you all day and all night, and you're ugly and peg-legged and must hear your mother go on about "niggers" till doomsday.

So I try not to arrest my characters in the end. I think they suffer from the nature of their choices and from their own characters, but I hope I don't make them suffer from my necessity to punish them for not being good Christians, good Jews, good Baptists in a story. I think one of my purposes as a writer is simply to understand as much of creation as I can and to communicate as much of that understanding as possible to as large an audience as possible. It even worries me when I sometimes see myself referred to as a "Christian novelist." Does this mean that Jewish people in America will not want to read me? Does this mean that all my Black Muslim friends are going to run a mile if they see a book by me? I'm not ashamed in any sense of being someone who is a believing Christian, but I do sometimes worry if it becomes a limitation on my audience.

That's a useful distinction to make between being a Christian and being a writer, and being a "Christian writer." When someone asks you if you are a "Christian writer," it puts you in a doublebind.

Yes. I don't think I'm a "Christian writer." I'm a Christian who happens to write. It's all a seamless garment. But I can never remember in any moment in my writing career, or in the practical writing of any given page, when I thought, Is it the Christian thing to do "a" or "b" at this moment in the story? Would it be immoral if so-and-so commits suicide? I once thought a character was going to commit suicide, and she just absolutely refused to do so. The woman I had made for the first two or three hundred pages of the book just would not commit suicide by the time I got her down to the page on which she was supposed to. The vitality that she had in my own brain as the character created itself just turned out to be the vitality of someone who would not kill herself. I did not avoid killing her because I thought it would have been an "un-Christian" or an "ungodly" act for her to perform. So I don't feel that my work is in any direct sense a missionary effort. Even in my child-hood, when people would stand up in Sunday school to take up a collection for missions, I felt uncomfortable. I didn't like the thought of someone grabbing people by the neck and saying, "You've got to become what I want you to become and if not, you're going to hell in a handbasket."

What you're repulsed by here, I think, is a certain form of arrogance.

Surely, and there's no way around it. If you read the Gospels closely, and certainly if you read St. Paul, there is a certain priority placed on preaching the good news to the world. There are those terrible passages in which Christ in the Gospel of John (and later Paul) says, "There is no way unto the Father except by me." Those passages give me a lot of trouble because I don't really think I believe that. I think I'm heretical in terms of orthodox Christianity in doubting that there's no way to the Creator but by a belief in Christ and in all the very complicated things Christ has come to mean to many different kinds of people in the last two thousand years. God knows, even Roman Catholicism before the Vatican councils and the liberalization of the church in the last thirty years had an entire category of people who might get to Heaven without benefit of Christ.

Was that for people who had died before Christ lived, or had not heard of Christianity?

It was the category of "invincible ignorance." You had invincible ignorance if you were a headhunter in New Guinea and I never reached you, or I did reach you, but couldn't conquer your ignorance about the faith. So a missionary I'm not. If someone said to me, "I've read your books and they strengthened my relationship to the Creator and to the creation," that pleases me. But it's not why I write. I can't think of a good novelist who does. There are some early novels of Graham Greene's in the thirties after he was converted to Catholicism that as much as I admire them, I feel as if a hand is reaching into my pocket for my wallet. He's trying to seduce me with the story and also have me to wind up down at St. Christopher's Catholic Church.

Converted. . . .

At the end of the day. But at his very best, he does very little of that. And I don't feel it as a subtle thing in Flannery O'Connor. If anything, the spectacle of belief in O'Connor is so radiant as to be potentially lethal. God in O'Connor seems almost like a nuclear plant out of control.

Yes! A meltdown.

Exactly. The closer you get to it the more chance you have of being melted down with it.

Yes, indeed. In her essay, "The Catholic Novelist in the Protestant South," O'Connor talks about the artist being of dual nature: the artist as creator and as believer.

I do feel (and it's a thing that finally may keep her from being one of the really great writers for me) that there's a mean streak in Flannery O'Connor which delights in the suffering of at least her characters, if not in that of other human beings. Of course, that's all part and parcel of her gifts as a satirist. I think she probably didn't want to be as much of a born satirist as she is. Satirists—great satirists like Swift and O'Connor—of necessity have to possess an awful lot of hatred. Walker Percy had heavy doses of hatred and rejection of the world in him.

Sometimes I've gotten put off by that rejection in his writing.

There's a lot of Percy I never felt comfortable reading or knowing about, in his reactions to certain things in the real world. It's
very hard for a Christian to be a satirist, I think, because you have
to keep those fires of resentment and hatred really banked to keep
on with good comic satire, with good denunciation; and that stoking
is not really all that congenial with Christianity as we know it, or
Judaism, as I understand Judaism.

*Also, to the degree that you have that mean streak, you run the
risk of distorting your characters artistically. They start doing
things they might not otherwise have done.*

Exactly. It leads sometimes in O'Connor to her setting up one more
time a kind of Flannery O'Connor repertory company: It's the ugly
daughter, the vicious mother, the ignorant but wily blacks who are
observing it all, the outlaw who comes in as the Bible salesman or
the Misfit, or whatever he is, and you begin to feel she's enjoying
sticking pins in these dolls.

They may become flatter than they ought to be.

The amazing thing is that right down to the last story she wrote,
she was capable of transcending that tendency. The story called
"Revelation" (which I think is the very last story she finished)—
it's about that old woman who goes to the doctor's office?

Yes, and the girl calls her a warthog from hell.

And the woman has the vision of the pigpen. I think that's just as
great a story as anybody ever wrote. And that story comes at the
end of her life, when, God knows, she had every reason to be full of
bitterness knowing that she was dying as young as she was. I think
she's a very heroic figure, but I think that it was her great problem
that she had the satiric gift. Take a quick look at the Sermon on the
Mount—it tells you you're not supposed to be mean to people, or
make fun of people, or judge people; and satirists are in the business
of doing just that. If they can't do that, they can't do anything.

*When you think of it in those terms, though, you also run the
risk of trying to make your thoughts, and therefore your fiction,
"meet code" or "do the right thing." It seems to be a risky proposition
to say that writers who profess to be Christian must exhibit in
their personalities, or through their fiction, fully Christian attitudes in order to achieve a fully realized artistic vision.*

Yes, that's true. And I think in the case of O'Connor the accounts get squared up much better when you've read her letters because you realize that this is a person who, in her own completely unde-monstrative way, did an enormous amount of practical good and charity in her life. If you read her stories you might think "It's going to be a cold day before I drop by to meet Miss O'Connor. Or ask Miss O'Connor to contribute to my college education." But we find, as a matter of fact, that she did an enormous amount of that sort of thing insofar as she could within her physical and financial limitations.

She counted herself among the warthogs from hell; she felt that she was in need of grace. And in that way, she maintained some sense of grace herself.

But, as with Graham Greene, I think she points up for me the classical problems of being an actual, dues-paying communicant in a particular creed or a particular cult, in her case, Roman Catholi-cism. And thus, to that extent her work has got to touch base with a very complicated belief and behavior system and code of discipline. We know from her letters that she would occasionally worry over whether she should read such-and-such a book because it's on the index of banned books; there are occasional moments when you really feel her wondering if she's made the right move in her career or in a piece of fiction she's working on. And I think that, for me, is when institutional beliefs become inimical to the creating that we as artists, as writers, are capable of doing.

It's at that point that an artist becomes self-censoring, to be con-scious of institutional proscriptions.

Yes, because again I think that we are meant to be witnesses, wit-nesses and recorders, and if there's a censor there called the pope, or the board of deacons of the Baptist church that can finally say, "You've witnessed this but we're not going to let you to say it, or in order to witness, you've got to put on these Presbyterian eyeglasses before we let you out of the church," then that's when I think the church becomes a system for causing lies rather than eliciting truth. It's all the more interesting because I think the end of fiction is mercy.

That's a wonderful idea.

I think that's another reason the novel is very much a Judeo-Christian form. The whole point of learning about the human race presumably is to give it mercy.

I think it's Lynn Veach Sadler who wrote about your work and your vision that you see, and describe, and in the end forgive, most of it, most of the world.

Well, it's the great thing that institutional Christianity constantly fails to do—that is, to remember Jesus's saying, "Do unto others," or when God says, "I will have mercy and not sacrifice," or "'Vengeance is mine,' sayeth the Lord, 'I will repay.'" Christian churches seem to be too busy getting vengeance on and sacrificing other Christians, not with mercy and forgiveness.

William Faulkner said, "The trouble with Christianity is we haven't tried it yet."

That's it.

Could it be said that as a novelist, you're attempting to see, to witness, and to write about a knowledge of God or an encounter with God through Creation?

Let me put it this way: I'm attempting to write about those portions of creation which present themselves to me as important and as worthy of communication to my fellow creatures, who I think, could be everybody alive and not simply everybody who's a member of such-and-such a church or synagogue.

And you are definitely not trying to loop in anyone to the fold.

Absolutely not, absolutely not. If you read all my novels and then come and tell me that you've gone and joined the Buddhist convent, I'm just as glad as if you'd told me you'd joined the Catholic church.

Or that you hadn't gone and joined.

Exactly. My purpose, if it's a moral purpose over and above the desire to entertain and inform you, is really to elicit understanding of and mercy toward as much creation I can present, and you, the reader, can manage.

May I read you a quotation from Susan Dodd of the Washington Post? *She says, "The Forseeable Future seems to testify to poet Howard Nemerov's view that novellas 'announce their intention of becoming sacred books.' Reynolds Price once again has given us a book that teaches, not by dictum, but by parable. These stories glorify all creation. Above all, though, they resound with implications of eternity and the promise of redemption."*

I saw that and was pleased. I would like to know the rest of the context of that Nemerov quotation because I don't quite understand what he means about the novella as a sacred thing. I certainly know that from the beginning of my own serious reading as an adolescent, I was always fascinated by the long stories, ones that were too long to be short stories, and not quite long enough to be novels— *Heart of Darkness, The Secret Sharer,* things of that length, the fifty-to-one-hundred-page length. Why Nemerov would think those are more nearly sacred texts than *War and Peace* I don't know. So I wouldn't be able to comment on that aspect of his statement. I don't think there is much I can say to what Susan Dodd says except to add that her comments are a hell of a lot better to listen to than some. They do seem to me a more accurate diagnosis of what's going on in my work than a lot of other descriptions I've heard or can think of.

But I'd also want to say very strongly that when I set out to write anything, those particular novellas or anything else, I don't have anything like that conscious a program. I really don't go into my room thinking, "Today I'm going to do something that makes the human race more merciful than it used to be," any more than a horse thinks, "I'm going to walk across this field and jiggle that barbed wire fence because I'm a horse." It's the nature of my mind, and it's what my parents reared me to be, and it's the operation of grace in my life and in my work that lets other people feel that this is the result. But again there's a very slender sense on my own part at the beginning of anything, that I've got a program here, that I've got an agenda.

What do you think about Susan Dodd's rather startling statement further on in her review that, like eighteenth- or nineteenth-century novels and plays, The Forseeable Future *is a book that teaches, that has a didactic purpose?*

I think it's something the novel has given up or literature has given up in recent years. At least what we think of as "serious literature," what we majored in in college as English majors. It became kind of square with the rise of modernism after World War I to think that poetry and fiction in any sense would lead to the improvement of the human race, or the behavior of "A" to "B."

But I don't have any trouble with thinking that I'm a better creature because I read *Anna Karenina* and *Madame Bovary* when I was a teenager in Raleigh. It deepened my sense of the complicity of all creation in some sort of joint enterprise, the sense of the boat that we're all in—from the amoebas and the AIDS viruses on up to brilliant nuclear scientists and the asteroids in outer space—they are all linked in some sort of design, I'm absolutely convinced. I've no sense at all that I know what that design is. I believe it was Einstein who said that reality is not only more complicated than we know, it is more complicated than we are capable of knowing, at least now, given our brains and our telescopes.

I think my work from the beginning until the present is a totally serious attempt to report honestly on what I see in creation. And I'm glad of that; my work has given me great pleasure and a great sense of reward. That doesn't mean that I think that I'm the greatest writer who ever lived. I think categories like that are utterly meaningless. But I don't have any big sense of failure, that I tried to do X-Y-Z in my work and have not succeeded. Up to the present, up to now in my life, I feel that the books that I've written have been the books I wanted to write, and that I'm proud of them in the way that a good cabinetmaker is proud of a beautiful table, a beautiful and very useful table.

You're not tormented, as some writers are, with a sense of having fallen short?

I don't have that. I know wonderful writers who do, and I feel great sadness for them, their sense of incompletion. I hope I don't have any kind of smug self-satisfaction either, but I don't have that curse of feeling that I always fall short of the goal.

You aren't plagued by that sense of falling short of the ideal that you've envisioned. You're speaking of your work as having a great sense of integrity.

Integrity and some importance. But I don't think writing fiction—or poetry or anything else we can write, by the way—is one of the most important things a human being can do. I mean, if you're saying, Is there more important work than writing poems and fiction? I would say yes, the more important work is being Mother Teresa or being whoever is at the community shelter today in downtown Durham. Or dealing with abused children in a hospital somewhere. I think those things are first. And I have enormous admiration for people who have the vocation for doing that and the physical stamina to do it. But, thank goodness, Christianity has always said from the start, everybody is not required to do everything.

We're each a part of the Body of Christ, Paul said.

That's right. And I'm not very happy usually with St. Paul because he's such a policeman; he's constantly arresting people and sending them off to hell in ways that Christ is not.

He's been said to be at war with himself.

Right. There were some things in the Gospels where Jesus says, "Inasmuch as you have done it unto the least of these, my brethren, you have done it unto me." And I feel that I should be down at the community shelter instead of sitting in my nice, clean study writing on my word processor. I then decided that maybe I shouldn't. My power is not to make the peanut butter sandwiches down at the shelter. My power is to write.

Yeats said that the artist "brings the soul of man to God." That suggests another dimension to an understanding of the artist's relationship to creation and to God.

In that sense, the artist's work explains creation back to God. The funny thing is, if you're Christian or Jewish, you're not supposed to think that God has any needs, that God lacks anything. But in practical terms it may be the great power of the Creator that It— He, She or It—not being a human, or a mouse or an AIDS virus, may simply benefit from hearing from a human, a mouse, or an AIDS virus.

The work of art as an offering?

Exactly. That's a large part of what needs to be said, I'm sure.

Let's talk for a moment about the South, the place we know and love and grew up in. In his book A Hidden God, *Cleanth Brooks said that southern religion influenced William Faulkner's imagination in fundamental ways, profoundly shaping that writer's vision of good and evil. One of the questions I have for you is: Do you think religion as it has manifested itself in southern culture has broken or in any sense muddied southern fiction?*

The fact that southern culture, even up until the seventies, provided us with a daily world in which religion played an omnipresent role was immensely important. We were constantly provided with the frequently horrendous and always comical spectacle of a culture which claimed that it believed and was doing a certain high thing which in fact it was constantly failing to do in the most awful way. The white South really wasn't involved in conscious hypocrisy; that may be too small a term. It was involved in an endless demonstration of the fallibility of human beings at least, if not the whole of creation. So we were constantly able to watch this fascinating pageant of announced intention and actual continual failure, ranging in scale from the horrors of slavery and its aftermath (which is still with us) to the comedy of the choir director having an affair with the preacher's wife, or vice versa. To that extent religion served the function in our lives of being the public arena in which human folly was continuously visible in interesting and instructive ways.

Above and beyond that, I think, for all of us who had any sort of gift or bent or vocation for belief, was the fact that church-religion provided us with a direct possibility of serious encounter with the center of things—the Creator. I can remember moments in the Methodist and the Baptist churches in Macon, North Carolina, which are moments of great importance in my whole life, and they occurred before I was ten years old. Had those churches not been there and had those dear racist cousins of mine not filled the rows around and behind me, I wouldn't be who I am and I wouldn't have done the work that I've done. And the work that I've done is much better than who I am.

I think it gets at the heart of the matter to look at the relationship between religion and racism. And the intensity of the exposure to religion. We were "immersed in it," as Doris Betts has said. It was still going strong in the fifties and sixties when I was coming up: Wednesday night prayer meetings, Sunday morning worship, Sunday night worship, memorizing the Bible verses on Sunday afternoon.

All those extra points you got in heaven for going to prayer meetings on Wednesday nights.

I and many others, I think, took that immersion dead cold seriously, too, for better or worse. I was going to hell if I didn't do this, this, and this, and so on. And part and parcel of all this were the impassioned sermons, the week-long revivals with preaching every night, and the songs. We became as southerners in the evangelistic

Protestant South, intimately familiar with the resounding beauty of the biblical language and the unmistakable rhetoric of sermons, the rhythm and meter, symbols, the metaphors, the cataloging of images, and the building up of tension in the narrative.

Oh yes, there's no question that that's true, and it's tremendously important. The thing I want to add to what Doris has said is that it wasn't just southerners who were in contact with the King James translation and all of its marvelous reverberations in our lives. New England had that; the Midwest had that. But I think that we perhaps capitalized on that in ways that other regions of America didn't, primarily because the white writers and preachers of our region were largely of Anglo-Saxon stock. We came from long, long generations of people who had spoken the English language, the Anglo-Saxon language. And our language had added to it, as a great leavening and enriching factor, something that British English never had—a profound involvement with African-American language. I mean if you ask me, "What does the South have that no other part of America had?" I would have to say it had southern Christianity and blacks. If you said, "What are the unique things about it?" they would be the only two unique things I think we've got. Everything else—southern cooking, southern social organizations, all that—exist in rich forms in the South; but they're not unique to the South. What was unique to the South was that very strange and intense and, as I said, frequently comical but also frequently transcendental brand of Christianity that we have built up over three centuries down here, along with the omnipresence of African-Americans. As an illustration, I grew up in a county which was almost seventy percent black, so I was in very intimate contact with large numbers of African-Americans from birth. A black midwife was in the room when I was born.

That's what John Shelton Reed might have been driving at when he said that the South has been crafted historically with a particularly painful awareness of, and tension between, race, class, and religion. That's the next level of what you're talking about: that from these omnipresent, mammoth forces of Christianity and race have come unique tensions that the South has been wrestling with throughout its history.

I very much regret, I lament, that we are rearing now generations of young southerners, not to mention young Americans, who are being brought up in an entirely—I hate to say "godless" because it sounds so judgmental—but are basically being brought up in an airtight atmosphere. My own nieces, who are extremely dear to me, and both of whom are wonderfully complicated and intelligent, good women, basically have had none of that very complex, bittersweet marination in religion that was available right on down through the fifties and sixties to the standard southern child. We now have the southern, urban, intellectual child to whom the church is simply a building down at the end of the street.

Lee Smith has commented on this loss as well.

With so many people who've been born in the South since the sixties and seventies, I see a demonstration of how enormously fragile the relation of human creatures to the Creator is. Something that would seem so indispensable, something that would seem so innate in us, turns out to be—for most of us who don't happen to be St. Paul, who is suddenly going to have a vision on the Damascus road—easily lost. For most of us, matters of that centrality depend very intensely upon where we came from and when we came from and who was behind us, who was cooking the meals and who was taking us places on Friday nights or Saturdays and Sundays. The human enterprise is an extremely fragile enterprise.

It's frightening to think what has been lost, to assess the dimensions of it. I wonder if anything has been gained?

It is frightening. Two friends of mine have just got back from substantial stints in Russia in the last month; and they both say that it's both the most exciting place in the world to be and also the scariest. One of the first things you discover is that there are millions now of what we would call intellectual Russians who have grown up with absolutely nothing to believe in. They knew they couldn't believe in their government, their official belief system of Marxist-Leninism; they secretly scorned that. But meanwhile they were offered absolutely nothing in its stead. They didn't have Russian Orthodox Christianity, they didn't have Judaism, they didn't have anything. And my friends say it's terrifying now to see all sorts of things springing up in the vacuum, like a huge interest in astrology and numerology and all kinds of cut-rate dumb brands of the occult and worse, the springing up again of anti-Semitism as an explanation of everything that goes wrong. Again it's just that the human enterprise is fragile. And by that I mean something beyond being merely a member of a species called *Homo sapiens*. I mean *Homo sapiens* is pretty damn tough. *Homo sapiens* (male and female) is likely to survive almost anything except nuclear disaster, but for us to survive as a fully human race is much more difficult. Basically barring those extraordinary moments when God breaks through to an individual creature, those things that make us most fully human largely occur, and are taught, in the way that table manners are taught. From mother to child. From father to son or father to daughter.

This is what you're talking about when you say that narrative is crucial to human survival, even before shelter. Through story-telling we are taught who we are as a species, who we are as human beings who can and must become more fully human.

Narrative is the only way that as human beings we've ever had of transmitting that knowledge from one generation to the next, from one mind to the next.

Stories about one another. Stories on one another.

Stories about creation, the whole of creation. I mean, having said that it's phenomenally fragile, I think the most hopeful thing we can say in the presence of all that is frightening is that the human creature goes on having this passionate desire for narrative and that this desire may well be our ultimate salvation. I've said in an essay that the need to tell and hear stories is the second most important need after nutrition, after food. People are going to tell stories, even if they're all alone on the streets of New York and schizophrenic. They're going to be babbling those stories to the wall.

We're talking about the need to tell and hear stories which might be called a narrative hunger, or a hunger for narrative, that you mention in A Palpable God. *And you've also written in the essay "Credible Light" in* Clear Pictures *about a passion you have had for the spiritual, that is, a kind of spiritual hunger, as being an apt way to describe your lifelong attitude towards God and His creation, the hunger for more.*

Yes. Yes! I'm a very hungry person; I always have been.

In that essay, you write that as a child you wished for complete spiritual fulfillment all at once — if only you could've seen it all in one big vision and just had it.

Yes, I was a very ambitious child. I always wanted to know everything, see everything, hear more and more. I always eavesdropped on my parents and my family. That's part of the given credentials of being any sort of artist—having that passionate curiosity, that gift for witness. Most people don't have a gift for witness because most people are, as I'm always telling my student writers, legally blind. They really don't see anything in the world unless you just bang them between the eyes and say, "Is this shirt red or blue?" And then they'll say, "Oh, oh okay, I guess it's red." But they wouldn't have noticed if you hadn't asked them.

And if it was a snake it would have bit 'em.

If it was a snake they'd be dead. And I think that my gifts (my basic equipment) were curiosity, a gift for paying attention to the world, and some sort of wiring system in my brain that made me good at the use of language. I'm not good at the use of figures and numbers or with my hands, but I'm good at using language. Those are my three talents. And probably the most important of those talents, if I had to rank them in order of importance, for my own life and my work and for my happiness as a creature, would be curiosity—the fact that I've gone on being absolutely fascinated by the world, in the broadest sense of everything in it. I mean, I can be bored obviously by all sorts of things in the world from a bad movie to a boring person, but basically I'm fascinated by life. If a writer ceases to have that fascination, he or she is in dismal trouble very fast.

That's when you start getting the tweed coat with the leather patches sewn in so you can "be a writer" rather than actually write.

Or you get the tragedy of the great writers of two generations before us—Faulkner, Hemingway, Fitzgerald, and to some extent Wolfe—who, for whatever extremely complicated reasons, wound up drugging their talent to death with alcohol.

Killing it.

Killing it. The greatest tragedy in American literature was the fact that Faulkner, Fitzgerald, Hemingway—as splendid work as they managed to do, had basically silenced themselves by the time they were forty. Hemingway and Faulkner went on writing after forty, but their great work was done, and to a large extent, they had put themselves off the air by age forty with a drug. They had silenced themselves.

That is a powerful way of putting it, "off the air." It's sad to think what stories might have been made. Let's go back to that need to hear and tell stories, that "hunger for narrative" you've talked about, and that spiritual hunger you write about—they are connected in profound ways. Can it be said that they are two ways of getting at the same thing?

No, not quite. But as you asked this, one of the things I think is that part of being a good human being or at least a good Christian is being as willing to listen to stories as you are to tell them. One of the things we mean by a "bore" is someone who would rather tell stories than hear them. You try to run up the chimney to get away from them when you see them coming. A satisfactory writer, a satisfactory verbal artist, is someone who is more prepared to listen to stories than to tell them because you've got to spend a lot more time observing and witnessing the world than in proclaiming. One of the terrible problems that's built into being a writer in the twentieth century is that the whole serious reading public is in a conspiracy to turn us into bores, into people who are constantly giving talks on National Public Radio, seminars, teaching classes, readings, doing workshops.

Anything but actually write.

Lots of times I want to say to myself, shut up and sit down and go home and write, or go sit in the bus station lobby and listen to people getting on with their lives. But the culture wants so much to turn us into these pundits, these experts, and after-dinner entertainers. It's a terrible temptation. Everybody likes to be loved (unless you're really deeply masochistic). And being loved as a writer tends to mean being asked to do those things which are not good for your work or your soul—that soul which is telling you you're talking too much, pretending you know too much, and above all, pretending you matter too much.

Without realizing it, you've been seduced by the phenomenon of "author worship."

Yes, indeed.

What areas of inquiry do you get excited about when it comes to

*talking about the interplay or the interconnections/intersections
between fiction and belief?*

It's something that I've very much consciously avoided doing or
talking about in my professional life. I'm always being asked to be
on panels about "The Christian Novel," "Faith and Art"—invited to
come to this conference or that. I almost invariably say no because I
feel that my work is done in my room and not out there theorizing on
panels. And as I've said, I have a deep, deep, innate revulsion to the
idea of being an evangelist. So my work is done at home in the study.

I certainly understand that.

So I wouldn't say that there's any kind of intellectual situation
relating to belief and art, faith and art, religion and art, that really
fascinates me. There are definitely things about faith and belief that
fascinate me and that I read about compulsively. I've been reading a
lot all my life, from the time I was a very young child and certainly
right down to this afternoon, about the figure of Jesus. Who was
this Jew? Who was this man who unquestionably existed for thirty-
odd years at a particular point in human history and who became
unquestionably the most influential human being who ever lived?
But the moment you start talking to me about what the Lord Jesus
means to you in your personal life, or the running of your business, or the rearing of your children, you're going to see my eyes
glaze over and I'm going to start nodding out fast.

And even with all my own basic allergy to churches, I've always
been fascinated by religious history or church history. The history
of the Reformation, the history of early Christianity, the early relationship between Christianity and Judaism are great sources of fascination for me in that they impinge upon spiritual matters of great
importance to me, as I think they are to the world. But again the
subject of "art and belief" is not something that I've let myself
spend a lot of time thinking about.

It might be that you are like the proverbial fish in the water.

Most practitioners of any art or any skill are fish in water. They
basically don't do a hell of a lot of thinking about "where are my
gills right now? Are my fins in the right place?" There are a lot of
mothers out there being mothers who couldn't tell you, if you
asked them, "How do you mother? How do you cook? How do you
make your biscuits?" They would simply say, "Don't know, I don't

measure anything, I just do it." It's the same with writing a story—my nerves either do or don't know how to do it. There's no way to describe it. You train yourself. You read and you expose yourself to the best practitioners of the skill you want to do, and then you either can or can't do it.

I feel, too, that I'm naturally graced with being a believer. I was located in the midst of a family all of whom were sincere believers or certainly sincere accepters of a tradition that was handed to them, which was Protestant Christianity, despite the fact that they were implicated in one of the great evils of human history—the enslavement of African-Americans. Most of them accepted their world (as I tried to explain in *Clear Pictures*) with about as much mercy as could be managed in the toils of an evil system. There were very few members of my family known to me who practiced what I would call an actively vicious brand of racism; they were passively caught in a situation that they saw no way to, nor did they have any desire to, change.

So I had a propitious environment around me. I had parents who left me pretty much alone. They provided me with a relaxed, sort of un-puritanical brand of Christianity. I can't ever remember hearing either parent say, "Don't do this, it's a sin" or "Don't do that, you'll go to hell" or "Don't do that, God will hate you." They weren't constructed that way. So I didn't have the problem of growing up in the kind of hateful, hypocritical, hellfire-and damnation sort of religious culture that I think an awful lot of Protestant southerners had (and which, I think, resulted often in their complete alienation from everything that they think of as religion). It's very hard to convince someone who grew up in a hateful Baptist, Methodist, Presbyterian or whatever background, that those brands of Methodism, Presbyterianism, etc., are not the whole of Christianity. I think the majority of people in this country who are atheist or agnostic are basically people who, if you said "Christianity," would see red, or see hypocrisy, judgment.

Self-righteousness and hate. Jimmy Swaggart's brand of Protestantism chills my blood.

Exactly. And that's enormously sad. That is part and parcel of my sense of whether I want to be known as a "Christian writer." A large number of people will simply not buy or not read a Reynolds

Price book because they perceive me as a "Christian" in the sense we're talking about.

Do you get letters excoriating you for using "bad" language and so on?

I don't get so much of that as I get the opposite which is people saying—how can I put this—feeling that they have some kind of extra relationship with me because they're religious and so am I. It's a kind of secret buddyism stemming from the fact that you have "found the Lord Jesus" and so have they. No one has an automatic claim on my time and sympathy just because he or she thinks they share a belief system with me. Of course, I have a Christian duty, a human duty to attempt to help people in need. But I resist people who assume that because they've read in a review that I'm a religious writer, that they have some sort of "in" with me. As a teacher, I get students who will come to me and say, "I'm taking your course because I know you're a Christian." And I always feel like saying, "Drop it fast because I'm going to challenge the hell out of you." And I do that. I don't try to turn them off from their beliefs, but I try to give them a kind of workout that I seriously doubt they've ever had in their Christian youth group.

All too often, today, as we've said, there is a vacuum of beliefs that you encounter.

Again, I think it's the fragility of the relationship of humankind to God. It's awfully difficult to convert someone who has had no religious background of any sort. The kinds of people that you and I run into who have suddenly "found the Lord" at age forty generally turn out to have only one way they can talk about it. When they get the glint in the eye and say to me, "I love the Lord Jesus too," I find that I have a deep revulsion to that. I'm not supposed to, I know.

It's the act, the behavior that you have a revulsion to, not the person's soul or anything like that. It does give me the willies, too. Thank you for answering that question. It sparks many areas for exploration. Earlier, I asked whether there are any ways that southern Protestantism has muddied or corrupted the artistic impulse of southerners.

Has my own work and my own spiritual experience suffered a lot from that? I don't think I'm the best person to say. I know a lot of awfully good human beings who are members of churches who feel that it's been a mistake in my life that I have not been able to find a fruitful relationship with an organized church. People whom I respect have said that to me. I'm prepared to grant the seriousness of their convictions, but I'm not prepared to do a whole lot about it. That's due, to a large extent, to the fact that I've been turned off by the racism of churches and the social clubbism of churches. Do I think that my vision of life has been in any sense distorted or mauled or trammeled by anything I've been taught? I can't believe that it has. I think on the contrary. The basic streams of love and mercy that are present in the whole Judeo-Christian tradition seem to me to have prepared me to be a more patient witness to the world than the reverse. And I'm also, on a bad day or at a bad moment, perfectly capable of exhibiting all the small and large sins that I observe in other people—intolerance, impatience, sadism. I'm not a candidate for sainthood.

You're describing a particular vision, your vision, of life. And when you say you are a witness to the world, I need to be very careful, because I don't want to have a too-literal meaning of that word to come into play.

That's good, because I don't mean the word "witness" in the sense of "I am a witness to the Lord Jesus." I could say that ultimately there is that kind of witness in my work. But I think it's a silent witness. It's the totality of experience that is presented in my work. When I've used "witness" heretofore in our discussion, I've meant literal watching or listening and watching the world, not standing up in church and testifying that the Lord Jesus kept me from getting drunk Saturday night. I say to my students every year when I teach Milton, "I think that I should tell you in advance that you are about to study *Paradise Lost* with someone who is a believing—though unorthodox—Christian. But wouldn't you have liked to study Homer with someone who believed in Zeus and Apollo? Wouldn't it be better understood, or at least more interesting that way, than to study him with someone who is an atheist or a Presbyterian?" I think I have a lot to bring to my students that's owing to the fact that I happen to be a Christian, though a Christian who would probably not be accepted as such by a lot of people who think of themselves as Christian.

It is important in understanding your theology and your work that you have given a great deal of thought to your faith and vision, rather than adopting a rote stance, or simply taking an attitude that you're a Christian because you've passed any given litmus test of belief or spoken a specific set of words like, "I accept Jesus Christ as my personal saviour."

And do I think that the fact that Jesus Christ is my personal savior makes me a better artist, or a better member of the human species than, let us say, the Dalai Lama? I would say no. I would say that the Dalai Lama may very well be, probably is, a better human being than I and probably a more valuable human being to other creatures than I. There would be a lot of Baptists and Catholics who couldn't hold with that. But I can because I just happen to think that the Creator, who triggered this whole unimaginably complex enterprise we call the universe (or this one of many universes) is not in the business of approving or disapproving creatures because of the insignia they happen to have on them— Baptist, Buddhist or whatever. I think that the Creator definitely has moral priorities, but are they about eating pork or not drinking wine? No, I don't think they are. I think they're about love and mercy and forgiveness and courage.

I was entranced by "Full Day" when I read it in Harper's *a while back (March 1991). I ended up reading it several times, for different reasons each time. It is a beautiful story. I also wanted to tell you that I read your essay on the Book of John in* Incarnation, *and gave my priest that book the next day. I told him that reading your essay was the closest thing I've had to a conversion experience in a long time, his sermons excepted, of course. [Laughter]*

I thank you.

It took my breath away because of how you engaged with the text.

I've translated Mark and I want to translate the Book of John, and teach a seminar next year in which we read Mark and John and try, insofar as we possibly can, to look at these things completely cold, as if they had just been dug up out of the ground. What is this book? What is it about? What does it say? What does it want me to do once I've read it? I've always loved John. I'd read a lot about

John through the years, in my hobby of reading Christian scholarship; but I'd never really sat down and dealt with it.

I'd always liked it because it seemed to me to be the wildest of the four Gospels.

It is the wildest book of all. And it turns out that so many of those things that Christians like to quote to each other—"For God so loved the world," and "In my Father's house are many mansions"—all come from John. Yet also John has the scariest things in it, all the scary moments when Jesus says things like "I'm God, get out of my way." [Laughter]

Is that when He withers the fig tree?

Actually I think that's in Mark; but in John He's always saying things like, "Before Abraham was, I am."

And raising Lazarus up after four days in the crypt. Your essay had me seeing that in new ways.

I think that Jesus' last resurrection appearance in John, when they're all out fishing at night, comes closest to proving the resurrection as an actual, photographable event more than anything else in the Gospels.

Yes! When Peter in his hysteria throws himself into the sea.

It's extremely difficult to believe that's an invented story.

You argue that its truthfulness is revealed in the ease with which the story can be instantly converted to first person.

And the fact that it retains its power when it's done that way. It's fascinating to me. You usually can't do that: "We were out fishing, dawn was breaking." Very weird stuff.

It means that this story goes deep, goes down to the bone.

Have you ever been to Israel?

No, I haven't.

Well, if the news calms down a bit, you really ought to go some time in your life. I went twice, in '80 and '83. I went with a friend; we just flew to Israel and rented a car, spent two weeks each time. It's enormously fascinating as a *place* where you can get in very direct contact with the sacred. If you've had the kind of intellectual and emotional raising that you and I had, there's an access there to the history of the place, the Jewish history, the Christian history, the Muslim history, which is amazing. You can stand right in what are literally the ruins of Peter's house in Capernaum—and they know it's Peter's house because it has all this first-century graffiti on the walls.

You have described in your writings the emotional impact of seeing the Basilica in Bethlehem at Christmas.

Absolutely. The Cave of the Nativity. And it's not like Williamsburg. You can also see how it's no accident at all that people have been in a state of semi-insane contention for the rights to this place forever, for as long as we can remember in human history. There is something truly sacred about the place that makes you see how it can drive people almost crazy if not truly crazy.

Can you tell me a little more about "Full Day"?

Yes. I don't know quite where it came from in the sense of what might have triggered it. I probably wrote it about three years ago because it was then that I decided to make myself a member of my own writing class. I started teaching a senior/graduate level class in writing, and I decided that I was going to make myself a member and do all the assignments that I'd asked the class to do, then ask them to discuss mine as I did theirs.

That's a great idea.

I think that "Full Day" started with my fulfilling an assignment which was to describe an action that occurred in no more than three hours of clock time and no more than ten pages of prose. I don't know why—certainly, all my childhood, my father was a salesman, and often a traveling salesman. Often he would leave home on Monday morning, and we wouldn't see him again until Friday night. He would be out on the road selling electrical appliances. And I used to think a lot of that part of my father's life as his "secret" life, and I'd wonder what he did. I'd invent all these scenarios—he had another family, he was a bigamist, and so on. All of which were totally wrong (my father was probably the best-behaved man you ever knew) but "Full Day" came out of that whole sense of giving my father the kinds of experiences which he probably didn't have.

The story seemed to be infused with a sense of celebration; it was, it seems to me, a portrait of ordinary people who were innately celebrating having been created and struggling to be good.

That's something that I think all my work is a witness to. And witness here in the sense of someone who stands up and says, "I want this to be *known* because it matters." From the very beginning of my work, I think my work is witness to the fact that there are an awful lot of good people in the world, many of whom are the kinds of people who would not be approved of by the official judgmental bodies of our culture (the churches, the courts and so forth). A lot of my characters are outlaws, emotional outlaws—people like Kate Vaiden or Wesley [in *A Long and Happy Life, Good Hearts*].

I'm crazy about Wesley.

They're outlaws, they're not officially acceptable people. But I think they're profoundly good people, and a lot of my work is in reference to that.

They are outside the bounds of the laws and societal norms which would say, for example, that a young matron should not lie down naked next to a strange man. That's the "right and wrong" of it, and yet it was, in a very real way, a beautiful act.

A beautiful experience.

And it became in the end, many years later, a tribute to the father, a description of a "full day" in the sense of a fully lived life.

My parents were just really fascinating people. And the longer I live, the more amazed I am at how many people will either tell you outright or circuitously that they didn't like their parents at all; a surprising number of people have parents whom they don't want to know. But my parents were fascinating, and I know I'm not crazy because my brother feels the same way. He and I both have said to each other on occasion (and we're very different from each other), that it's almost detrimental to have parents who were as interesting as ours because it's made us both almost snobbish about relationships in our lives. We had these giving, kind, funny, loving, narratively skillful, affirming people there at our cradles. It makes a lot of other people not too easy to put up with.

You can view it as verging on snobbish, but I think that it may mean that you simply don't feel a need to settle for destructive or less-than-satisfying relationships.

Of course I'm being hyperbolic. But we did have our standards for human companionship set very high very early in our lives. That's probably the single fact that is true about both of us.

As I study some of your works, and view them as a whole, what would you suggest I look at? I'd like to read Kate Vaiden *and reread* A Generous Man, A Long and Happy Life, *and* Good Hearts

*and deal with them in some way that has to do with the relation-
ship between Jewish traditions of narrative and Christian traditions of narrative as they pertain to fiction in our southern culture.
Does that ring any bells?*

Surely. It sounds congenial to the kind of work I've done. I think
that I've become aware in the last five or six years of something
that seems to be going on forever in my work (which I wasn't especially conscious of before) and that is the degree to which my work
has dealt with what I might call "Christian outlaws," or "believing
outlaws," the "virtuous" or "saintly outlaw." Wesley, Kate—I
have a new novel coming in May which is the first-person, life
story of a man named Blue Calhoun (the novel is called *Blue
Calhoun*) who is born and reared in Raleigh. And Blue is an outlaw.
He works in a music store on Fayetteville Street in Raleigh, but he
ran away from his wife and daughter, ran off with a sixteen-year-
old girl; a thirty-six-year-old man. He's done a lot of bad reckless
stuff in his life, but basically I think he's an enormously good and
careful person. I think Kate Vaiden is like that.

I guess it goes back again to some kind of relation to my parents,
both of whom saw themselves as outlaws. My mother was an
orphan. Her parents died when she was a young child. She was
reared in her own homeplace by an older sister, so she never had to
go to an orphanage or foster care. The people who were supposed to
have taken care of her—her parents—didn't, though not through
any choice of their own, but because they died. It made her always
have that slight sense that she didn't belong to the world. And my
father somehow never integrated into his own family the way his
brothers and sisters did. I think he always saw himself as a kind of
sojourner alone in the world. I don't think it made him terribly
unhappy; I just think it was the way he saw himself.

It's an exciting idea. Wesley in Good Hearts *is a good-hearted
outlaw.*

Wesley is a real outlaw when he runs away. A real outlaw.
Wesley and Kate and Blue Calhoun are the three big outlaws. To
some extent Milo in *A Generous Man* is.

Yet, he closes down prematurely.

It's like what happens to so many people in the country world where I and other southern writers like Clyde Edgerton and Kaye Gibbons grew up. Some of those country kids had to become grown men when they were sixteen. Dad was dead, you must run the tobacco farm, and you also had to take care of Mama and Brother. Maybe my own fascination with what I call the "outlaw" somehow arises out of my witnessing them in my childhood. And I'm an outlaw in all sorts of ways. But then everybody likes outlaws better than they like churchgoers. ✝

3

LARRY BROWN

Proceeding Out from Calamity

Larry Brown was born in 1951 and raised in Yocona, Mississippi, a cross-roads community near Oxford. After graduating from high school in 1970, he served a two-year stint in the marines, returning home in 1973 to marry and raise a family. From then until early 1990, he served as a member of the Oxford fire department, attaining the rank of captain in 1986. In 1990, Brown left the fire department to write full-time. He and his wife, Mary Annie, and three children have made their home outside Oxford on farmland that was Mary Annie's family homeplace.

Before he became a firefighter, Brown had worked variously as a house-painter, carpet cleaner, lumberjack and carpenter. In 1980, at the age of twenty-nine, he decided, as he puts it, to "do something with my life" and began teaching himself the art and craft of fiction writing. An avid reader since childhood, Brown began reading every kind of fiction he could find, from detective thrillers to Henry James and William Faulkner, studying how they "did things." He cites Raymond Carver, Flannery O'Connor, Tobias Wolff, and Stephen King as being particularly influential. By 1990, while he was still employed as a full-time firefighter, he had completed over one hundred short stories, five novels, and a stage play.

In 1988, Brown published a short story collection, *Facing the Music*, to critical acclaim. His first published novel, *Dirty Work* (1989), was awarded the Mississippi Institute of Arts and Letters Award for fiction. In 1990, his second collection of short stories, *Big Bad Love*, was published. A television production of *Dirty Work*, for which Brown has written the screenplay, is currently being developed by *American Playhouse*. His work has been represented in anthologies including *Best American Short Stories 1989*, edited by Margaret Atwood and Shannon Ravenel, and has appeared in magazines such as *Chattahoochee Review, Easyrider, Fiction International, Mississippi Review, Paris Review, St. Andrews Review*, and *Southern Exposure*. His nonfiction book, *On Fire*, about his life as a firefighter, will be published in 1994.

In his first collection of short fiction, *Facing the Music*, Brown introduces us to people who seem to be paralyzed by calamity, and who eventually must learn, often with only the slightest glimmer of understanding, how to deal with it—through resignation, denial, or a wan faith. The stories themselves are written with a command of the craft and an authenticity of dialogue that is sophisticated and effective. In the novel *Dirty Work*, Brown creates two distinctive narrative voices (one of Walter James, a white man, and the other of Braiden Chaney, a black man, both from Mississippi). Lying side by side in a veterans hospital, both having sustained severe, permanent wounds in Vietnam, they seek deliverance from suffering in one another. The second collection of short stories, *Big Bad Love*, examines with acrid bitterness and humor the inexorable death of love in marriage.

Larry Brown's characters are poor, plain people who are leading lonely lives characterized by alcoholism, suicide, poverty, and despair. His stories often depict the violence and horror of loss, whether of "the end of romance" (the theme of one violent, supremely ironic story of the same title), or of the aftermath of war. "The characters in my stories are all proceeding out from calamity. We are all striving for the same things, for some kind of love," he observes. In his fiction Brown shows a moral world, and though it is filled with brutality and despair, it is a world in which ordinary people struggle to do what is right, to understand their suffering. His fiction succeeds because it reveals meaning but avoids pat moral preachments: at the heart of his stories, just as at the heart of religious truths, lies a mystery. †

A Roadside Resurrection

Story opens, Mr. Redding is coughing in a cafe by the Yocona River, really whamming it out between his knees. He's got on penny loafers with pennies in them, yellow socks, madras shorts, a reversible hat and a shirt that's faded from being washed too many times. His wife, Flenco, or Flenc, as he calls her, is slapping him on the back and alternately sucking her chocolate milkshake through a straw and looking around to see who's watching. She's got a big fat face, rollers in her hair, and she's wearing what may well be her nightgown and robe. Fingernails: bright red.

"Damn!" Mr. Redding coughs. "Godamighty . . . damn!"

Flenco hits him on the back and winces at his language, sucking hard on her straw and glancing around. Mr. Redding goes into a bad fit of coughing, kneels down on the floor heaving, tongue out and curled, veins distended on his skinny forearms, hacking, strangling, and the children of the diners are starting to look around in disgust.

"Oh," he coughs. "Oh shit. Oh damn."

Mr. Redding crawls back up in the booth and reaches into his shirt pocket for a Pall Mall 100, lights it, takes one suck, then repeats the entire scenario above. This goes on three times in thirty minutes.

Customers go in and out and people order beers and drink them at the counter on stools, but Mr. Redding lies back in the booth while his wife mops his feverish forehead with wetted paper towels brought by a waitress from the kitchen, along with another milkshake just like the last one. The hair on Mr. Redding's forearms is dark and scattered like hair on a mangey dog just recovering, and his sideburns sticking out from under the reversible cap are gray. Twenty years ago he could do a pretty good imitation of Elvis. Now he's washed up.

"Oh crap," he says. "Oh shit. Oh hell."

Flenco mops him and sops up his sweat and sucks her big round mouth around the straw and looks at people and pats him on the back. Truckers come in with their names on their belts and eat eggs and ham and wash down pills with coffee and put their cigarettes out in their plates, stagger back outside and climb up into their sleepers. Flenco looks down the road and wonders what road she'll be on before long.

"Oh shit," Mr. Redding wheezes.

Miles away down the road a legendary young healer is ready to raise the roof on a tent gathering. Sawdust is on the floor and the lights are bright and a crippled boy in a wheelchair has been brought forward to feel his healing hands. The boy lies in his chair drooling up at the lights, hands trembling, the crowd watching on all sides, spectators all piled up along the back and sides and others peeking in the opened opening, some lying on the ground with their heads stuck up between the tent pegs. The crippled child waits, the mother trembling also, nearby, hands clasped breastwise to the Holy Father Sweet Mary Mother of Saints heal my child who was wrong from the womb Amen. The lights flicker. The healer is imbued with the Spirit of God which has come down at the edge of this cotton field and put into his fingers the strength of His love and healing fire. Outside bright blades of lightning arch and thunderclouds rumble in the turbulent sky as the healer goes into his trance. His fine dark hair is sleek on the sides of his head and he cries out: "Heeeeeel! Heal this boy, Lord! Heal him! Dear sweet merciful God if You ever felt it in your heart to heal somebody heal this boy! This boy! This one right here, Lord! I know there's a bunch of em over there in darkest Africa need healing too Lord but they ain't down on their knees to You right now like we are!"

The healer sinks to his knees with these words, hands locked and upflung before him. Ushers are moving slowly through the crowd with their plates out, but nobody's putting much into the plates yet because they haven't seen the boy get up and walk.

"Lord what about Gethsemane? Lord what about Calvary's cross? Lord what about Your merciful love that we're here to lay on this child? There's his mama, Lord. I guess his daddy's in here, too. Maybe all his brothers and sisters."

"He's a only child," the mama whispers, but nobody seems to notice. The rain has started and everybody's trying to crowd inside.

"Neighbors? I don't believe there's much faith in this house tonight. I believe we've done run into a bunch of doubting Thomases, folks who want to play before they pay. Maybe they think this ain't nothing but a sideshow. Maybe they think this boy works for me. Because I don't believe they're putting in any money to further our work."

The ushers make another pass through the crowd and collect six dollars and fifty-two cents. The boy lies in the wheelchair, legs dangling. This child has never walked before. The mother has told the healer his history. He was born with spinal meningitis, his heart outside his body, and she said God only gave him one kidney. She said on the day she goes to her grave she will still owe hospital bills on him. The healer can see that the congregation thinks nothing is going to happen. He can almost read their faces, can almost read in their countenances the unsaid accusations: *Ha! Unclean! Imposter prove your worth! Make him walk!*

The healer comes down from the podium. The fire of God is still in him. The wheels of the wheelchair are mired in the sawdust. The mother has already begun to feel what has come inside the tent. She faints, falls over, shrieks gently. An uncle stands up. The healer lays his hands on.

"Now I said *heal!* I don't give a damn! About what's happening over there in Saudi Arabia! I don't care what else You got on Your mind! You got to heal this boy! Either heal him or take him right now! Heal him! Or take him! We don't care! He's with You either way!"

The child wobbles in the wheelchair. The healer digs his fingers down deep into the flesh. More people stand up to see. The mother wakes up, moans and faints again. The lightning cracks overhead and the lights go out and then come back on dim. The ushers are moving more quickly through the crowd. An aura of Presence moves inside the tent to where everybody feels it. The child grips the armrests of his chair. His feet dig for purchase in the sawdust. He cries out with eyes closed in a racked and silent scream.

"Yeah!" the healer shouts. "Didn't believe! Look at him! Watch him walk!"

The boy struggles up out of the chair. People have come to his mother's side with wet handkerchiefs and they revive her in time to witness him make his stand. He rises up on his wasted legs, the healer's hands octopussed on his head.

"Heal! Heal! Heal! Heal! Heal! Heal! Heal!"

The boy shoves the hands away. The mother looks up at her son from the dirt. He takes a step. His spine is straight. He takes another step. People are falling to their knees in the sawdust. They are reaching for their purses and wallets.

Mr. Redding has to be taken outside because he is bothering the other customers. Flenco lets him lie on the seat of the truck for a while and fans him with a Merle Haggard album.

"Oh shit," Mr. Redding says. "Oh arrrrgh."

"It's gonna be all right, baby," Flenco says.

Mr. Redding is almost beyond talking, but he gasps out: "What do . . . you mean . . . it's . . . gonna . . . be . . . all right?"

"Oh, Flem, I heard he'd be through here by nine o'clock. And they say he can really heal."

"I don't . . . believe . . . none of that . . . *bull*shit!"

Mr. Redding says that, and goes into great whoops of coughing.

A lot of money in the plates tonight. The mission can go on. But some helpers have wives back home, trailer payments have to be met, others want satellite dishes. The healer requires nothing but a meal that will last him until the next meal. He gives them all the money except for the price of steak and eggs at a Waffle House and heads for the car. The road is mud. The tent is being taken down in the storm. The memory of the woman is on him and he doesn't feel very close to God.

"Oh shit," Mr. Redding says. "Oh damn oh hell oh shit."

"Baby?" Flenco says., "Don't you think you ought not be cussing so bad when you're like this?"

"Li . . . iii . . . iiike what?" Mr. Redding spews out.

"When you're coughing so bad and all. I bet if you'd quit smoking them cigarettes you wouldn't cough so bad."

She pats him on the back like she saw the respiratory therapist do and feels she knows a little about medicine.

"Oh crap," Mr. Redding says. "Oh *shit!*"

Flenco mops his sweaty head and fans hot air with her hand. She had heard that the healer drives a long black Caddy. They say he refuses to appear on network television and will not endorse products. They say he comes speeding out of the dusty fields in his dusty black car and they say the wind his machine brings whips the trousers of the state troopers before they can get into their cruisers and take pursuit. They say he lives only to heal and that he stops on the roadsides where crippled children have been set up and where their mothers stand behind them holding up cardboard placards painstakingly printed HEALER HEAL MY CHILD. They say that if the state troopers catch up with him while he is performing some miracle of mercy on one of God's bent lambs, the people pull their cars out into the road and block the highway, taking the keys out of the ignitions, locking the doors. It's said that in Georgia last year a blockade of the faithful ran interference for him through a web of parked police cars outside Waycross and allowed him to pass unmolested, such is the strength of his fame. Flenco hasn't a placard. She has rented a billboard beside the cafe, letters six feet tall proclaiming HEALER HEAL MY HUSBAND. Telephone reports from her sister-in-law in Bruce confirm the rumor that he has left Water Valley and is heading their way. Flenco imagines him coming down out of the hilly country, barreling down the secondary roads and blasting toward the very spot where she sits fanning Mr. Redding's feverish frame.

"Oh shit," Mr. Redding says. "Oh God. . . dang!"

"Just rest easy now, honey," Flenco says. "You want me to go get you some Co-Coler?!"

"Hell naw I don't want no goddamn Co-Coler," Mr. Redding says "I want some . . . want some goddamn . . . I want some . . . shit! Just carry me . . . back home and . . . goddamn . . . let me die. I'm . . . goddamn . . . burning up out here."

Flenco hugs his skinny body tight and feels of his emaciated wrists. Hands that used to hold a silver microphone hang limply from his cadaverous arms, all speckled with liver spots. She wants him to hold on a little longer because she doesn't know if the healer has worked his way up to raising the dead yet. She knows a little of his scanty history. Born to Christian Seminoles and submerged for thirty-seven minutes in the frigid waters of Lake Huron at the age of fourteen, he was found by divers and revived with little hope of ultimate survival by firefighters on a snowcovered bank. He allegedly lay at death's door in a coma for nine weeks, then suddenly got out of his bed, ripping the IV tubes out, muttering without cursing, and walked down the hall to the Intensive Care Unit where a family of four held a death vigil over their ninety-year-old grand-mother fatally afflicted with a ruptured duodenum and laid his hands on her. The legend goes that within two minutes the old lady was sitting up in the bed demanding Fudge Ripple on a sugar cone and a pack of Lucky Strikes. Fame soon followed and the boy's yard became littered with the sick and the crippled, and the knees of his jeans became permanently grass-stained from kneeling. The walking canes piled up in a corner of the yard as a testament to his powers. A man brought a truck once a week to collect the empty wheelchairs. He made the blind see, the mute speak. A worldwide team of doc-tors watched him cure a case of wet leprosy. The President had him summoned to the White House, but he could not go; the street in front of his house was blocked solid with the bodies of the needing-to-be-healed. People clamored after him, and women for his seed. The supermarket tabloids proclaim that he will not break the vow he gave to God in the last few frantic moments before sinking below the waters of Lake Huron: if God would bring him back from a watery death he would remain pure and virginal in order to do His work. And now he has come South like a hunted animal to seek out the legions of believers with their sad and twisted limbs.

"Flenc," Mr. Redding coughs out, "How many goddamn times I told you . . . oh shit . . . not to . . . aw hell, ahhhhh."

The tent is down, the rain has ceased. The footsteps of many are printed in the mud. He's had to sign autographs this time, and fighting the women off is never easy. They are convinced the child they'd bear would be an Albert Einstein, an Arnold Schwarzenegger, a Tom Selleck with the brain of Renoir. Some tell him they only want him for a few moments to look at something in the back seat of their car, but he knows they are offering their legs and their breasts and their mouths. He can't resist them any more. He's thinking about getting out of the business. The promise has already been broken anyway, and the first time was the hardest.

His bodyguards and henchmen push with arms spread against the surging crowd and his feet suck in the mud as he picks his way to his Caddy. All around sit cars and pickup trucks parked or stuck spinning in the mud as the weak sun tries to smile down between the parting clouds.

He gets into the car and inserts the ignition key and the engine barks instantly into life with the merest flick of the key. The engine is as finely tuned as a Swiss watchmaker's watch and it hums with a low and throaty purring that emanates from glasspack mufflers topped off with six feet of chrome. He tromps on the gas pedal and the motor rumbles, cammed up so high it will barely take off.

He hits the gas harder and the Caddy squats in the mud, fishtailing like an injured snake through the quagmire of goop. The crowd rushes the bodyguards, pushing their burly bodies back and down and trampling them underfoot, stepping on their fingers, surging forward to lay their once-withered hands on the dusty flanks of the healer's automobile. Faces gather around the windows outside and the healer steers his machine through the swampy mess of the pasture and over to a faint trail of gravel that leads to the highway. Many hands push and he guns the big car and mudballs thwack hollowly and flatten on the pants and shirts of the faithful left gawking after him in his wake. They wave, beat their chests to see him go. Liberated children turn handsprings in the mud and perform impromptu fencing matches with their useless crutches and these images recede quickly through the back window as the car lurches toward the road.

The healer looks both ways before pulling out on the highway. Cars are lined on both sides all the way to the curves that lie in the distance. Horns blare behind him and he turns the car north and smashes the gas pedal flat against the floorboard. The big vehicle takes the road under its wheels and rockets past the lines of automobiles. Small hands wave from the back seats as he accelerates rapidly past them.

The needle on the speedometer rises quickly. He eyes the gas gauge's red wedge of metal edged toward FULL. He finds k. d. lang on the radio and fishes beneath the seat for the flask of vodka his bodyguards have secreted there. The prearranged destination is Marion, Arkansas, where droves of the helpless are rumored to be gathered in a field outside the town.

He takes one hit, two hits, three hits of vodka and pops the top on a hot Coke while reaching for his smokes. His shoes are slathered with mud and his shirt is dirty, but fresh clothes await him somewhere up ahead. Everything is provided. Every bathroom in the South is open to him. The Fuzzbuster on the dash ticks and he hits the brakes just in time to cruise by a cruiser hidden in a nest of honeysuckle. At 57 mph.

He feels weak and ashamed for breaking his vow, but the women won't let him alone. They seem to know the weakness of his flesh. A new issue of *Penthouse* is under the seat. He reaches over and takes his eyes off the road for a moment, pulls the magazine out. He flips it open and the pictures are there, with nothing left to the imagination, the long legs, the tawny hair, the full and pouting lips. With a sharp stab of guilt he closes it up and shoves it back under the seat. He can't go on like this. A decision has to be made. There are too many who believe in him and he is the vessel of their faith. He knows he's unworthy of that trust now. It's going to be embarrassing if God decides to let him down one night in front of a hundred and fifty people. The crowd might even turn ugly and lynch him if he's suddenly unable to heal. They've come to expect it. They have every right to expect it. But they don't know about his needs. They don't know what it's like to be denied the one thing that everybody else can have: the intimate touch of another.

He lights the cigarette and cracks the vent as a smattering of raindrops splatter across the windshield. He turns the wipers on and passes through a curtain of rain as perpendicular as a wall, crosses over onto a shiny darkened highway with tiny white explosions of water pinging up on its surface. He tromps on the gas pedal and the Caddy's tires sing their highspeeded whine. Small heads on front porches turn like tennis spectators as a black flash shoots down the road. He waves.

Mr. Redding lies near comatose under the shade tree Flenco has dragged him to, and people coming out of the cafe now are giving

him queasy looks. Flenco knows that some good citizen might have
an ambulance called.

"Just hold on now, baby." Flenco says. "I feel it in my heart he's
coming any minute now."

"I don't give a . . . give a good . . . a good . . . a good goddamn . . .
I don't give a shit who's coming," Mr. Redding hacks out. His lips
are slimy with a splotching of pink foam and his breath rattles in
his chest like dry peas in a pod. He quivers and shakes and licks his
lips and groans. Flenco cradles his graying head in her ample lap
and rubs the top of his hat with her tremendous sagging breasts.
Her rose-tipped nipples miss the passion that used to be in Mr.
Redding's tongue. Flenco deeply feels this loss of sexual desire and
sighs in her sleep at night on the couch while Mr. Redding hacks
and coughs and curses in the bedroom and gets up to read detective
magazines or rolls all over the bed. She's ashamed of her blatant
overtures and attempts at enticement, the parted robe, the naked
toweling off beside the open bathroom door, the changing of her
underwear in the middle of the day. Mr. Redding appears not to
notice, only lights one Pall Mall after another and swears.

She has sent a little wide-eyed boy inside for another chocolate
milkshake and he brings it out to her under the tree where she
holds the gasping wheezebag who used to belt out one Elvis song
after another in his white jumpsuit with the silver zippers. He'd
been nabbed for bad checks in Texas, was on the run from a Mann
Act in Alabama, but Flenco fell in love with his roguey smile and
twinkling eyes the first time she saw him do "You Ain't Nothing
But A Hound Dog" at the Junior/Senior Prom. His battered travel
trailer had a cubbyhole with a stained mattress that held the scent-
ed remnants of other nights of lust. But Flenco, pressed hard
against the striped ticking with her head in a corner, found in his
wild and enthusiastic gymnastics a kind of secret delight. Shunned
by her schoolmates, sent to the office for passing explicit notes to
boys, downtrodden by the depression caused by her steady eating,
Flenco was hopelessly smitten in the first few minutes with his
hunk of "Burning Love."

Now her lover lies wasted in her lap, his true age finally showing,
his wrinkled neck corded with skin like an old lizard's as he sags
against her and drools. She's not asking for immortality; she's not

asking for the Fountain of Youth; she's only asking for a little more time. The hope that burns like a bright flame in her heart is a candle lit to the memory of physical love. She wipes his hot face tenderly with a wadded napkin soaked in the cold sweat from the milkshake cup. Mr. Redding turns and digs his head deeper into her belly. People at the tables in the cafe are staring openly through the windows now and Flenco knows it's only a matter of time before somebody calls the lawdogs.

"Can I do anything for you, baby?" she says.

Mr. Redding turns his eyes up to her and the pain buried in them is like a dying fire.

"Hell yeah you can . . . do . . . something . . . goddamn . . . do something . . . oh shit . . . for me. You can . . . goddamn . . . oh shit . . . . you can . . . just . . . hell . . . by God . . . shoot me."

"Oh baby, don't talk like that," Flenco says. Her eyes mist up and she covers his face with her breasts until he reaches up with both hands and tries to push the weighty mass of her mammary monsters up out of the way.

"Goddamn, what you . . . what you trying to . . . trying to . . . I didn't say . . . smother me," Mr. Redding says.

Flenco doesn't answer. She closes her eyes and feels the former flicks of his tongue across her breastworks in a memory as real as their truck.

The road is straight, the cotton young and strong, and the Caddy is a speeding bullet across the flat highway. The needle is buried to the hilt at 120 and the car is floating at the very limit of adhesion, weightless, almost, drifting slightly side to side like a ship lightly tacking on the ocean in the stiff edges of a breeze. The blue pulses of light winking far behind him in the sun are like annoying toys, no more. The healer dips handful after handful of roofing tacks out of the sack beside him and flings them out the open window, scattering them like bad seeds. The blue lights fade, are gone, left far behind. Others of like bent are waiting probably somewhere ahead but he'll deal with them when the time comes.

Fruit and vegetable stands flash by the open windows of the car, junk peddlers, mobile homes, stacked firewood corded up on the sides of the road for sale, waving people, fans. It is these people he heals, these people crushed and maimed by the falling trees, by the falling house trailers, by the falling cars and junk. These innocents carving a life out of the wilderness with their hands, these with so much faith that he is merely an instrument, a transmitter to funnel the energy required to make them stand up and throw away their braces. He thinks of the promise he made going down reaching for the surface of Lake Huron. He gets another drink of the vodka and lights another cigarette and shakes his head as the hubcaps glitter in the sun.

"Lord God I wouldn't have touched her if I was the Pope!" he suddenly screams out into the car, beating his fist on the seat. He turns his head and shouts out the open window: "Why didn't you let me die and then bring me back as the Pope? Huh? You want to answer that one, Lord?"

He takes another quick suck of the hot vodka. His shoulders shiver, and he caps it.

"I cain't cure everbody in the whole world!"

He slows down and rolls to about 15 mph and shouts to a God maybe lurking behind a dilapidated cotton pen and guarded by a pink Edsel with the hood on the roof.

"You ought not made it so tough on me! I ain't like Jesus, I'm human! I can't do it no more, they's too many of em! They's too many women! I take back my promise, I quit!"

The long low surprised face of a farmer in a 1953 Chevrolet pickup with a goat in the back passes by him in slow motion, his head hanging out the window, a woman looking over his shoulder, seeing, figuring the black car and the haranguing finger poking out at a telephone pole, gathering her wits, her thoughts, her breath, to point back, inhale, scream: "It's HIM! PRAISE WONDERFUL GOD IT'S HIIIIIIM!"

The healer looks. He sees the old black pickup grind to a halt, the one brake light coming on, the woman hopping out the door, arms waving, the farmer leaning out the window waving. For the first time ever the healer is tempted to burn rubber and leave them smelling his getaway fumes, leave behind him unheard the story of their huge drooling son, prisoner of the basement, chained in the garage at the family reunions. But the faces of these two parents are lit like rays of sunshine with the knowledge that a modern messiah has chosen the road that borders their alfalfa patch to receive his Divine instructions.

The woman runs up to the side of the car and lays her hands on the fender as if she'd hold it to keep the car from leaving. Her beady eyes and panting breath and hopeless eternal hope-filled face tell the healer this woman has a task of such insurmountable proportions she's scarce shared the secret of her problem with minister or preacher or parson, that this one's so bad he can't quit now. Holy cow. What pining cripple on his bed of mouldy quilts with his palsied arms shaking lies waiting nearly forever for his release? What afflicted lamb has lain behind a curtain to be hidden from company all these years? Here, he sees, are the mother and the father, the suffering parents, here with their pain and their hope and their alfalfa patch and cows and fishponds, their world struck askew by the birth or the affliction or the accident that befell their fallen one, with neither hope of redemption or cure available for what might be eating mothballs or masturbating in old dirty underwear and hiding it under his mother's mattress to be discovered when the springs need turning, might be roaming the pastures by night creeping stealthily upon the female livestock.

"Healer," the woman asks. "Will you heal my child?"

He's not coming, Flenco suddenly decides. In a burst of thought process too deep for her to understand, a mere scab on the broad scar of telepathy which man's mind forgot to remember eons ago, she knows somehow that another emergency has detained him. She knows, too, that they must therefore go find him. She gets up and catches Mr. Redding under the armpits and drags him through the dust toward the truck, where now in large numbers on the other side of the cafe windows people stand gathered to track the proceedings and place wagers on the estimated time of arrival of Mr. Redding's demise.

"Oh hope, there's hope," she chants and pants. His heels make two trails of dust through the parking lot but his loafers stay on like a miracle or a magic trick. Flenco gets him next to the running board and stoops to release the precious burden of him, opens the door, gives a hefty grunt and hauls him up into the seat. Mr. Redding falls over against the horn of the truck and it begins to blow as Flenco shuts the door and runs around to the other side. She yanks open the door and pushes him erect in the seat and reaches across him and locks the door so he won't fall out and hurt himself any worse. Those cigarettes have a hold on him that keeps him from eating, from gaining weight, from not wheezing in the early morning hours when she awakens beside him and lies in the dark staring at his face and twirling the tufts of gray hair on his chest around her fingers. But maybe the healer can even cure him of his addiction, drive the blackness from his lungs, the platelets from his aorta, flush the tiny capillaries in their encrusted fingers of flesh. She seat belts him.

Mr. Redding sits in a perfect and abject state of apathy, his head keened back on his neck and his closed eyes seeing nothing. Not even coughing.

"Hold on, baby," Flenco says, and cranks the truck. Truckers and patrons stand gawking at the roostertail of dust and gravel kicked up by the spinning wheel of the truck, then it slews badly, hits the road sliding and is gone in a final suck of sound.

With stabbing motions of her arm and hand, index finger extended, the mother directs the healer into the yard. A white picket fence with blooming daffodils belies the nature of the thing inside.

"Please, he's a baby, harmless really, come, in here, behind, I just know you, please, my mother she, my brother too they," she gasps.

The healer turns in and sees the black pickup coming behind him, the goat peeking around the cab as if directing its movement, this Nubian. Before he can fully stop the car, the woman is tugging on his arm, saying, "In here, you, oh, my husband, like a child, really."

He opens the door and starts out as the truck slides to a stop beside him, dust rising to drift over them. The healer waves his hand and coughs and the woman pulls on his arm. The farmer jogs around the hood on his gimpy leg and they each take an arm and lead him up the steps, across the porch, both of them talking in either ear a mix of latent complaints and untold griefs and shared blames for the years this child born wrong and then injured in the brain has visited on this house. The healer is dragged into a living room with white doilies under lamps and a flowerful rug spread over polished wood and a potbellied stove in one corner where a dead squirrel sits eating a varnished walnut.

"Back here, in here, he," the woman rants.

"You know, he, by golly, our field," the farmer raves.

The healer is afraid they're going to smell his breath and he turns his face from side to side as he's dragged with feet sliding to the back room, inside the closet, down hidden stairs revealed by a trapdoor. The farmer unlocks a door in the dark, hits a switch. A light comes on. Gray walls of drabness lie sweating faintly deep in the earth's damp and they're hung with old mattresses brown with spots. The furniture in the room is soft with rot, green with mold. A large, naked, drooling hairy man sits playing with a ball of his own shit in the center of the room, his splayed feet and fuzzy toes black with dirt and his sloped forehead furrowed in concentration. He says, "Huuuuuuuurrrrrnnn . . . . . ."

The healer recoils. The hairy man sits happily in the center of the floor amongst plates of old food and the little pies he has made, but looks up and eyes his parents and the paling youth between them and instantly his piglike eyes darken with total ignorance or like the darkest of animals an unveiled hostile threat.

"Hurrrrr," he says, and swivels on his buttocks to face them.

"Sweet Lord Jesus Christ," the healer whispers. "Get me out of here."

"Not so fast, young fella," the farmer says, and unlimbers from a back pocket a hogleg of Dirty Harry proportions, backs to the door behind him, locks it, pockets the key deep in his overalls.

It doesn't smell nice at all in this dungeon and the thing before him begins to try to get up on its knees and make sounds of wet rumbling wanting deep in its throat. The eyebrows knit up and down and together and apart and the healer draws back with his hands up because the man is sniffing now, trying like a blind calf to scent his mother, maybe remembering milk.

Mr. Redding lies back in the seat not even harumphing but merely juxtaposed into the position his wife has seated him in like a form set in concrete while the truck roars down the road. Flenco slurps the sediment of her shake through the straw and flings the used container out the window into a passing mass of sunflowers' bright yellow faces. Her right hand is clenched upon the wheel and her foot is pressed hard on the gas.

"Hold on, baby," she says. "I don't know where he's at but we're going to find him." Her mouth is grim.

Mr. Redding doesn't answer. He sits mute and unmoving with his head canted back and lolling limply on his neck, the squashed knot of his reversible fishing hat pulled down over his ears. He seems uninterested in the green countryside flashing by, the happy farms of cows grazing contentedly on the lush pasture grass, the wooded creeks and planted fields within the industry of American agriculture thriving peacefully beside the road.

Flenco reaches over and gets one of his cigarettes from his pocket and grabs a box of matches off the dash. She doesn't usually smoke but the situation is making her nervous. Afraid that his rancid lips might never again maul her fallow flesh, she scratches the match on the box and touches the whipping flame to the tip of the Pall Mall 100. Deluged with the desperation of despair, she draws the smoke deep and then worries her forehead with the cigarette held between her fingers. Her eyes scan the fertile fields and unpainted barns for a gathering of cripples miraculously assembled somewhere to seek out the ultimate truth. Somewhere between the borders of three counties a black Caddy runs speeding to another destination and she must intercept it or find its location. The rotting fruit of her romance lies hanging in the balance. The sad wreck of her lover must be rejuvenated. All is lost if not.

Flenco remembers the early years with Mr. Redding. Through him the ghost of Elvis not only lived but sang and whirled his pumping hips to dirges engraved on the brains of fans like grooves in records. He could get down on one knee and bring five or six of them screaming to their feet and rushing to the edge of the stage, the nostalgic, the overweight, the faded dyed ever-faithful. Now this sad wasted figure lays his head back on the seat with his lips slightly parted, his tongue drying.

Flenco smokes the cigarette furiously, stabs the scenery with her eyes, roars down the left fork of a road where a sign says HILLTOP 10 MILES. Dust hurtles up behind the pickup as it barrels down the hill. Flenco has the blind faith of love but she panics when she thinks that she might not find the healer, that he might be out of reach already, that he might have taken an alternate road and be somewhere else in the county, doing his work, healing the minions who seek him out, laying his hands on others less fortunate whose despair has eclipsed hers. But as long as there is gas in the truck, as long as Mr. Redding draws breath, she will drive until the wheels fall off the truck, until the cows come home, until they piss on the fire and call the dogs. Until hope, however much is left, is smashed, kicked around, stomped on or gone. Until Mr. Redding is dead.

Flenco eyes him and feels uneasy over his stillness. She's never known him to be this quiet before. She mashes harder on the gas and her beloved sways in the curves.

"Hold on, baby," she whispers.

The healer stands unmoving with the hard round mouth of the pistol in his back. The man on the floor is growling low and grinding his tartared teeth. His hairy arms are encrusted with a nameless nasty crap.

"Aaaarrrrr," he says.

"Yes, darling," the mother coos. "The nice man has come to help us. You like the nice man, don't you, dear?"

"He likes to play," the farmer says. "He plays down here all the time, don't you, son?" the farmer says. "We just keep him down here so he won't scare people," he explains.

The parents see no need to recite the list of stray dogs and hapless cats caught and torn limb from limb, dripping joints of furred meat thrust mouthward without mayonnaise. The six-year-old girl still missing from last year is best not spoken of. The farmer now makes use of a pneumatic tranquilizer gun before laying on the chains and padlocks at night. Delivered at home beside his stillborn twin like Elvis, the hairy one has a headstone over his undug grave.

The warped and wavy line of his dented skull is thick with a rancid growth where small insect life traverses the stalks of his matted hair. He sways and utters his gutteral verbs and fixes the healer's face with his bated malevolence and grunts his soft equations into the dusty air.

"He wants to play," the mother says. "Ain't that cute."

"Cute as a bug," the farmer says, without loosening his grip on the pistol.

"I can't heal him," the healer says.

"What did you say?" the farmer says.

"Did he say what I think he said?" the mother says.

"I think you better say that again," the farmer says.

"I can't heal him. I can't heal anything like this."

"What are you saying?" the mother says.

"You heard what he said," the farmer says. "Says he can't heal him."

"Can't?" the mother says.

"I can't," the healer says, as the man on the floor drools a rope of drool and moans a secret rhyme and moves his shoulders to and fro and never takes his eyes off the healer's face.

"I bet you'd like to know what happened to him," the mother says.

"Horse kicked him," the farmer says.

"Right in the head," the mother says.

"Turned him ass over teakettle," the farmer says. "Kicked him clean over a fence."

"Like to kicked half his head off," the mother says. "But you've cured worse than this. That little girl over in Alabama last year with that arm growed out of her stomach and that old man in the Delta who had two and a half eyes. You can heal him. Now heal him."

"We done read all about you," the farmer says. "We been trying to find you for months."

"And then he just come driving right by the place," the mother says. "Will wonders never cease."

The man on the floor is trying to form the rude impulses necessary to gather his legs beneath himself and put his feet flat on the floor. He wants to stand and will stand in a moment and the farmer reaches quickly behind him for the coiled whip on a nail.

"Easy now, son," he says.

A low uneasy moaning begins at sight of the bullwhip and the bared teeth alternate with that in a singsong incantation as he totters up onto his knees and rests his folded knuckles flat on the floor. The hair is long on his back and arms and legs. His face is transfixed with an ignorance as old as time, yet a small light burns in his eyes, and he has a little tail six inches in length entending from the coccyx bone with a tufted tip of bristles. He slides forward a few inches closer to the healer. Old bones lie piled in corners for safe-keeping with their scraps of blackened flesh.

"You might as well go on and heal him," the farmer says. "We ain't letting you out of here till you do."

"He's been like this a long time," the mother says.

"You don't understand," the healer says. "I've never dealt with anything like this."

"You cured cancer," the farmer says.

"Raised the dead, I've heard," the mother says.

"No ma'am. Ain't nobody ever raised the dead but Jesus Himself," the healer says, as the thing begins to look as if it would like to grab his leg. He tries to retreat, but the gun is in his back like a hard finger.

"What you think, mama?" the farmer says.

"I think he's trying to pull our leg," she says.

"You think he's a false prophet?"

"Might be. Or maybe he's used up all his power?"

"What about it, young feller? You used up all your power?"

"I known it was him when I seen that black car," she says.

"Lots of people have black cars," the healer says dully, unable to take his own eyes off those dully glinting ones before him. What lies inside there will not do to look at, it won't be altered by human hands, probably should have been drowned when it was little. "Don't let him hurt me," he says.

"Hurt you? Why he ain't going to hurt you," the mother says. "He just wants to play with you a little bit. We come down here and play with him all the time, don't we, daddy."

"That's right," the farmer says. "Hopfrog and leapscotch and like that. Go on and lay your hands on him. He won't bite or nothing, I promise."

"He's real good most of the time," she says. "We just keep him penned up so he won't hurt hisself."

"I can't . . . I can't . . ." the healer begins.

"Can't what?" the farmer says.

"Can't what?" the mother says.

"*Touch* him," the healer breathes.

"Uh oh," says the farmer. "I's afraid of that, mama."

"You people have got to let me out of here," the healer says. "I'm on my way to Arkansas."

"Wrong answer, mister," the farmer says.

"Definitely the wrong answer," the mother says.

Their boy moves closer and his snarling mouth seems to smile.

Flenco stands in her nightgown and robe and curlers, pumping gas into the neck of the fuel tank located in the left rear quarter panel of the truck. Years ago Mr. Redding took a hammer and screwdriver to it so that it would readily accept a leaded gasoline nozzle. Flenco pumps five dollars' worth into it and hands the money to the attendant who wiped no windshield and checked no oil but stood gawking at the rigorously mortised figure of Mr. Redding displayed in the seat like a large sack of potatoes. The attendant takes the five and looks thoughtfully at Flenco, then opens his mouth to ask:

"Lady, is this guy all right?"

Flenco starts to go around and get behind the wheel and then when she sees the beer signs hung in the windows of the gas station thinks of the twenty dollar bill wadded in the pocket of her robe like used facial tissue.

"Well he's been sick," she says, hurrying toward the door of the building.

"I don't believe he's feeling real good right now," he says to her disappearing back. When she goes inside, he watches her heading for the beer coolers at the back of the store and steps closer to the open window of the truck. He studies Mr. Redding from a vantage point of ten inches and notices that his lips are blue and his face is devoid of any color, sort of like, a *lot* like, an uncle of his who was laid out in a coffin in the comfort of his own home some two weeks before.

"Mister," he says. "Hey, mister!"

Mr. Redding has nothing to say. Flenco comes rushing back out the door with three quart bottles of cold Busch in a big grocery sack and a small package of cups for whenever Mr. Redding feels like waking up and partaking of a cool refreshing drink. She eyes the attendant suspiciously and gets in the truck and sets the beer on the seat between them, pausing first to open one bottle and set it between her massive thighs. She leans up and cranks the truck and looks at the attendant who steps back and holds up one hand and says, "Don't mind me, lady, it's a free country." Then she pulls it down into D and roars out onto the road.

Flenco gooses it up to about sixty and reaches over briefly to touch Mr. Redding's hand. The hand is cool and limp and she's glad the fever has passed. He'll feel better now that he's had a nap, maybe, not be so irritable. Maybe she can talk to him reasonably. His temper's never been good even when he was sober which hasn't been much these last twenty years. Flenco wonders where all those years went to and then realizes that one day just built into another one like with a mason stacking bricks. All those nights in all those beer joints with all that singing and stomping and screaming and women shouting out declarations of desire for the frenzied figure that was him just past his prime blend together in her mind and spin like carousel horses in a funhouse ride. They billed him as Uncle Elvis, and he's told Flenco a little about his one trip up the river and how they'd hit you in the head with something if you didn't act right, but those days are long gone and what does it matter how since the cars he stole were transient things and even now probably lie stripped and rusted out in some junkyard bog, a hulking garden of flowers adorning their machinegunned sides?

Flenco feels guilty for feeling her faith sag a little when she thinks of all the miles of roads the healer could be on and how easy it will be to miss him. She wonders if it was smart to abandon her big billboard sign by the side of the road and take off like this, but she was feeling the grip of a helpless sudden hopeless inertia and there was nothing to do but put some road under her wheels.

Flenco glances at Mr. Redding who is still oblivious to everything with the wind sailing up his nostrils. She takes a hefty slug of the beer between her legs. She nudges him.

"You want some of this beer, baby? You still asleep? Well you just go on and take you a nap, get rested. Maybe you'll feel better when you wake up."

Flenco hopes that's so. She hopes for a clue, a sign somehow, maybe that gathering of the crippled in a field like she's heard happens sometimes. If she can find him, she'll deliver Mr. Redding into the healer's healing hands herself. But if she can't, she doesn't know what she's going to do. She feels like the eleventh hour is fast approaching, and her beloved sits on the seat beside her in stony silence, his mouth open, his head canted back, the wind gently riffling his thin gray hair now that his reversible cap has blown off.

"I think maybe they need a little time to get to know one another, mama, what do you think?" the farmer says.

"That might be a good idear," the mother says. "Leave em alone together a while and maybe they can play."

The healer looks for a place to run but there are no windows in the airless chamber of what his good work has brought him to and no door but the one the farmer guards with the point of a gun.

"You can't leave me down here with him," the healer says, and he searches for some shred of sanity in the seamed faces of the farmer and his wife. His playmate edges closer.

"You could even eat supper with us if you wanted to after you heal him," the mother says. "Be right nice if we could all set down at the table together."

"He makes too big a mess for him to eat with us very much," the farmer says, a little apologetically, gesturing with the gun. "Throws his food everwhere and what not."

The farmer turns with the key in his pocket and fumbles down deep in there for it. He takes the key out and has to almost turn his back on the healer to get it in the lock, but he says, "I wouldn't try nothing funny if I was you."

"If you're scared of him biting you we'll hold him and not let him bite you," the mother says.

The key clicks in the lock and the farmer says, "I just don't believe he's much of a mind to heal him, mama. We can go up here and take us a nap and when we come back down they liable to be discussing philosophy or something, you cain't never tell."

"You people don't understand," the healer says. "He's beyond help. There's nothing I can do for him. I don't deal with the mind. I deal with the body."

"Ain't nothing wrong with his body," the mother says. "We just had to slow him down a little."

"His body's in good shape," the farmer says. "He's strong as a ox. Why I've seen him pull cows out of mud holes before. I don't believe he knows how strong he is."

"We'll be back after a while," the mother says, and out the door she goes. "Come on, daddy," she says back. The farmer backs out the door holding the gun on the healer and then the door closes. There are sounds of the other lock being affixed on the other side. The healer backs hard into the corner and eyes the mumbling being in front of him.

"Jesus would heal him if He was here!" the farmer hollers through the thick door. "I done read all about what He done in the Bible! What They've done, They've done laid this burden on us to test our faith! Ain't that right, mama!"

"That's right, daddy!" the mother shouts through the door.

"We been tested!" the farmer screams. "We been tested hard and we ain't been found wanting! Have we, mama!"

"You got that right, daddy! Lot of folks couldn't put up with what we've put up with!"

"Just don't make him mad!" the farmer shrieks. "Don't try to take nothing away from him if he's playing with it! He don't like that! He's a little spoiled!"

"He likes to rassle but don't get in a rasslin' match with him cause he gets mad sometimes! Don't get him mad! We'll be back in about an hour! Talk to him! He likes that!"

A rapid clump of footsteps climbing up the stairs fades away to a slammed door above. The healer flattens himself in the corner with his arms bracing up the walls.

"Don't touch me, please," he says, then adds: "I'm not going to hurt you."

The prisoner has made himself a bed of soiled quilts and assorted bedding and he pillows his head with a discarded tire. His nest is knotted with hairs and his lair is littered with lice. The farmer has snipped his hamstrings and Achilles tendon on alternate legs and cauterized the severed sinews while the mother kept the head restrained and the howling muffled with towels rolled and stuffed over his mouth one midnight scene years ago when they became unable to control him. He moves toward the healer, slowly, hard. The healer watches the painful stance, the shifting feet, the arms outspread for balance, and he walks like a man on a tightrope as he makes his way across. Perhaps to kiss? His dangling thangling is large and hairy, swaying there like a big brown anesthetized mole.

The healer watches him come. On the edges of the wasted fields of the South and stuck back in the roadless reaches of timber where people have trails like animals, the unseen faceless sum of mankind's lesser genes quietly disassemble cars and squat underneath trees talking and back of them lie small dwellings of rotted wood and sagging floors where strange children sit wrapped for hours on end slavering mutely and utter no words from their stunned mouths. Pictures of porches full of them all shy and embarrassed or smiling in delight turn up now and again here and there, but no visitor but the documenter of the far less fortunate comes to visit again. It is not that they are not God's children, but that mankind shuns them, bad reminders of rotted teeth and mismatched eyes, uncontrollable sexual desire turned loose in the woods to procreate a new race of the drooling mindless eating where they shit. He is like them, but even they would not accept him. An old midwife who knew anything would not allow the question. In the first few desperate moments the hand would smother the mouth, pinch the nostrils, still the heaving chest trying to draw in the first tiny breath. The brother and sister above know this. They have known it for years.

The thing comes closer and the healer looks into its depthless eyes, eyes like a fish that lives so deep in the dark black of the ocean and has no need to see. He thinks of the woman's legs in the back seat of the car parked behind a Walgreen's in Sumter and the strength of the promise of God. He thinks not of retribution or outrage, and not even fear any more. He thinks of mercy, and lambs, and he brings his hands out from his sides to suffer to him this outcast. His fingers teach and they touch and he clamps them down hard over the ears. Dust motes turn in the air. They stand in stillness, hardly breathing, locked by the touch of another hand. Their eyes close. The healer fills his chest with air. He prepares to command him to heal.

Flenco sits sobbing beside the road in a grove of trees with a cool breeze wafting through, gently moving the hair on Mr. Redding's head. It's a nice afternoon for a nap, but Flenco has no thoughts of sleep. The search is over and he is cold like a slice of baloney, an egg from the refrigerator. The state troopers cluster behind her and slap their ticket books along their legs, heads shaking in utter solemnity or undisguised amazement. The ambulance crew waits, their equipment useless, still scattered their ambu bags and cardiopulmonary cases over the gravelly grass. The sun is going down and the legendary speeder has not appeared, and the roadblock will soon be broken up, the blue-and-white cruisers sent out to other destinations like prowling animals to simply prowl the roads.

But an interesting phenomenon has briefly materialized to break the boredom of an otherwise routine afternoon, a fat woman drunk and hauling the dead corpse of her husband down the road at ninety, sobbing and screaming and yelling out loud to God, and they wait now only for the coroner to place his seal of approval so that the body can be moved. One trooper leans against a tree chewing a stem of grass and remarks to nobody in particular: "I been to three county fairs, two goatropins and one horsefuckin, and I ain't never seen nothing like that."

Some chuckle, others shake their heads, as if to allow that the world is a strange place and in it lie things of another nature, a bent order, and beyond a certain point there are no rules to make man mind.

A wrecker is moving slowly with its red lights down the road. Doves cry in the trees. And down the road in a field where someone has stood them stand three giant wooden crosses, their colors rising in the falling sunlight, yellow, and blue, and tan. †

Interview

My interview with Larry Brown took place over the course of three meetings, in the Mississippi towns of Tula and Taylor and in Durham, North Carolina. Though we had met before this, our talks about religion and fiction began in July 1991, when my family and I came to Mississippi for a visit on the occasion of Brown's fortieth birthday.

Having met Richard Howorth (to whom the story "Facing the Music" is dedicated) at his Oxford store, Square Books, my husband and I followed him to Taylor, about ten miles south of Oxford, to surprise Larry at a catfish place where Mary Annie, his wife, had told us they would be eating supper. Kudzu was growing two or three stories high on both sides of the state road between Oxford and Taylor. There were no billboards, roadsigns, or markers to guide us along the twists and turns on the backroads—nothing for miles, it seemed, but dark kudzu in the summer twilight.

Taylor Restaurant is situated at a sharp bend in the road; it and a one-room post office constitute most of downtown Taylor. Worn, sagging wooden steps lead to its narrow porch. One solid wooden carpenter's bench sits outside the entrance; on the other side of the black, double screen doors is the drink box. People come here from all around to eat catfish and drink beer, especially on Friday nights after work. Huge live oak trees—"must be two hundred years old," someone said—brood over the sandy sideroads and walks. We waited in the heat in the gravel parking lot (though it was past seven in the evening, it was still over 90 degrees and humid) until we saw Mary Annie and Larry go inside. A moment later, we walked in to find them in a booth in back.

Larry Brown is a slightly built but strong and wiry-looking fellow, whose face shows years of hard work and pain. He has fine features (a long thin nose, sad hazel eyes) and sunburned skin from many years in the Mississippi sun.

Sitting at a long wooden table big enough for the eight people who had gathered to celebrate, we ate fresh, fried catfish, french fries, cole slaw, hush puppies, and homemade fried apple pie. The slatted floors creaked as customers walked to and from the combination bathroom/broom closet in back; ropes of exposed wiring crawled up the walls to the pressed tin ceiling and over it like snakes toward two or three overburdened outlets. Stark puddles of light emanated from bare bulbs in the high ceiling.

The waitress brought platters of fried fish, as fast as the owner could fry them, to the tables from the grill that ran the length of one side of the room. Initials and hearts, names and platitudes, were carved all over the boothbacks and walls. Larry was in a bemused and philosophical (though by no means solemn) mood. He talked readily about the meaning of his fiction, and of the good life—what it takes, who's got it, who doesn't, and why; after about the third platter of food and that many pitchers of beer, we concluded that truth in fiction, and truth in friendship, not to mention truth *in vino,* figure prominently. Our booth was near the jukebox; we played "I Fall to Pieces" and "You Don't Know About Lonely 'Til It's Chiselled in Stone" for Larry—Patsy Kline and Vern Gosdin easing him into his forty-first year.

That fall, Brown came to give a reading from his novel *Joe* at the Regulator Bookshop, an independent bookstore in Durham. Dressed in his usual Lee jeans, baseball cap, tweed jacket, cowboy boots, and a Flannery O'Connor t-shirt (he opened his jacket to display the front—a large caricature of O'Connor clutching a Bible, with a comical-looking peacock in the background), he smoked Camels and looked a little nervous. "I always hate it on the road," he says. "I don't sleep too good away from home."

People began to drift in for the reading an hour and a half early, some visiting a moment or two with Brown, a few asking him to sign books. The store owner showed us a sun-filled room in back where we could talk quietly for an hour or so before the reading. As always, I was struck by Brown's quiet manner—he speaks in a low, soft Mississippi accent, an undertone of sorrow ever-present in it; his hazel eyes seem to look far off and deep within as he talks. When he speaks about ancient myths and the lure and power of storytelling in ancient cultures, it strikes me that he's been there. He is an "old soul."

Let's talk about "Facing the Music." People not only seem to react very strongly to that story, but there seems to be a remarkable disparity in their reactions. Some decry it as unrealistically bleak;

others see it as a story about redemption — or at least that its end-
ing redeems the bleakness by suggesting hope in the midst of loss.
What were you thinking as you wrote this story and what is your
reaction to it now?

It's true that most of the stuff I write about does come from
things I've seen, or lived through myself—with the exception of
"Facing the Music." It's funny. People think that story is autobiographical. I get letters all the time about that one from people consoling me and my wife about "her mastectomy." But this story is
really about pain and loss wherever you find it. I just believe that
my fiction, anybody's fiction, is simply supposed to illuminate the
human condition, tell us something about ourselves. I did see it as
having a hopeful ending.

Your fiction does seem to reach its fullest power when you are
writing about what lies at the heart of human suffering. One of the
most powerful scenes in your first novel, Dirty Work, *occurs when*
Jesus comes to Braiden at his hospital bed. As Jesus lights a ciga-
rette for him, the paralyzed Braiden asks how long he must continue
to suffer. This scene portrays a startlingly human Jesus who suffers
along with the world in sorrow and grief.

Some people get upset about that scene. They want to know
whether the scene is actually occurring. Is Jesus actually there, or is
it a vision, or something in Braiden's mind? To tell you the truth, I
don't know. Braiden—he's helpless. He's tired. He wants suicide.
But he has no way to do it. He doesn't think it's wrong any more.
He believes in it. By that I mean, he believes God is merciful, and
that he's suffered enough; he can't stand any more. He longs for
death. It's not a sin in his case. I can understand Braiden. But I
believe the Lord don't ever put more on you than you can bear.

Some people just have harder lives than others. I've got an aunt who
I figure is probably one of the most devout Christian people that there
is in the world. I know a lot of other people who profess to be that, but
who don't live life—I don't believe they live it—or practice their religion the way that she does, and her mama before her, my grandmother, all my aunts. Some people have such a harder time than other
people do, some people have to pay more in life, I don't know why.

It makes you understand why one might consider giving up, or
suicide. Some of your fiction seems to deal with this notion.

For a long time, I've been trying to understand suicide, and I do see how it is not a sin for some people, in some cases. The story "Old Frank and Jesus" is drawn from a man who used to cut my hair. One day, he borrowed a pistol and shot himself through the head. I knew him well—I'd picked cotton with him and things like that. There was no outward indication of any trouble. That was when I began imagining, What is the pressure? What would cause someone to do that? Years later, I learned that he had been losing his land to taxes. He'd lost twenty, thirty acres. Mr. P. in the story was concerned with two things he couldn't understand: How could anybody be so mean to Jesus? How did he let his wife talk him into shooting his old dog? That kind of despair was what I was thinking about in "Samaritans," too. Since then, I've known others who were caught in something like that.

Does the story end in despair?

I was thinking about despair when I wrote that story. Mr. P. was at the end of his rope. There was no help for him, the pressures were too much. I wanted to show how the loss of love can bring it on, can bring on very strong emotions. Grief can kill you, I mean literally, it can. When Harry Crews talked about his boy drowning, he said you think you are going to die. That you couldn't survive that. Most of the time, you can, but sometimes you can't. When our baby died, in 1977, I didn't think I would survive. It was a very rocky time . . . tough. You meet other people who have suffered the same thing. It comes up in conversation—it's the same each time—you never get over it.

But my fiction is about people surviving, about people proceeding out from calamity. I write about loss. These people are aware of their need for redemption. We all spend our time dealing with some kind of hurt and looking for love. We are all striving for the same thing, for some kind of love. But love is a big word. It covers a lot of territory. I try to tell it in a fresh, new way, to be innovative.

Several of the titles of your stories refer to biblical images, maybe in an ironic way. Tell me about the origins of the titles "Old Frank and Jesus" and "Samaritans."

Even though "Samaritans" has a suggestive title, it's not a "message story." I wanted it to say a lot of things, some contradictory. Like, it's about the futility of helping people who do nothing to help themselves, the outcasts of society. But it's also about that it's a good thing to try. That's what Jesus would have done. It's an ironic title.

Partly because it's in the plural. Only one character in the story actually acts like the Good Samaritan of the parable, yet the title suggests that other people in the story, including the itinerants, could be considered Samaritans. Do you see your stories as growing out of a particular view of God and humankind?

I'm asked about this a lot of times, and I always say I think it's evident in my work, in some of it anyway. I don't take a specific stand about things like that, but it's in there, in certain stories, in certain models. I think a lot about God in the humanity of Jesus, like with the conversation between Braiden and Jesus. It helps me. But most of my stories aren't directly concerned with religion—except for "Roadside Resurrection." Now that is a religious story. It's about a real faith healer, someone who really heals the afflicted. It's all about faith and trust, where they come from. This famous healer has lost his faith, but no one knows it yet. It has humor in it, too. There is an ex-Elvis impersonator who needs healing.

It is, in fact, a very funny story.

I've always thought being able to write humor is the mark of a superior writer, but it's going to ruin me. People think I'm mocking their beliefs, and I'm not. I have a strong belief in God.

Tell me more about that. What do you believe are the origins of your belief, for instance?

I was raised in the Methodist church in Memphis. That's where all my cousins, aunts, and uncles went. When we moved, we went to a country church, Mama's church, for a while. We belong to a Methodist church here, but I don't go like I should. My faith has gotten deeper over the years. It seems to have developed because of the suffering I see—of mine and of others. I believe suffering is here to make you strong. See what you can endure. Some are weak, some are stronger.

It is often said that your experiences as a firefighter shaped your vision as a person and as a fiction writer. How about your beliefs?

I write about life-and-death situations in my nonfiction book that I am working on now, *On Fire*. Sometimes things would happen where you'd get put in an utterly helpless position. When it was really bad was when everybody would be looking at me: What we gonna do, Captain Brown? So, when you've got the rank, and you're drawing the pay, it's up to you. Somebody's life can be in your hands, and it's a heavy responsibility.

The bad thing is, you've got fifty or a hundred people standing there watching you, watching every mistake you make, ain't going to miss a thing. They ain't going to walk off and leave. And you got to do something. And you're going to hear all this noise, people second-guessing you afterward. I could hardly stand to do it, sometimes, the situation would be so bad, but I had to kind of detach myself from my feelings about what the person was going through. In most cases, I could not concentrate on their pain, I could only concentrate on the speed and efficiency of my crew in removing the person from the situation, so that they could go to the hospital.

If you thought about their pain, you wouldn't be able to move them because it would hurt them too much.

That's right. And you know, you sometimes have people there screaming, "Y'all are killing me, you're killing me!" What can you do? You're there to try to help them and remedy the situation. But it's a very nerve-wracking business to be in. But it wasn't the excitement that I left, it was the boredom. The hours sitting there with nothing going on, and I was wishing I was home writing.

You got caught between two worlds?

Yes. But I didn't back off from anything I ever got sent to. I always preferred to be the first one there, so that I could size it up, and figure out what was going on, whether I had to call in more people, or certain pieces of equipment, or whatever.

Many southerners speak vividly of the time when they were "saved" as being as emotionally intense an experience as they have ever undergone. Have you had such an experience?

I've felt I've been saved many, many times. No joke. Once, when I worked as a fireman, my partner, a black guy, and I worked a long time together—for hours, one night, to get someone out of a car that was wrapped around a telephone pole. It was a boy who had this terrible, terrible wreck. Inside the city limits. Normally, you wouldn't have that bad an accident inside the city limits. I can't remember whether this boy was running from the police, or what, but he'd wrapped his car completely around a telephone pole. It was on the right side of the street, headed the wrong way, so the driver's door was up against this pole. His chest was all broken up internally, he was bleeding out the mouth, ears, nose, and everywhere else. This nurse was in the seat with him, trying to clear his airway with a piece of surgical tubing, which was steadily getting clogged with blood. So the boy was in real danger of dying right there, but there wasn't any way for him to come out. His legs were in this door behind him, and his body was lodged over up against the shifter. That's what had him caught. This nurse was screaming at me to do something; I was in charge of the crew. But I just couldn't see any way to bring him out. He was going to lay right there and die before we could get him out. Only thing I could see was that he couldn't come out sideways, he'd have to come out straight up. So I said, Okay, we'll chop the windshield out, reach in and bend the shifter off of him, and bring him out.

That's what we did. We covered him up in a blanket and took our fire axes and chopped around the windshield, pulled it out, and throwed it out on the street. I climbed up on the hood and reached down for the shifter, but I couldn't bend it. So, Mack was there, the black guy who worked with me. I told him to get up here and help me. I said, "Put your hand on top of mine, let's bend the shifter, that's what's got him hung." He nearly crushed my hand with his, but the thing started moving. We bent it on over. We both fell down into the floorboards, but we got it off of him. Then we put the backboard on the boy, pulled traction on it, and brought him on out. They loaded him in the ambulance, took him on down to the hospital. He lived, too. When things like that happen, it makes you really realize the preciousness of life. The whole rescue depended on the strength of this one guy's arm pushing the gear shift out of the way.

It's about life and death—the real thing. I had another experience one time like that that I would call a conversion experience. It was a truly religious experience. When my partner—that black guy I was telling you about—died, he died while he was rabbit hunting, real quick. Had a stroke. I went to his church for the funeral. And the ladies coming in, and they're starting to sing; they don't have any hymnals in their hands. It was in the summertime, and it was this church, way way out in the woods. I mean off this sure-enough tiny pig trail. We had to take the fire trucks up there, and it was muddy. It was really bad. And the place he was buried in was a really scrubby little piece of pitiful land with these stunted trees and weeds and just wasn't a pretty place to be buried. But they all had this faith, and the way it came out was that this preacher stood up and started preaching and then he got to moving and he got to kind of rocking and rolling and people started getting excited. They'd jump up and holler, "Amen! Yeah brother, tell it!" You know, we were just sitting there just looking around with our white faces. And it just made me see how strong they were, how much faith they had, and it also made me realize that God ain't got no color. It's something I wouldn't ever forget. One God, no particular color, one God for everybody.

Your fiction reveals this same intensity of feeling.

All kinds of things have a deep meaning to me. All kinds of experiences. They move me. When I write, all I'm doing is trying to tell a story. Above all is the art. Your art must evolve from your experience and it must evolve as art.

You have told me that some folks have criticized the violence, the alcoholism, and the graphic language and so on in your work. They point to the "brutality" in your work, its sexism, and the so-called "antireligious" nature of it.

I can't be concerned about who's going to think what. I try to make as good a story as I can, and let the chips fall where they may. I can't write to please others; I must please me. I must trust my own judgment, and above all, I must be honest. Your art must evolve from your honesty, your experience. If they are seeing only negative things in my fiction, then they aren't reading it right, not seeing what's there.

What do you think impells you to create fiction?

At around age thirty, I realized that I was still being bossed by someone else. I had done about everyhing I could think of, being a fireman, setting out trees, a carpenter's helper, and so on. I was married and had three kids by then. I realized I must do something else with my life, make something of myself. I had always loved books and reading; it was what I cared most about. I figured writing was the only thing I could teach myself to do on my own.

I checked out books from the library by the armload—Flannery

O'Connor, Raymond Carver, William Faulkner, Harry Crews, Cormac McCarthy. I found out that I wanted to write "literature," the kind of stories that I had read over and over again. At first, I thought it would be simple. It's not. I think everybody who wants to write well has to go through an apprenticeship, with a blind faith that says you can't take no for an answer. In a way it was like the Marine Corps—it's all in your mind. To be successful in boot camp or in writing, you must become an automaton: keep going, keep working, keep believing. And I've always believed in the trash can as a valuable tool. I burned a novel one time.

You did not.

Burned it in the back yard. I sure did. I felt like I had to.

How come?

Wasn't any good. And there wasn't any saving it. I had it finished and it didn't work. I said I believe it's a kindness to take that into the woods and burn it, lose it forever. I think the main thing was that in destroying it, I knew that I was never going to see it again or be able to. Once I made that decision, it was irrevocable. That work was up in smoke just like the paper was.

Did burning it free you?

Yes. I wrote two more bad ones, wrote five bad ones altogether, before *Facing the Music* was published. Over time I came to love the act of writing, the inventing, the imagining of a character. Now, it's not even work, and when it's going well, it's pure recreation.

Let's talk more about "Roadside Resurrection." It has just recently come out in the Paris Review. *What are some reactions you've gotten to that story?*

People seem to be spellbound by it. It's the idiot, I think. In fact, I'm spellbound by it. It's a wild story. The writing of it was a process of discovery, one of those things that just started telling itself. The first draft took a week—it was really cooking, burning to be finished. The rhythm of the words developed a life of its own; it assumed its own way of being told. I revised it at least six times to take out stuff and tighten my control on the language. The story just came—it was as if I were just a transmitter.

The main character, the youthful healer, is ambiguous. He's lost his faith. He is caught up in a dilemma. What is he going to do? Has God turned his face away from him? Flenco, the ex-Elvis impersonator's wife, is on a quest of faith, too, but she doesn't get what she wants. She believes if she can just find him then everything's going to be okay. But the faith healer has no awareness that this woman's looking for him. It's not even a part of his life.

Tell me about the ending of the story. The crosses on the roadside—what did they suggest to you?

The crosses at the end of the story are a mystery to me. You see them all over the South, along the sides of roads and interstates. I've seen them in Mississippi, Alabama, Georgia. Nobody knows where they come from. Who puts them up? Nobody ever sees them being put up. It's a great deal of trouble—they're huge, like telephone poles.

It may be stretching it a bit, but just as those crosses might be seen to be imposing a startling image of faith on the consciousness of those who are driving by, do you see your stories as possibly posing startling problems of faith for the reader?

Yes, I do, sure do. I think any literature, if it's going to be any good, has to be about right and wrong, good and bad, good versus evil. Like my novel, *Joe*. Joe must do something bad to get rid of the evil in his world. He must do what he does (he gives them plenty of warning, too), but he must do what he does as a moral imperative. Even though he wasn't directly affected, Joe felt he must take care of the problem. Joe knows that evil is real, not some abstraction. Whatever good is in this world has to have teeth in it if evil is to be dealt with.

Is there redemption in this suffering, any hope for these characters?

You can't tack a happy ending on tragedy. Braiden in *Dirty Work*, for example, loves his life. It was what he wanted all along. But his problems are too much. He wants release. In his case it is not a sin to seek suicide. The ministers I've talked to about this story agree with me. God wouldn't punish Braiden; God would pity him. Braiden has a strong, unwavering faith in God. He seeks release and peace.

Why do you think so many southern writers write about religion? Somehow it always seems to come up, whether it's Faulkner's sermon in The Sound and the Fury, *or the three crosses and the faith healer in "Roadside Resurrection," or simply in a title that gets you thinking, like "Samaritans."*

Well, I think in my case religion crops up so much because I heard it all my life. From the earliest times I can remember, I was in the church, raised in the church, went to Sunday school, vacation Bible school, church on Sunday night, church on Sunday morning, all that stuff. And my whole family was heavily involved in it. I think probably the reason it crops up in so many other southern writers' works is for the same reason. Because they were exposed to so much of it at an early age, it makes an impression on them.

Harry Crews has said that he feels matters of life and death, and suffering and meaning, so deeply that he has to write about them in his fiction, sort out these emotions through his characters. The characters themselves start talking to him about their struggles.

Yeah, I've seen other writers that are doing it, too. Cormac McCarthy's got a couple of lines—this preacher is travelling around, doing this talking, and he said, "A blind feller hollered out one day and said, 'Look at me' (and he only had one leg). He said, 'Look at me, legless and everything; I reckon you think I ought to love God.' And the feller said, 'Yeah,' said, 'I reckon you ought. An old blind mess and legless fool is a flower in the garden of God.'"

Fiction, you were saying, has to be about some kind of moral problem or faith problem. Southern writers seem to say that about fiction more often and more openly than writers of other regions do. Notable southern writers, you and others such as Robert Penn Warren and William Faulkner, have talked very compellingly about the moral imperative of fiction, that is, that it must deal with these ultimate questions of good and evil, life and death.

Yes, that's what my fiction is about and I guess that's what religion is all about, too. The basic concept is either to be good or to be bad. And in order to be good you got to fight the bad. So those are the issues that most of my characters are struggling with. They are struggling to be good people. They know the difference between good and bad, and right and wrong. They don't always do what's right, because they're imperfect, like all of us. Like all people. And I try to give my characters those human traits that we all recognize and all have and all feel. I try to make them as real as I can. And therefore, very simply, a story's about a person who has a problem, and he or she will either resolve that problem or they will not resolve that problem. The problems may be many-faceted, especially in the course of a novel. In a good novel there is always something going on: either they are not satisfied with their life, or they have some major problem that's disrupting their life. I mean if you go along happy-go-lucky, one scene to another, nothing ever happens, there's never any trouble, everybody in the world is nice and treats everybody with kindness, that's not representative of the real world, and it's not representative of a real novel, either. It's got to be a major struggle. More than one, nothing simple.

And you pile them on, too.

Yes, I pile 'em on. I think you should sandbag your characters—load 'em up with as much as you can, then see what they do. That's why I make things so tough on them. I want them to have some kind of conflict going on within themselves and with the other characters around them. I think the thing to do is pull the character in early in the first few sentences and keep him. And once you get him by the throat, don't let him go. Don't let him go until you're finished with him. The way I look at a novel, the way I tell a novel's finished, is the point when I think I have done all I can for them, have helped the characters as much as I can, helped them all I can.

And these characters mostly, well, all of them except Wade in the novel, Joe, and that idiot-monster in "Roadside Resurrection," it seems to me, are basically well-meaning people.

I have some bad people in my stories, but they're there as antagonists. They're the ones who are making the problems.

And even Wade is human.

Yeah, he's human. He doesn't have very many redeeming human qualities about him—

Can't think of any.

Can't think of a thing.

He's incorrigible, yet, it doesn't come across as if it's being done for effect. He, unfortunately, is all too human.

He's got some concerns. But his are mainly selfish, pertaining to himself only.

Atavistic, primitive concerns. Right now, I am reading in Joe where Wade has killed a black guy for his food coupons. Wade laid his hands on something in the grass, picked it up and knocked the man's brains out.

Yeah, Joe and him have difficulties, a hard time.

In the book I'm doing, I'm ascribing a chapter title to each author which will try to capture what each author is about. Reynolds Price, for example, said that most of his characters might be termed "saintly outlaws," that is, good-hearted people who live and act, nonetheless, outside the norms of society. Harry Crews talks about the writer as shaman or healer in a society because he sees that the sacred role of the writer in the community is to tell stories about who we are. How would you describe your characters or your role as writer in this regard?

Some of my work is on the other side of reality sometimes. Maybe you would want to describe my work in terms of myths and dreams. *Dirty Work* involves so much myth you're not able to tell what's real and what's not, sometimes.

Myths and dreams.

Yes, and that's the way I want it to be. I wanted the reader to be uncertain what really was occurring, what was fantasy and what was reality.

When I read the *Iliad* and the *Odyssey* when I was little, on my own, it got me thinking in terms of myths and dreams; I was really into Greek mythology, all the battles and gods, what each one did and what each one was responsible for. They formed the core of my belief about storytelling.

What do you see as the importance of storytelling?

I think people depend on storytellers down through history to carry on the stories of things that came before. When Alex Haley went all the way to Africa chasing down his ancestors, he got finally to that village where Kunta Kinte was from and the guy there told the story that many years ago, there was another person in our tribe named Kunta Kinte who went into the woods to get wood for a drum and we never saw him again, and that was the day they kidnapped him and put him on a slave ship and brought him to America. That was the storyteller's job, to keep all the information and to relay it—the whole history of not only his tribe but also the individual families and what all had happened before. And once he made that connection, he knew irrevocably that this was his family; he knew where he was from and thus who he was.

Before we go, can you tell me how you think living where you do, in Yocona, Mississippi, has shaped your writing?

Well, for one thing, I'm the real native son of Oxford. Faulkner wasn't from around here. He was from Ripley, sixty miles away. Seriously, though, living in the country shapes my whole life and work. My writing is formed by the people, by the lives they lead around here, and the land. In the country, you can swim, fish, ride your bike on dirt roads. I hate cities. I lived for ten years in Memphis, and I was not happy. Things here are peaceful, quiet, no hassles. When I spent some time in Los Angeles, I got downright scared. It's depressing.

That's where my fiction comes from, I think. I use everything: memory, imagination, and what people have told me. Like with "Waiting for the Ladies"—the guy in that exposed himself at a dumpster. There was a real guy like that and I followed him once. He was simply not right in the head. †

4

SHEILA BOSWORTH

On Being Southern, Catholic, and Female

Sheila Bosworth was born in New Orleans, Louisiana, in 1950. Raised in a family of "steadfast" and "practical" Roman Catholics, she attended convent schools and weekly Mass among the old French and Irish families of the Crescent City, an intense social milieu that she describes as almost a "Catholic dynasty." In 1971, she graduated from Tulane University. She lives in Covington, Louisiana, with her husband and two sons.

In her fiction Bosworth blends together a haunting sense of the past, of family, and of deeply ingrained religion; with her keen grasp of the manners and customs of New Orleans, she creates a painful vision of what it means to grow up southern, Catholic, and female in contemporary society. This vision was shaped in part by her friendship and long conversations with Walker Percy, Bosworth's neighbor in Covington. Her novels *Almost Innocent* (1984) and *Slow Poison* (1992) depict contemporary southern families awash in the intoxicating and toxic effects of tragically flawed family love. A third novel in progress, *To Ransom the Captives*, concerns loneliness and entrapment.

Like the old-fashioneds their parents drink, the lives of Clay-Lee (*Almost Innocent*), and Rory (*Slow Poison*) are marked by sweetness and bitterness. "To a Southerner," Bosworth writes, "sweet and sad mean the same thing." In *Almost Innocent* Clay-Lee is forced to confront at too tender an age the horrors of her father's ineffectual naivete and her mother's obsessive love, a love that culminates in a pact with what Walker Percy termed "pure evil" in the form of Clement (Uncle Baby), a family black sheep who is bent on destroying all vestiges of trust and belief in a family he despises. The outcome leaves Clay-Lee crushed by her own dark guilt, doomed to spend the rest of her life in a grey half-light of detachment, regret, and grief. In *Slow Poison* we are allowed inside the life of the almost visionary young Rory as she remembers the horrors and joys of her youth in New Orleans. Before she is twenty-one years old she has suffered the deaths of her mother, her stepmother, and her father. Love in flawed families—the complicated, sometimes heady, slow poison of it—is shown to be immeasurably destructive.

Although her novels are not explicitly "Catholic" in message or intent, Bosworth allows that her themes concern nothing less than the wounding and healing of the immortal soul. Irreparable damage and loss can occur. Sacred promises are made and broken; holy innocence is fostered, then betrayed. "I don't really feel that I write 'Catholic novels,' but Catholicism's influence on me is huge," she maintains. Her ambivalent feelings toward her Catholic upbringing have engendered emotions ranging from ironic detachment to outright anger. What she found most disturbing was the Catholic teaching that one must always thank God for the good that befalls one in life, but never blame Him for the evil. In her fiction, Bosworth's characters wrestle with issues of the nature of God and the meaning of catastrophe and evil; their struggles are anguished and personal. "This doctor in *Almost Innocent* strikes me as a character who . . . probably did blame God, in a quiet way," Bosworth notes. God, who is the Great Instigator or Permitter of all Tragedy, would probably be to blame for the "little mistakes" that the doctor has witnessed daily in his practice. Yet, once he realizes that Clay-Lee may be implicated in her own mother's death, he reflects, "Not even God should have to take the blame for this one." Constance's death, he sees, has resulted from a blend of guilt and innocence, malevolence and victimization, predation and self-destruction that reaches beyond the realm of tragedy to the inexplicable, blasted heath of despair.

Bosworth's ambivalence and anger are particularly potent and productive because they spring from the confluence of her identities as a woman and a southerner as well as a Catholic. "Southern women are taught not only to believe [in God] but to have faith that God, or our fathers, or our husbands, 'Daddy' in one form or another, will protect us. God does not protect us," Bosworth maintains, and illusions of male protection collapse like a house of cards for the women in both her novels. The sardonic attitude toward her culture and its issues of gender and religion recalls the satiric vision of Flannery O'Connor. But Bosworth feels less affinity with O'Connor, who as a Catholic chose to write only about Protestants, than she does with the late Walker Percy, whose characters and thematic concerns more closely resemble her own. Bosworth enjoyed lively discussions with Percy about their disparate experiences with Catholicism (she a "cradle" female child in the Catholic church, and he an adult convert) and how fiction might be regarded by the writer in light of a serious Catholic faith.

Throughout her fiction, Bosworth's characters seek clarity and deliverance. They inhabit a world created by an artist whose deep rootedness in the rich and toxic soil of her religion and culture and whose fiercely individual eye have enabled her to feel the tragedy of the human condition, and the hope, if sometimes wan, of redemption within shared suffering. "What I feel I am there to do is to use whatever gifts I have to create art that convinces someone, as many people as possible, that we're not in this alone, that the truth is that we're all in this human condition together, and that there's hope in the very communal nature of that."

From

Slow Poison

Years earlier, when Grandolly was dying of cancer, Rory had known she had the power to save her. She knew the secret: all she had to do was to make the infallible nine-day novena to St. Jude, the patron of impossible cases, and name Grandolly.

The trouble was, Rory couldn't seem to get cranked up on the novena. She knew the situation was critical—"It's in her blood-stream!" she had heard Aunt Tippy whisper, mysteriously, to Merrill, whose horselike jaw had gone slack with hopelessness—but still she was immobilized, and couldn't even do the first day of the novena. After Grandolly died, Rory had confessed to Etta, in confidence, that she, Rory, had murdered Grandolly through the sin of omission.

"What?" said Etta. Her voice was shrill with impatience. "You ain't murdered her! You just got too much sense to believe in that novena shit. You know it don't work and you was too polite to bring it up to St. Jude and embarrass him. Now go put your funeral skirt on."

Rory had written off St. Jude, but in 1967 she still held a belief in certain gentleman's rules for the Creator, a certain cosmic code of ethics. She still believed that tragedy confers transitory immunity from further tragedy, that trouble intrinsically, if temporarily, precludes more trouble. Thus, a nursing mother won't develop breast cancer. Loved ones don't drop dead at another loved one's funeral. A victim of acute appendicitis is not subject to menstrual cramps. And a young girl whose husband has just been blown up in an obscene war certainly does not receive in the mail an obscene letter from the dead man's mother, along with a jaunty posthumous message from the dead man himself.

"Damn!" said Etta, handing the two letters back to Rory. Etta and Rory were out in the yard, sitting on the same bench Jane Ann had collapsed onto an hour earlier, soon after the mailman's visit, and just before Eamon had returned home. "What your daddy says about these letters?"

"Nothing yet, that I know of. He's in the library with Judge Montcrief. The judge is calling up people in Washington, trying to get better information on what happened to Charlie."

"What do it matter what happened to him? He's dead, ain't he? I hope your sister sleep a long while from whatever was in that shot the doctor give her. Sleep till I can find me a job someplace else. I can't stand around here and watch this shit. How long you figure we got till the crazy mama-in-law bust in on us from Alabama?"

"About twenty minutes."

"Girl, quit it. All this working on my nerves. Go ask your daddy what must we do. I'm going out to the kitchen and find me some lunch."

When she heard the word "lunch," Rory realized that Johnny Killelea had failed to show up for it.

Eamon was alone in his study, eating a sandwich at his desk. He had a small refrigerator in his study that he kept stocked with baked ham from Mother's Restaurant on Poydras Street in New Orleans, along with a selection of sharp cheeses and hot peppers and some pungent mustards. Eamon liked his eating to involve some pain to the tongue.

"Hello there, kid," he said when Rory came in.

"Where's Judge Montcrief?" said Rory. She sat down in the big armchair of cracked maroon leather that smelled of years of trapped cigar smoke.

"Walter? He just left, thank Christ. Get this. Walter believes Charlie Monroe was taken prisoner by the North Vietnamese. Here the poor bastard disintegrates in front of four eyewitnesses, but old Walter's convinced he's somewhere out in the jungle, wearing a striped suit with a number on the front."

"Prisoners of war don't wear uniforms," said Rory, sinking deeper into the leather chair, delighting in the sound of the calm voice, in the sight of the remote hazel eyes, in the sweet miracle of the sobriety.

"They don't wear uniforms? Certainly they do, some of them. When I was in the Philippine Islands, we had some German and some Japanese prisoners. The Germans sat around in their undershirts, playing poker. Hell, they knew they'd lost the goddamn war; they were just waiting for the whole show to be officially over. The Japs, though, they demanded the right to march up and down the prison yard twice a day, in full uniform. Never say die, boy. You had to admire the poor crazy sons of bitches."

"Daddy? What are we going to do about Jane Ann?"

"Nothing we can do, kid. Let her know we're here, that's all."

Let her know we're here? But how long are you planning to be here, Daddy? That is, in your right mind? I miss you, and you aren't even gone yet.

"No kidding now, kid. I don't want you taking all this on your shoulders," said Eamon. "You leave this to the guy in the sky."

"The guy in the sky? Give me a break."

Eamon raised his eyebrows while he finished swallowing a bite of his ham sandwich.

"You're mad at God now? What are you, an atheist? The atheists are the true believers, you know. Nobody gets that mad, expends all that energy, at Somebody they don't even believe exists."

"Anybody with any brains is either mad at God or afraid of Him.

I think afraid is worse. You talk about prisoners of war, that's what Mrs. Buck reminds me of, a prisoner of war."

"Who the hell is Mrs. Buck?"

"She's a friend of Aunt Tippy's. A much younger friend. She had this baby born with its heart on the outside of its body, and something's wrong with its brain, too. Now Mrs. Buck acts like she's afraid of God. She goes around saying, Isn't God good! every other sentence, in case He's listening and is in a bad mood again. It gives me the creeps."

Eamon looked at her. "You know what would be a lot easier on you, kid? Just buy the whole program, no questions asked. You've got to believe in something, right? Why not the grand old Church of Rome?"

No use your doubting me, and thinking blasphemy besides. "I believe in you," said Rory.

"And I appreciate that," said Eamon. "However, I'm not much good in the miracle department. I can't bring dead Navy fliers back to life. I wish to Christ I could."

Abilene came to the door. "Dr. Plaisance is in the sun parlor," she said to Eamon. "He want to talk to you about Jane Ann."

"I'm coming," said Eamon. He lit a cigar, puffed on it briefly, then stubbed it out violently in the ashtray on his desk. "God *damn* Fidel Castro," he said, on his way out.

Rory fell asleep in the leather chair and dreamed it was the day of Jane Ann's First Holy Communion. Cato and the other part-time musicians from the Club Sorrento were serenading her as she stood on the gallery outside her bedroom in her white organdy dress and veil, the sunlight glinting on the crystal and silver of the rosary wrapped around her hands. The song the Negroes played for Jane Ann was "The Old Rugged Cross," but Jane Ann didn't like that song; it frightened her. She started to blow on a silver police whistle. Rory, standing next to Cato in the yard, looking up at her sister, saw that Jane Ann's rosary was really a snake, and the silver snake's cross-shaped head was biting into Jane Ann's thin wrists, again and again, while Jane Ann screamed and blew on the police whistle and "The Old Rugged Cross" played on.

Abilene woke her, shaking her.

"You ain't heard the car drive up? It made enough racket. I think he hit a couple of squirrels in the driveway. Johnny's got here. He's out in the kitchen, drinking coffee with Arabella."

Rory jumped up and ran along the freshly waxed floor of the hall, skidding toward the kitchen so fast that Abilene had to call out the rest of her news. "I heard him telling your sister he got him a notice in the noon mail about how he have twenty-four hours to report someplace for his Army physical examination."

Rory suddenly lost her balance and hit the floor on one hip. It didn't hurt. The floor felt like a giant banana peel.

"Well don't break your neck over it!" Abilene yelled. She lifted Rory up off the floor by one elbow, and stood her on her feet.

Interview

Sheila Bosworth has an ethereal air that suggests an artist's life filled with sweet poignancy and a past (possibly tragic) shrouded in mystery. Slender, with long blond hair, clear, pale skin, and luminous eyes, Bosworth seems like a fragile romantic heroine, simultaneously aloof from and over-whelmed by the jarring vicissitudes of modern life.

We met for our interview in a small, glassed-in conference room in the corner of the lobby at the Holiday Inn in Nashville, Tennessee, in October 1992 during the annual southern Festival of Books. Bosworth had been invited to the festival to read from her latest novel *Slow Poison*, a book whose epigraph (from Ivan Turgenev) reads: "Beware the love of women; that ecstasy, that slow poison." Bosworth's appearance and manner (like her fiction) evoke a quiet elegance and mystery undergirded by a subtle strength. The circumstances under which we had to conduct the interview, though, were almost humorously antithetical to any expression of elegance or subtlety in any form.

The first task we faced was overcoming the scratchy Muzak which garbled forth from a two-inch speaker in the ceiling above us. Then, the tape recorder suddenly and inexplicably wouldn't work (a dead wall outlet—a sound technician from the local television station saw our puzzlement through the glass as he passed by and rescued us with the grand gesture of moving the recorder's plug from one outlet to the other). After the technician left, Sheila and I dragged two heavy, upholstered wing-back chairs across the carpet away from the Muzak and closer to the conference table where the recorder was now running smoothly, recording every thump we made.

We sat across the conference table from one another and began what was to be a freewheeling conversation about religion, art, politics, and the meaning of life.

Despite her seemingly otherworldly manner, it is clear that Sheila Bosworth is, in fact, situated quite squarely in this one. She is witty, sardonic, strong-minded, and intelligent; she is a master of the raised eyebrow, the quick laugh. She clearly cares deeply about her art, as well as about issues of gender, class, and culture; she articulates her thoughts with quiet forcefulness, often spiking them with ironic wit or understatement. A month later, having read a transcript of the interview, Bosworth wrote: "I shrieked when I read it—I'd never read a transcript from a tape recording, and after having done so I now believe Richard Nixon was innocent."

Though the meeting room was like a fish-bowl (curious hotel guests and friends would wave at us, mime-like, through the glass as we carried on our conversation), through her empathic, keenly observant presence Bosworth evoked the paradoxical ambiance of her native New Orleans—a city that is, as she says, at once compelling, sensual and "very, very Catholic."

Can you tell me about growing up in New Orleans where you were born and raised, especially with relationship to the religious culture of that city?

New Orleans is maybe the only city in America that is run by Catholics; it's a very, very Catholic city. Instead of having prejudice against Catholics like you do in much of the Protestant South, you've got almost a Catholic dynasty there. The oldest French families there are Catholic, and some of the English families as well. My own family is Catholic as far back as I know of, and I can't really understand why because my father's side of the family is English. My mother's side is totally Irish, and my father's mother was Irish, but I can't figure out how a name like Bosworth, which is very British, could have gotten Catholic.

As far as the Catholic church, I can't imagine anything that's been as far-reaching in my life as the church has been. It's like breathing or eating; it has been simply a fact of my life, as long as I can remember. From the time I was five years old I went to a Catholic parochial school. It was run by the Sisters of Mercy. Then after fourth grade I went to the Sacred Heart Convent in New Orleans. I stayed there all through high school and then that was the end of my Catholic education. I didn't go to a Catholic college; I stayed home and went to Sophie Newcomb. I can't ever remember my parents missing Mass, or any of us, for any reason, ever. Yet, I would not say that they were particularly pious people or devout people. We never said grace before meals, including Thanksgiving. I always felt that they were quiet followers of the Catholic faith, steadfast, without any question. They didn't talk about it any more than you talked about the fact that you breathed or said, "Look we're breathing. Let's all breathe together." My grandmother, my mother's mother, was very devout. I can remember her sitting in the rocking chair saying her morning prayers; she had a little book of prayers that she would read. But she was very practical, too. She would never say, "You have to go to church even though you have a cold." If you didn't want to go to church it was all right with her—that is, if you were sick. They were all very practical people, very quiet Catholics except for one aunt who entered the convent at the age of fifty-three, after she had become a widow. She eventually left because of ill health.

This is your mother's sister?

My mother's sister. We did have a priest in the family. My mother's cousin was a priest. My father was educated at a Jesuit high school in New Orleans. I don't know what it is about a Jesuit education; it seems to "take" for life.

I noticed in Almost Innocent *you grapple with some very complex theological and moral issues in the voices of several of the characters, particularly the young Clay-Lee. For example, when the doctor says, "Not even God himself should have to take the blame for this one." What do you think about that?*

I think the Catholic church—and maybe all Christian religions, maybe the entire Judeo-Christian tradition—makes a great show of thanking God for things, but of never blaming God for anything. I feel that it's a matter of logic that if you thank God for the good weather for the church fair, you could also say the opposite: He didn't do it right if the weather doesn't come out. The issue of blaming God is an unusual one. This doctor in *Almost Innocent* strikes me as a character who's probably seen a lot of God's little "mistakes," shall we say, and probably did blame God, in a quiet way, and yet, this particular incident he's referring to is so awful and so tragic, that even the Great Instigator of Tragedy, which would probably be God, even the Great Permitter of Tragedy should not have to take the blame for this.

In Portait of the Artist as a Young Man, *Stephen Dedalus calls God, among other things, a "corpse chewer." Dedalus grapples very deeply and very honestly, I think, with the concept of the Divine not always being benevolent.*

I think that the more belief you have in the existence of God, the angrier you get and the louder your voice becomes; you're hoping that He will hear. It reminds me of book critics. I often get the feeling that when I'm reading an angry, negative review of someone's book, it's clear that the critic wrote it just for that author, and the critic's heart would be broken if the author didn't see it. I think that's true of a lot of people who rail against God, especially atheists. In my second novel, *Slow Poison*, one of the characters says that all atheists are true believers—nobody puts that much energy in trying to "get somebody," who doesn't really believe in who they're trying to get. So I think a lot of the "corpse chewer" business is, "Are you listening to this, God? Quit it." And I think a lot of the anger in people who are believers stems from the fact that we are also taught not only to believe, but to have faith that God will protect us. That's the big thing that I was taught as a child.

"Consider the lilies of the field; they do not toil nor spin, yet even Solomon in all his glory is not arrayed as one of these." If you have four children in an accident, and three die but one doesn't, what does that tell you? That God loved the one and not the others?

It suggests to me that God is a monster.

Yes. What does it mean? And the question of would it be more comforting to feel that you are walking through the forest without anybody in charge, or walking through the forest with a monster in charge? It's awful. He might help you, then again He might harm you.

Yeah, it's the capriciousness of it all that's so frightening. You said a moment ago that that God does not protect us.

I can't see it; I can't see that's part of the plan. And yet, I think I got a lot of the anger out in the second novel, *Slow Poison*. Now I think I can go on to something else. But as far as the melding of religion into my fiction, it's such an advantage. I don't really feel that I write "Catholic" novels, but Catholicism's influence on me is huge; there's just so much information that I just happen to have, and the structure of the church is a real plus for a writer. I use it over and over again in all kinds of different ways. So I think it'll always be there to some degree.

I'm sure people have asked you this before, so you don't have to answer this, but what do you think about your debt to Walker Percy or Flannery O'Connor? Or the influence either has had on your development as a fiction writer?

I'm not a very big reader of Flannery O'Connor. I read *Wise Blood* and was not particularly taken with it. Plus, she's a Catholic woman who writes about nothing but Protestants, which I can't see. It would be like a woman writing only in a man's voice. I mean, what's the "prob"? But as far as Walker's concerned, you know, I knew him personally, in the last ten or so years of his life, and we used to argue all the time because I was a cradle Catholic, and he was a convert. He was born in 1916 and converted in 1947 so he was thirty-two or thereabouts when he converted.

Yes. He was an adult convert.

His church and my church were two different churches. Sometimes we would argue about laughable things. For instance, I would tell him about something that a nun had done that cost me a great deal. And this sounds very funny to talk about mean nuns, but when you're a six-year-old baby leaving your mother for the first time and going to school, and you've got a nut at the helm, it can cost you big. And he didn't understand that. He didn't understand what it was like to be a female child in the Catholic church in the 1950s. He'd say, "I thought all nuns were like Loretta Young." He wrote me, cautioning me not to be too critical of the church and to have a set of beliefs I could hold on to. I think he decided he could not make it through the world unless he held onto the promise that if he acted in a certain way in this life, he would be rewarded in eternal life. Because this life was not his thing. He struggled day by day, I think, just to get through. The best way to get there he thought, the best road map, is contained in the Catholic church. He wouldn't take no for an answer.

And you had long conversations with him about these things?

Oh yes. I had told him I thought my Catholicism had cost me a lot. I think—perhaps this is my fault because of the way I am constructed—but I was frightened to death as a child, frightened to death. I remember my first confession which I've treated in *Almost Innocent*. It was a rainy day, just a horrible, gray day, and the priest that we were to confess to was a very gruff priest. He was known for yelling at us from the pulpit—not just the children, grown-ups too. "Don't call the priest house," he'd say. And we were expected to go into a little dark room and tell this man how bad we were, what we had done, and I was frightened silly to the point where I couldn't think straight. Now, a lot of kids would have gone there and thought of it as an adventure. I didn't.

You had a kind of sensitivity, and I think a lot of creative people do, that makes you take things very seriously.

Yes. And I resented it. I resented babies being hurt, and for what purpose? And suddenly in the 1970s the church was saying "God is Love." Well, that wasn't what we were taught; we were taught that God will love you if you were good. I mean God's love is universal but you got the impression that you yourself were pretty worthless. And the only thing you could do was admit it and try to go on from there and then maybe you had a chance.

Do you see similarities between that kind of Catholicism and fundamentalism?

No, no, I really don't. As a matter of fact I'm a terrific Catholic snob when it comes to the beauty and the intellectual grandeur of the Catholic church. Fundamentalists make me very, very nervous and I get almost a sick feeling because of their judgmental tone. I've often heard Catholics accused of being judgmental, yet in all the years that I grew up as a Catholic, I never heard anyone, a nun, a priest, a fellow Catholic say anything against any other religion, ever. It was not "those crummy Baptists," or "those fire-breathing Methodists," or "those awful Lutherans," never. The judgmental nature of the fundamentalists is what frightens me. In the Catholic church, you judged yourself, and it's reflected in the Mass before Vatican II. The Catholic Mass before Vatican II was a very private affair. It was done in communion with others—you were standing next to someone—but you followed along in the missal, and it was more of an individual thing. Some people said the rosary all during Mass. Vatican II sought to redress those grievances against community by having us turn to one another, speak English, and shake hands during the sharing of the peace. That was very much against the Catholic grain, it seemed to me. But you didn't find Catholics judging. I know there was an undercurrent of "We are the one true faith," but the invitation was there to join. This is the Catholic church, historically founded by Christ, no one could argue that, the other religions were offshoots of that, historically if nothing else. There were abuses certainly, but historically we knew it went back to one man. I think the Catholic church has a lot of historical integrity going for it. No, I don't see that the Catholic church has any direct connection to fundamentalism, thank God.

I was thinking about the fundamentalist image of God as a wrathful judge, as in the famous Protestant sermon of Jonathan Edwards, "Sinners in the Hands of an Angry God," who determines whether your soul is judged either to heaven or hell.

But I've never met a fundamentalist who seemed to feel that his own soul was in any trouble; it was other people's souls who were in trouble. There's a sign next to me at my house in Covington, beside a fundamentalist church—it is the church Jimmy Swaggart was in?

The Church of God, I think.

On their marquee every week, they post things such as "Four conversions, two reavowals, praise the Lord." And it's as if they're saying, "We're all okay and if you dark sheep out there come in, you'll be okay, too."

Tell me about the epigraph you gave from the poet Seneca to Almost Innocent: *"He who is penitent is almost innocent."*

We have this belief in the Catholic church that when you go to confession and you get absolution, it's as if the sin were not committed. But what about purgatory? You still have to pay. You're not quite innocent. Let's assume you're sinless until you attain the age of reason, which is seven, and on your seventh birthday, you commit a mortal sin, make a perfect confession, and then die. Then you go, I guess, straight to heaven. But on the other hand, even though the sin is gone, you still have to pay for it according to Catholic doctrine, so that's not quite totally innocent, is it? You're penitent, so you're almost innocent, and not guilty anymore, but you're not innocent, either.

It's interesting, that statement was made by a Roman poet, someone who was not of any Christian faith.

The moral behind the epigraph seems to be that repentance takes care of only so much. You still must pay in some way. The "karma" aspect of it all, if you will.

Catholic karma. [Laughter]

Your soul is not lost, but you still must pay. And we were always taught that you paid in the afterlife, in purgatory.

It's clear in Almost Innocent *that Clay-Lee pays every minute of her life, thereafter.*

A lot of people have asked me who the "almost innocent" refers to. I think that that can be left open because there are a lot of people there that are penitent, and who are sorry for the mistakes that they have made. Rand, for instance, is certainly not guiltless; he commits sins of omission, the sin of lethargy, the sin of sloth.

I have always been interested in that sin. It seems so benign; how in the world could sloth be a sin?

Throughout the Gospels, Christ is very vehement about that sin: "I will spew the lukewarm out of my mouth."

He gets fed up with them?

Yeah, it's a bad one because it gets in the way of everything else.
Like a black hole, it sucks everything around it in.
That's right.
Any kind of positive energy, or initiative.
And we all know about idle hands and idle minds.
There was a passage in Almost Innocent *that I was especially taken with — the description of the break-in and its aftermath, the profound effect that it had on Constance and Rand's marriage. Perhaps that passage is talking about this sin of sloth?*
Yes, or the failure to protect, as God fails to protect. Constance had been taught that Daddy is going to take care of her—"Daddy" in one form or another, whether the Father in Heaven or the actual birth father, or her husband who acted like a father, who carried her upstairs to bed like a baby. But this house of cards collapsed on her. Her father certainly didn't take care of her. He died and left her helpless.
He was actually doing very little protecting or nurturing even when he was alive — he took her to bars with him when she was a child and let her eat maraschino cherries and olives for supper as he drank.
Yet the message is: "You have nothing to worry about. Leave it to me." That was the message that Rand gave her, too, and she had no reason to doubt it. It was brought home to her very brutally that she was on her own when the break-in occurred. She had to rely on the strength of her own hand; her own neck was on the line.
You know, we had a similar incident happen to us in our house.
It happened to me. That was very true to life; I mean, I embellished it but I was the one down there. I was the one who said to my husband, "Let's get out of here." I felt totally alone, and I was seven months pregnant. I didn't care what happened, frankly; I was getting out of there with the baby and me. And I remember as I beat on the window of the people next door, thinking very clearly—I was not thinking in a panicked way—"If they don't come, I'm going to go over the balcony." Because I knew I wasn't going back in my house. There was someone *in* there.
It's life or death, a question of survival. My entire view of what "women were capable of" changed profoundly in those kinds of moments. And the change deepened when I actually had a baby.

Isn't that amazing how simple that is?

Yes.

It's very odd—that we would end up talking about this.

Yes, it's interesting the commonality of experience, physical and emotional, of two southern women, how we were brought up. I was very drawn to the sadness of Almost Innocent. *At the end of the novel, the grown Clay-Lee says of her father, "Why has he never learned that the healing of a soul is not guaranteed in return for fees paid with sorrow and with time?"*

Right. And it isn't. There just isn't any "fixing it." I remember a line from Hemingway—I think it was in *Islands in the Stream*. He says there are many things that can make sorrow better, work is one of them and sometimes drink, but if anything makes it go away, then the chances are it wasn't true sorrow to begin with. Sorrow is something you learn to live with.

The grief is lifelong.

You learn to adjust, or to live despite it. But you can't imagine that even time would heal anything completely, anything that is drastic. For instance, the loss of a child. I can't see that anything, anything would heal that. There'd just be this constant crying in the night inside.

As you wrote, tears wouldn't heal it, time doesn't heal it. I think that perhaps you become an adult when you realize fully for the first time that some griefs are forever.

And, of course, that's one of Rand's problems—he'd never grown up. He was a "golden boy" so he still doesn't know. He's just going along like, "I'm going to be okay tomorrow; everything's going to be okay tomorrow."

Perhaps that's what the entire book is about, about the healing and wounding of the soul. Is Slow Poison *about that, too?*

Yes, it is. It is, and I wish I'd thought to put it that way. Yes, and it's about coming to terms with things, seeing people as they truly are. And that's not always pleasant, and seeing the choices that you make based on early events in your life. I think women especially make choices in life, not exactly blindly, but perhaps while looking backward. They reach out with one hand while looking backwards. And sometimes you have to look forward again and ask, "What made me do this?" And not blaming anyone, not saying, "He made me do it," but just asking, "What were the factors in my life that allowed me or drove me to make certain decisions that are so costly?"

Would you say that these women characters are believing lies? Would you go so far as to say that, for example, Constance is believing the lie that her father told her: "Don't worry, I'll take care of everything"?

There would be some recourse in anger if you thought you had deliberately been told a lie. But worse than that, it's as if the people who perpetuated this belief were not ever aware that they were lying but were simply doing what they thought was necessary for the protection of women, for the well-being of these fragile creatures who really shouldn't be told what's going on because how will they cope? And it's not as simple as a calculating "I think I'll lie to her and then see what happens."

Yes. Fathers and husbands and sons may help perpetuate these illusions in order to protect themselves from the spectre of weakness or failure.

That's another thing, surely. If I tell myself enough times that as long as I'm here, nothing will happen to anybody, maybe I can believe it. It must be a scary situation to be in, to be the one that everyone looks to, and to know down deep that it's all shaky. The foundation is shaky. How can you protect people from things? You can't.

You would have to be a rock. You would have to be forever and always strong.

And what comes at the price of being a rock? You have no feelings.

Right, you're a rock. [Laughter] Early on in the novel when Uncle Baby is making out the will for the Home for the Incurables, Sis, the black cook, says, "You don't have to be strapped to a hammock to be an incurable." Isn't she referring to the soul, do you think?

Oh, absolutely. We all can be invalids, you know, emotional invalids. Or in another sense, incurably romantic or incurably optimistic.

Or incurably naive. And I think that that's how Sis saw Rand. I mean, here is this guy that you know even as his uncle is making out the will to someone else was still probably swinging along in his own proverbial hammock. Of course, Rand was not completely convincing himself because he was leaning on alcohol more and more toward the end of the novel, perhaps to be able to perpetuate this dream that he kept telling himself.

How firmly entrenched in being southern, in being from New Orleans, is all of this business about the fragility of women and the illusions men and women maintain to protect themselves?

I think the South is such a male-dominated society from the bloody hunt on down, or on up, and it's a very convenient, thing— they're in charge.

Did you see Thelma and Louise?

Yes. That awful husband in the beginning was just marvelous. I just finished reading Susan Minot's new book. It's about Boston Brahmin women around 1917 and goes up through the thirties. And it's exactly the same sort of thing. The men being in charge to the point that they're punishingly in charge. You will obey me, not just my daughters will do so, but also my wife. And it was the wives who were dipping into the sherry. They went about it a lot more quietly than southern women would. Southern women may go along, but they can be pretty vocal in the process. And they're going to go along only to a certain point.

Did you see a movie called Sherman's March? *It's a documentary, and the filmmaker, Ross McIlwee, is tracing the path that General Sherman took on his march from Mississippi through Georgia to the sea. In the process, McIlwee ends up interviewing many of his old girlfriends, southern women, all, about their lives.*

It sounds great.

It's pretty incredible what he ends up with. When he goes back up to Boston he realizes in a yearning and perplexed kind of way, that southern women are strong, and vulnerable — and crazy.

In the South? Crazy in what sense? Does he feel that they're crazy or that they're driven crazy?

Driven, in a way, by their culture's complicated, often contradictory expectations, and in the bittersweet, tragic thwarting or skewing of such dynamism and energy in its women.

Yeah, maybe so. I noticed in Susan Minot's book there was only one actually "crazy" woman in that book, and she was the artistic type. She had a lot of creative, artistic sensibility. The other women just seemed to be zombies, much less dynamic than southern women, just almost stupid. I don't know if you've ever read *Mr. and Mrs. Bridge,* or *Mrs. Bridge?*

No.

A friend of mine gave me *Mrs. Bridge,* and I couldn't bear the main character, Mrs. Bridge. She was such a stupid woman. Then when I saw the movie, Joanne Woodward was such a fine actor that she made the character sympathetic, and I tell you what, she should have gotten an Academy Award for that one. Unless you've read the book you have no idea what a job Joanne Woodward had on her hands. I just wanted to kill Mrs. Bridge when I was reading the book because she was such a stupid woman.

Drinking from the river Lethe.

Oh boy, yeah.

I think it's true for most southern women that they have never been able to be truly passive.

Southern women historically have learned that they are capable of making it without men. During World War II, of course, women all over the country worked in airplane factories and that sort of thing, but southern women literally had to meet the enemy on their front porch and deal with that in the Civil War, while their husbands and brothers were away at the front.

Their farms and homes were occupied by enemy troops.

That's right, they were the only American women who have ever had to face occupation by enemy troops—men who were out to burn their houses over their heads, and did.

And ransack their smokehouses and barns. Southerners all have been handed down stories, especially in the Deep South. They have been passed down from great-great-grandma on. I guess a good way to sum this up would be to quote Lillian Hellman, as you did in one of the sections of Almost Innocent: *"You ain't born in the South unless you're a fool." It's an interestingly ambiguous statement.*

That's why I liked it.

What do you think about that?

It's just sort of a shaking of the heads among us, among the southerners. Times when you get impatient you think, "I must be crazy" but you don't want anybody else to say you must be crazy.

Lillian Hellman said it, but you know if John Updike had said it, I wouldn't have liked it.

Yes. The imaginative sensibility you have, the fact that you're a woman, the fact that you were born and raised in the South, and the fact that you were born and raised a "cradle" Catholic is an interesting and perhaps volatile combination.

It is. The message of Christ, supposedly, is love; the "new law" is love, and yet I felt precious little of that in the Catholic church when I was growing up. I don't ever remember feeling loved, by any nun, by any priest, but of course, by my parents, I certainly did. But it was not this outpouring of "Come let me tell you how the good news is: if you're upset in this life you're going to be with the baby Jesus in the next." It was never that. You had to struggle, and to watch your step, and you were always on the verge of a precipice. It scared the hell out of me. Robert Hughes, the art critic, was raised Catholic in Australia. *The New Yorker* had a piece by him recently called "Fetus Don't Fail Me Now."

Yes? [Laughter]

He writes that suffocating guilt, the byproduct of suffocating guilt, is skepticism. It's simply a defense. You can only feel so frightened and guilty for so long. You know when you frighten a child badly enough with abuse, then the child's mind, her psyche, splinters. That's what multiple personality is, a coping mechanism, an escape valve. And it's the same thing with religious training. If you lay on the guilt too heavy with these children and women, it's just going to be too much.

That defensive reaction is an attempt to preserve life, isn't it?

The same mechanism happened in communist states. "This is such a wonderful idea, so good for humanity, but at first we might have to beat them over the head with sticks to get their attention," and that becomes abuse of power. You can't have communism without a dictator and therein lies its destruction. The Catholic church has got to watch out for that dictator mentality in the name of good, because it will all fall apart if the rules and the guilt become so suffocating that the escape valve blows and that's it.

It presupposes a rather dim view of human nature to hold to the conviction that you have to beat people over the head with a stick to get them to "see the light."

Yes, but that's the whole doctrine of original sin.

Oh yes, let's talk about that.

I'm innocent.

Sure you are. [Laughter]

The idea of the son literally being damned for the sins of the father is an amazing thing when you think about it. Of course, you get a child young enough and you can teach him anything. It never occurred to me to question that.

In Almost Innocent *(and also for the characters in* Slow Poison*), it happened that indeed Clay-Lee had to suffer for the sins of her parents.*

Right. In Clay-Lee's family no one was at the helm, she was the child of two children. So she had to take on the burden of worry and the old rescue fantasy of "I'm going to save Daddy, and if I can do this, then Mommy will pat me like she does the dog."

I really liked what you did with the image of the sailboat too. The fact that "no one is at the helm in this family" is painfully true; she's left to her own devices.

That is one thing the children really catch on to quickly because the child's main question in life, no matter what happens is, "Who is going to take care of me?" They are smart enough to know that without a caretaker, they will soon die.

That's indeed a most crucial question for a child. What do you think got Constance and Rand together in the first place? You talk about this a little in the novel. Can you elaborate on it?

I remember once reading a Kurt Vonnegut book. It was called *Bluebeard.* A woman in the book was involved with a horrible man and Kurt Vonnegut says—the narrator says—"I guess you're wondering how Maralee and her lover got together, and why they stayed together, and the answer is: 'She was in love with him and he was in love with her.'"

Yes.

But I see what your question is. Rand was older, for one thing. She met him under very dramatic circumstances, as a rescuer. Then she sees Rand Calvert for the second time on horseback, a few months later, riding through the streets of New Orleans cloaked as

a magical prince in a Mardi Gras parade. The first time he's the rescuer, or superman, or what ever you want to call it.

"Here I come to save the day."

Yeah! Mighty Mouse. So that was pretty powerful, and being an
artist, Rand was not full of these Catholic . . . he wasn't Catholic, he
was Presbyterian. And so he didn't understand what Constance was
talking about as far as her trying to be a good Catholic. To Rand it
was simply, you love someone, you feel a certain way. She was
swept away by him. And she was only eighteen; she wanted to be
swept away.

Yes, you're pretty vulnerable at that age.

He's Prince Charming, and then he rescues you; he's an older
father figure.

Tell me about Uncle Baby, the name. That's a wild name.

There are so many names like that in the South, Uncle Son, and
Aunt Baby Sister. I actually knew an Aunt Baby Sister. I didn't
know her, but a former friend of mine in Mississippi had an Aunt
Baby Sister. She was her mother's little sister, and all the people in
the family called this woman "baby sister." Somebody else in New
Orleans had an Aunt Mama, and an Aunt Baby. In the first version
of *Almost Innocent* before I revised it, Uncle Baby was really disgusting. He was fat, and when he ate gumbo, okra hung out of his
mouth in strings. He was gross, and I wanted Constance really to
have to toe the line for this bargain she'd made with him, but my
editor said he's so disgusting, can't we just make him a little more
physically attractive? So I just didn't put a lot in about his physical
disgustingness.

*I think you captured very well what it was like when he became
drunk, he would go from being okay to true meanness.*

He was a bad drunk, a mean drunk.

*How very dangerous that person really was. I like the fact that
he was a bit of a roué and a cad and attractive in that way.*

Yeah, and he was in a way a roué and a cad, but—and here's the
difference—here was Rand who was so lovely and he couldn't handle
a damn thing, whereas Uncle Baby who was a roué and a cad was
the one who saved the baby Julie the time she choked and he ran the
children off who were frightening Clay-Lee. So, he's confusing.

And he was rich; he made money.

He knew how to do that, too.

So I could see how Constance would feel. You have to be able to see how she would be willing to go through with her bargain.

Well, it's truly a bargain of pure evil, pure evil. I remember Walker Percy telling me that, after he'd read the scene where Constance and Uncle Baby are out on the porch in the eye of the hurricane. He said to me, "First I absolutely believed in the bargain she'd made, and secondly, that was pure evil on that porch."

What do you think he meant?

That it was the giving up of goodness for evil gain, it was betrayal, it was dishonesty, it was carnal depravity, the selling of a blessing for filthy lucre. I used the image of Rumpelstiltskin. The spinning of straw into gold for which she has to give up her child.

He's a pirate, too. He robs her.

I've always felt that his main motive was to castrate Rand. Through some sort of self-hatred.

Therein lies the essence of the evil. He did, it seems to me, want to castrate Rand, and why? For the hell of it. Because he could.

Right, because Rand was this golden boy and probably he was annoyed by him. Yeah, or maybe it was just a male self-hatred. Look at what's going to happen here, look what I can do. Let me do this to him before somebody does it to me.

That's the essence of a power trip, I guess. What do you think happened to Clay-Lee after the book ends, as she becomes an adolescent? She's still a child as the book ends, but she's not innocent.

You asked about the "almost innocent" in the epigraph: babies who die unbaptized are almost innocent, because according to Catholic doctrine they go to limbo, a place which Jonathan Edwards once described as the "easiest room in hell."

Indeed.

And in a different sense, Clay-Lee is given the easiest room in hell for the rest of her life. And although she is not guilty in any way, she was a child who was driven temporarily out of her mind by the sight of her mother on that porch with Uncle Baby. And all the truth comes through to her at that moment; she's a very smart child. And I think that her sentence was—what she sentenced herself to—was a life in limbo, the easiest room in hell, because nothing really happened to Clay-Lee after that night. Her life is in limbo, going back and forth across the causeway. There had been so much drama, and she had played such a part in it. She says at one point, "I was the spectator who jumps on stage and interrupts the progression of a scene." She was sentenced to simply watch for the rest of her days. I know Walker Percy asked me about that, too. He was disturbed about that. And yet, I didn't want to tie it up neatly.

It's honest; it seems to me it's the only thing you could do.

Obviously she has no real life.

Isn't she a part-time lecturer in English?

Yes, that's limbo, huh?

That's limbo, all right. What passages from Almost Innocent *or* Slow Poison, *would you recommend as passages that seem to get at the heart of the conflict, the anger and the ambivalence, that you've been experiencing with regard to Catholicism?*

There's a passage in *Slow Poison* in which Rory asks her father why God allows certain things to happen. It goes from page 171 to 175. There also is a set piece in *Slow Poison* that takes place on a typical day in the parochial school that this child attends. When Florence King wrote a review of *Slow Poison* for the *Washington Times*, she treated the novel as a pure comedy. It was a very good review, but the only thing she couldn't laugh at was that day at school—that's where the true craziness occurred.

Violence to the psyche?

I took the most outrageous events that I could think of that happened to me in parochial school and compiled them into one day. A day in the life.

Sounds like a very bad day.

Yeah.

You mentioned earlier that you don't think of yourself as a Catholic writer, and most of the writers I've interviewed, understandably so, do not wish to be called a "Christian writer." Is there anybody who is, and what is the aversion to being one?

Andrew Greeley. I mean I don't think he writes literature but he's a Catholic writer. I think that Walker Percy was a Catholic writer, and he took it to a level of genius, but unless you have that level of genius, watch out. Then you get into didacticism, and author's message, and that sort of thing, and even Walker Percy's *bête noire*, his pet peeve, was that people not call him a philosopher or a religious philosopher who was using the novel form to make a point. In fact Shelby Foote, at his memorial service for Walker Percy in New York City that I attended (Shelby Foote who was his friend from the time they were eleven years old) spoke and very vehemently said that Walker did not want to be thought of as someone who used the art of the novel for a vehicle to preach. I think that's what the aversion is. Religion is so linked up in the reader's mind with the preaching end of things. What you are there to do as a novelist, or what I feel I am there to do, is to use whatever gifts I have to create art that convinces someone, as many people as possible, that we're not in this alone, that the truth is that we're all in this human condition together and that there's hope in the very communal nature of that.

Is that why you write?

Can't seem to help it.

Yes!

Someone once said that writers are always complaining, "Oh, I never have time to write, oh it's so hard to write." And yet if you told the writer he could never write again, it would be, "What!?" Because it's what you do, it's just what you do. I imagine it's why a painter paints; it's such a part of your blood that it's simply what you can't help doing, and if you didn't have any other outlet, you could just write letters all day. But you have to play with words and you have to use the words in a way that's going to get at the heart of something. My daughter asked me once, "What's the difference? You're always talking about something not being literature; what's the difference between just a book and literature?" And I said, "Well, it's what I call the 'Aha!' effect. When you're reading literature, your mouth falls open every few lines if you're lucky, every few pages if you're a little less lucky, and you say, Yes! that's just how it is." It's the writer's angle of vision making things a little clearer for you.

Someone asked Eudora Welty why she wrote and sought to get published, and she said, "Why do you have a telephone?"

Exactly, exactly, because there has to be that other person out there. Some writers say they write just for themselves, but I don't think that's true; there has to be that third party. It's the material, and then the writer, and then that reader.

Do you actually feel pressure building up when you haven't written, or when you're thinking about something?

Oh, I am so miserable most of the time. Someone said to me, "You're so lucky to have been published," and I said, "Sometimes I think it is the best thing that ever happened to me, other times the worst thing." Let's face it, your life is ruined; my life is ruined. Not only because of the outside things that have happened to ruin it, but because of the inner pressure of feeling that no matter what you're doing it's not enough, and most of the time it is damn well not enough; I know I'm not just imagining.

The anguish of inadequacy.

I think the most frightening aspect of it is the knowledge that you don't want to face how much time it takes, and how much of you is going to be required. And every time I finish a book I think, Oh, the next one's not going to take so long. I bet if I sit in a room and work for three months straight, it will be ready—and that's crazy. It's a long, long haul, and you never know whether you're going to be able to do it again. If you go to medical school and you don't go blind, and you pass, you know you're going to be able to operate in the morning. If you're a graduate of law school, and you don't have a stroke, then you're going to be able to help people through the practice of law. And if you're a writer, all you can hope for is that you can find that muse again, that you can do it again.

That's a terror. It's like stepping off a cliff every time you search for a word and waiting for something to come out of the mist.

It's so easy to forget that as you sit there and do it that things happen that you have no control over, no prediction of. That's the hardest thing for me to remember. I'm never sure it's going to happen again.

Do you remember those toy eightballs they used to have in the fifties?

Of course.

And you sit there and ask a question and the answer would float into view?

Oh, I remember it so well. You know what always came up for me? "Answer hazy, try again." Remember that one?

Right!

"All signs point to yes." I always wanted to get that one and I never got it. I can't believe you had an eightball. I can't believe it. "Answer hazy, try again." Too much!

That to me is a good metaphor for writing, for the creative process.

That's a great metaphor.

When did you grow up?

I was born in 1950 so I grew up during the fifties and sixties. I'm reading a new novel that was written by Ann Padgett, who's twenty-eight, twenty-nine years old, now, which means she was probably writing it when she was twenty-five, so smart, so brilliant. . . .

But don't look back.

No, because when I was that age, I was raising kids, I was having babies.

How many kids do you have?

Two. Do you have more than two?

I have one. She sometimes seems like two. Do you live in New Orleans now?

No, six years ago we moved across Lake Ponchartrain to Covington. It's about thirty miles out of New Orleans.

What's that like?

Covington used to be what Walker Percy called a "nontown." It was mostly woods and one little main street with a train depot. Now, with the white flight from New Orleans it is just growing so unbelievably with its overpasses and expressways. I live in a house that's within the city limits but it's down a lane and up in the woods, so that's really nice. It's the best of both worlds. It helps just to get twenty or thirty miles from where you were raised. To me it's a big difference.

Have you ever lived or worked outside the South?

I lived in California briefly when I was first married. I've never been away to camp; I've never been away to school. I married somebody from California, of all places.

That must be interesting.

Yeah, but he went to school at Tulane, and that's where we met.

What was it like going to Tulane?

Well, it wasn't like I had imagined college to be. I was living at home. I look back on it and I think, given my temperament, I don't think I could have lived in a small room with another girl; I would feel so trapped. I remember thinking, I'm so glad to get in my car and leave this campus and go home, or go to the movies. I'm a real loner and I'm so claustrophobic. If the only place I could go after school was back to the dorm, I think I would have crumpled under it.

Do you raise your kids Catholic?

They were both baptized Catholic and have gone to Catholic schools. I have one at the University of the South, now; that school, of course, is Episcopalian. They went to Sacred Heart as I did when I was in New Orleans and when we moved to Covington, they went to the Catholic school there, St. Scholastica.

What do you think about their Catholic upbringing these days in contrast to yours?

It's different; there's a lot of emphasis on ethics and values instead of on Christian doctrine. They know very little about Christian doctrine as far as I can tell; they don't know the Gospels; they don't know the New Testament, the Old Testament, they're not versed in the fine—what is the word—the academics of it. Compared to me they're intellectually worse off and emotionally probably better off.

What about your study of the Bible? Many writers in the South have commented on the fact that they were highly influenced by the King James version of the Bible, that in Sunday school, they memorized scripture.

We were not encouraged to read the Bible. That was more of a Protestant thing: Let's all read the Bible, the family Bible. The Bible in the Catholic church was not emphasized in that way at all. But if you went to mass every Sunday or every day as I did when I was in high school, then you heard all the Gospels week after week after week, you had all the Epistles, and so on. I know it backwards and forwards. We did study the Old Testament in school. But it was never a Bible-oriented sort of thing. Of course the King James version, you couldn't look at that one, the one with all the beautiful language, the Douay-Rheims version was ours.

Did you read, or were you told lives of the saints? The saints and martyrs?

Oh yes. Saint Theresa, Little Flower.

Yes.

Are you Catholic?

No.

You know so much about it, I thought perhaps you were.

Thank you. I've always been interested in Catholicism, but I was raised a Presbyterian, and now I'm Episcopalian.

We had certain events in school called retreats. Do you know what that is? It's an intense sort of a turning inward at school and you'd keep silent for a three-day period, even during meals. You'd have a day that's divided into private prayer and devotions, and three or four lectures on different subjects, like on the first day the thrust of the lectures would be everlasting life, the second day would be hell.

I'm sure that was the last day.

And a priest called the retreat master would conduct this retreat. You were encouraged during the free time of the day, when you weren't allowed to talk, to read certain books and pamphlets, and I cannot tell you the influence they had on me.

Which ones do you remember most vividly?

The one about St. Therese of Lisieux, who was called "the little flower of the child Jesus." She died from tuberculosis at twenty-four. I don't know if you know anything about the Carmelite order?

No, not very much. Was it St. Theresa of Avila who was the founder of that order?

Yes, I think so. Well, St. Therese of Lisieux, from the moment she was born, knew she wanted to be a Carmelite nun. They are completely cloistered, which means that when you enter the convent at Carmel you never see your family again unless through a thick iron grill. You never come home again, you never write, you never call. It's a contemplative order which means that your day is spent in prayer and simple garden work or baking, enough to keep the convent going. A very severe order. But the little flower died a happy death because she was so in love with Christ, and was going home to him. Her body has been preserved intact. I've always wanted to see it, but I can't recall where it is. Lisieux, maybe. Another one of those retreat pamphlets, I remember, was about a young girl who had gone away to college, to a non-Catholic college.

Uh-oh.

Yes, and that college had robbed her of her faith, yes, I'm afraid it had. And all of it just made you want to die a martyr's death, to be spotless and holy. It was very compelling, romantic stuff. But then you have the down side, the religious version of cocaine withdrawal. You are very high, and then dangerously depressed. Because you're never quite good enough.

I always wondered about that desire to be true and holy, that yearning. I never had it.

You're probably purer in heart than anybody who ever wanted it.

No, I think not. [Laughter]

It shows in your eyes. Oh, as Catholic girls, we had benediction and incense and the white veils, and let's cleanse our souls, and oh, it's very interesting, yes.

Didn't Ingrid Bergman play a nun?

Yes, she was a nun in *Going My Way* with Bing Crosby. And Loretta Young.

That's the closest I ever got to yearning for the holy life.

She was so jolly and wonderful, wasn't she?

That's true. You've been describing how Catholic writings influenced you profoundly. What are some works of fiction or authors who have influenced you in the fiction world?

That's always one question that sets my head reeling because I've read so many different things, and I just hate to narrow it down. I just go blank.

You don't have to name anybody in particular but it's often very revealing if you can.

Right now, I'm really appreciating Nabokov of all people. His later work that he wrote in English, *Lolita* and *Pale Fire*—just the beauty of his style, and he's so funny! So funny, and yet very dark. And that's one thing that I have always found coming out in my own work—no matter how serious I set out to be. I have to have a little humor for some reason, or as my friend the novelist Nancy Lemann said: I start out to say something and then I can't help being silly.

Tell me more about this humor that comes through in your work; it seems to "bubble up."

Well, it's a defense and I have to watch it. Like this movie coming out called *Mr. Saturday Night*—he is the absolute epitome of the person who is no longer able to say a single sentence without its being a one-liner. He's so defended and so rigid and so trying to avoid his pain that the only way to do that is through humor. You know I've never known anyone who was witty who didn't have that wit spring from pain. That's the price you have to pay. There are a lot of people who have been in pain who don't turn out to be witty, but I've never seen the converse to be true.

Do you suppose that's why there are so many Jewish comics? And so many southern writers who are noted for their humor?

Yes, they've been discriminated against—both cultures have. Southerners are patronized. Someone in the *New York Times* recently in a review of Cormac McCarthy's new book, said for a while he had fallen into the "southern trap" or something. If you have to fall into a trap, I guess that's the one to fall into. In this rave review of her book, in the *New York Times*, Dorothy Allison, who has been nominated for a National Book Award, was described as walking in a minefield of southern cliches; she succeeded in not falling into this pit—what in the world? I don't get it. You know, nobody's saying you have to be silly all the time or act like you're milking the cows or something. You are who you are, and to me it's an advantage.

I think the humor of Almost Innocent *is that vein that goes all the way down deep into the philosophical understanding of what's going on in life.*

Yes, I think so. I hope so.

One thing I really liked, too, was the way you worked in descriptions of New Orleans food and cooking throughout the book. I was hungry all the way through.

When I was little we used to read and read, and my sisters and I would say, Oh, is that a good food book? Does it make you hungry?

I want to try some of those roux, and the biscuits.

I always try to get some food in the book. I think it's a sensuous pleasure to read about food. Reading itself is such a sensuous pleasure, the feel of the book in your hand and the smells and the sights it evokes, even the look of the print. I remember when I was little I used to read some series of girls' books, and midway through the series, they changed the typeface. And I was just devastated. I used to really *look* at that type. I liked the way the c's were formed and the o's.

Well, what about these sensuous pleasures now? This is definitely not Catholic. I mean, they should at least be guilty pleasures.

When I go into a bookstore, I get so excited I feel sick. Somebody who interviewed me once said maybe that's a form of Catholic guilt. I mean, here's all this pleasure at your fingertips and that wave of sickness that you feel is really guilt—you're going to have all this wonderful, sensuous experience. I knew a priest who had been a priest since he was a young man. He was elderly when I knew him and he had a stomach out to here. It's because we are all sensuous creatures. You have to take the pleasure some way, and if you don't have a sexual outlet, then you have eating. After all, Christ instituted the sacrament of the Holy Eucharist at the Last Supper. He chose that, he chose that setting for the Eucharist, of the feast. Feed the body as well as the soul. And reading does that. I mean reading is an incredible outlet for that; as you said, it's a sensuous outlet.

Oh yes, that's right. Reading itself is a form of sublimation of passion, I think, if you're a voracious reader.

And so is eating. People say now that there really is something in chocolate that makes people feel better mentally—some substance, I don't know what it's called. I don't want to know.

I do get a beatific feeling when I eat chocolate; I just love it. With chocolate in hand, I'm looking forward to reading Slow Poison.

Oh, well, it's very different from *Almost Innocent.* I wanted to get away from lyricism and description and poignancy. *Slow Poison* is what I think Vonnegut might call a "sad comedy." That is, it's funny but you can't laugh without crying, and it is sad but you can't cry without laughing.

Sounds like an effective way of dealing with suffering.

Dealing with suffering. A Catholic specialty.

5

Sandra Hollin Flowers

Something's Got a Hold on Me

Sandra Hollin Flowers was born in Yuma, Arizona, in 1947, the daughter of a homemaker and a mail carrier who was an active member of the NAACP and other community groups. Her grandfather on her father's side was a Pentecostal minister, but Flowers maintains that her family was not a "church-going" one. A significant event in her teen years changed the course of Flowers's life: in 1960, when she was fifteen, her family moved to a segregated neighborhood and were soon pressured to move out. The family was forced to split up. The children were sent to live with a Baptist minister in a neighboring town for a time until another home could be secured. That summer when she was literally homeless was a watershed for Flowers, who learned not only about the power of racial prejudice but about the value of religious faith by becoming a part of the church community of her host family.

In 1965, Flowers entered the University of Arizona and studied business administration but dropped out in her junior year. She moved to Atlanta, where she worked as a secretary. Ten years later in 1977, the divorced mother of a ten-year-old boy, she returned to the University of Arizona to finish her bachelor's degree. She changed her major to creative writing, graduated in 1979, and went on to earn her M.F.A. in creative writing from Arizona in 1981. Keeping a promise to her son, Eric, she moved them both back to Atlanta and enrolled in a Ph.D. program in African-American studies at Emory University, completing this degree in 1989 with a dissertation called "The Poetics of the Poetry, Drama, and Fiction Associated with Afro-American Nationalism, 1963–72."

During her graduate studies she served as director of the Writing Proficiency Program at Clark College (1983–87), director of the Communication Skills Center at Clark-Atlanta University (1988–90), and as the Brittain Fellow in Writing (1987–88) at the Georgia Institute of Technology. Publications include "Hope of Zion," selected for *Prize Stories 1981: The O. Henry Awards;* other short stories, including "I Heard the Doctor Speak," in *Breaking Ice: An Anthology of Contemporary African-American Fiction* edited by Terry McMillan (1990); and critical studies in *Studies in Short Fiction, Quest: A Feminist Quarterly, Contemporary Literary Criticism,* and others. Since 1990, Flowers has taught literature at Mercer University in Macon, Georgia.

Although she is not a native southerner, Flowers has made her home in Georgia nearly all of her adult life. She came to the South by choice as a young woman, she writes, "virtually penniless, without job, friends, or known family, having simply come as an expatriated descendent of slaves from the Carolinas and Alabama."

The evocative power of this southern heritage springs in significant ways from the region's religious legacy to her not only as an African-American but also as a woman. She writes: "I notice that the congregations of most of the churches I've attended in the South are predominantly female while the leadership is almost universally male. . . . I would add that what being a woman brings to my religious experience is the pain of being a black woman in America. Black women still labor under the culture's perception of themselves as tough and matriarchal . . . [and] inordinately sensual."

Along with painful cultural issues of gender and race, Flowers has grappled with reconciling serious fiction writing with her faith: "These days I want to get better acquainted with what some have called 'Christian writers'— C. S. Lewis and Flannery O'Connor, for example, and take a look at how they may have reconciled their personal, religious values and their professional, aesthetic values without losing anything artistically. . . . I am beginning to understand that I serve God through my writing. . . . My writing is a natural outgrowth of my life as a Christian."

Flowers attributes her survival and strength as a black woman against overwhelming societal odds to prayer and the power of the Holy Spirit.

Although still in the process of understanding and appeciating her heritage in the black church as an institution, she recognizes one of its livelier aspects, gospel music, as having been for her a powerful means of experiencing the sacred: "Through music we have a direct experience with the holy. I had always gotten more out of the music in church than from any sermon." †

Hope of Zion

Each year when Veronica returned for Hope of Zion's home-coming, she entered the church with a fervent prayer that something would have changed. Perhaps there would be new stained-glass contact paper on the windows, new offering and attendance banners, a different version of the Last Supper emblazoned on the wall behind the pulpit. And each year the prayer went unanswered.

This year, however, the change was in her, for today marked the last time she would make the eight-hundred-mile trip for home-coming. During the last six years she had resented her father's unarticulated assumption that she would be there. And as she approached the crooked, whitewashed building she felt good knowing that as her father beamed on her from the pulpit he'd have no idea that she'd made up her mind never to suffer through another of his meaningless, meandering sermons. Sermons (if they could be called that) of no use to any but Zion's dead and dying.

Let the dead bury their dead; but as for me and my house . . . Ah, she was mixing testaments again in the fashion of her father. Because she was embarrassed about being a bit late, she accepted, along with a program and an offering envelope, an extra hug in the fleshy arms and deep bosom of the head usher. "Hugging Sister Thorpe" she was called, her meaty arms always so extremely ready to enfold some body. Veronica had permitted these embraces more graciously as the years passed; and now, approaching her twenty ninth birthday, she was more charitable than Hope of Zion had ever seen her. She pulled away from Sister Thorpe and tiptoed respectfully to her seat, third bench, left row, under the window.

Hope of Zion's lemon-oil-shined benches creaked under the unaccustomed weight of a full house. Unless sick or out of town, the faithful came every Sunday. The others, by far the majority, came on Christmas, Easter, Mother's Day and during hard times. And those, like Veronica, whose out-of-town addresses proclaimed them truly lost sheep, came for home-coming, the Sunday of Thanksgiving weekend.

In childhood Veronica had often spied on her father, the Reverend Douglas Fairfax, as he prepared and practiced his sermons. She remembered, with some anguish and embarrassment, how he would pore over his Bibles and clergyman's periodicals, searching for those certain passages that would make Mother's Day and home-coming messages meaningful to somebody's mother. And how those mothers worshiped him for it! Outside after service they led their grown, God-strange children by the sleeve: "You remember my little Eugene (or Melvina or what-have-you), don't you, Rev?" Written all over the mother's face and sometimes spilling from her mouth: "Bless my baby—just say one word to keep him on the path." Written all over the baby's face: "Damn, I sure could use a smoke."

The deacons, rising at the end of passionate prayers delivered into dry, ashy hands, brought Veronica back to the service. Immediately a sharp *ding!* from the silver offering bell signaled the ushers to admit the latecomers. While these filed in, a saint in the front row began a garbled wail:

"*BeforethistimetomorrowImaybeonmywaytoglory . . .*"

And the congregation, dissecting the dirge, drew each word out to its infinite possibilities, achieving harmony and logic without trying. Furtive glances were cast over perfumed and furred shoulders. Who was coming in; what were they wearing?

Latecomers seated, the choir halt-stepped up the center aisle, resplendent in red and gold.

"*The Lord is blessing me*
Right now — oh, yes, he is!"

When they reached the altar Veronica's father also blessed them, simultaneously bringing the congregation to their feet with a majestic sweep of black-robed arms. He prayed for all those who had got out of their beds this morning to come to the House of the Lord and for all those who had otherwise been summoned to the House. He blessed the comings and goings of all people everywhere; and he invoked a particular blessing for the sick and the shut-in. With a last blessing he released the choir, who marched on, singing, into the choir stand.

"He woke me up this mor-aning . . ."

Rev. Fairfax knew the song to be one of Veronica's favorites. Had he asked the choir to sing it? she wondered uneasily. He might do that, she suspected, to make her feel remorseful and penitent about what he called the sin-filled life she led in Los Angeles. She craned her neck to get a look at him on the other side of the pulpit. His eyes were cast upward and he appeared lost in the ecstasy of the music.

Within a few minutes it was time for the first offering. The choir slipped smoothly into a soothing, lulling melody about the joys of giving. By the infrequency with which silver could be heard clinking against copper, Veronica judged the offering to be a generous one. Still blessing and praising, Rev. Fairfax approached the pulpit again.

"Our lesson this morning," he said, "comes from Luke fifteen. You know the story—hear me, Church. Say, 'There was a man who had two sons; and the younger of them said to his father, "Father give me the share of property that falls to me." And he divided his living between them. Not many days later, the younger son gathered all he had and took his journey into a far country, and there he squandered his property in loose living. And when he had spent everything, a great famine arose in that country, and he began to be in want.' "

Rev. Fairfax finished in a precise, low voice, slowing the words as though hypnotizing a reluctant subject. He paused and ceremoniously closed the Bible, fixing his stare on the door in the manner of one awaiting a long desired visitor. The pianist tinkled some forlorn notes, which the choir picked up and turned into a mournful humming. The humming had a shape, the shape a song whose words need not be articulated, for everyone knew them.

"Coming home," they hummed, *"coming home, Lord, I'm coming home. . . ."*

Veronica refused to hum with the others, though she could not keep the words from tumbling through her mind as the song moved inexorably on. If they had stopped humming in mid-chorus, she would have been forced to finish out the song in her head; and this, she knew, was what was expected of her, what she had been conditioned for. "Train up a child," her father loved to quote to the despairing parents of his congregation, "in the way he should go, and when he is old he will not depart from it." Recalling the many times she had heard him issue that advice, Veronica tried to reason herself out of feeling that she had betrayed him, had even—she winced at the thought—betrayed God.

Rev. Fairfax was proceeding with his message, summarizing the parable and its happy ending. His voice, patient, compelling, was just as it had been the day Veronica told him she'd signed a contract as a back-up singer with a blues artist. But the note of desperation it had held then was missing now. This morning's listeners, hearing him that day, would not have believed him to be their pastor, God's voice with a ready, unvarying answer to every earthly problem. He had been objective at first, talking about the harshness of life in a big city. She answered all his arguments—she had a place to stay, a roommate waiting for her, a job, some savings to keep her going until her first check. Switching tactics, he had asked her what she knew about the life of "show people." She countered by asking where his faith was in his "train up a child" motto.

"I have built this church for you," he'd finally said in exasperation. "From a prayer circle of six souls to what it is today."

"And what is it?" she had asked. "A raggedy, patched-up hut I'd be ashamed to have strangers step into."

"Then you would be like Peter. But remember what the Lord said on the Mount: 'No man can serve two masters; for either he will hate the one and love the other, or he will be devoted to the one and despise the other. You cannot serve God and Mammon.'"

"Well, suppose I don't want to serve God?"

"What are you saying?" he had cried, throwing his hands over his ears. "Take it back right now, lest the anger of the Lord be kindled against you and he destroy you—"

"—from off the face of the earth," she interrupted, finishing the Scripture. "For God's sake, Daddy! You walk the paths of righteousness like a policeman on patrol. I don't want to do all that. I want to live before I die into your kind of eternal life."

"Veronica! You are blaspheming, you are dishonoring your father—"

"I know that!"

"Well, God protect and forgive you."

"But you drove me to it!" she shouted.

"Then God protect and forgive me," he said, slumping into his chair.

No, his congregation wouldn't have recognized him, she thought now, watching him pace himself through his sermon. She glanced at her watch, surprised that nearly ten minutes were past and he had not yet launched into the singsong harangue that all except her accepted as the Lord working through him for their souls' salvation. Today he was calm and delivered the message his text had promised.

"How many of us," he was saying, "would accept the return of the prodigal, or—and this is the real test—reward it? I hear what you thinking! 'What's that you say Rev—reward the ungrateful spendthrift, reward a disobedient child for being a fool?' Say, 'That was all right in the Bible days when there was plenty to go around, but things pretty tight now.'"

"All right!" Hugging Sister Thorpe said with a short, rhythmic handclap.

"Well, sir," Rev. Fairfax continued, "go on and call your own child a fool; that's between you and the Lord. But while you acting contrarywise and refusing to reward your prodigal, remember that you have been told to 'answer not a fool according to his folly, lest you be like him yourself.' Proverbs twenty-six: four!"

"Amen!" and "Say on!" rang out among the younger worshipers while the elders offered a tentative, low-pitched "Well-l-l. . . ."

Veronica stared at her father questioningly. He avoided looking toward the row where she sat. She remembered his letters from the first few months after she'd left home, full of blistering pain couched in the guise of Biblical wisdom. He'd done everything short of opening his letters with "Dear Fool."

"The wise of heart will heed commandments," he had written once, "but a prating fool will come to ruin." That had been in response to someone's showing him an article in a rock magazine in which Veronica had given advice to youngsters who wanted to be back-up singers. Her few words, she felt, hardly deserved his accusation that she had switched from winning souls for the Lord to winning them for the devil. After trying unsuccessfully to pray over the question, she'd finally written back that she didn't see it his way. Immediately he responded that "the way of a fool is right in *her* own eyes, but a wise *woman* listens to advice." She began to dread his letters, letting them go unopened for days at a time.

And now he was saying it in public. Or was he? she wondered as he continued. "And you remember, don't you, children, that the prodigal, after wasting his inheritance, said to his father, 'I am no longer worthy to be called your son.' What ought we to do with a child who is not worthy, people? What would Jesus do—what would be his answer? Search your hearts, Church, and if the answer's not in there—search your Bibles!"

The "amens" got louder, the "wells" got longer, the old sisters in the saints' corner started tambourining their sturdy black shoes against the floorboards. Veronica grew uneasier. Her father was preaching as though to her, as though he had guessed her intention of never coming home again. She could almost believe that he did know, for he often had visions. When she'd been involved with the church, she too sometimes had had visions. Not clear, graphic ones like her father's, but distorted puzzles that he would help her rearrange and interpret like dreams. These days, though, she had nothing that could even pass for a vision. A sign of her weakened faith, she assumed, feeling a sense of loss and regret.

Shifting restlessly on the bench, she became annoyed. In Los Angeles such thoughts never occurred to her, but here there was no escape from them. Even the Fairfax home, which she had helped decorate years and years ago, seemed like an accusation: ceramic praying hands, crosses, pictures of Jesus with little shaded light bulbs over or under them. "Bless This House" and other prayers hanging from all the walls, in doorways, plastered under the glass of tables. Everywhere she turned she felt fingers pointing at her—backslider, backslider, they accused. Those that weren't pointing were beckoning her to come back to the fold.

Last month she had called to wish her father happy birthday, having forgotten, as usual, to send him a card. By this time, they had reestablished enough rapport for him to tease her about her forgetfulness.

"But," he had said, "with me going on seventy, you won't have to be bothered with remembering too much longer."

He'd said it lightly enough, but the point was, he *had* said it. Rev. Fairfax had been widowed when Veronica was only ten, and since that time he had used his age as a sort of cold-war weapon whenever she showed signs of growing away from him. Born late into an until-then-childless marriage, Veronica had no one to share the burden with. She might have borne it well enough except that when she became a teen-ager, her father had begun sounding her out on the question of going into the ministry and carrying on Hope of Zion.

And the birthday call revealed that he'd not given up the idea, even with her having been away from home six years.

"I just don't want you to lose sight of what's here for you," he'd said. "I had my will done over yesterday—do that every year just before my birthday, you know. There's a lot here for you, baby—a lot more than you know."

"I'm sure you're right, Daddy, but at this point I just can't see coming back there."

"You might look at the church," he continued as though she hadn't spoken, "and think it's not much to whoop and holler about. But the land—now, the land is worth something. Why, you could tear the old building down and put up a new one—"

"Daddy—"

"—or leave the old one standing so you'd have some place to worship while you built a new sanctuary alongside it."

"Why won't you understand that my sanctuary is in Los Angeles?"

"Some young man?" he asked.

"That's not what I meant."

"Are you going to church?"

"Sometimes." It wasn't a full-fledged lie. Wasn't she always there at Hope of Zion's home-coming?

He said nothing for a moment. Obviously he was coming to some realization, for his voice was tired, discouraged, as they

finished the conversation. She imagined the lines deepening in his
face, felt his spirits declining with each sentence. Guiltily she hung
up as soon as she decently could, resolved to quit holding out false
hope to him by returning to the church once a year like an absentee
landlord. . . .

Rev. Fairfax had concluded his sermon and was basking in the
warmth that even Veronica could feel flowing through the congregation. What she had heard of his message had moved her, which
she found surprising, for she long ago had stopped listening to his sermons, once she discovered that he never really *said* anything. His idea
of preaching was to recite scriptures, call down blessings and remi-
nisce over wraths that Job and Noah and the rest had suffered—as
if he'd been right there by their side. All this was accompanied by
shouts and posturings and frequent dabbing of his forehead with a
neatly pressed handkerchief that doubled as a bookmark for his Bible.

Today, though, he had talked, had made himself accessible to the
congregation, as though admitting he had no advantage over them,
had had no secret meetings with God, or at least not any that they
themselves couldn't bring about. She felt kindly toward him for
making her last Hope of Zion service something worth remembering.

"Rev preached this morning, didn't he?" she heard one of the
missionaries behind her whisper.

"Did," another answered. "But it was right strange, wasn't it?
Nobody even got happy!"

Veronica rolled her eyes. Got happy! That was another thing
that she had not missed about Hope of Zion—frenzied shouting
and jerking that sometimes erupted into wild dancing and diving
over benches. They would do that, some of the older women, when
her father howled at them and when he was, as Veronica saw it, at
the height of not making sense. It seemed to worry her father that
she was apparently untouched by the spirit of the Lord during services, for he occasionally asked her if she ever felt anything at
church. "Sometimes," she had admitted. But she didn't tell him
that what she felt came from the music, not the preaching.

It was a strange feeling, and it made her so uncomfortable that
she'd physically restrain herself to keep it from overpowering her.
During these times she diverted herself by intellectualizing what
was going on. An emotional overload, probably a tired body, a word

or a chord that struck a charged nerve and set off an excess of adrenaline and ended in a physical reaction. And that, sisters, she mentally said to the missionaries, is all there is to getting happy.

Remembering the many times she had reasoned this out, Veronica smiled and felt the tension ease from her body. Surely God would find a subtler, more private way to touch her if He felt the need. She trusted His wisdom on this point; He knew what she needed. Hadn't He just led her father to a complete forgiveness and release of her? For thinking back on it, she felt sure now that that had been the meaning of his sermon. Pleased, she settled herself more comfortably, admiring the smoothness of her father's altar-call technique. One more offering, the benediction, and her last Hope of Zion service would be over.

Suddenly, as she was sometimes apt to do, as though overcome with the power of being able to make music—suddenly the pianist went wild. She pounded out a refrain on the bass keys, shouting as she played. Hugging Sister Thorpe gave one mighty yelp from the back of the church and Veronica heard what sounded like heavily clad feet running up the back of a bench. By this time, the choir and some of the congregation had started clapping and rocking to the music. Then, having gone from one end of the keyboard to the other, the pianist worked her way back to the choir's key and played a few bars of introduction. Eagerly the choir sang:

"*Something*
   got a hold — got a hold
   on me;
Oh, yes it did, right now!
Something . . ."

In seconds the whole church was afire, singing and clapping and shouting as Veronica had never known it. Her father was on his feet again, singing joyously, a radiant smile on his face as he directed the choir, the deacons, anybody who would look at him. Veronica knew the song; it was a favorite at Hope of Zion. But had she ever heard it sung with so much—what? So much urgency?

My God! she thought, looking around, feeling genuinely frightened, as though waking up to find herself in a place she'd never been. Have they gone crazy? The church sang as though the song would be taken from them any minute:

"I went to the meeting last night,
and my heart was not right —
ooooh — "

Veronica felt her knees knocking together. Her hands grew cold and clammy; the blood pounded in her head. They were drawing her into it; she was getting happy, she realized. And with that knowledge she remembered something her father had told her long ago: *If you ever get happy just once, baby, you will be the Lord's from then on!*

"No!" she cried into the shouting and singing. She pressed her thighs together; interlaced her fingers tightly; clenched her teeth, which had started to chatter. She gripped the edge of the bench, but the trembling and pulsating, the itching in her hands, the chills and the urge to weep, of all things, wouldn't go away.

The pianist hit the bass keys again, coming halfway up the scale, and broke into a new, faster rhythm as she went into the bridge. The hand clapping switched effortlessly to double time.

"*It was the Holy Ghost*," the choir sang; "*. . . Holy Ghost*," the congregation answered. Veronica saw her father lean across the pulpit rail, his hands outstretched to her. "Jesus will make a way!" she heard him shout. She shook her head, "Oh, yes!" he insisted.

"*The Holy Ghost*," the choir chanted; "*. . . Holy Ghost*," the church responded. Rev. Fairfax clapped his hands fiercely and shouted, "Thy will be done!" And the choir began prancing and shouting.

"*It made me walk right —*
  Holy Ghost!
Talk right —
  Holy Ghost!"

As though thrust from the bench, Veronica sprang up, her fists clenched, arms waving stiffly in the air, head thrown back and mouth stretched open in a silent scream of horrified joy. †

Interview

Sandra Hollin Flowers's rich, soft voice and musical laugh invite you to talk with her about matters both spiritual and temporal in a language and vocabulary not often used in this secular society. When we first began to talk with one another, Flowers spoke with candor and quiet conviction about the Holy Spirit and His transformation of her life. At issue is nothing less than life or death; Flowers takes as a sacred trust the knowledge that all human endeavor must be directed toward loving and serving God with the will of the Holy Spirit as it acts in individual lives. In the past few years she has been seeking to reconcile the tenets of academic scholarship she holds with the will of the Holy Spirit for her life as revealed in scriptures and through prayer. She speaks slowly and thoughtfully; the letter she wrote to me expanding on questions I'd asked her was both scholarly and impassioned, reasoned and personal. It is as if she lives at the crux of a tension between faith and reason, feeling and abstraction, that forms the core values of her life as a teacher, writer, and religious woman.

It is indicative of her lack of self-preoccupation or vanity that Flowers had no pictures of herself on hand when I asked her to send me a photo of herself; she had to ask someone to take a couple of Polaroids. She is a tall, attractive woman with honey-brown skin, gracefully arching brows, and a slightly mischievous smile that says, "I know." Sitting behind her desk in her office at the college, reading glasses on top of a stack of student papers, she is looking up at the photographer with an expression that suggests a blend of seriousness, forbearance toward even her more callow students, and an uncanny ability to see right through you—I would like to be one of her "A" students coming for a conference, but would dread having to explain why I'd cut class.

Though Flowers has fought great battles in her life against the evils of sexism and racism, she does not complain; she speaks softly but without equivocation about the suffering that black people, especially black women, have endured in this society. She wrote me: "As I think about the truly 'strong' black women I know as compared to those who are merely tough or resilient or resourceful, I make the distinction on Biblical grounds: 'The Lord is close to the brokenhearted and saves those who are crushed in spirit' (Ps 34:18 NIV). What black women have endured in this nation from every quarter—and endure even today, everyday—is enough to break anyone's heart and crush even the supposedly indomitable spirit."

Flowers possesses an earnestness that suggests how seriously she takes the dilemmas she confronts concerning her faith, her teaching, and her fiction writing. She wonders if fiction writing is compatible with her life of faith. Is it possible to write good fiction and be a true Christian? Or is fiction, in its fundamental assumptions, antithetical to the life in the Spirit?

Underlying her quiet explorations of these questions and her introspection concerning her past and future as a fiction writer is an unusual openness to the possibility of mystery beyond rational understanding. From these deeper wellsprings of intuition and feeling comes her love of music of all kinds, especially gospel. Her voice became lighter, more energized when I asked her about different forms of gospel, what she liked about each of them: Sandra Hollin Flowers is attuned to the power of music to reach, heal, and transform the soul of the listener "where nothing else can."

Let's start with where you are today in your teaching and writing. You are now teaching at Mercer University. Do you find that your world view and teaching philosophy are compatible with that of the university as a whole?

Yes and no. In my composition courses, for example, I used to discourage my students from writing about religious themes. Often, when inexperienced writers attempt to tackle religious themes, they fall into "witnessing" for their own beliefs. That kind of composition, as you can imagine, is very difficult to grade. I wanted my students to learn how to do so-called "academic" writing—to develop logical arguments systematically. Yet, grading according to the conventions of argumentation seemed to me inevitably to constitute an attack on my students' faith. This was quite a dilemma for me. It began to seem as if the principles I'd learned to cherish as an academic were in direct conflict with those I've come to cherish in my faith. Then I read a wonderful book about Christian scholarship. It's called *Loving God With All Your Mind: How to Survive and Prosper as a Christian in the Secular University and Post-Christian Culture.* It has been most helpful to me in my efforts to help students, especially Christian students, reconcile their academic training in logic and scholarship with their faith and beliefs. Now I feel much freer in my approach, in what I teach my students, in how I interact with them. Now, I don't want them to shy away from a moral stance; in fact, I want them, if they feel this way, to take a strong stand against prevailing norms. Christian students are often intimidated or even harrassed for expressing their beliefs in the university setting.

Even at Mercer, an avowedly Baptist university?

Yes, I know because I, for one, harrassed them with my policy. I think a better approach is to teach them how to apply biblical perspectives to their academic learning. *Loving God With All Your Mind* enlightened me on the biblical tradition's place in the academic enterprise. The book's argument that knowledge and intellectual ability are from God was especially helpful to me.

Has this process of reconciliation of the religious with the scholarly perspectives — if that's an accurate way to term it — affected your approach to fiction writing?

That's a good question. I am still in the throes of deciding what to do about my fiction. I have not been able to write much in the past few years in part because of this dilemma. How can I write good fiction and be a true Christian? These days, I want to get better acquainted with what some have called "Christian writers" — C.S. Lewis and Flannery O'Connor, for example — and take a look at how they may have reconciled their personal, religious values and their professional, aesthetic values without losing anything artistically. After all is said and done (or read), however, I know that I want to direct my life and my work to Christ. I want to see just how my writing and my teaching—my work—can be directed this way.

How do you think your early religious upbringing or experiences are figuring into your struggle with faith and reason now?

Surprisingly enough, I didn't grow up with a good grounding or education in church. My brothers and I went to church, but we didn't get a solid grounding in scripture; I didn't get what I call a good Christian education. My church, a small-town Baptist church, was very similar to the one I describe in "Hope of Zion." We knew the term "Holy Ghost" and elderly women often "got the Holy Ghost" on Sundays, but I can't remember anyone actually teaching or explaining about the Holy Ghost. To show you how mysterious the concept was to me, I grew up thinking that the Holy Ghost was a thing, not a person. As such, "it" was akin to those things my paternal grandmother used to scare us with in late-night ghost-story-telling sessions. It was full of those who were "professing," not "practicing." I believe neither they, nor I at the time, knew the Holy Ghost.

Did your fiction writing as a young woman figure in to your search for knowledge of the Spirit?

Not really, because at the time I didn't know enough about the Spirit to be searching for Him. I wrote "Hope of Zion" in response to James Baldwin's *Go Tell It on the Mountain.* His story, it seemed to me, didn't ring true. Baldwin, I thought, was too distanced from the subject. I wanted to see what a character feels who actually experiences the Holy Ghost. And, as I have said before, it is through music that this so often happens. Through music we have a direct experience with the holy. Music is the medium. When I wrote "Hope of Zion," I was playing gospel music in the background—The Voices of Faith Choir, I believe it was, and James Cleveland's "Something's Got a Hold on Me." That song was so completely convincing that, in a sense, you could say my story was structured around that song. And yet, it's also an autobiographical story.

Tell me more about that. Where did you grow up?

I was born in Yuma, Arizona. My mother was Baptist, and my father was Pentecostal. He was a mail carrier and he was quite socially committed—an active member of the NAACP, the PTA, and so on, but he was not a churchgoing man. My grandfather, his father, was a Pentecostal minister. An uncle, my mother's brother, was a Baptist minister during my adolescence.

It sounds like an interesting combination of community involvment and a heritage of religious faith from both your mother and your father.

I suppose my parents did have a heritage of faith, but since we were not a churchgoing family, I didn't grow up with that heritage realized. However, in 1960 we moved into a segregated neighborhood. You see, the neighborhood where we lived was not really integrated. We were the only blacks in a lower-middle-class all-white neighborhood, and the neighbors drove us out through some kind of manipulation of the sale—probably pressure on the previous owners of the house. I'm not sure of the details.

We were literally homeless. My parents went to live with a local Baptist minister. The children, my two brothers and I, went to live with another Baptist minister in Yuma, a few miles away.

Your family was split up?

Yes, for a time. After that summer of 1960, since I was living in the home of a Baptist minister, I became a regular churchgoer. I went throughout high school (but stopped for a while in college) and was baptized at age twenty-two.

You must have felt alienated during that time, justifiably so.

Yes, but I always had a sense of God in the background. My relationship with Him consisted, more than anything else, of my petitioning and grieving—asking Him for help, for understanding, crying out in grief. But my father found another home for us by the end of the summer—this one was in a white neighborhood, too— and we were reunited. But it was to be for only a relatively short time. My father died five years later, in 1965, when I was nineteen.

What a terrible time. Were you able to continue with your schooling?

Yes, somehow my mother found money for my tuition and expenses.

How did you become interested in writing fiction?

I wanted to major in literature, in creative writing, simply because I loved reading. I had taken a correspondence course through the magazine, *The Writer's Digest,* and that had piqued my interest greatly. I'd dropped out of the University of Arizona in my junior year and moved to Atlanta. In 1977, as a thirty-year-old, divorced mother of a ten-year-old son, Eric, I returned to Arizona—the scene of my academic crimes ten years earlier—to get my degree. My reasons were partly vocational (I couldn't move permanently out of the secretarial field which had always been my livelihood, without a degree); partly atoning (I had let my family down by dropping out); and partly psychological (I needed to bring closure to that unhappy and unfulfilled period of my life in order to look forward to the future). Once I resumed my undergrad work with a new major—creative writing instead of business—I made close friendships with several of my teachers. They inspired me to consider a career in college teaching. So, when I finished my B.A. in 1979 and M.F.A. in 1980, I kept a promise to Eric and moved us back to Atlanta. There, I enrolled in a Ph.D. program at Emory University. I finished my Ph.D. in 1989.

When did you start teaching?

I started teaching full-time at Mercer in 1990. In the meantime, the combination of working and going to school—both full-time— took me further from writing. My son is now grown. He graduated from West Point in 1990 and is serving with the 82d Airborne at Fort Bragg. He's a wonderful person and a cherished part of my life. I'll always be grateful to him for his love and constancy.

You must be very proud of him. No wonder you haven't been able to write as much as you'd like. Earning a Ph.D., working full-time, raising a child as a single parent.

Working became all about surviving. Maybe because of that outlook, I found that there was nothing I cared enough about to write about meaningfully.

Now that things have settled down a bit, have you begun working on something new?

Yes, it's coming. A couple of years ago, I started a novel called *I Heard A Crazy Woman Speak*. It's a retrospective look at the 1960s, a period which left the narrator psychologically unsettled. It was a way of resolving some issues for me. But Christianity has resolved those issues so resolutely that I don't think I'm going to be able (or need) to finish the novel. It seems to speak to me to have something meaningful to say. I learned something I'll never forget at the M.F.A. program at Arizona. The teachers in the M.F.A. program were all truly excellent (Arizona was then often called "West Iowa"). They taught me all about craft, meaning, and the significance of a story. They taught me that the purpose of a story is to illuminate meaning.

Other stories you have written?

The only other published one is "Awakening in Arizona," in *Redbook*, October 1980.

Tell me about "Hope of Zion," how it came about, what it has meant to you.

I wrote the story when I was finishing my undergraduate program at Arizona. The whole story sort of fell out of the blue. It was truly a gift. And lo and behold, it won the O. Henry Award. I was taken aback. What was this award? I went to the library to find out. I was absolutely stunned. I felt compelled to write to that standard again, but also frightened. The main character, Veronica Fairfax, is the daughter of the Reverend Fairfax, minister of Hope of Zion Baptist Church. She turned out to be one of twelve characters whose stories comprised my master's thesis. I compare the thesis to a kaleidoscope; it is a collection of black women's experiences in this culture. I see it, now, too, as a way of looking at how the Holy Spirit works. It is just *there*. Always.

Did any short story writers influence you in particular while you were at Arizona?

Not consciously, though I do remember studying Flannery O'Connor, especially *Mystery and Manners*. It seems to me now when I look at O'Connor that she was making deliberate attempts to bring the truths she saw to her fiction. But at the same time, she was focusing entirely on character. I must take a character and follow her. I never write from an outline or preconceived notion of what I want to convey. I also was struck by an idea that seemed to capture O'Connor's imagination as well, and that is, once you are in touch with God, once He speaks to you, there is no escape.

In that sense, it can be said that Veronica's experience might be compared to that of Hazel Motes in Wise Blood.

Veronica wanted to pursue a singing career, a secular singing career as a blues artist. As the story opens, she is a backup singer in a blues band in Los Angeles. This was part and parcel of the generalized struggle going on in her life. Her father had taught her that she could not serve two masters. She could not serve God and serve the world. She was in a very real struggle. She was feeling the guilt. The conflict was that one kind of work, one kind of singing, glorifies the world, the other kind glorifies God. The story ends by her being sought out, captured by the Holy Spirit.

You mentioned earlier that this story was autobiographical. To what extent is Veronica's experience like yours?

I wrote it twelve years ago, but now it strikes me as being prophetic. I have been struggling with the same choices in my own art, my writing, for the last ten years without understanding actually what the struggle was.

Is this what you meant when you said you could not find for a long time any subject that was meaningful enough for you to write about?

Yes. While I was pursuing my degrees, I read widely. My teachers at Arizona exposed me to all kinds of literature, and my studies at Emory led me to the realm of political thought. And then there was all the critical theory that went along with the disciplines and all the pedagogical studies (teaching concepts and theories) that I had to read to do my job as a writing-across-the-curriculum director in Atlanta. Whatever I was studying, that's what I was most interested in at the time, what I was most committed to. But that was the problem: everything was "interesting" but nothing was "me." Everything seemed equally important—the literary, the political, the pedagogical. Some people have managed to combine all three into a workable career—feminist literary critics, for example. But, again, that wasn't me. In fact, the more I studied, the more cynical and disinterested I found myself becoming. What did it all mean? What did it all matter? What was really worth doing? This sense of being intellectually lost made it really hard for me to finish my doctoral program, and for a couple of years in the mid-eighties, I just floundered in the morass of all I'd been exposed to. I survived that, but in the process I completely lost touch with my writing—and, though I didn't know it at the time, with my faith as well. Toward the end of 1991, it became clear to me that I had lost both my passion for writing and my understanding of faith. It never was especially orthodox, in any case, but I would give myself daily meditations, and readings of affirmations. Last year, though, I found myself more and more unable to find spiritual comfort in this practice. I felt more and more distant from God, more and more purposeless and directionless. Feeling bereft, I prayed to have my faith restored. For several months, things seemed to get worse. Then, I had an unforgettable experience this past summer—in the end, God gave me my faith—on terms similar to Veronica's. I had to make a choice. He said, "You must live for Me, or for the world."

Did the choice involve a sacrifice, as it seemed to for Veronica?

For a time, it seemed as if it would. It seemed that my life would be circumscribed, that God would overshadow my individual freedom. Veronica had charged her father with "walking the paths of righteousness like a policeman on patrol." Would my life be just like Veronica's vision of things? Must I give up being a writer? If I insist on writing, must I consign myself to being a "Christian writer"—which I thought at one time meant being a part of a sub-sub-genre, doomed to obscurity and mediocrity?

I also grappled very seriously with the question of whether I had committed the unpardonable sin of blasphemy in "Hope of Zion." The possibility alarmed me. I have come to understand that I did not because if one has repentance or remorse for something which seems to deny the Holy Spirit, then that presupposes that the person believes in Him.

"I Heard the Doctor Speak" is a wonderful story that seems to have no overt religious intent; it does seem to have an intent of poking fun at patriarchal institutions such as psychiatry, law enforcement, marriage, with its satire pointing to a larger truth.

In the late seventies, when I wrote that story, I was a very strong feminist. I am today still quite sympathetic with struggles women face in our culture, especially black women. "I Heard the Doctor Speak" is reflective of that, I think.

Let's go back to the idea of sacrifice in talking about faith and fiction writing.

Well, yes—I'm beginning to believe that it isn't necessary to sacrifice one for the other. Nor to sacrifice my self. My transformation has simply involved a crystallization of the conflict between my faith and fiction writing. But I am beginning to understand that I serve God through my writing. I do my scholarly research and my fiction writing as part of living from the perspective of being a Christian. My writing is a natural outgrowth of my life as a Christian. I have a feeling of excitement. It's a wonderful feeling; life is full of prospects. "Getting happy," as Veronica did in "Hope of Zion" is something I've never experienced. But when I regained my faith, it was very much a sense of "horrified joy." I felt completely overwhelmed. It was a sense of "this is wonderful—but what must I do now?"

A powerful element in "Hope of Zion" is the power of music to reach Veronica when nothing else would. Would you tell me more about the role of music in your life and belief?

Oh, yes. I had always gotten more out of the music in church than from any sermon. That is a great tribute to the musicians and what they have done in my life. In the churches I grew up in, there was truly a ministry of music, though I didn't understand it as such at the time. But that's what it was for me—it was a continual revealing of the Holy Spirit through music.

What kinds of songs, music, do you remember hearing in the churches you grew up in? Titles? Generally, how was music incorporated into the worship?

The service always opened with a devotional period—the deacons praying and "lining out" unaccompanied lyrics, usually mournful ones about dying or how hard life was. The only ones of these I liked and remember the names of were "Amazing Grace" and "Guide Me, O Thou Great Jehovah." Not many people came to the devotional. It was as though the service didn't really start until the choir marched in singing something like "The Lord Is Blessing Me." There'd be a prayer from the preacher, some announcements, and a collection, during which the choir would sing again in the background with anyone free to join in. Then, the choir would sing a couple of songs before the sermon. Some of the songs I grew up hearing were "Highway to Heaven," "I Had a Talk With God," "Higher Ground," "Must Jesus Bear the Cross Alone," "Walk Around Heaven All Day," Every Time I Feel the Spirit," "Just a Closer Walk With Thee," "In the Garden," "What a Fellowship," and "Something's Got a Hold on Me." Then during the altar call, the choir would sing something like "Coming Home." The service usually closed with "Blest Be the Tie That Binds" or "God Be With You Till We Meet Again." I remember those songs, but not one sermon, not one message from the pulpit, not one lesson that elucidated rather than just reiterated scripture. For me, as for Veronica, music was the medium.

Do you enjoy playing music yourself?

I wish I could sing. I'm not a musician, though I've owned a couple of pianos and taught myself to play. But I have a passion for music, for listening, and hearing all that music can give you. I'm crazy

about traditional gospel music and I've quite a collection. Music has
been at the heart of my transformation these past few months.

*I recently attended Sister Shirley Caesar's Gospel Convention,
and there I heard music by the West Los Angeles Church of God in
Christ Mass Choir. One of their albums is called "Saints in Praise."
Do you know anything about them?*

Yes, I know that choir. They do a combination of gospel and
"praise and worship" music. I generally like old-time gospel more
than praise and worship music, although I get the impression that
praise and worship is supposed to be or is considered a higher form
of sacred music.

*What is praise and worship music? How is it different from tra-
ditional gospel?*

It is a relatively new form, available in instrumental or vocal for-
mat. Some soloists and churches use taped instrumental of the
genre in place of on-site musicians, a feature which completely
represses the opportunity for spontaneity or personalizing the
music in my view. The lyrics focus on God instead of the believer.
Many lyrics are drawn from the Psalms. Traditional gospel is more
believer-centered, with an emphasis on the individual's direct relationship to and experience of God, though it, too, can have a praise
orientation. It can touch the listener where nothing else can.

And I am still receiving the power, sorting things out. This
process, this struggle only has to do with the quality and meaning
of the rest of my life.

Sandra Hollin Flowers and I completed our interview in late October. In
November 1992, I sent her a transcript of our interview accompanied by a
letter in which I asked her specifically about her views on the role religion
has played in African-American life, especially among African-American
women, and about her particular identification with southern culture and
heritage.

I've lived in the South only since 1972, so my entire southern experience has been of the New South. And it wasn't until I had lived
here about ten years (interrupted by a four-year return to Arizona)
that I developed any sense of an identity with the South. Too, that

identity is based more on my empathy with my slave ancestors than on my own experiences of living in the South. So I certainly wouldn't regard myself as a southerner in the sense of women like Fannie Lou Hamer or Rosa Parks or Coretta Scott King or Flannery O'Connor or Eudora Welty. The South has not shaped my sensibilities, my world view, or my work as it did theirs; it has not taken from me or given to me what it took from or gave women such as these. Further, unlike native-born southerners, I am here by choice rather than circumstance. In fact I am here despite circumstances, having come to the South virtually penniless, without job, friends, or known family, having simply come as an expatriated descendent of slaves from the Carolinas and Alabama. Now, however, when I think about the fiction I want to write, the South and southern sensibilities are far more evocative and inviting to me than those of the West.

As far as your question about how religion (by which I assume you mean Christianity) informs the work of black women writers, I'm not sure that it does. Alice Walker dedicates *The Color Purple* "To the Spirit: Without whose assistance/ Neither this book nor I/ Would have been/ Written." But, despite the Dear God letters, I don't know how to read that dedication, how to interpret the Spirit, because after the text of the novel, she says, "I thank everybody in this book for coming. A.W., Author and medium." Similarly, although the canon of black women's fiction is not without religious references, for the most part the references are just that references and not central themes. A couple of exceptions which come to mind are Arthenia Bates's *The Deity Nodded* (which is about the rejection of Christianity) or Barbara Neeley's "Spilled Salt" (in which Christianity shares thematic significance with other issues). I certainly haven't read everything everybody's written, but I can think of more black male than female authors whose fiction explores religion and spirituality. Perhaps this phenomenon reflects the male dominance of the black (or any) church.

Turning back to your question about religion in the lives of southern black women in general, as an outsider I can't offer an authoritative answer. I notice that the congregations of most of the churches I've attended in the South are predominantly female while the leadership is almost universally male. I've seen very young women—teen-agers—get happy in church, and in professional settings I often hear women talk about church responsibilities. On the whole, it seems to me that religion is central to the lives of women who were raised in southern black churches. Especially the elderly women, the church mothers, the missionary boards and deaconesses.

To this supposition, I would add that what being a woman brings to *my* religious experience is the pain of being a black woman in America. Black women still labor under the culture's perception of themselves as tough and matriarchal and—far worse for the consequences it too frequently brings when acted out—inordinately sensual. The political and economic underpinnings are too familiar to need reiteration here.

However, as I think about the truly "strong" black women I know as compared to those who are merely tough or resilient or resourceful, I make the distinction on biblical grounds: "The Lord is close to the brokenhearted and saves those who are crushed in spirit" (Ps 34:18 NIV). What black women have endured in this nation from every quarter—and endure even today, every day—is enough to break anyone's heart and crush even the supposedly indomitable spirit. Those who pray and have an abiding faith become strong. Others manage to survive, but not without cost. People often describe me as strong. I don't see myself that way. At most I might be resilient. Even so, I say in all candor that I would not have survived much longer had I not turned to Christ and found in Him the fulfillment of the psalm's promise. In that sense, then, my identity as a black woman has become inseparable from my identity as a spiritual person.

But being a black person of either gender adds yet another dimension to religion. At the heart of this dimension is the heritage of the black church. I am still in the process of understanding and appreciating the black church tradition and don't consider myself qualified to offer critiques of it. There is, however, one aspect of that tradition on which I can speak confidently, and that is gospel music.

Nowadays there are so many strains of black gospel music that the term evokes any number of images. I'm not talking about variants such as urban hip-hop, sociology gospel, rap gospel, or what Yolanda Adams described as "songs where you can be talking about your husband or you can be talking about Jesus." I consider the heart of black gospel to be that which celebrates or appeals to God and Jesus and the Holy Spirit. It's the traditional strain that evolved from the style of soloists and small groups—Mahalia Jackson, Sam Cooke and the Soul Stirrers, Marion Williams, Rosetta Tharpe, the Clara Ward Singers, to name a few exemplars. Their contemporary heirs are people like Shirley Caesar and Dorothy Norwood and Albertina Walker. Simultaneous with the emergence of these women singers was the choral tradition shaped by choirs such as those which sang with the early James Cleveland. That tradition survives in some of today's community choirs, state choirs, and congregational and mass choirs under the leadership of their own pastors. In any analysis of black spirituality, I would say that the spectrum of gospel music is a vital part of what makes black spirituality so rich and intense.

In general, then, being black colors (no pun intended) my religious experience profoundly. Early black Christianity made much of the parallel between African American slaves and the children of Israel in bondage in Egypt (hence the spiritual, "Let My People Go," for instance). For me there is an equally powerful parallel between the Roman persecution of Christians in the first and second centuries and the development of the Jim Crow South of Reconstruction at the turn of this century. That parallel gives me yet another level of identification with the South. †

6

WILL CAMPBELL

Mississippi Madness, Mississippi Magic

Will Davis Campbell has been described as "one of the most challenging and controversial civil rights figures of our time." Born in Liberty, Mississippi, in 1924, Campbell recounts spending a good portion of his childhood writing stories sometimes underneath the covers at night after the household had gone to bed. Campbell earned bachelor's degrees from Wake Forest College (now university) in 1948 and from Yale Divinity School in 1952 with graduate work at Tulane University. Pastor of a Baptist church in Taylor, Louisiana, from 1952 to 1954, he became director of religious life at the University of Mississippi in Oxford, and was a consultant in race relations for the National Council of Churches, from 1956 to 1963. He has been a writer and "preacher-at-large" (as he describes himself) from 1962 to the present. In addition to these careers, Campbell served as an army sergeant in World War II, and was a self-described "itinerant social worker," farmer, and tour bus cook for a country music band.

A memoir of his tragic relationship with his brother, *Brother to a Dragonfly* (1977), won a Lillian Smith Prize, a Christopher Award, and a National Book Award nomination. Other books include the novels *The Glad River* (1982), which won the Friends of American Writers Award for fiction. Other fiction includes *The Convention*, a novel (1990), and a novella, *Cecelia's Sin* (1983). Nonfiction work appears in *Race and Renewal of the Church* (1962) and *Mississippi Writers: Reflections of Childhood and Youth* (1986); a memoir about his work in the civil rights movement is called *Forty Acres and a Goat* (1986). Through use of imagination, research, and oral history, Campbell's tenth book, *Providence* (1992), chronicles the 170-year saga of a small tract of land in Holmes County, Mississippi, which was once the homeland of the Choctaw Indians, then became a cotton plantation and later a racially integrated communal farm of socialists and Christian visionaries, and is today a game preserve for the U.S. Department of the Interior.

Campbell, who has brought a message of radical salvation to his fellow southerners, both black and white, to prisoners on death row, white supremacists, and Vietnam War resisters, has been awarded an honorary Doctor of Humanities degree from Wake Forest University and an honorary Doctor of Literature degree from the University of the South. His collective works were awarded the Lyndhurst Prize in 1980. Robert Coles has said that because of Campbell's penetrating vision and life's work, he has been aptly described by historian Thomas Connelly as "the soul of the South." Recently, he was honored as the first recipient of the Alex Haley Award for distinguished Tennessee writers. He and his wife of forty-seven years, Brenda Fisher Campbell, have lived on their farm near Mt. Juliet, Tennessee, since 1956, but he enjoys traveling widely throughout this country and abroad giving speeches and talks. On occasion, one might find him singing and playing country music with old friends Waylon Jennings and Tom T. Hall.

Of his many books, Campbell admits that *Cecelia's Sin* is perhaps the work that lies closest to Campbell's heart. Now a novella, this little work was originally part of a larger manuscript of *The Glad River*. In the central character, Cecelia, one finds the embodiment of the passionate commitment and purity of vision that lies at the core of Campbell's own pilgrimage. As Campbell himself describes the creative process and its relation to his life's work: "Ultimately, I think the greatest freedom—if not the only freedom—is freedom from religion. . . . Jesus wasn't a religious person, as I see it. I am not a 'religious' person. . . . True Christianity implies faith and discipleship, not a subscription to a creed or a list of beliefs. There are actually about as many gods around as there are people to worship them and about as many beliefs around as there are gods. The characters in my stories grapple with these things. . . . [These characters] come from where I came from, from my southern heritage, my spiritual heritage. They are part of the genes, tissue, and sinews of me."

Although he has said he is seeking "freedom *from* religion," in another lifetime, Will Campbell might have been himself an Anabaptist, one of a sect of fiercely independent believers that existed in Northern Europe in the seventeenth and eighteenth centuries, about whom *Cecelia's Sin* was written. The Anabaptist faith and creed were radically simple, and defiant of the political status quo. Forced to meet in secret, they suffered persecution and imprisonment for their anti-establishment beliefs. Some were executed as political criminals, martyrs to the cause of religious freedom. †

From

Cecelia's Sin

Goris had wanted to tell them earlier of the rumors of the streets, the things he had heard in his shop from those who were friendly, but Cecelia had decided that the story should be told in two languages. So for more than a month he had watched them as they worked, correcting, adding to, deleting from what was written. As she read aloud Pieter translated and copied her Dutch words into German. Sometimes they worked through the night, stopping only when one of them fell asleep at the table. As they did their work, Goris dozed beside the fire, jumping up at the slightest hint of a need. He had continued to work in the shop, the only income they had. He also prepared the meals, ran the errands, supervised the house, quietly closing the door of each day as it passed. When there was time and it seemed appropriate to him, he sat with them, listening, making suggestions when something was not clear to him. And more than they, he waited.

"Where's the church?" he asked from where he lay on the floor, not even opening his eyes.

"The Church is here," Cecelia said, answering in the same casual tone as he had asked the question. She turned immediately back to the paper in her hand, reading a sentence to Pieter.

"Why here?" Goris asked, still not opening his eyes.

"Where two or three are gathered," Cecelia said. She glanced down at him and then quickly read another sentence.

Goris pulled himself up onto one elbow. "What about one?" he asked.

"One what?" Cecelia said, looking impatiently at him as he shifted his weight to the other elbow.

"One person. You said where two or three are gathered. Why not one?"

"One person cannot be the church," she said. She whispered and smiled, like one trying to quiet an inquiring child's questions.

"Why?"

"Just because," she said, growing more impatient now.

"Because what?" he said.

"Because the Book says where two or three are *gathered*. One person cannot gather." She had put the sheet down and was looking at Pieter, seeking his aid in quieting Goris.

"It takes two or three to gather, Goris," Pieter said, humoring him, continuing to copy the last sentence she had read.

"What about four?" Goris said. "What about where four or five are gathered?"

"I don't know," she said, whispering and smiling again. "Jesus just said two or three. I assume He meant at least two or three. It could be more."

"Then why didn't He say that?" Goris said, sitting upright, an itch in his own voice now. "Why do we think Jesus didn't say just exactly what He meant? We're falling into the same trap as the priests. Always having to say that He meant more, or meant less than what He actually said. Was He not fully as smart as they? Or as we?"

"Are you being frivolous, Goris?" Cecelia asked, less sure of her ground now.

"I think he is not being frivolous," Pieter said, putting his quill in the well and walking over beside him.

"I am not being frivolous. I think two or three. But not four or five."

"Why?" Cecelia asked, trying to mimic Goris at first, then quickly asking it in her own voice. "Why?"

"Because when there are more than two or three they start looking for a leader. He's in the midst of two or three but not four or five or eight hundred."

"Perhaps not. Perhaps so," Cecelia said, speaking sharply again. Then adding, "That's a nice lesson, Goris, Now, will you let us get back to the story?" Pieter had returned to his seat at the table.

Goris stood up, walked to the table and sat down between them. He placed one hand on the stack of parchment in front of Cecelia, reached over and placed the other one on the stack before Pieter, his palms turned upward. They sat looking at the big hands, big enough to cover the sheets without spreading his fingers, hands clean and strong and supple from the years of practicing his trade. Neither of them spoke.

"No, my sister. My brother. But it is not I who will not let you get back to the story. Our story is done. They are coming for us tomorrow." He said it without affect, as if reporting some minor event of the city.

Without a word Cecelia left the room and started down the stairs. Pieter moved to go after her but Goris placed his hand on his knee. "Let her be."

"Do you know this for sure?" Pieter asked when she was out of sight.

"Wait until she returns," Goris said. "We will be what we are. We are three. Three gathered have no secrets."

"But I have a secret," Pieter said. "She had her secret and I have mine, and you have yours. You have known that they were coming."

"Then tell it to me now," Goris said. "Tell me your secret before she returns."

"I am afraid. I have fear."

"What is your fear? Tell it to me before Cecelia returns."

"I had hoped the cup would pass. Now that hope is gone."

"Then you have no fear," Goris said, gesturing through the window with his hand.

"But I do," Pieter said, leaning to stare him directly in the face.

"You cannot have it both ways, my brother," Goris said. "It makes no sense to fear without hope. Fear is lost when hope is lost. You may have fear if you still have hope. But if you have no hope you can have no fear."

"Well, of course, I have hope in the perfect love of God. But that is not what I mean."

"First John, four, eighteen," Goris said, gesturing to the big Lutheran Bible on the cupboard. "Look it up."

Pieter moved across the room, taking one of the candles with him to the cupboard. He opened the Bible and turned the pages until he found the passage. He read it to himself in German, recited it under his breath in French. Then he turned to Goris and said it aloud in Dutch. "There is no fear in love, for perfect love casteth out fear." He closed the book but continued to stand beside the cupboard. "She taught you to read well, didn't she?" he said.

"Yes," Goris said. "She taught me to read well."

They sat on the bench together, gazing into the fire but saying nothing until Cecelia came back.

"Do you know this for sure?" she said, sitting on the bench between them. She was dressed as they had never seen her before. She was wearing a heavy gray kirtle, full length, with sleeves tied about her wrists. A high collar, made of the same material but separate from the rest of the garment, covered her neck and was held in place, directly under her chin, by a plain silver pin. A white linen apron, reaching almost to her ankles, was tied tightly about her waist. A knitted bonnet of coarse black wool with a light shawl attached covered her head and fell over her shoulders like a tippet. Her shoes, black leather with slight heels, were hooked above the ankles; not even the black stockings underneath were showing. Her brown hair, washed and brushed to a lustrous hue, a tinge of red glistening in the light of the candle behind her, fell straight down her back, unbraided. As she entered the room the smell of soft cleanness followed as she strolled.

"Yes," Goris said. "I know it for sure. They have the list and the bailiff has given sanction to fifty armed horsemen to find everyone on the list. But he will come for us himself. He knows that Pieter is here. And he knows about the project. It is my fault. Someone I brought for the interview was not of us."

"Where two or three are gathered they do not apologize," Cecelia said. "It is not a matter of fault."

Cecelia stood up and began to move about the house. With a feather duster she cleaned the furniture, wiping each chair, bench, table and cupboard with a piece of broadcloth when she had dusted it. She folded bedsheets, handcloths, two tablecloths, and a dozen table napkins, all made of linen, and placed them in a neat stack on top of a large oak chest. All the blankets, except those on the beds, were stacked on an eight-sided table beside the chest.

"These must be distributed before they come," Cecelia said.

"Blaisus knows they are coming. I told him you would leave them in the peat closet. He will get them later."

"That will not do," Cecelia said. "The sentence will call for the confiscation of all my possessions. If I give them away before they come they are no longer my possessions. To do it later would be to steal what already belongs to them."

"They will remain your possessions until after the sentencing," Goris said. "Not even the Anabaptists are guilty until the judges give the word. Blaisus will distribute it all properly."

She moved into other parts of the house. Silver buttons, a few ornaments of gold—earrings, hair brooches, a medallion and chain— were placed in a small basket. A few pieces of decorative porcelain and several buckles, beakers, and head ornaments were added.

She walked about straightening and dusting several paintings hanging on the walls. "It would be risky for Blaisus to place these on the market," she said. "The curtains and fireplace coverings had best stay as well."

After the things she had collected were placed in the peat closet she walked through the house again, making sure that each room was orderly. When she had finished she reached in the cupboard and got the decanter containing the wine which had been poured for Gillis the night the project had begun. She placed it in the center of the table.

"Does that mean you have forgiven him?" Goris asked.

"For betraying us?" she asked.

"No," Goris said. She looked at him but did not answer.

She came and sat by the fire and began to talk. "What power do they have over us? Even as they come for us they see us because God has trimmed the wick of His lamp to light the day. The rivers and canals are melted not by their bidding. But ours is not the first innocent blood to stain the streets of Amsterdam, nor to breathe our last in Amstel's waters. So let them act according to their laws. Surely it is better to die innocent than guilty."

"But we are guilty," Goris said. "We have done all the things they will charge. And more."

"But they are not wrong things," Cecelia said. "Our hearts are pure before God."

"But it is not God who will kill us. When the tormentors set their minds, the sword falls, the flames leap up, the waters fill our bellies. It does not have to do with purity of heart. It has to do with offense to their laws. And of that we cannot plead innocence. We will not baptize our young, punishable by death since Justinius. We will not swear. We will not bear the sword for them . . . and we share our goods. Community of goods—I think you are right. From the talk I hear, it is for that that they hate us most."

"But we do not really do that," Pieter said. "We are not really *der Kommunists.* You said so yourself."

"But they believe we are communist," Goris said. "And that is enough. If they think we are seditious, we are seditious. That is what sedition is. It is what they say it is, what they think it is. The bread is risen when it is risen, but it is baked when I say it is risen. The dough is not lord of the baker. The baker is lord of the loaf."

Cecelia fell into a spell of deep sighing. At first it was nothing more than heavy breathing, her shoulders and breasts heaving and falling with no sound. But suddenly the room was filled with the gripping sounds of lamentation and distress. "Ohhohohoho. Ohhohohoho." Goris and Pieter were making the same sounds as Cecelia. Between the thrusts of shouts and sobs there could be heard some brief recitation from one or the other of them. "For our light affliction, which is but for a moment, worketh for us a far more exceeding and eternal weight of glory." Then all together again, guttural moans of unutterable hurt. "There shall be no death, neither sorrow nor crying, neither shall there be any more pain, for the former things are passed away. Ohuhuhuhuhu. If God be for us, who can be against us?" Then more agonizing screams of anguish. For a time they were simply milling about the room aimlessly, sighing, moaning, each one making their individual noises of passion.

Cecelia lifted her hands and head and voice toward the ceiling and called out, "Let the sighing of the prisoner come before thee." Goris followed with the same motions and called out, "According to the Greatness of thy power." Pieter did the same, adding, "Preserve thou those who are appointed to die."

They formed a circle and with their hands still lifted, repeated the words in unison: "Let the sighing of the prisoner come before thee; according to the greatness of thy power preserve thou those who are appointed to die."

The lamentation moved abruptly and without interruption into sounds of joy and exultation and celebration. They embraced and patted each other and spoke congratulatory words, dancing, laughing more loudly than they had wept. For more than an hour they sang and frolicked about the room, sometimes playing follow the leader as they pranced through the house, up and down the stairs, twice sliding down the banister, crawling under the table on hands and knees as if it were a tunnel. Sometimes they joined hands and skipped in a circle like children, moving first in one direction and then the other.

"Let's go visiting," Cecelia said, getting their coats from the hall, not even waiting for them to reply. Goris and Pieter followed her into the night without question. They stopped for a few minutes beside Harlaan's tannery, a place they had often gathered for their meetings.

"Shall we awaken him?" Pieter asked.

"No," Cecelia said. "We shall see him soon enough. He needs his rest."

When they reached Goris's shop he unlatched the door and they followed him inside. He checked the ovens as he had done each night for twenty years. It was plain that he had not baked for several days. The ashes in the furnace were cold and white. With Pieter's help he shoveled them clean, emptying the ashes in a pit behind his living quarters. Cecelia took the few remaining loaves and placed them on the ledges facing the street. "Let the stray dogs eat," she said to herself, putting two loaves on the lower ledge. "And this is for whomever takes them." She stacked the other loaves on the higher shelf.

Goris chuckled when he saw what she had done. "Something for the bailiff?" he asked.

"Maybe," she said. "Bailiffs eat too."

"Yes, I suppose they do. 'Inasmuch as ye have done it unto the least of these.' Caesar's bailiff must surely be the least. Until now that passage had always given me trouble."

"Through a glass, darkly. Now face to face," Cecelia said, looking into the night, not talking to Goris.

Pieter and Cecelia watched as Goris placed his simple possessions in order. He took two stalks of barley from underneath the counter where he displayed his bread and laced them into a wreath shape. "I saved them from my first baking," he said. He opened the door to the second oven and peered inside for a moment. "The bread is rising," he whispered.

Pieter turned his good ear to Cecelia and asked what he had said. She cupped her hand to his ear and said, "He said the resurrection is certain." Pieter did not answer.

Back in his living quarters he took a flat package from a large trunk and unwrapped it. He held up a faded painting in a silver frame, oval shaped with small blossoms embossed around the edges. He held it near the candle and the two of them moved to see it clearly. It was of a young woman, very dark, with fine black hair captured in two buns on either side of her head. The painting itself was of poor quality but the natural beauty of her countenance showed through. "My father did it," he said. He wiped it clean and placed it on a mantel near his bed. "It was after they were married," he said, looking at it again before he walked away.

The clock in the tower of St. Nicolas Church struck three o'clock. They moved in the direction of the sound. No one spoke when they reached the arc leading into the well-kept churchyard. They stood close together, looking at the very tip of the spires silhouetted against low hanging clouds, clouds which at times seemed to smother the steeple itself, hiding it from view almost completely. "Do you want to go in?" Cecelia asked.

"Do you?" Pieter said.

"It used to be so beautiful," Cecelia said, moving away, neither answering the question of the other.

"It is too big to be beautiful," Goris said.

They paused in front of shops and stores as they walked. "That was my father's business," Cecelia said, pointing to an upstairs office. "And there is where we were baptized. I wonder where old Gillis, the baptizer, is tonight. He dipped water from the well with a gourd."

"If he had waited one month there would have been plenty of water," Goris said. "But leave the gourd for Jonah."

"Yes, I remember that flood. We even got blamed for that," Cecelia said. "They said it was heresy that brought the strong north-west wind during high tides. I remember the dikes breaking on this very spot, the waters rushing in on every side, rolling with resistless fury, sweeping houses, trees, men, and cattle in its wake."

They stopped beside the canal where Goris had his boat moored. "You have served me well," he said, pulling the boat through the slushy ice which broke in pieces as he pulled it to him. When he had removed all the lines he pushed it away with his boot. "Don't stop until you float to Emden," he said, watching the retreating tide pull it away. "Someone there will treat you well."

"What will ever become of our Netherlands?" Goris said as they began walking in the direction of Cecelia's house. "Will she ever blush for what is happening to us now?"

"She is no worse than the others," Cecelia said. "The lowering clouds of despotism and superstition hang dark over all of Europe today. Scenes of violence, of bloodshed and oppression are rampant everywhere. That's the story we have written. But a land which gave us an Erasmus will one day grant us liberty. And when that meridian splendor makes its rounds it will light the way for all the world. Whatever the private interests of the princes, one day they will be a rare occurrence, and the fear they engender will be no more. A people who could snatch this ground from the sea will not let it be forever ruled by tyranny and falsehood. The blood of some may be in vain, but the red blood of Holland's martyrs will paint the corners of the earth. I would die for my Lord anywhere, but I am happy that He will let me die in Amsterdam." They had not heard her speak this way before; neither of them answered.

It was almost dawn when they climbed the stairs to the room where they had written the book. Cecelia put two small pieces of wood on the fire and blew on it until the coals flamed up. She walked to the table and picked up the thick manuscript Pieter had translated to German and handed it to him. She took the Dutch version, written in her own elegant hand, and sat on the bench facing the fire.

She began to pray aloud, looking straight ahead, not bowing her head and not closing her eyes. "Grace, joy, and peace from God the heavenly Father, and our Lord Jesus Christ, who loved us, and washed us from our sins in His own blood, and hath shined bright in our hearts, and translated us into Goris and Pieter and Cecelia in Amsterdam. We thank thee for the story. We thank thee for the Church of two or three gathered, for the assurance that whosoever loseth his life for thy sake and the Gospel's the same shall find it hereafter in life eternal. We thank thee for the words of our brother Paul who said, 'Whatsoever things were written aforetime were written for our learning.' And let us not fear men, which must perish like grass; but let us fear God, whose story shall abide forever."

She moved from where she sat and stood directly behind Goris and Pieter, holding her right hand over their heads, still holding the manuscript in the other. "Herewith I commend you to the Lord, and to the story of His grace. May He comfort, strengthen, stablish you all with His Spirit, that you may finish that whereunto you are called, to the praise and glory of the Lord, so that we may rejoice together, and sit down at the Lord's table, where He shall serve us with new wine, in the kingdom of God, His father."

She did not say Amen when she stopped but took her place again on the bench. She turned the stack of paper face side down, so that the last page she had written was on the top, the writing away from her. She motioned for Pieter to do the same. Taking the top page, the last words she had written, she leaned forward and dropped it quickly into the flame. "Jacob Cool was right," she whispered. "May he and God the Father forgive me for my sin. Writing the story is not the *Story*."

"Is it what you wish?" Pieter asked, watching the flame of the parchment as it filled the room with light, not dropping the sheet he held.

"Is it what I wish? No. It is not what I wish," she said, adding, "*Thy* kingdom come. *Thy* will be done," then pausing as she watched Pieter hold the end of the sheet in the fire, holding it until the flame was almost to his fingertips.

"Perhaps the smoke from what we do will float over all of Europe," she said, her voice the same as when she was praying before." And also to England. And the new world as well, new as it is. For no land will long survive without its tyrants. May it be a testament to all who breathe it that God wills us free."

They continued to burn one page at a time. Sometimes Cecelia called a name aloud when she supposed a page contained a certain person's words. Goris sat rigidly upright between them, staring out the window at the white smoke flying and scattering in the early morning wind, blowing downward into the city streets, upward and away in the direction of the North Sea, skipping and dancing like a kite.

Page by page they slowly fed the fire, Pieter waiting each time until Cecelia had dropped a sheet before following.

Suddenly Cecelia was a little girl back in the convent in East Friesia. She heard herself intoning words from the Latin funeral Mass. Her voice was steady and loud, but slow, saying a few words with each burning page. "Per dominum nostrum . . . Jesum Christum . . . filium tuum qui tecum . . . vivit et regnat . . . unitate Spiritus Sanctus . . . Deus per saecula saeculorum."

As she spoke she could tell from the corner of her eye that Pieter was watching her, listening to her, and wondering. "Some of it was beautiful," she said, as if Pieter were about to challenge her, continuing to burn the pages, not looking directly at him.

"Yes," he said. "Some of it *is* beautiful."

As she began to repeat the words, again in Latin, Pieter recited them in German, Goris joining them in Dutch, in perfect unison with both of them. "Through our Lord Jesus Christ, thy Son, who lives and reigns with you in the unity of the Holy Spirit, one God forever and ever."

"A finished story which has no ending," she said as they reached the last page which was the first. "We have reached the beginning. There is no ending," she said, as if to clarify what she had just said. Goris continued to sit between them, whimpering softly, making no effort to conceal the sound. "That was the error of Rome and Wittenburg. Of Geneva and Zurich. And almost us as well. To end the story. The end of a story can only be defended with violence. Nothing else is left."

Pieter sat now with his arms folded across his chest, watching with Goris as the smoke blended with the gathering clouds, the clouds accepting and embracing it like a vacuum. Cecelia continued to speak, softer now. "The tattered coat can never be possessed."

The wind had shifted and a slight gust down the chimney livened the coals, blowing a wisp of the white smoke, the very last of it, back into the room. Cecelia leaned into it and inhaled deeply. Goris and Pieter did the same, saying nothing, Pieter no longer sobbing. "Until we came together we knew the words," Cecelia continued. "Now we know the tune." †

Interview

Will Campbell lives on a farm in Mt. Juliet, Tennessee, about fifteen miles outside Nashville. On the outer boundaries of Music City, this place seems to be a fitting location for a self-described "good ol' boy" and country songwriter. Though probably better known as a "preacher of radical salvation," Campbell clearly delights in his persona as country balladeer. His songs are naturally flavored with homespun wisdom and social protest springing from his upbringing in rural Mississippi and his travels throughout the world in connection with civil rights. One song's yearning yet pointed refrain goes, "When we was born we was all kin/When we're dead we'll be kinfolks again/Let Mississippi madness be Mississippi magic again."

The sixty-seven-year-old Campbell wears jeans and a western shirt, a string tie, and an emblematic black parson's hat; he walks with a gnarled cherry cane. I talked with him at his daughter's house, a brick bungalow on a quiet side street in suburban Durham, North Carolina. (He was there to visit his thirteen-year-old grandson, Harlan.) At my house later for a meal of turnip greens, cornbread, and ham, Will told us how to make moonshine whiskey (use hickory and oak sticks, very dried out, branch water and, of course, the copper kettle to avoid danger of lead poisoning). As we sat and talked that evening, Campbell's passion and wit illumined his finely boned face; his blue eyes twinkled when he remembered some

human absurdity, or turned steely when he recounted some of the very
real injustices he'd witnessed in years past. Like many other independent
thinkers, Campbell was ready with strong convictions and remarkable stories of the courageous people and events that make up his life as preacher,
activist, and storyteller. "I have no pulpit. My vocation is not to be successful, but to be faithful and to live out in the world." Though smiling a
bit, his face has the look of one who has seen perhaps too much of human
foibles and suffering.

Campbell's friends and associates, some "outlaws" in the strictest sense,
have at times been the subject of controversy during the years in his work
as a civil rights activist (he was the only white founding member of the
Southern Christian Leadership Conference and a troubleshooter for the
National Council of Churches). In later years, Campbell invited scorn and
criticism when he publicly announced his friendship with Ku Klux
Klansmen. He recently told a National Public Radio correspondent, "I
have befriended all sorts of unsavory characters. I am pro-Klansman
because I am pro-human being." Having been described variously as a
Christian anarchist, maverick, and curmudgeon, as well as by other,
stronger sobriquets, Campbell cuts to the heart of the Christian message
when he says, "There is something sacred about every human being. To
me, the notion of grace and redemption means we're all bastards but God
loves us anyway."

*I'd like to talk to you about your fiction—why you write fiction,
what purposes it serves for you that memoir does not, for example.
Your little novella,* Cecelia's Sin, *is quite an interesting book.*

Cecelia's Sin is a story about the Anabaptists that was originally
part of the manuscript of *The Glad River.* Do you know about the
Anabaptists? When you look at where the Baptist movement came
from, you can understand a lot by looking at these folks.
Originally, the Anabaptists would not go to war. They were vehemently opposed to the death penalty. They would not take an oath,
either, so they would not serve on juries. And, most provocatively,
the Anabaptists wouldn't baptize their babies, in part because they
saw it as a way their government would keep track of them, a kind
of enrollment of new citizens. They firmly believed in separation of
church and state, as you can probably gather. But my editor said,

"The Anabaptists may be the greatest thing since sliced bread, but I never heard of them and they don't belong in this novel," so out came a hundred pages from *The Glad River*. Now, I did manage to keep the story alive in the novel, though I'm not sure how I did it. It was the guts of *The Glad River*, in my view. But, I had too much invested in it by then to throw it away, thank goodness. Then Mercer University asked me to do a book for them, and I worked up that hundred pages into the novella. They called it *Cecelia's Sin* and published it.

And then, of course, there was *The Convention*. It's been called a parable, but it's more of a parody. People say, "You were so prophetic in that book." It's easy to be prophetic when the people you're writing about have short memories. By God, those things had already happened. Now the book is just beginning to be read. The fellow who edited it called me last night. I don't know if you saw in the paper that the Disciples of Christ recently had their annual convention in Tulsa. The guy who was in the running for the presidency of it came out in favor of ordination of women and the ordination of gays and lesbians and so on. Wild as it may sound, he was almost elected. But during the debate, this editor told me, someone stood up and said, "Everyone at this convention, all six thousand of you, should have read Will Campbell's book, *The Convention*, because we are doing everything he talked about in that book." But again, I knew I was up to something with that book; I was having too good a time.

What do you think you were up to?

Well, I was up to sounding a warning, certainly. Briefly, the story of that book is about Southern Baptists (of course, my convention was something called the Federal Baptist Church and not the Southern Baptist Convention). The Southern Baptist Convention several years ago, you may remember, said in a resolution, or whatever they have, that women should not be ordained ministers because man was first in creation and woman was first in the "Edenic fall." Isn't that cute? The Edenic fall. It has a nice ring to it, whatever it is. So I had this character who was a holdover from *The Glad River*, Doops, who by then had become a technician with audio-visual things. Doops said that by that logic, *only* women should be ordained because they discovered sin first, they've been at it longer, and thus they should be more adept at identifying it and casting it out. Well, anyway, these three women decided that they were urbane, theologically educated people, and so on, but they had only little nickel-and-dime jobs like music director, or some other thing that they let women do. They realized that those in charge didn't say they couldn't be *president* of the whole thing, so they ran one of their own. She was an ordinary housewife from Mississippi who wore a dotted swiss dress every day (that she ironed in her room), who had brought a skillet with her to the hotel where they were staying to make her husband's meals, who wore a little bun, and so on. In the book, they succeeded in getting this woman elected president. But I won't tell you what happened after she was elected.

It sounds wonderful.

It was fun to write and, of course, I don't know if you followed the Southern Baptist Convention fight or not, but Judge Pressler from Houston was the one who figured out how to take over and he pulled it off. He had begun by establishing that all boards and trustees and committees and commissions are to be appointed by the president on a rotating basis, so if you elect a president for ten years running, you've got it all, all the seminaries, all the hospitals, everything. And he did it.

He's a right-winger, isn't he?

Oh, God, yeah.

They get more right wing every time they convene, it seems to me. Who is the man from Atlanta?

Stanley. Stanley was one of Pressler's henchmen. In my book (my lawyer read it before it was published), I had a character named Senator Perdue who was a great friend of the president of the U.S. He had the president come down to speak at the convention when he was afraid he might not win that year. There was a fiasco in the hall that Doops had caused. Doops had figured out a way to kill the sound and project subtitles up on the screen behind the speaker without the speaker realizing what was happening. So, what the speaker would be saying and what the audience would be reading could be diametrically opposed. Of course, the president didn't know what was going on. So, everybody was surprised he was saying all those things—he was coming out against the death penalty and against war, favoring women priests and all this. But Doops wasn't as good an electrician as he was supposed to have been, and the main speaker system got a short in it. There was this "pop!" in the ceiling, and suddenly all the secret service men who surrounded the president were all over him, examining him. They thought he had been shot because he had at that point "fell out," you know. They couldn't find any wounds, though he kept saying, "Hail Mary, full of grace, blessed art thou among women, blessed is the fruit of thy womb, Jesus." A big Irish, ex-Notre Dame football player, secret service guy said, "This guy's a damn closet Catholic. And he's down here preaching to these Baptists." It's a fun book. So that's what I was up to, just making fun of 'em.

I noticed that Cecelia's Sin *is a very somber tableau; there's no parody there at all. Literary historian Linda Weaver Williams has suggested to me that she believed* Cecelia's Sin *might be the work that was closest to your heart.*

Probably so. Yes. I am sorry it got cut from *The Glad River.* Walker Percy was a good friend of mine; he would always read my stuff, and I would read his. Of course, he would criticize mine but I wouldn't dare criticize his. One day we were talking about *The Glad River* and he said, "It doesn't work." We were sitting down on Lake Ponchartrain, just across from the theater where he got the idea for *The Moviegoer.* We talked for three hours sitting there drinking whisky, one day, and he never would tell me why the book didn't work.

I was really shaken, you know. I thought he was talking about the technique and my use of the language and so on. So finally he said, "You committed the greatest of Christian heresies in it." And I said, "Which is what?" And he said, "The Romantic Heresy." So, I had to ask him to explain what that meant, you know. So he quoted something in Latin, "The efficacy of the sacrament is not dependent on the morality of the priest," or some such.

See Doops, he was never baptized. He grew up Baptist but he said that he couldn't ever find a real Baptist to baptize him. Finally, he was baptized in jail by a little Cajun guy named Model-T Arceneau who had stepped on a land mine during the war. The explosion had blown out one of his eyes and one of his ears, and he wouldn't agree to any plastic surgery or anything like that. Once, the surgeons

said, "We can make you an ear," and he said, "Well, can I hear out
of it?" The surgeons told him, "Well, no. But we can fix you an artificial eye." And the little Cajun guy asked, "Can I see out of it?" They
replied, "Well, no, it's cosmetic." The result of his affliction was
that he couldn't look at you and listen to you at the same time. If
you were talking he'd have to turn his head one way, and if he were
talking, he'd have to turn it back another way. So he went through
the rest of his life just shaking his head to the whole damn world.

Anyway, before Model-T was executed for murder (which murder I never could figure out whether he actually did or not), Doops
got him to baptize him. Well, Percy's point was that he should have
let that no-good Baptist preacher a while back in the story go ahead
and baptize him. When the book came out, Percy called me one
night (I suspected that it was during toddy time), and he said, "I
just finished *The Glad River* and it's a great piece of work." I said,
"Wait a minute, you said you didn't like it," and he said, "You fixed
it." I said, "I changed one paragraph." He said, "Well, that's all you
needed to change." I said, "Why the hell didn't you tell me in the
first place that's all I needed to change and save me some grief?"

You see, the way I fixed it for Percy was I had these three characters: Doops was one, and Model-T Arceneau, and a fellow named
Smiley (Smiley was a Catholic, too). And they were talking to
Doops one day after the war was over and Doops said, "Why don't
you just go ahead?" (because his mama was forever bugging him to
be baptized, and she would pray over him at the revival meetings
that he would be converted to Baptist). And Arceneau says, "Yeah,
why the hell don't you go ahead and let them baptize you?" and
Smiley looked at Model-T and said, "That's the way we do it, isn't
it?" and he said, "Yeah, yeah." That little change served the purpose of saying it's the sacrament that counts, and the priest's character doesn't have anything to do with it. He's just a technician
anyhow.

And he liked it from then on?
Yeah.
*Do you suppose, being a preacher as you are, it would be fair to
say that you've been captivated — or caught in the throes of — what
it means to be a thoughtful, authentic Christian in twentieth-*

century life? Many writers, southern writers especially, seem to be. What do you think it is that holds you, that has such a grip on you?

It really does go back to being a southerner. It's something we intuitively do—it's not something we consciously do, I think. It's just in our genes, our bones.

As southerners you mean? How so?

It's a disease. To be southern and Christian. Of course, I'm not religious—I don't go to church; I wouldn't know where to go. I don't go to the steeples, I don't know what "the church" is. Yet, I do have a very high doctrine of the church. I think when Jesus said he would build his church and the gates of hell wouldn't prevail against it, I believe that, but he didn't ask me to build it, and he didn't ask First Baptist by the gas station to build it, and he didn't ask Judge Pressler to build it. But we do. We're always kingdom-building. We build these steeples, these edifices, which seem to me to be a great denial. I mean it's all a long way from Bethlehem.

When you say "kingdom-building" you're saying that this is synonymous with church-building?

Yes. They call it kingdom-building, but they're building steeples. It's brick and mortar. Then they buy busses to bring more people in to build a bigger building to get more money to buy more busses to bring more people. And the man in the ditch is dying.

It's a self-perpetuation of the institution that you deplore; the institution feeds on itself while the needy go hungry.

Always. Always and inevitably in all institutions, and it's too much to expect or hope that the church would be any different. All institutions, or most institutions, begin for a good purpose but pretty soon they begin to exist for themselves.

I see what you mean. What brought you to write fiction about all this?

I don't know. I've always liked dabbling in fiction. When I was a little boy I was the runt in the community, in a rural community, and I was invariably the last one to be chosen when we were playing ball Saturday or Sunday afternoon. You know, the two captains were always Robert Lee and Scott who were great big country boys. They would choose the next biggest, and then on down. I was called Dave when I was a boy since my middle name is Davis. And I'd be standing over there, you know, about that tall with my head down. I knew I'd be the last one called over. Finally whoever was choosing would say, "Well . . . Dave."

They'd have to take you. That's a terrible feeling.

There were two of us. One was a boy who was fat, you know. He couldn't run, he couldn't catch the ball, and so he and I were the last two to be chosen. The fattest one and the littlest one. So I would, I'd sweat it out. After a while, I'd just stay at the house and write cowboy stories. All I'd ever read, except the Bible. And I was pretty sure I couldn't improve on that. When we would be assigned a theme in school, in six or seventh grade, usually it would be half a page on a Blue Horse tablet about going to your grandmother's house and seeing a chicken snake or seeing a hen lay an egg, or whatever. Well, I'd stay up all night around that little kerosene lamp, until my mama made me go to bed, writing these long, elaborate cowboy stories. I still remember some of them. And the other kids would just pray that Dave would be called on first to read his theme because that would shoot the whole time, and they wouldn't have to read about seeing a chicken snake at grandmother's house. Even *Brother to a Dragonfly* was partly fiction since I don't have total recall and conversations had to be reconstructed, the dialogues and so on. But the story line—those things did actually happen. It's the same way with *Forty Acres and a Goat*—I got some criticism on that.

Why?

I had a character called T. J. Eaves, a black character. The epigram I wrote about him says that the fact that T. J. Eaves appears in more than one form makes him none the less real. One day he might be John Lewis, the next time he may be Dick Gregory, or Julius Lester. All those things happened in actuality, but of course in real life, they didn't happen to just one person. So, I had chosen to make it a composite as a more tractable arrangement. I would have had to write a twenty-thousand-page book to develop that many characters. Some of the reviewers didn't like that. Reviewers would also say, "Well, this is not good history." Well, I'm not a historian.

Yes. You're talking about the sometimes blurred lines between fiction, memoir, history, and "real life."

And I'll probably run into the same thing with this book I'm working on now. I began by trying to write a history of one section of land in Mississippi which has become a Persian rug of a tale. I wanted to write about that section of land because in 1955 there was a group there, a little group of socialists, Christian visionaries, who ran a medical clinic and organized federal credit unions, and co-ops and so on. Anyway, the White Citizens Council ran them off and the land's been there unused ever since. The time came, a couple years ago, when we as board members of the organization had to decide what to do with it, give it away or sell it, or what. I wanted to give it back to the Choctaws. There was strong sentiment on the small board (five or six people), but then two weeks after that, the Department of Interior decided that they wanted it, as if we might be up to some mischievous precedent giving land back to the Indians. And they got it. The Department of Interior got it for a game management program. Against my vote, but that's not the first vote I've lost.

So I decided to write a history of that section of land, having no idea what had happened there before the commune. This little interracial, cooperative farm is what my book started out being an account of. These folks had bought it in 1935. But when I started researching it, I ran into some fascinating characters. The first non-Choctaw owner was a fellow named William McKendree Gwin whose father, James Gwin, was a Methodist preacher from Tennessee, who was a next-door neighbor and close friend of Andrew Jackson. And Andrew Jackson took him to New Orleans. Before he became a Methodist preacher, Gwin had been quite a well-known Indian fighter in Kentucky and Tennessee. In the War of 1812, Andrew Jackson took Gwin as his chaplain to New Orleans, but when he got there, apparently Jackson found he was more in need of fire power than he was exhortation for the troops and he put Gwin in charge of fourteen hundred sharpshooters in the second line of defense in the Battle of New Orleans. Then as a reward, when he became president, Jackson appointed Gwin to be U.S. Marshal for the Mississippi Territory, a very lucrative and exceedingly influential political office. And Gwin became a congressman. He wanted to be a senator but didn't get along with the governor. Gwin already had plenty of gold, but he wanted to campaign for statehood for California with an eye to being the first United States senator from that state, and within eight months he had accomplished his mission of being elected. He was arrested twice during the Civil War for being a Confederate sympathizer (which, no doubt, he was). He never actually did anything to betray the Union but was imprisoned twice and pardoned twice, once by President Lincoln and once by President Johnson.

And another character who lived on that piece of ground was a fellow named William Pinchback who in 1840 took a slave woman named Eliza Stewart and five children to Philadelphia. There he manumitted them and brought them back to Holmes County where he had a large plantation and where they lived peacefully with the neighbors. Ironically, a hundred years later, here they were running these little Christian missionaries off who were not concerned with miscegenation at all; they were just practicing medicine, and education, and trying to help the poor blacks of the county. When this William Pinchback died, his son and family went immediately back to Cincinnati because the white relatives would try to disinherit them and reenslave them. They did disinherit them. One of the children was named P. B. S. Pinchback. They called him Percy Bysshe Shelley but that wasn't his real name. I guess today they'd call him Public Broadcasting System.

Yes, I would think so.

That's probably more about that project than you want to know, but it shows just how these little innocent projects blossom into fascinating stories.

They really do. Have you got a title for this book?

Well, I'm calling it *Return To Providence,* but the publisher just wants to call it *Providence.* That was the name of the plantation when William McKendree Gwin had it. When the missionaries got it, they called it Providence Farm because it had been called Providence Plantation, also owned at one time by a four-hundred-pound man named Richard Davis who was a cousin of Gwin's. The land has remained in the Gwin family one way or another, not in a direct line, you know, but hopping around.

These people must come back alive when you've been on their trail for a while.

Yeah. Colonel Dick Davis.

Speculate if you will, on the perspectives of other writers, like Walker Percy, for example. He's one of the most outstanding writ-

ers *we've had from the South, and he is known for writing from a Catholic perspective. Do you think he did?*

I think he did, but I don't think he was trying to. That's what I told him when he quoted that Latin to me, you know. I said, "I'm not trying to write a Catholic novel, Walker, I'm trying to write a Baptist novel," and he said, "There's no such thing as a Baptist novel." And I said, "Well, that's a helluva note. You're known all over the world as a Catholic novelist." He said, "Not by me." And I recall that in that interview that he did with himself in *Esquire* some years ago, he asked himself, "Are you a Catholic novelist?" And he said, "Well, I'm a Catholic and I'm a novelist, but I am not a Catholic novelist." I don't know. I would question that because he was not a "cradle Catholic." I can write out of Baptist genes. Percy had those Calvinist genes to overcome or live with, before he was converted. I do think he took his Catholic faith very seriously and was consciously trying to write out of that wellspring. But I don't know, he would deny it.

I imagine he didn't want to feel or have it considered that he was compromising his art for dogma's sake in any way.

Yeah, get typed, you know. I'm willing to say I was up to something in my fiction and he would say, "Well, I was just writing a story."

And he would be very scrupulous about that. He was just writing a story. Well, when you're up to something, are you a Baptist novelist?

Well, I think maybe I'm an Anabaptist novelist.

Yes!

There aren't any Baptist novelists—I think Doops was right. I stumbled up on him by accident, but he said, "There aren't any Baptists left," and I don't think there are. When you look at where the Baptists—what tradition did you grow up in?

Associate Reformed Presbyterian, but now I'm Episcopalian.

Oh, my God. Well, I'm a Seventh Day Horizontalist, I reckon. You know, the Anabaptists would not go to war but now, my God, any time there is the least little skirmish, the Baptists are the first to rush down and join in. The Anabaptists were against the death penalty, but now any time any prosecuting attorney wants to fry somebody, he's delighted to get twelve staunch Baptists, preferably deacons, on the jury because, by God, they'll hang the boy. Used to be, they would not serve on juries. Well, now man, we'll serve on their juries, we'll put our hand on the Bible and swear to anything. And it was the Anabaptists, really, more than any one else, that were responsible for the First Amendment to the Constitution. Two Anabaptists, Isaac Backus and John Leland, were the ones who pressured and lobbied their friend and neighbor, Thomas Jefferson, about religious liberty.

So, if you ask if I am that kind of Baptist novelist then the answer is no. I did wonder myself, and then I went to the Southern Baptist Convention when it was in St. Louis. And I came away about as near clinically depressed as I've ever been in my life, with the exception of when my ex-sister-in-law sued me over *Brother to a Dragonfly*. And I couldn't figure out what it was that was bothering me so much. I thought I'd walked away from all that thirty-five years ago, or it had walked away from me. Why do I give a damn? And I finally agonized through it and figured out that the Baptist heritage—not the Baptists of today—but the heritage, is such a glorious one. All those things are things that I sought then, they're gone; they died and that's what I was seeing in St. Louis at the convention, a death. There was no talk of discipleship; it was all doctrine. Are you familiar with a little book that Edith Hamilton wrote toward the end of her life called *Witness To The Truth*?

I know only her work on classical mythology.

That was her field, but towards the end of her life she wrote a little book about Plato and Socrates and all that bunch, and she had a brief chapter on the church. She wasn't a religious woman, to my knowledge. That one brief chapter on the church which says so much to me. She said the great church of Christ was founded by good men, saintly men, men who loved Christ, often loved Him enough to die for Him, but they did not trust Him. They could not trust Him enough to build the church by His way of doing things. So they set about to make it safe in their own way, and that's when creeds and confessions of faith, doctrine, and theology, and so on entered the picture to protect it. That was the beginning of the end, actually, she was saying. She argued that the church became strong, it became powerful, and it became rich, but weaker and weaker until today, it's hardly distinguishable from any other social organization.

A good outfit, mind you. I've never said it was bad. Anytime we're looking for a good outfit, we have the Boy Scouts, the League of Women Voters, the Red Cross, and the church right in there. It's an amazing little book, I think.

I will read it. It sounds as if she "hits the head on the nail" as a student I knew used to say.

Well, you think something's good if you agree with it, you know. I just agree with it so strongly. It kind of says where I am, anyway. I'd never heard of the book, I'd never read it, I just ran across it by accident. By contrast, this guy, Larry Wright, wrote a thing about me in *Rolling Stone* which, I think I told you, I didn't read.

I've got it right here.

Well, I don't want to read it. I don't know why I didn't read it. I know there's a thin line between arrogance and humility, but for whatever reason, I just decided not to read it. But now he's coming out with a book. A collection of these stories he's written about religious figures, I being one, and Jimmy Swaggart being one, and Madalyn O'Hair. I don't know if he ever wrote one on Mother Teresa or not, but if he didn't, I'm thrown in there with a bunch of two-headed calves.

[Laughter] Jimmy Swaggart is quite something, isn't he?

Yeah, I'm afraid he's had it, but maybe not, I don't know. He's a powerful actor. But Larry Wright called me the other day, and he said that *Rolling Stone* had edited out about half his original copy (which of course they do), and he wanted to put it all in this book. He kept pressing me about what to put back in, saying things like, "Well, do you believe this? Do you believe this? Do you believe so and so?" And I wouldn't answer him. So finally he got kind of exasperated and said, "You're being evasive, as if you're afraid to be quoted for what you believe." And so finally I said, "Well, for me to answer these questions, which are bordering on sounding like those of the Grand Inquisitor, would be to negate what I've been saying to you the past six or eight months you've been following me around: I'm not a creedalist. If I check a box that says I believe a certain thing, then I become a strict creedalist and I have already told you that I am not a creedalist." There is a difference between belief and faith and this I had always felt in my gut, but had not articulated as succinctly as Edith Hamiliton does in this essay of hers.

And that's what affected you so deeply at the Southern Baptist Convention?

That's right. This is the main reason I was so depressed in St. Louis. There was no talk of discipleship, but only of belief. To say I believe that a whale swallowed Jonah, so I'm going to heaven, and it doesn't matter if what that means is that it's not important who your next-door neighbor is, or who your shop foreman is, or who your daughter marries. The story of Jonah and the whale to me is a story about justice. But belief doesn't require you to do anything. Faith is active, belief is passive. Belief, it seems to me, leaves no room for discipleship, for going out into the world and doing something about the Good News. That's my story, and I'm sticking to it.

That's a great story and a great truth. Let me ask you this: Do you see your writing fiction as an act of faith, as an action that you do out in the world about the Good News, or in response to it?

Yeah. Yeah, I do. Everything you do is, I think. Now if you ask if this is a soap box only, then I would demur there because it also has to do with my glands, with my being a runt as a boy and all that, that I decided I would write stories—because I can't play ball. I'm aware of that too, but I think everyone who writes is a propagandist, and people who say, "I just write, I don't care if anybody reads it or not" are lying. You are trying, even if it's pornography, to say something, to make a statement. Well, maybe some people just say, "Well, I just write to get rich." Well, they're in for a jolt. I haven't gotten very rich by writing books, and not many people do.

You talked earlier about your faith being in your genes. Flannery O'Connor once commented that she didn't think she could have been a Catholic if she had had to convert to it as an adult. She said you had to be "brung up" to it, from the cradle onward, because it contains so many incomprehensible mysteries that you do have to come to it as a little child. She was very admiring of her correspondent, "A.," who was baptized and confirmed in the Catholic church as an adult. Tell me about that. What was it like being a Southern Baptist boy "brung up in" the evangelical Baptist faith? What was it like in your everyday life with the Bible and the church?

Well, of course we read the Bible every day at home, my daddy did, and we read the Bible every day in school. We were, in essence, a parochial school, paid for by the state of Mississippi. The school was next door to the church just as you have in parochial parishes. Everyone, everyone in the consolidated school was not only Christian, not only Protestant, but Baptist. We had no Presbyterians. We had no "Reformed's." We'd never heard of them. There wasn't a Catholic on our side of Natchez. There wasn't a Jew on our side of New Orleans. And there wasn't a Methodist on our side of McComb City, twelve miles away. One itinerant Holiness family came through, but they didn't stay long. When someone died, we were lined up, and all marched into the church for the funeral. If there was going to be a revival meeting in the winter (which there seldom was), we would be taken to these special services, you know, during school hours, and that's all I knew. And intermarriage meant marrying a Presbyterian or a Methodist. It didn't mean marrying a Catholic, or a Jew, or a black. That was unheard of. Occasionally, someone would move down to New Orleans and their children, we'd hear, would marry a Methodist, or some such. You'd hear someone say, "Methodists don't believe in baptism. They don't baptize, they just sprinkle."

Oh, that's right. Methodists do just sprinkle, don't they?

Yeah, and that's not baptism. Plus, they do it to babies. Now, along with all that I've described, there were staunch lectures on separation of church and state, but what that meant was we'd hear that over in Louisiana they had nuns teaching in the public schools, sometimes. Now, we saw absolutely no inconsistency in any of this, and half the time our principal would be a part-time Baptist preacher, and that was all right.

Did you read scripture every morning and then pray the Lord's Prayer?

Well, not necessarily the Lord's Prayer—if you prayed the same prayer every day, that could be kind of papist. But the principal would read the scripture every day and usually it was about the different talents or a "time for all things"—that was another all-time favorite. I must say I don't think it hurt us.

That's what was done in the Atlanta public schools. Do you understand some of the objections being raised today about organized prayer in school?

I understand it. But I really—I just don't think it hurts and I think there are ways to cope, you know, even in this pluralistic society we live in. I remember some of the stories of Sonny Evans told in his book, *The Provincials*. You know Eli Evans? His father was the mayor of Durham, North Carolina, a couple of terms when Eli was a boy. He went to public school and all that same thing went on there and he told me about how he managed Christmas. One time he wrote a letter to Santa Claus, under the covers, at night. He wanted a pair of cowboy boots. He was walking to school and after hanging around the mail box a little while, he dropped the letter to Santa in and took off. He learned how to deal with being Jewish in a predominantly Christian society. When he graduated from the eighth grade, he was the class marshal. That's the one that walks in front, you know, and leads the singing and it's always "Onward Christian Soldiers." But, the leader doesn't have to sing; they may just be waving their hands, so he'd say, "Onward *um um* soldiers." But the real insight he got was when he was with his daddy in a tent meeting and they'd asked the mayor to come up front during the prayers. Now, his dad was running for reelection and Eli was wondering about that, about how his daddy would handle all this talk of Jesus. His daddy was standing there, his hat in his hand, while they were praying to Jesus. Eli looked up at his father, he was just a little fellow, and he saw what his daddy was doing, just "getting along." When his daddy saw Eli looking at him, he gave him a long, drawn-out wink. That incident opened everything up to him, he said. He realized that this was a matter of expediency. So kids learned how to deal with that, somehow. I have mixed feelings about it, but I must say, looking back, I'm not about to get out and campaign and crusade for prayer in the schools because what you'd end up with is not prayer. After all, if God is omniscient, then every thought is a prayer. One of things that people ask is, do I believe in prayer? Well, no. I don't believe in prayer. Prayer is just a word for frail, human utterances.

Before our time is up, what have I not asked you that I should have asked you?

Oh, I don't know. I think we started out by saying I'm up to something, and then I've concluded by saying I'm not up to anything. I'm trying to survive as a human being and not be a robot. I am a human being. I tell a story about this because my wife gets embarrassed sometimes at some of the crazy things I do. The cane I carry, you know. Did I ever tell you that story?

No.

I think it illustrates how I think about things. Half the time, when I'm in airports, I walk through the upright sensors, you know, and the guy down there at the end of the row says, "Go back and put your cane on the roller," which makes no sense. If there's a gun or a sword in there and you walk past these upright sensors it's going to sound. I think I was in Dallas and so was already kind of out of sorts and they said, "Go back and put your cane on the roller," and I said, "O.K." So I went back through the uprights and put it on there and just stood there. Then the guy says, "O.K., Mister, come on down" (and it was a long roller too) "and get your cane." And I said, "No, no you bring it back to me." He said, "Can you walk without that cane?" and I said, "No, no we don't pay you, *we* don't pay you to comment on the state of our health. I pay someone else to do that. Now I have done what you asked me" (people backed up behind me, clearing their throats). "Now will you do what I'm asking you? I'm asking you to bring the cane back." And he said, "If you want your cane, come down here and get it." So I got down on my hands and knees and crawled through. My point was made.

And your point is that you are a human being, not a cog in the airport's security system.

I am a human being. We must always shake our heads or our fists at the powers and principalities, shake the dust off our feet. Ultimately, I think the greatest freedom—if not the only freedom—is freedom from religion.

Do you see it as a form of liberty from arbitrary rules?

I do. I'm seeking freedom from religion. Jesus wasn't a religious person, as I see it. I'm not a "religious" person. I am Christian, but I do not consider myself *a* Christian. True Christianity implies faith and discipleship, not a subscription to a creed or to a list of beliefs. There are actually about as many gods around as there are people to worship them and about as many "beliefs" around as there are gods. And the characters in my stories grapple with these things.

Where do these characters come from? How do you make them real?

I get them where I came from, from my southern heritage, my spiritual heritage. They are a part of the genes, tissue, and sinews of me and my family. I am just now realizing how much influence my father had on me, on my way of seeing things, for example. Even families who these days are termed "dysfunctional" don't realize the full extent of the influence we have on our children. I had always thought of my father, when I was a young man, as saccharine and pious—I thought of myself as quite a maverick compared to him. Now, looking back I see things he did that were amazingly courageous and clever at the same time. Here's a story about what I mean. One time there was a rededication call going on during the church service where my family worshipped. Everybody was going down front, to get rededicated, to live a pure life from now on, and so on. My father was the only one to refuse to walk down the aisle to the front. He said he wasn't going to act any differently today than yesterday, so he wasn't going to be hypocritical about it and fool like he was.

Another time, there were about seven or eight deacons in this little country church. One of them had gotten a divorce and married another woman. Both of them were eminently decent people. They had just gotten divorced. So there was a movement by the preacher to have this deacon reprimanded by the church because he had sinned. At the crucial meeting, before the issue was raised, the deacon in question stood up and said, "I hereby resign as the church treasurer." "I move we accept," someone said. The preacher said, "All in favor?" And the deacons said, "Aye, aye." Very ceremoniously, the deacon turns over the books to the pastor, the church records, and sits down. Then, he stands up again and says, "I hereby resign as director of music." "Move we accept?" "Second." "All in favor?" "Aye." So he turns all the musical material over to the pastor and sits down again. Then he gets up a third time and resigns the deaconship. "I hereby resign as deacon." "Move we accept?" "Second." And then he sits down. Well, the young preacher, smelling blood, and thinking that he had the other deacons' support said, "I just think that we ought to go back to the old ways where we would discipline people in the church, so that when someone sins like this, they've got to come before the church and repent and ask for forgiveness, and then the church decides whether to restore them to fellowship or to 'disfellow' him"—you know, kick him out. And nobody said anything. Finally somebody asked my daddy, "Brother Lee, what do you think? You're the senior deacon." And he said, "Well, if you hadn't asked Uncle Lee, Uncle Lee wouldn't have told you, but since you did, Uncle Lee is a-thinking, who's gonna make the motion? And who's gonna second it?" And that's all he said, but they knew then, like a mule had kicked them in the belly, as they looked around, that every one of them, except daddy, was either divorced themselves or was married to a woman who been divorced, who had a living husband. That's all he said. The sermon, "He who is without sin, throw the first rock," was implied. So, all this stuff that's considered rebellious about me, well, I know where I got it.

From your daddy.

Yeah, I just caught it like a condition from my daddy. My daddy never taught it. He didn't say, "Be a rebel, Will, be an ass." †

7

DORIS BETTS

Resting on the Bedrock of Original Sin

Born in the cotton mill town of Statesville, North Carolina, Doris Betts for the last three decades has lived, worked, and raised three children with her husband on the horse farm they own in rural Chatham County fifteen miles south of Chapel Hill. An award-winning and beloved teacher and faculty leader at the University of North Carolina at Chapel Hill, Betts at the same time has earned a distinguished place in American letters as a novelist and short story writer. Beginning with *The Gentle Insurrection* (a collection of stories) in 1954, Betts's fiction has explored the complexities of love and loneliness in human relationships. Other short story collections are *The Astronomer and Other Stories* (1966) and *Beasts of the Southern Wild and Other Stories* (1973), which was a finalist for the National Book Award the following year. Her novels include *The Scarlet Thread* (1964), *The River to Pickle Beach* (1972), and *Heading West* (1981). A Guggenheim Fellowship (1958–59), a North Carolina Award (that state's highest honor), the American Academy of Arts and Letters Medal of Merit in the Short Story (1989), and numerous other literary honors and awards for public service throughout her career are testimony to Betts's achievement in creating finely wrought characters, in conveying a feeling for place and time, and in demonstrating a true, unerring sense of structure and technical control. Deciding that perhaps the short story form "sacrifices for intensity the slower truths," Betts in recent years has focused with characteristic energy on the novel. At this writing one novel,

Souls Raised from the Dead is forthcoming from Knopf in 1994, and a second, *Wings of the Morning,* is in progress.

Betts cites her exposure to the awesome power of Calvinism in her Associate Reformed Presbyterian upbringing and a saturation in biblical language and story as the origins of her art and vision. In her piece "The Fingerprint of Style," she writes, "An awe of the magical power of words was conditioned in me long ago and in a peculiarly religious manner. . . . I believed that language was the real mark of God's image within us. . . . In my church, word was like sacrament; words can pull cripples to their feet." And, as is true for most southern writers of this and earlier generations, the structures, style, and poetry of biblical narrative contribute to the shaping of her fiction. "Biblical narrative turns everything to purpose; events occur against a backdrop of eternity," she says in "Southern Writers and the Bible." In this framework, she says, she is able to experience the process of writing, of storytelling itself, as being "a struggle for faith and rescue." Stories must deal with matters of ultimate truth and must have meaning. If endings are ambiguous, there must also be the suggestion of a mode of redemption, if the story is to be a true one.

Betts has a great deal to say about the love, loneliness, and suffering that are part of human experience, particularly in relationships that seem offbeat and unorthodox, that occur in the context of unlikely situations. It is through struggles with others and through suffering that Betts's characters find self-identity and identity within family and ultimately within the universe. Sue Laslie Kimball characterizes the upheaval and transformation that Betts's characters undergo in Betts's terms, as "gentle insurrections." Kimball writes, "From the characters assembled by Doris Betts in her short fiction, we learn that no life is without hope; that it is not meet for one person to attempt to control the destiny of another; that the world is full of lonely, desperate people; that we can never completely escape our roots; and that all human relationships are to be respected and sought."

Betts describes the writing process itself as deceptively simple at the genesis of a story, but as ultimately concerning nothing less than matters of life and death: "I'm astonished by people who cope with plenty of pain and do so with real grace. To write about that and not sentimentalize, to tell the truth, the tragic truths, is what I'd like to do as a mature writer." †

This Is the Only Time I'll Tell It

Maybe we should never have given Zelene the baby.

Except for me, everybody else on those rocky farms had more babies than they could feed.

Tom Jamison could have fed his—he'll never get that excuse from me—that man was always crazy. After his wife died he got drunker and crazier, and it was nothing but accident that Zelene Bolick was walking past his house and heard that baby scream and keep screaming. She beat on the locked front door, she called, and finally ran on the wraparound porch to a kitchen window in time to see him sticking the baby headfirst down a bucket. How Zelene got inside she never said much about. That woman must have exploded through the glass. As usual, she wore half a blanket for a shawl; I guess she wrapped up her head and dove straight through the panes.

Tom, maybe thinking the whole wall would come next, let go the baby's feet and ran out the back door while Zelene yanked the baby's face out of the water and blew breath through the mouth. That picture—her with a scatter of bleeding cuts and her blanket shining with broken glass bits while she matched her big lungs to those little ones—well? It affected us. The baby, a girl, was nine months old.

When she had brought back breath and screams, Zelene opened her clothes and fixed that naked baby flat against her naked breasts and buttoned her tight inside and started running to the crossroads with the blanket wadded to her front. The lump was still glittering with glass when Zelene ran yelling into my store. Blood on her forearms had stained down to the elbow points and dripped off.

While we waited for the Sheriff, she laid the bare baby girl on my counter by the cash register. "Give her your coat," said Zelene, breathing hard.

I wished that wooden surface was softer when I saw the bruises. Would you drive off a sparrow with a log? I just can't tell you.

The Jamison baby cried through my red wool coat. "He's bringing the county nurse," I told Zelene.

"O.K.," she said, stepping back to shake a few bits of glass to my oiled floor. "I'm going back and kill him." Before I could move, she lifted the biggest ax off my shelf and was gone.

She didn't find Tom Jamison, of course. Nobody did for six months, and then in another state. By the time he was safe in prison the baby was better, her arm bones grown back shut; and we Presbyterians had voted her to Zelene and told the State what we called a *righteous* lie about next-of-kin. There's nobody can lie like a Presbyterian if he thinks good sense requires it. My wife's people, Baptists, are a lot more soft-headed; one of them would have read his Commandments wrong and weakened someday.

But we had 37 lifetime Presbyterian mouths gone flat against their teeth till Judgement Day, and 20 of them—not counting mine—had been heard to declare it was a shame Zelene had not drove home her ax.

Before the Jamison baby, see, Zelene had been pitiable herself. She was 38, and built like a salt block. Even the widowers needing a good worker in the house never thought of courting her. I don't believe her broad mouth was ever put to another human mouth until that day in Tom Jamison's kitchen; I don't think more than a washrag had ever touched her chest before. She owned an old cabin her daddy had left, two cows, some chickens, hogs, a garden to can from, one hound dog so dumb it split one ear and then two on the same barbwire fence. She had lived up the road so long alone that she went by touch and not talk. I know I often shouted the weather at her in the store—her nods and pointing made me nervous. She would pinch, too, if you took down sugar when she wanted tea.

But Zelene was a Presbyterian—God, yes.

Yes *sir*, I ought to say. On foot to church and prayer meeting, snow or not. Coming through the rain with her wide face wet, and leaving empty a whole back bench or two around her goaty smell. Bringing, not money for the plate, but one of those oakstave baskets that she wove, full of squash, beans, or wild fox grapes, for the preacher's table. The basket stayed with the food; I thought he must have dozens getting brittle in his loft.

She brought her own cow on a chain to be bred; she birthed the calves alone and slaughtered a hog in November and cured her own hams. Everything at Zelene's moved through the circles: what seeds she planted she had dried and saved; the cow's turds went straight to her garden rows; she never wrung a rooster's neck until the young cock had whipped him once. I sold her everything on trade. She put good handles on those baskets; I've carried stones in some of mine.

Zelene couldn't read—my wife brought that up at the special church meeting. Two of the elders rolled their eyes away from that Baptist flaw and toward me till I had to stand up, fast, and brag on the memorized Scripture any of our members knew by now. Somebody else said school buses would stop for anyone's children waiting by the road.

Before the health nurse brought the baby back, our whole church cleaned out Tom Jamison's house of whatever Zelene could use, even the mantel clock my wife would have liked to own. We carried the stuff a long way uphill to her front yard. Zelene came out wearing a blue dress I didn't know she owned, her mother's maybe. We formed a wheel of people near her woodpile for a baptism with cold water dipped out of the Bolick spring. The preacher bent, whispered to her, waited, poured a cupped handful on the head which now belonged to Silver Bolick. The people were expecting some choice more Biblical. My wife said the name would have better suited a cow.

All of us shook Zelene's big crusty hand. My wife told her Silver would never remember all of that early pain. A blessing.

Zelene shook her cropped brown hair. "The pain went *in* her."

Her fierce voice surprised us, she spoke so little.

"I wouldn't ever tell that little girl a thing about it," said my wife, avoiding the baptized name.

Nodding, Zelene only ran one finger down the thin arm that crazy man had broken, saying in silence that the mark was made, made deep, that water meant for drowning had gone inside this child, that no grown body—at any size—would ever be fully dry of that knowledge.

Oh, yes, Zelene, a Presbyterian.

Listen. It's true. Count them by hundreds; terrible things are true. It's all I can take eating Christmas dinner with my wife's stribbly kinfolk. They live on *should be;* I live on *is.* Open your Bible; which Testament is longer? There's not a single good argument against Jesus picking His time back in Egypt, when the Jews really needed Him. Forty years His ancestors wandered to Canaan; He never needed but 33 to set up the whole system. If you were planning all along to walk on the water, why not to Noah?

First time I ever scattered a dandelion seedhead, I knew how much life was planned to be wasted. Right away, Abel was blown on the wind?

I slid my fingers once on the baby's damp hair. "Let's go home," I said to my wife.

You can't make Ruby see anything. She jumps from Genesis 1 to Luke 2 in a breath, and all the heathen before and since those times pass through her mind in some kind of blur, without counting. I see their one-by-one breakable faces, so much like mine. Waking many a night, I have laid furious in my own bed, certain I could have run the whole thing with some speed and a lot more kindness. But you have to be Presbyterian to feel that bitter in the dark.

My wife Ruby sleeps sweetly through the nights like a Christian and prays over sins too small for a man like Adam or me to notice.

All that was back in the thirties. Ruby, who still thought she could pray out a child of our own, let that one go to Zelene with a smile. We have been waiting ever since.

I kept a close weekly eye on Silver Bolick, carried as she was through all weathers to church. When she could walk, I would keep her outdoors during services. We wrote and drew in that packed, hard dirt with sticks, while the high singing voices at our backs bounced through "By and By," and cut by tenor and soprano the Depression down to size.

Sometimes, at the courthouse, I put down a little on Zelene's land taxes. Sometimes for her I turned back the scales at my store. I told her people in town had paid cash for the baskets my mules were then eating from. Ruby wanted to carry the woman and child her own butter and pound cake; she is never going to live in these hills like a native.

All of us natives took on our voted jobs. Some, during church
hour, forked more hay into her barn; others would lift Zelene's
hens and add eggs. My job was to watch Tom Jamison, keep track of
where the State sent him next, when he would come up for parole
and how to keep him from winning. One time the guards found a
knife in his mattress; I am not going to tell you how I did that.

When she was six, Silver stood behind the organ and said to the
whole congregation the Children's Catechism. Thirty-one pages.
Not a lip in the house failed to move through the words while she
answered those questions, then to mouth prayers one syllable
behind her voice. "Give me neither poverty nor riches," she said in
this wire-thin voice of hers, "feed me with the food that is needful
to me; lest I be full and deny Thee, and say, Who is Jehovah?"

All of us shared the recital except Shank Evans; that was his
Sunday to cull out Zelene's two sickly piglets and replace them as
near matched as possible. By August, Silver was half through the
harder Westminster. That year, she got off the school bus at my
crossroads and swept my clean floor every day till her shoes were
paid for.

Slowly, I learned what her life with Zelene was like. Kerosene
lamps blown out early, though by now the electric tower stood in
her own pasture. Each eggshell saved to be fed to the chickens, each
chicken bone sucked dry and crushed and sent back mixed with
their feed. When the straw ticks went flat, they were emptied on
the clean stable floor; what had been shoveled out steamed down
their cornrows; every brown corncob started the morning fires.
Wheel in a wheel. The girl could learn worse, I thought.

As she grew tall and got long in her limbs, I would try to tell
which had been broken. You couldn't see it.

One time she told me her daddy had frozen to death just before
she was born. Who would have guessed our Zelene could have
thought of that? I passed it on. During cold winters, we took to
recalling him for Silver. It was a night like this. So was the ice in
the creek that day.

The talk molded Zelene's blunt face to a widow's. With her hair
streaking now, with her head thrown back, she had gotten her
beauty long past any practical use to her, at a time when our other
women were pinching inward.

How to explain this. Well, have you ever walked up on a feeding deer and had your breath stolen? Knowing the deer had no slight intent of beauty, he was just eating grass? Like that.

With Silver, the good looks came early. She could give feed sacks a shape. Where Mabel Jamison's hair had been sparse and pale, Silver's was full as a wheatfield and the edge curled under like a soft hem. Behind that swirl of yellow hair she had a brain you could almost hear humming; I would listen anytime she hugged me. She could outwrite and outspell the low-country children. Nobody else read the Psalms as well. Once when she did parts of Isaiah, I had to go outside and stand by myself in the heated air. She was reading from the late chapters, what they call The Rhapsodies. "The voice said, Cry. And he said, What shall I cry? All flesh is grass." I stayed out there until everyone else had, on her voice alone, mounted up with wings as the eagles.

Did she remember, through some mended crack in a full-sized bone, anything at all? Was there a spot in her trained from the very first to know, some part that ticked far away to the words she read? I could see nothing hurt or frightened in her, and her voice warmed up that whirlwind.

Then she was seventeen, and in my store trading rag dolls for cornmeal, when the man came in.

He looked at her. He was my age. He took a cold wet bottle from the drink box and paid for it in coins.

They did not look alike—let's settle that now.

"How you doing, Coley?" he said to me.

Even the voice sounded different. Last time I heard, he had fought with a prisoner and that fighting canceled his appeal.

"I don't know you," I said, and started Silver to the door. My hand was pushing on her back where the hair touched.

"Jamison," he said. He touched himself on the chest as easily? Well? I have seen flies set themselves down harder than that. He said, "I'm looking for Zelene Bolick. She still live up the road?"

Broke out, I thought, although they've got a lot of Baptists in State Government these days.

Naturally, Silver turned to see him better. I thought he searched her over for the marks that might have been there.

"She's home," said Silver, but I shook my head at her. My

telephone was in the very back of the store. Once I thought that was better; you could call in while the thieves were still scraping back the screen.

How she did stare at him! Maybe her bones were looking. Maybe below her ribs there moved a memory of water. What if she raised against this man the arm that knew his hand had broken it? Well?

I kept my axes still on the very shelf. It was so light, the one I chose, that I felt a whole crowd of us had lifted it high, and swung. She did not scream until after he burst to the blade.

Babies should not be beaten; I do not care Who made this world. †

Interview

On a warm day in early fall, Doris Betts and I met at the Carolina Coffee Shop in Chapel Hill, a restaurant near the campus that has been frequented by students and professors at Carolina for generations. We sat in a dark booth near the bar; a tiny lamp provided light enough to read our menus by. Dark panelling along the walls, a massive mirror framed in carved mahogany spanning the length of the bar, starched table napkins, heavy white porcelain coffee mugs, and a Brandenburg concerto playing a little too loudly over the radio gave the place a sense of timelessness and warmth. We ordered large spinach salads and the shop's specialty, home-made yeast rolls.

As we talked, several of Betts's colleagues or former students dropped by the booth to speak. She greeted each person by name, and in asides to me afterwards told me who they were, what class she had taught them in, what year. Cracking jokes, her dark eyes sparkling, Betts savors the ironies of life without cynicism; after one former undergraduate, now in his thirties and with two school-age children, bemoaned encroaching bald spots and bifocals, Betts turned back to her salad and laughed, for both of them, it seemed, telling me, "Cheerfulness is the only stance with which to approach old age."

Esteemed by folks in her community (when I asked the bartender to turn down the volume on the radio a bit for our interview, he obliged willingly when he realized I was interviewing Doris Betts), Betts has clearly loved her teaching over the thirty years she has taught freshman surveys and creative writing at the university. On this day, just as classes had started back up for the fall semester, she told me, "I am enthusiastic. There are some truly dedicated, talented students I've got this time." I have a hunch that she has greeted every semester's new crop with a similar response.

As we settled in to the business at hand, Doris inquired about my family and my childhood church. Like her, I was raised in the Associate Reformed Presbyterian church, a small, southern sect characterized by its particularly austere form of Calvinism. "Associate Reformed Presbyterians are the All Right People, my mother always told me," Betts said. "She thinks the 'plain' Presbyterian church I go to now is pretty radical."

As the waiter brought iced tea, I asked about her family. A grandchild was baptized this year in the small Episcopal church in Pittsboro, the country town near her farm. "At St. Bartholomew's they do things differently. The baptism was at sunset, for Easter Vigil. There were tambourines, a bonfire, a procession into the old church, musical bells. The grandbaby just squiggled and squirmed the whole time. But it was good to see so many people in the community, some I hadn't seen for a while." This keen awareness of all that's going on and sense of the need for connectedness suggest the origins of her loving genius for character, place, and story. When a chicken truck turns over on the highway, Betts empathizes with the chicken; a story about death and life among those who, trapped by fate, suddenly find themselves painfully free, ensues.

Betts's strength of character and droll wit infused our time together with laughter and sharp insight. The time flew by until mid-afternoon, when she headed out into the sunlight toward her three o'clock seminar. She hugged me, saying, "Give my love to your family," and turned toward the campus. A few steps down the sidewalk, two students called out to her, and she waved to them to walk with her toward her office.

Tell me about your new novel, Souls Raised From the Dead. *Many folks have been asking with great enthusiasm what this novel is about, but I'd like to ask what did you consider yourself to be about in the writing of this novel?*

I think it is a religious novel. I mean in the sense that it's exploring those old questions—if there is a benevolent God, why is there so much evil and suffering in the world? Why does God allow the innocent to suffer? Of course, I don't give anything but my usual ambiguous answers at the end. It involves the death of a child and that's the worst thing you can bear—but I do think the end is not really ambiguous, because the novel follows one character, the father, who is moving forward. I meant that to be a point of positive recovery, at least a slight rise from the depths of despair. The endings that came to me at first were all so Pollyannaish they were unbearable. They made light of the suffering of people who really have lost children. You just can't do that. It really is a lifelong blow. Even though you may learn to survive, the damage goes very deep, I think. I remember one evening after I had read from the novel, a minister came up and said that he had lost his teen-aged daughter in an automobile accident years before. He told me,"Whatever you write, don't write that you get over this because there are some mornings that I get up and it just happened an hour ago." And I was really in tears listening to him. And I thought, you just can't play false to that by giving any kind of glib catechism answer. You either have to turn to hope, thin though it may be at the time, or you just have to say: "To hell with this life" and cut your throat. That's why it has taken me so long to finish this novel. I wish I'd never started it. I got to the point where Mary had to die, and I just balked. I wrote descriptive passages and I prolonged the girl's illness; I did character sketches of minor people; the novel got longer and longer without getting the least bit better. It just hid. And finally I just had to come back and do her final scene, where she does die, and it's not even two pages long. I just had to beat around the bush a long time to write those two pages.

What about your novel-in-progress, Wings of the Morning?

I'm not sure. I don't like it as well as I did when I last put it down. To my horror, there has now been another novel published with that title, which is, of course, from the Psalms, and that shook me. I haven't rekindled to it. It was ("was"—that was an interesting past tense)—it *is* about an orphan, abandoned at Barium Springs Orphanage, who grows up to be a Presbyterian minister. His life roughly parallels the twentieth century, during which he watches religion lose its power in American life, as I do think it has. I think I'll finish it, but it has problems.

Also you probably need to hear about the first one.

You haven't quite cut the umbilical cord until they say something. And then there may be changes. I'm not at all a prima donna. I usually get good editorial advice and I usually listen to it.

I enjoyed reading Beasts of the Southern Wild, *and I'm absorbed in* Heading West *now. What do you think about* Heading West?

Well, it seems to me it was okay when I wrote it. There are lots of things that I would change now. In November I am going out to talk to the Western Literature Association. That's what they want to hear about—a southern writer using western themes. So I've been reading a lot of western literature and also Jane Tompkins's book, *West of Everything*, which is fascinating. The essays are lively, and I've also seen it attacked for feminism and vegetarianism. For me, the importance of *Heading West* is that it was a less "southern" novel, that Nancy Finch got out of the South even though she returns to it.

You mentioned during a reading at the time that you wondered why no one had written fiction about the Grand Canyon.

It's like the ocean, one of the great natural images. And one of the great images of the abyss. Do you know Loren Eisley's essay about in going down in the cliffs in the earth, you also go down through the layers of time?

"The Immense Journey"?

Yes! And the canyon is a huge experience of that descent. And if you're ever to feel that there can't be anything going on here except geology and microbiology, you will then, because the canyon is dwarfing. You can die in it in no time at all. I quote Carl Sandburg about the canyon because he looks at it differently. He has this line everybody else loves, "There goes God with an army of banners." Well, really that's *not* what you think when you look down in there; you think there might not be any God anywhere in the world or the universe. Nihilism. So I was interested in going down into it and coming out.

You've described the Associate Reformed Presbyterian Church in which you were raised as "a tribe, descendants of Abraham, Southern W.A.S.P. division—Scotch-Irish, mill-workers, All Right

People." Is the Presbyterian Church you attend now an A.R.P. church?

No. It's plain. And in fact now that my mother has moved down to Pittsboro, she really finds it pretty radical. [Laughter] So each time I go to a worship service I sort of have one eye on the preacher and one eye on my mother. But fortunately she's getting deafer and she misses a lot of social emphasis which is probably a blessing. The ARP's . . . I still get their monthly magazine, thanks to Mother. They haven't changed at all. There are still no women elders, much less ministers. They still speak of homosexuality as a sin, period. There are no gradations. There's no place to move from; you're either in or you're out. They remain everything that I both loathed and benefitted from simultaneously, because I did benefit from it. I wouldn't trade anything for the knowledge of the Bible or for their love of the Psalms, a predilection which is a total contradiction to their standard Calvinist bent.

In "Fingerprints of Style," you write that "paradox sung on that eerie, praising note of the Psalms" is how the "incredibly magical power of the Word" was conveyed to you as a child.

These psalms—they are mostly joyous. Once in a while you have one of those "smite mine enemies" psalms, but in all the denomination's determinism, mostly their songs are songs of praise.

Another paradox always puzzled me (I was raised in an Associate Reformed church, too). I've always wondered about the Associate Reformed Presbyterian creed. Our church used to have altar calls. Did you all have altar calls?

We did used to. And we also had spring and fall reunions and both had altar calls. I always felt guilty that I was not going forward again. Didn't you?

To rededicate? Yes!

Especially if the invitation went on and on, and nobody came forward. They always played "Just as I Am."

I've always wondered how getting saved in this manner fit in with Calvin's teachings about the doctrine of the elect and predestination. I never did figure this out even though I did get saved by coming forward during an altar call.

I don't think you can work with this paradox very long. I assume that if you came forward you were in the "elect" even though you had not known it until now, unless it was not a true conversion, in which case you had always not been elected. Really when you start examining it, you can't work it out. The one thing that I would say is that I've come to look back at that doctrine as having an ugly truth in it, something to do with the commandments. I've always objected to that "visiting sins unto the children of the third and fourth generation" business except that in real life, I see that sins do get visited: that if you're a drunk, those children are penalized by it, or if you're a child abuser you've passed it on; and to that degree, I would say there is an almost genetic predestination. Sometimes an environmental one. Americans as a rule think everything can be fixed, but I don't think that.

Americans on the whole seem to abhor the idea of original sin.

That's right. They have a childlike faith that everything can be cured by science or technology. But in recognizing that all cannot be cured, that's a big difference from acquiescing to fatalism, and I always thought the A.R.P.'s acquiesced to it; and some of them, indeed, felt pleased by retribution. Whereas I want, I prefer, to be like Job and shout, "What are you doing!" shaking my fist at heaven. I don't want to give in.

The notion of God choosing and not choosing the elect for salvation and not revealing who's who.

I don't see where you get that out of anything Jesus said. You don't see it in the Gospels.

An Episcopal priest once told me that when he talks about original sin, he says it's not that we're depraved, but that we are broken human beings—not broken and thus "fixable," but broken in terms of being wounded or injured. And in the wounding we wound others and we need the grace of God to become whole.

I might go even further than that. Something about rearing children has made me think that in all of us is a perversity and a self-centeredness that, if it is not schooled out of us, or if we are not helped to shed or mitigate it, we do turn into rather terrible, self-centered adults and do lasting damage. Some criminals didn't get schooled out of it. Think of the children who've got to grow up without a chance to make that switch. I believe any child would torment an animal and go on to worse from there unless taught otherwise. You have to be taught that somebody else feels the pain you feel. I don't believe you know that automatically, and dogs and cats don't either. And in that sense that's what I mean by "original," that biologically you are programmed selfishly inside your soul, but with a human nervous system and the ability to teach one another, we can see this centering on self. The dogs and cats don't see it.

Our obligation, then, is to reach it and teach it. So many people say, "I can't stand being a Christian or think about going to church, because it talks about people being wretched and sinful, and I can't accept that."

Most of us grew up hearing more about hellfire than about how we could be kinder to one another.

I was definitely afraid of John Calvin. I memorized the Bible verses, and did everything I could think of to try to keep from burning in hell and then I realized at about age eleven that getting saved so you could be sure to go to heaven could be regarded as nothing more virtuous than taking out an insurance policy.

And what could be more selfish or more self-centered! I just read this biography on Calvin, by Stephen Zweig, and clearly Zweig hated him. It's a hatchet job. But what may have "done in" Calvin forever with me is something only a woman would hate. It was what he said at his wife's funeral—and this was his sole accolade—"She never interfered with my work." Wouldn't you like to go back through history and whip the man?

That's awful. I think he ought to be throttled. But at least he was able to say that art is of God and not of the devil.

Yes. And I was relieved to hear he drank a little wine. But he still did some terrible things. That stern pietism is probably what I wanted to get away from. But I ought to add that the touchy-feely extreme alternative also strikes me as being wrong-headed.

As you have pointed out, "Sometimes to rest with a grin on the bedrock of original sin can be downright relaxing."

I think that is true—perfection is not required. And in fact Hugh Holman taught me something that helped me with original sin. He thought the route of brotherhood was never through the perfectibility of man, because nobody ever got to be perfect. But if we all admitted we were fallible, then we had to be gentle and forgiving with one another, not because everybody was as good as everybody else, but precisely because nobody was any better than anybody else. One view leads to pride, the other to humility. Now that happens at the end of *Heading West*. Nancy leaves home being very judgmental about her family (and indeed they have a lot wrong with them) but when she comes home, she has learned she also has a lot wrong herself, so does everybody. It's in that context that we can care for one another, not because we expect perfection. That shift has been very helpful to me because youth is judgmental, and I was a very judgmental kid.

Mark Twain remarked once how astonished he was to see his father grow smarter as the younger Twain turned twenty-one. I've been reading your essay, "Southern Writers and the Bible," in which you talk about the southerner's keen sense of "standing in the need of prayer" in the aftermath of the Civil War.

We not only lost, but moral people thought the South deserved to lose if the Bible meant what it said. Certainly the church was used to justify slavery, but of the southerners who stood strongly against it, most did so out of religious conviction. They just couldn't work slavery into the Sermon on the Mount. I still remember to this day when I was maybe twelve or thirteen we had a radio program on a local station in Statesville called "Youth Views the News." This was back when they used wire recorders, and students met at one another's houses to record the program each week. I would get two from this school and two from another and we would all discuss whatever—and we didn't know beans, of course. The time came when we invited students from Morningside, the black school. My mother had always served us Co-Colas and potato chips at our house. When I told her that students would be coming from Morningside this Saturday, I could see her face stop. She'd never really had black people coming in her front door, sitting down on her living room couch, and having Co-Colas and potato chips. And then she said—and this is so elemental—but it's the basis of a good starting place beyond racism—she said, "Well, I guess it won't be any different in heaven." She'd made that leap, perfectly. That's ultimately the leap that even uneducated Christians had to make if they believed in any kind of literal way. I don't see how they could prevent making that leap.

That reveals to me a bedrock understanding of the Christian message.

Yet, look how hard integration was in the South, in this Bible Belt. The civil rights movement did have its roots in the black church; the white church had none of it. That failure is part of what has hurt the church with young people. It didn't take leadership in the biggest moral issue of this century for Americans.

Your characters have been said to be "misfits who are somehow deserving of understanding and love: A simpleminded girl awaiting faith healing, a retired mill worker searching for the heavens and his own heart, a kidnapped librarian who heads West into a landscape of desires and discoveries." I've been tracing a motif that seems to be recurring in writing by southerners. Reynolds Price dubbed it in his own works as the notion of "the saintly outlaw."

Oh, I like that.

I wondered what you thought about your characters as misfits or saintly outlaws?

The surprise is: if you're on the side of the outlaws, you don't know they're outlaws. To me, they seem like the real citizens; the others seem like the outlaws. I'm always surprised when somebody says "I like your eccentric character." I wonder what's eccentric about that character? I mean, she's me. Or at least she seems to me normal. I've done various old women that people have called eccentric, and I thought, no, I'm going to be just like that. I prefer people like Walker Percy's characters who in some way are willing to ask questions, or to take a risk. They haven't settled down or given up. The worst thing I could think of is that you should be self-satisfied and not open to challenge or change. Even if you have to be kidnapped to have it, you know, like Nancy Finch. There are many ways to skin a cat.

The name of the father in the new novel?

His name is Frank, which is really for Francis Thompson who wrote *The Hound of Heaven.* I am trying to imply that even in the worst of circumstances, I do believe one is being sought. Being pursued.

Really? Tell me more about that.

Yes, I do believe that. I do believe there is an overarching love that seeks out the soul.

In Lee Smith's new book, The Devil's Dream, *a character named Katie Cocker sings a song called "God Stood Waiting by the Side of the Road." In my Episcopalian-but-deep-down-Associate-*

Reformed-Presbyterian heart, I sat down and wrote the music and lyrics to the song.

Oh, wonderful! I want to hear this.

It begins: "When my soul was tempest tossed/ When all hope in sin was lost/ My Saviour came to find me . . . ."

See, that's the reformed message. Look how old-fashioned you are! You're theological. But isn't that better than thinking that we either have to do or be something wonderful in order to attract the attention of the universe? It's hopeless, if that's true. Reformed theology does make one less judgmental of everybody else in the same fix. It has its benefits.

Yes! Katie Cocker winds up finding this little church out in the country with a preacher and a number of women elders and deacons who are healing by laying on the hands and praying.

Because the way grace so often occurs is through other people. My new book wants to deal with that, even though I let the child die. I finally realized that I wanted her to die on the page, in one of those out-of-body experiences. But I'm not going to pronounce on whether that's a physiological experience or a supernatural one. The reports from patients who "come back" are at least comforting—there is a light, there is a journey. I don't care if the experience is physiological—it seems a very generous thing for plain old biology to have done for us, to have provided that means to go out. And I mean the book's theme to be: Though grief is horrible, and though you will never get over losing your daughter, nonetheless, Francis lives on and is changed (not because suffering is to be sought; I'm not of a hairshirt mentality), but suffering does come. The question is whether through it, or beyond it, something else is operating. I think something else is.

In the context of this deeply rooted faith, what brings you to write fiction? What do you think are the origins of your wanting to write fiction?

Oh, Bible stories, beyond question. They're the most marvelous stories. Besides being wonderful stories, they make the place where you live nontemporal; it is always possible that if an angel showed up on a threshing floor, appearances could happen anywhere. It makes you feel that the ordinary is not ordinary. Flannery O'Connor wrote about incarnation, or immanence, in a whole different way. She would have the red sun seem to be God peeping over the pines. I don't go that far. I don't trust God as magic. It's not something I see every day. I am more likely, on a day when I feel down and in need of help, to come home at the end of the day and think, how remarkable that so-and-so called me today and said that good thing. Wasn't that a gift? Yes, that was a gift. If you're looking for grace, you see it. If you're not looking for it, you won't see it. Graham Greene's novels say this. So seeing grace is not proof. I do not believe you can persuade anybody of God's presence, but maybe you can encourage them to consider the option, to choose to look.

Did you memorize Bible verses and stories as a child? Did your mother tell them to you?

Constantly.

Did you have sword drills?

Oh yes, we had to memorize books of the Bible and had to find things fast in the Bible in teams. My first real book was *Hurlbert's Bible Stories*, which Reynolds Price often mentions. And it's full of dreadful engravings. You do have David holding Goliath's head by its hair. And when I show these pictures at Sunday school (I taught four- and five-year-olds last year), they were only interested in the blood. They wanted Absalom to hang by his hair in the tree.

And Jezebel with nothing left — but the palms of her hands. I love that one myself.

I read the book of Esther, recently, for the first time straight through.

Isn't it a wonderful book? And God's name isn't mentioned in it one time. God isn't the problem. See, that indicates a sense of humor in "inspired" scripture, to omit Oneself.

The first two or three verses of that book talk about the rich blue tapestries and the glorious food that is laid out for a banquet. They feasted and drank wine for five solid days. It's full of sensuous detail.

Oh, it is, like fairy stories, too, with details that are really significant. I like, too, the presence of a lot of truly bad people in the Bible, what writers call "round characters." Again we're back to the comfort of imperfection. Here's Jacob, he's really a mess, you know, not a hero at all, a cheat, if anything. Even a hero makes a big mistake, even David, the big King David with Bathsheba; everybody makes some sort of mistake. It's a great comfort. And it teaches you how to make characters in fiction. The best advice I've heard about creating characters I heard in a sermon. It was about "Thou shalt love thy neighbor as thyself," and I thought, "Well, I don't have to listen to this; I've heard this." And the Reverend Louis Patrick said, "Bear in mind that you don't always love yourself," and I thought "Uh-oh." He said, "You're often ashamed of yourself, or angry with yourself, or even feel like you'd like to get rid of yourself." He said, "Even in those moments you make excuses for yourself, you put things in context, you justify; you say, "I had a headache," or "He asked for it." What that text asks is that you make the same kind of excuses for other people that you make for yourself." And I thought: "That's how you create characters; you put yourself in their position and figure out what their excuses and rationalizations would be." We all feel that if we went to heaven and got to explain everything about our lives and errors we'd be forgiven! Even murderers. I do think that religion helps you think about people in a different, more truthful way because you lose your illusions about yourself.

In your writing fiction you distinguish yourself from Flannery O'Connor, suggesting that she tends to use broad, loud symbols to get people to pay attention to what she says.

She draws these dark, stylized lines around people, like Rouault, and I really prefer ordinary people who are muddling through. They're the only kind I know anything about.

But you don't set out to write a "theological" story.

No. I don't think of anything; I don't even think of the theme at the time, much less anything theological. The book about the child dying got started because of this chicken truck wreck out here on the highway. I had no idea where that was going to go. But in retrospect I saw that those very real chickens were symbolic. Frank Thompson's wreck was coming two hundred pages later. You know, at moments like that, even those starter-moments are like gifts. Something comes along that hits what you're ready for—if you're patient.

If you can hold on long enough.

And the novel ends with a wreck in the Haw River, which I made deeper and wider than it really is. I'm going to get letters correcting that. And I'm going to say: poetic license.

Now, here's something you said that I would love for you to elaborate on: "Any writing must be a struggle for faith and rescue." You were talking about the difficulty of writing, that even the difficulty had a theological dimension to it.

When you start writing a story, it is like the chicken truck; there is no meaning. It's only a spark for a story. And even many pages later a novel is like your own life; if somebody came along and said to me today: What is the meaning of your life? I would fall out. No one knows an answer, but somehow in a book the writer knows that there has to be something a story is here for—and if it's not, then it was just a vignette; it doesn't add. It doesn't matter. I don't mean an ending that cites a moral, so much as makes a point or fulfills the whole in some way. Yet, you almost never know what the sum of it is going to be. And you proceed (I think I was comparing the process to what was required of Abraham and Isaac), you proceed in writing this book thinking: It might be up there. If I keep climbing, there might be a ram in the thicket, an end to this book, even though I don't know what. Some writers do know what their ending will be; some know what theme they're working with. For me, it's as if I were the reader going through it for the first time, and I'll go back to page one, fix and direct it more, but while writing I almost need that anxiety of being uncertain whether this story makes any sense at all. I need it.

And it's a horrible anxiety.

One needs it. That's where the adrenalin is. That may also be Presbyterian. There may be writers who can get adrenalin and impetus out of joy, but I can't get it out of joy. I need to be prodded by uncertainty, even a pretty sure sense that it's probably not going to work.

You are prodded out of a sense of impending doom?

That's right.

When you've finished a work, do you always have a sense of being dissatisfied?

Always.

I asked Reynolds Price that question and he said, "Oh no, when it's done, I'm satisfied with it. I know I did my best and couldn't have done any better than that."

Bless his heart. That's like Billy Graham saying, "Once I was saved, I never had any doubt again." No, it's never as good as I wanted it to be. It's never even what I thought it was as I approached the end, when I thought, "Oh that's it!" I write the last page, and then I say: "That's *it*?"

It may make you dread writing.

Yeah, it does. My attitude is: I'm going to fail at this, too, but it's a better failure than the last one.

And there may be a few breaks in the clouds.

Yes, there are moments. And I've learned something from doing it. The process does sound very Presbyterian, doesn't it? It's the old pilgrimage motif transferred to whatever you do in life. You don't arrive. You just keep moving.

"Life is but a passing moment on a never-ending trail," as the old Primitive Baptist hymn says.

It's true. I grew up believing that and in spite of years of arguing otherwise, life relentlessly said to me, "You was right the first time!" I threw it all away, but essentially, if you pay attention, you have to come back and admit, well, this creed or this belief resulted from the experiences of thousands and thousands of people who were looking at the same things I'm looking at, year after year, life after life.

They were on to something.

Sounds like Will Barrett!

It's that soul-searching, that sensitivity.

And it doesn't have anything to do with how educated they were, just with how vividly they lived. How much they paid attention. Religion makes you pay attention. Do you know Madeline L'Engle's essay where she's looking after her grandmother, and she says, "And now I will go on loving her as long as this dwindling may last." Dwindling, I thought, that's the best word, and the loving that can cope with that is the best, too. But "dwindling"; when I read it, I just shook. Some words are so right, they do feel sacred. See, that's one place where I find a link between scripture and other kinds of writing: that sacredness of words in works that are ostensibly secular, when I think, yes, there it is! When he's talking about reading prose, John Gardner says you can tell where the power turns on and off. Even my students can do it. They can't do it all the time—who can?—but you'll be reading along in a paper and there it'll be, right there, the lively, sacred word. That's a moment of real truth.

In your essay, "The Fingerprint of Style," you talk about the word "indwelling." I thought, "Oh, I haven't heard 'indwelling' in so long" and it's such a powerful word, filled with rich connotations.

A sacred word!

You have written that "Biblical narrative turns everything to purpose; events occur against the backdrop of eternity." Are you aware of this happening in your fiction, too?

I read to a college audience once, and someone asked, "Do you always make your stories have so much closure?" I suddenly understood that he meant closure in a really pejorative way. I don't want to have strict closure, but I do feel that if fiction doesn't in some way satisfy the appetite it has raised, the story hasn't been worth reading. Many postmodernist stories don't. Though I may love them while I'm reading, by the end of the week I've forgotten all content. I can't tell one from another because I am not able to summarize, to say it's a story in which "x" happens. There's no nutshell except situation, and situation doesn't move. That's very old-fashioned. I still prefer in fiction that something changes between the beginning and the end. It may not be a big plot twist, but something becomes either larger, or deeper, or altered, and altered in some significant way, or else why'd you bother to write it? That is one profound influence the Bible had on me. Usually Jesus would stop in the middle of a parable. He just gave the parable and then his listeners were stupid, so he had to explain it. I like the parable you don't have to explain, but the reader gets the sense that a parable is there.

When Jonathan Yardley was talking about Heading West—

Yes, that was really one of the most interesting reviews. It was a thoughtful review. I have a lot of respect for him.

He maintained that the novel became an argument between "masculine" and "feminine" points of view.

I think it is. Most of the novels by women do have more closure. Besides my religious sense, women in general have a tendency, if not to solve the problem, then at least to solve the nature of the person who has to live with it. That's very female, because women have never been able to pick up and just leave their problems behind. Either they go off to the asylum or they stay home and feed that baby, tend that old woman, wash that dead body. They don't go to sea or the French foreign legion. Coping produces a different attitude. Yardley really would have preferred, in fact he says so, that Nancy went down in the canyon where she had an experience of existentialist despair, and the novel left her there. He felt that to bring her out, certainly to have her get married, which seems neither feminist nor liberated, and then to come back home and deal with her awful family turned a literary novel into what he called "women's fiction." I do know what he means. I wrote him and just said, "I haven't learned how to do that well enough yet." I don't believe it's that reductive if it's well-written. Anne Tyler is doing it, that classic endurance of making the best of everyday life. Many women whose writing I like a lot are doing it. If it feels like *Cosmo* or *Redbook*, then I haven't done it yet; I've copped out. But I want to learn how to write that reality well, because I'm tired of despair. Gloom was more fun when I was young than it is now. It's not the mood I want to carry with me into my last decades which are going to be tough enough anyway. I do see why as you get older "cheerfulness breaks in." What are your options?

"Old age is not for sissies," as the saying goes.

By then all the weak ones have dropped away or been killed, some of them even slaughtered, absolutely slaughtered. I used to characterize the hope in Christianity as merely wishful thinking. Now I think it is hope. Not certainty, but hope. And I find hope sufficient. I'll settle for maintaining a hopeful attitude. When you live or write that really well, it isn't as sappy as it sounds when I say it now. It turns into courage.

It's a unifying attitude that Dorothy Hill has written about Lee Smith.

Oh, yes.

The book talks about unification, about healing the ancient cultural split between mind and body, flesh and spirit. And you were saying in that connection that Smith's fiction has a darker side that may go unnoticed.

People assume Lee Smith is "just" funny. She is funny but she's not funny, funny but serious; she's very serious. I have more in common with Lee Smith in some ways than I do with Flannery

O'Connor. Lee, too, believes that you can tell serious stories
through the voices of beauticians. You don't have to go all the way
to the saint or to the Oxford don; the issues are the same. Christianity taught democracy about equality of souls, that despite
worldly condition, nobody is more or less innately worthwhile, or
more or less curious or pained than anybody else. I wish I had more
of Lee's humor—I don't have it. It wells up out of her personally,
and it wells up on her pages.

*You've remarked upon the fact that Calvinist thought, austere
though it was, has such a generous view of God's grace. You
described it as being like an alpine floral mat at a chilly high alti-
tude.*

Even in these cold reaches of Calvinism there's something blooming.

It reminded me in an odd way of what Alice Walker said in The
Color Purple: *God wants to woo us, and is angry if we don't notice
a field of purple flowers.*

What Shug has is very old, natural religion, that feeling that in
the earth there is a spirit omnipresent. C. S. Lewis said the convenient thing about that religion was that it didn't ask you to *do* anything. Just walk by the ocean and say "Wow!" And that's the point
where Alice Walker and I probably part company. But we outdoor,
rural southerners have had an opportunity of seeing enough nature
so we can still see what Wordsworth meant. We're not in the Alps,
but we're not all humanists in big cities, either. The actual Grand
Canyon is realer to me than the grand canyons of New York City,
where I see crowded human beings at their worst and at their least
compassionate for one another. In a rural state we live close to
nature, and natural images, which again are biblical. We are still
open to them though we're losing that rapidly to malls and high-
ways and suburbs. Ironically enough, much of the Old Testament is
couched in terms of that kind of austere, rocky, dry landscape. No
wonder Jehovah is such a vengeful thing. Whereas in the New
Testament you have more of the Jordan valley and things soften a
little bit. You have a little bit of green grass, and it is a place where
sheep can safely graze. Landscape makes a difference. In the southern landscape where we can be outdoors and nearer to animals, we
can feel there is a rhythm which we do not create and do not con-

trol, and that affects what we think in a way that if all your milk comes from the dairy, you're not affected like the man who bred the cow to freshen her.

If the chickens always come in little plastic wraps, you don't see them in the same way as you do when you have to wring their necks and dress them for tonight's supper.

Most consumers don't have to kill anything. They don't have to have any mixed emotions. Part of the decline of religion may be just that simple. A whole way of life has changed. The peasantry is disappearing. Now if you quest after religious belief, your journey will be more like the experience of Walker Percy's characters although he sends them down into caves and into desolate places, too, when he has to. But in our time it will be more of an intellectual search, very lopsided, but better than nothing.

Have you read Harold Bloom's American Religion?

Yes. It's gotten some strange reviews but he's right; Americans seem to prefer gnosticism.

You mentioned something about leaving religion behind for a while; you didn't go to church for a while.

A long time.

What was going on then?

I lost it pretty much in college where I found atheism much more intellectually appealing. It seemed brave, the way Camus was brave, and Sartre was brave; they were willing to face that abyss of nihilism. To be like Sisyphus, to climb up there and push that rock. I concluded that Christianity was a form of whining that was necessary for weaklings and stupid people. It didn't occur to me to recall the sin of pride. That attitude lasted a very long time. But I fooled myself because even during those years, having persuaded myself that prayer was only a psychological delusion, it was just a way of discussing things with the superego, I nonetheless went on "discussing things with myself" before I went to sleep. And I justified prayer by saying, "This is efficacious; this is cheaper than therapy." I finally thought, "You're just lying, aren't you?" That's Calvinistic training, the lifelong suspicion that you're probably not telling yourself the truth.

You have to be pretty hard on yourself.

You do. And that's probably a gift, I think. Although it's sometimes discouraging, I would prefer self-scrutiny to the alternative. So I was gone a long time. Really I was gone twenty years.

What brought you back?

What brought me back is just one small version of what brings most prodigals back, just being in a situation that I couldn't control—in this case being at the point where my children were growing up and away and I was worried about them and they were understandably not listening to me. In worrying about adolescence and rebellion, I caught myself praying for them, because nothing else was working. And I do believe those prayers were efficacious actually, though not because I asked for "x" and "x" happened, but because in some way the good you petition for other people floats around and gets sent back like a light. Prayer certainly helped me. Even anxiety helped me. Until then I thought I had been running my life very well.

That's a wonderful story. I have been reading about conversion experiences.

Which I can't say I had. I just kept edging back, grumbling all the way.

And you remain struggling and questioning?

Some days it doesn't seem to make much sense to believe. Everybody has days when indeed one feels like these children will never grow up, probably you ought not to stay married, your job is rotten, your friends are disloyal, and so on. On the scale of the "dark night of the soul"—the blues are really kind of small. You just plod on until they go away.

When you were away from the church did you feel bereft of it? When I was not a part of any church, I thought I was having a pretty good life. I was like the Misfit. I was doing all right by myself.

Me, too. Exactly. And I wasn't under any particular stress. I didn't feel especially guilty. In fact, I felt enlightened and superior. I used to think that you couldn't go to church unless you had everything settled in your mind about belief. I had defined faith as certainty; now, faith is simply my decision to proceed in a certain direction. To try it, to give it your best shot.

When I was growing up, I was afraid that religion, perhaps even God Himself, was going to do me in.

It has done a lot of people in. But as you said about Mark Twain and his father—don't you find the church better now than you ever dreamed it was as a child?

It is, indeed.

Churchgoers seemed such hypocrites when I was an adolescent; now they seem remarkable, all things considered. But I couldn't have been in this church twenty years ago. That realization brings me back to a wish somehow to do justice to good people like the ones I know in my church. Many of them are leading courageous lives, lives that are not big, but how big do you have to be to bear what they bear, and do it with remarkable good cheer? That's not sentimental; there's something very potent in goodness. But it's very hard to write about without getting sappy.

Oh, I know it is, even to talk about.

It turns sugared candy on you, but virtue matters just as much as existentialist despair, though admiring virtue is out of style, and writing about it feels like false optimism. That's why I both respected Jonathan Yardley's review and was also troubled by it. I was trying to say something about suffering and compassion—Nancy did start out as a Pharisee, did come back as a Publican, did learn something. The canyon made her able to be generous. And if that's just "women's fiction," God, I'm going to have a hard twenty years ahead!

"Women's fiction." That phrase was the kiss of death.

Nowadays, to write "feminist literature" is the kiss of love.

These labels in book reviews can be awfully facile.

One thing I did not like about the review of Lee's book in the *New York Times*, which as a whole was a lovely review, was that near the end, it said that you can "draw up your chair on the front porch and get your sweetened ice tea and listen to a born story-teller," and so on. It's a reductive stereotype. It makes Lee less than she is, though I know he meant it as a compliment.

And you can't take it apart. It's a phantom. Once you start trying to say, "Well, the reason why that is reductive or condescending is . . ." It's difficult to be from the South, and writing about your own place.

And it's doubly difficult to be from the South with religious interests. Since now the one special interest group that's fair game are Christians, who are always represented by the worst possible examples.

Jim and Tammy?

Exactly. That's what a southern Christian looks like in Manhattan. And I don't have any earthly way to show the difference between Oral Roberts and the people I know in the pews—I don't know where to begin in explaining this difference.

Reynolds Price talks about how his family, his racist cousins filling the pews behind him, about how can it be that these people speak and act in such a racist manner and yet are there at the same time tending children in a loving way and acting compassionately in the community among both blacks and whites.

There's just a hole in many southerners. There's just a hole. You can walk right up to it and fall in. It's like the San Andreas fault.

And you find yourself staring down into the abyss.

But I think we will see that go. There's still a lot of racism, but it's differently based. It will wane.

You mention in your essay "Southern Writers and the Bible" that some of the best writing seems to come about when a given culture is in decline.

Somebody told me that; that's a theft. When I tested it, I did think that was true. Homer's *Iliad*. Even Milton's *Paradise Lost*, for instance; you are already sliding towards the Renaissance by that time. I do feel religion slipping away, and if there is something worth saving, there is an urgency to save it. And that animates what is written. I believe that John Bunyan felt it slipping; I don't think he was preaching to the choir. There continue to be needs and hungers out there that no institution is dealing with very well. When churches get involved in social action, some conservatives complain the church should focus on worship. In the split between faith and works, people line up on one side or the other. We have lost the unity of body and soul, faith and works together. Because it's the best synthesis around, I cling to the church. What will people do in a hundred years if there is no church? Are they going to marry and bury and christen out of city hall? That tribal necessity to solemnize, even at so simple a level; its loss will produce, is producing, psychological unhealth, disease. Not every Tom, Dick, and Harry can push that stone uphill with the existentialists. That's what Flannery O'Connor's Misfit says.

The metaphor of disease and healing you used is a useful one. I think that much healing occurs when we realize that we are universally human beings with ancient stories that are to be felt and reenacted in communities.

And we've moved death into a mechanistic setting—out of sight. Yet in the end, there is a body. Who handles that in any sense well but the church? Even in Graham Greene's funny book called *Travels With My Aunt*. That crematorium chapter is dead serious. Greene is illuminated, I would say, by a vision of what really matters and he cannot keep it out even from his comedies and spy stories.

Tell me about "This Is the Only Time I'll Tell It."

It's based on a true story I heard on the car radio one Thanksgiving. It was a news report about the murder of a little baby, except she was drowned in a sink rather than a bucket as I have it in the story. I came home, sat down, and wrote the story straight through, though I did not know where it was going at the time. The story does violate the premise of "Vengeance is mine, I will repay, saith the Lord," because the narrator commits the vengeance in an act of rage which I fully understand. But by making that Who capitalized in the last line, I really meant to say that the narrator is a believer though he has a long way to go. That little story also has something to do with the novel because both are about doing something inexcusable to a child. A very human reaction is to strike back as Coley does. But the novel is trying to reveal a different and, I think, a better reaction. My reflex when I heard the story on the radio was that somebody ought to kill that fellow. That was my honest, unredeemed knee-jerk response. Any religion in the story is not in the revenge murder at the end, but in the raising of the child and the fact that the community provides her a family. That's the redemptive act. That's the real religion. †

8

RANDALL KENAN

Ancient Spells and Incantations

Although Randall Kenan was born in Brooklyn, New York, in 1963, from the time he was less than eight weeks old, he was raised as part of an extended family of farmers and preachers in Chinquapin, North Carolina, a tiny community in the eastern part of that state. After graduating in 1983 from the University of North Carolina, Kenan worked as an editor at Knopf. His first novel, *A Visitation of Spirits,* was published in 1989. Honors include a New York Foundation for the Arts Fellowship and a MacDowell Colony Lila Wallace Reader's Digest Fellowship. Kenan currently teaches creative writing at Sarah Lawrence College and Columbia University. He is at work on a nonfiction book based on interviews conducted throughout the United States about contemporary African-American culture in this country. His most recent fictional work, a collection of short stories entitled *Let the Dead Bury Their Dead,* was published in 1992.

A Visitation of Spirits introduces the inhabitants of Tims Creek, North Carolina, a fictional hamlet as rife with intrigue and tragedy as Yoknapatawpha County, Mississippi. Tims Creek is a rural community of singular personalities, both black and white, earthly and supernatural, whose comic relationships often have tragic consequences. Using layers of richly allusive language, Kenan tells how Horace Cross, a young man tortured by real or imaginary demons, recapitulates in one night's wild vision his young life among the people he has loved and hated so passionately. The nighttime visitors ultimately force Horace to confront his tortured homosexuality, the treacherous relationships between blacks and whites, and the hellish undercurrents of condemnation and wrath boiling beneath the surface of his elders' self-righteous preachings.

In *Let the Dead Bury Their Dead,* Kenan returns to Tims Creek. In this collection of short fiction, angels, ghosts, and demons are active, vocal citizens who are intimately involved with the lives of human townfolk in a full hierarchy of the natural and supernatural, flesh and spirit, in an eerily credible cosmology. As Valerie Minor wrote in *The Nation,* throughout these stories "reclaiming life history—whether through apparition or scholarship—is a healing process of personal and cultural recovery."

Kenan's religious experiences as a child and adolescent were potent shapers of his imagination: "I took the whole thing very seriously . . . all that hell-fire preaching. For me this was just a very simple formulation. If God exists and if the Bible (especially if it is inerrant) is to be taken on any level as the truth, you have this profound spiritual tension between good and evil." In his fiction, Kenan blends secular philosophical influences from his adult life in New York City with the Calvinistic worldview of his youth: "I wanted to blend in my own way the southern gothic (which is how people describe my sensibility but I don't really see it that way), and my Down East spirituality with this understanding of the world. And it occurred to me, existentialism actually dovetails with Calvinism ironically—how bleak the world is, and so on." †

The Strange and Tragic Ballad of Mabel Pearsall

Mabel going down the road. Mabel in her car. Mabel's mind a flurry. Mabel's mind like Mabel's car. Racing. Down the road. Down, down, down. Mabel. Mabel. Mabel thinks:

Peculiar. That was the word he had used. *Peculiar.* She could not believe that man. That man had actually sat her down just to call her—peculiar! Not troubled. Or strict. Or tired. Which she was really. Tired. All those bad children running around the classroom. All day long. Five days a week. Then back home to cook. Wash clothes. Clean up after everybody. Fuss at them for not cleaning up after themselves. And then to run to church to help out with one group or the other. The choir. The Women's Club. The Usher Board. The 4-H Club. The Finance Committee. Every night. Some group. Some organization. No. Not tired. That ugly old white man. Sitting not a yard from her. *Peculiar*. To her face. Oh, he tried to be compassionate. Puffing that cigarette. Always puffing that damn cigarette. Trying to be kind. Still she couldn't believe the sheer gall. That he.

A deer leaps in front of Mabel's car. Magical. Graceful. Lithe. From the woods. From the blue. Like a sign from God. Mabel gasps. So hard she thinks she might pass out. In front of her with its hind legs in the air. Its tail up. Then gone. She jerks the wheel hard to the left. She stomps on the brakes. The car lurches. Screeches. Her head barely misses the wheel. The car slides roughly into the opposite lane. The front left tire bites into the grassy shoulder. Followed by the rear left tire. The long blue car halts only inches from the gully. A jerky stop.

Mabel doesn't linger over what would have happened. What could have happened. If a car had been in the other lane. She stops to say a word of thanks. To her Lord Jesus. Her mind's eye fixates on the tail. It all happened so fast. All she had clearly seen was the snowy tail. That sparkling white tail. Like a star. Mabel cannot think. Only see. See the tail. Searing into her mind. A brand. Charring the center of her brain. Hotter. Brighter. Until it becomes a pain. At the base of her skull. Thud-thudding with the force of a hammer.

A few cars whiz past. No one she knows. No one stops to see if anything is wrong. Why is she like this on the side of the road? Slowly she begins to remember. To feel her heart beating like a frantic bird. To realize that her car is partially off the road. Stopped. Facing the wrong direction. She tells herself she must right the car. Continue on home. About her neck are gathered all the aches and sorrows of the day. The pressures. The tiny scars. The minute wounds. Pains. They all rise to the center of her head. A balloon expanding up and behind her eyes. She refuses to let it push through. Mabel is afraid. So she sits. Trying hard to push back the throbbing. To keep that hoard of hurts behind her face. One slips through. Hot. Another. And another. Until like a broken dam. A cracked dike. She weeps. Sobs. So relieved. Mabel is finally crying. Mabel collapses in the seat. Closes her eyes. Mabel has wanted to cry for so long.

Mabel in homeroom. Earlier that day. Mabel taking the roll of her seventh-grade class. Phillip Pickett taunted Felicia Jones, who sat across from him. An impish white girl with longish blond hair. Phillip picked at her and pulled her hair. Felicia constantly whining: "Mrs. Pearsall! Mrs. Pearsall! Make Phillip leave me alone! I'm gonna hit him!"

"You ain't gone hit nobody, gal." Phillip looked round to his running mates. Mabel's stomach churned. These boys giving so much attention. To this silly girl.

"Phillip, leave that girl alone. This minute. You had better be studying for that test this—"

The intercom cut her off. It snapped and crackled on so sharply. It made her start. Embarrassed to jump before the children.

"Mrs. Pearsall?"

"Yes, Mr. Todd?"

"I need to see you this afternoon after the buses leave."

"Okay."

"Thank—" The old speaker gave the same electric fire-snap-crackle.

What could he want with me? Perhaps it's something about one of the students. But which one? Or maybe it's about the girl they found lice on the other day. Or one of the three children flunking? Or that little girl whose father regularly beats her and her mother? Or . . .

So much. Mabel could not bear waiting six hours to find out. She was sure it was some little thing. Something about one of her students. But his tone. He usually had an impatience in his slow drawl. But there had been something else in his voice this time. Something too nice. Too.

All day she kept her ears and eyes open. What could Mr. Todd want? She scattered hints like bread crumbs when she talked to the librarian. She dangled bait before the cafeteria people. She coaxed her fellow teachers as if sprinkling birdseed to sparrows. No one bit or nibbled at any of her hints. No one volunteered anything. No one dispelled her not knowing. They all smiled. Nodded. As if they didn't know.

Lies. They knew. She knew they knew. All the "Good morning, Mabel"s. All the "How you feeling today—how's Allen?"s. All the "Sure is a pretty day, isn't it?"s. All said behind normal smiling everyday faces. Behind eyes reflecting placid routine. Behind cups of stale instant coffee. They knew. And behind their raisin buns and chicken salad sandwiches they talked. Snickering. Laughing. At her.

Wasn't it about her? Of course. It had to be. She had seen it coming. She had felt the change in people. Whispering behind her back. Like wind in the grass. Concealing. Conjecturing. Condemning. Her.

The day went on. The tension grew worse and worse. A headache threatened but never fully came. The children rowdy as hell. Throwing paper airplanes. Getting into fights. Talking when she was lecturing. Shooting spitballs. Throwing books. She sent five boys into the hall. Reprimanded ten girls for talking.

Finally the last bell rang. Children scampered out to the lines of yellow buses. Like rodents into blocks of cheese. She sat in her room. Absorbing all the festive colors all about. The puppets. The posters. The maps. Bright. Intended to entice children to learn. She inhaled. Smelling the chalk and the dust. She wondered who she had been at twelve years old. She watched the afternoon sun through the tall oak trees. Beyond the high windows that lined the wall. Thick with a milky and distorted film. She sat waiting. For the proper moment to get up. To go down the hall with the dark wood floors. Down the creaky, ancient stairway. Down the hall to Mr. Todd. Mabel felt dread. Noxious as black coffee in her belly.

"You can go on in, Mrs. Pearsall." The overweight secretary grinned. She knew. The thing Mr. Todd concealed. Mabel always felt better when in the same room with that cow. She made the few pounds Mabel could not lose seem light.

Smoke in the hot room attacked Mabel. Rushing up her nostrils. Forcing her to cough. Mr. Todd sat at his desk as though a part of it. Motioned to a seat in front of his desk. He did not rise as a gentleman should. He did not ask her about her health. Her family. Her state of mind. Or what she thought about the weather. He did not look at her. As if talking to a child. Staring out the window. Onto the schoolyard. Now showing signs of spring. He was puffing his cigarette.

"Mrs. Pearsall. I've been receiving a few complaints." He paused. Puffed on his cigarette. Stubbed it out.

"Complaints?"

"You see, some of the parents have called in. Said their children have been . . . have been saying . . . *things* about you."

"Things?"

"Yes. And I wouldn't have said anything if there hadn't been . . . so many."

"I don't—"

"And then, you see, some of your colleagues . . . well, they have added to that and have suggested that you . . . that you might not be . . ."

"Mr. Todd . . ."

"That you weren't quite yourself."

"I don't understand what you're talking about."

He cast an impatient look at Mabel. She had always considered him an ugly man. Now he was more so.

"Do you feel okay, Mrs. Pearsall? Is there anything we can help you with? Some problems you've not told us about?"

"Mr. Todd. Exactly what are you talking about? . . . I don't . . . there's nothing wrong with me—"

"Well, why are you behaving so . . . so peculiar? You seem to be . . . well, a bit . . . preoccupied, shall we say? Perhaps you should consider . . . Well, to be frank. You're beginning to frighten the children. And I've noticed it myself. I'll tell you—"

"Mr. Todd, I—"

"Now please don't get angry or anything. Do you need some time off? Is that it? I can understand that, Mabel." He actually called her Mabel. The first time he had ever been so familiar. She found herself resenting it. "You've been here for twenty years. I've been here for eleven of those twenty. And I've noticed a significant change in—"

"Mr. Todd, like I said, I didn't realize that I was behaving . . . abnormally. I—"

"Well, you have . . . downright peculiar, to be honest . . . peculiar . . . and . . ."

Mabel. Mabel. Mabel. Mabel down the road. In her car. Stalled on the road. Now salt water bathes Mabel's nutmeg cheeks. The image of the deer's tail still burns in the back of Mabel's mind. Mabel comes to see what has befallen her. She is powerless. She cannot understand it. Cannot help it. But she feels it. In the morning when she rises to cook breakfast. She looks out the back window into the rising sun. But she feels no joy. Her heart feels hollow. Numb. A fear and a longing have taken up residence in her soul. She prays to the sweet Lord Jesus. Please lift me up. Praying does not help. She prays. And prays. And prays. Like the old people. Rising only to fall to her knees in the morning. Bending her knees before she sleeps at night. She remembers everyone she can think of in her prayers. But for all her supplications she has been ignored. Nothing has changed. She knows the sun shines for free. She knows she has food to eat. A fine place to live. Good clothes to wear. Why does she feel so forsaken then? So wrong?

Mabel wipes away her tears. Retouches her makeup. Using the mirror behind the sun visor. She notes her face. Sagging. No longer taut and ripe. Not wrinkling. Just sagging. Her eyes now red. She turns the car back onto the highway. Feeling not better. But less sad. Numb. Again. The bright tail still flashes in her head.

The late-afternoon sun paints an abstract color. Across the sky. Explodes. Ambers and coppers and violets and infinity. Over corn and soybeans. Vivid. Alive. Fire and water. Mabel wants to be there. Where the fire is. Mabel's numb is like the sky. Mabel. Mabel. Mabel.

Mabel turns into the lonesome road leading home. An old red car ambling to meet her. Down the road. Patricia. Mabel does not understand why the Good Lord has chosen this day. To test Mabel so. Patricia. The last person she needs. Wants. To see.

Patricia stops her car. Rolls down the window. Smiling that sweet lemon-juice-and-marigold smile.

"Miss Mabel! How are you?"

"How you doing, Pat?"

"Just fine. Just fine." The flash at the base of Mabel's skull grows. Brighter and brighter. Mabel lets her smile grow with the pain. An opening blossom.

"You think you'll be able to keep Alexander tomorrow night,

again?" Patricia has rich skin. Like good earth. Mabel just knows it yields soft. Goosedown-soft.

"Of course, Pat."

"How's Allen?"

Mabel does not flinch. Mabel's eyes do not quiver. Her smile blossoms more. "Oh, he's fine. Working hard. But he loves hard work, you know."

"Well, I better go on. Tend to the baby."

Mabel continues to smile. As she heads toward home. The blossom-smile finally drops off. Petal by petal.

She turns into the yard and sees the lawn mower. Sitting abandoned. No grass cut. That boy, that boy. She gathers her book bag and her purse. Hurriedly. She marches into the house.

"Perry! Perry!"

No answer. She walks into the family room. There they both sit. Before the television. Stuffing their mouths with chocolate bars. Perry fifteen. Now weighing two hundred pounds. No taller than five feet ten. Anne, his sister, there too. She a plump one hundred and sixty. Shorter than Perry.

"Boy, didn't I tell you to mow the lawn? You were supposed to do it yesterday."

Perry does not move his eyes. "*G-Man's* on now. I'll do it a little later."

"*G-Man* was on yesterday." The pain in Mabel's head gives a strong throb. She winces. "*G-Man* will be on tomorrow, and the next day. And after *G-Man, Sanford and Son* and then *People's Court,* and then it'll be too dark. Get up *now.*"

She walks over to the television. Switches it off.

"Ma." Perry frowns. Mabel puts her hands on her hips. Akimbo. He gets up and switches the television back on. "In a minute."

Mabel runs her hand over her face. "Anne? Did you do the laundry like I asked you?"

"No."

"Why?"

"In a minute."

Mabel stands there staring. Afloat in her pain. Rage. Humiliation. She can only fume. Finally she asks: "Where's your father?"

"Shed."

They can't even speak in full sentences. Me a teacher. And they can't speak in full sentences. She flees the room. Why can't I get them to cooperate? To stop eating? It's Allen's fault. He.

"Allen, why didn't you make Perry cut the grass?"

Allen. Tall. Slender. A bit of a paunch forming. Just a little. He bends over the open hood of an old Buick. The innards of the car stare at her. Angry metal monsters. Mabel knows they hate her. "He'll get to it, honey."

"It took him two weeks last time."

"You want me to talk to him?"

"Yes."

"Okay."

"When?"

"Christ, Mabel. Does everybody have to drop every damn thing the minute you say? I'll talk to him, I said."

Mabel goes back to the house. Into the kitchen. Of course Anne has not started supper. Mabel checks the beef she left out to thaw. She thinks of everything that happened today. Of the Simpson boy calling her a witch. Of the look Frances Miller gave her in the cafeteria. Of the way Mr. Todd spoke to her. Of the way Patricia flounced before her. Of the way her own issue are ignoring her. Of the tone in Allen's voice. Of the deer. Of the car's wrenching. Of the light in the back of her mind. Mabel. Mabel. Mabel.

Mabel sits down. Mabel wrings her hands. A child. She feels exactly like a child on a ride. A high scary ride. She wants to get off so desperately. Whom does she tell? She starts to pray. Then stops. No one is listening. Why? Is she so bad? Peculiar and evil like everyone is saying? She closes her eyes. Just closes her eyes. Calm yourself, woman. Won't do any good to get all worked up. No good. No good at all. The light begins to shrink. Slowly. Like a plane into the distance. Smaller. Into a tiny pinprick of light. A morning star in the north of her brain.

> *Ain't no reason to sit and cry.*
> *You'll be an angel, by and by.*

"Ma, what's for supper?"

Part of her wants to throw a chair at him. Yet she remains motionless. Her eyes closed.

"Roast beef and rutabaga."

"Ugh."

Mabel ignores him. Gets up and starts the laundry. Seeing Anne has no such intention. She thinks about cutting the grass. No. Allen. Maybe later.

Mabel goes about fixing dinner. The peas. The mashed potatoes. The rutabagas. The iced tea. She calls them in at a quarter after six. Again at six-thirty. At twenty minutes to seven she huffs into the family room.

"I told you twenty-five minutes ago that supper was ready, didn't I? Didn't I? I work hard all blessed day. Come home. Nobody's done anything. Nobody *will* do anything. I have to wash the clothes, clean the house. I cook and you don't have the respect to come eat before it gets cold. I swear you'll all drive me crazy. I—"

"What's the matter, honey?" Allen walks in behind her. Wiping his wet hands on a clean white towel. Smearing it with engine grease. Mabel almost bites through her cheek. To stop herself from yelling at him. She has told him before.

"Supper's ready and they just sit here. I told them—"

"Perry. Turn that TV off and go eat your supper. You too, Anne."

Sluggishly the two rise. First Anne. Then Perry. Perry mutters: "Always fussing."

"Boy, don't you talk back to me. And don't talk ill about your mama."

A graveyard gloom hangs over the table. Perry complains about the rutabagas. Declares he will not eat them. Mabel demands he eat them. Allen grunts. Perry doesn't eat them. Mabel tries to tell Allen about the deer. About Mr. Todd. About. But though he grunts he doesn't hear a word. He never does. He doesn't have time to listen to her. She knows. He knows Mabel's peculiar too. He hates her. His mind on that damn car. Some blessed carburetor. And that woman.

Perry and Anne fight over who is to do the dishes as they do every night. Mabel hangs out the clothes. In early twilight. The pain no longer pounds at the back of her skull. The light twinkles on the horizon of her mind. The hanging of clothes soothes her. It always soothes her. The smell of the fabric softener. April-fresh. What an odd way to describe it. The feel of moist terry and cotton and nylon. The sight of a stretched sheet rolling in a slight breeze.

Mabel has no papers to grade tonight. No church meetings. No community meetings. No choir rehearsals. Nothing to run off to. She sits with the family in the family room and watches television. Sipping iced tea. Allen falls asleep after the game shows. He snores bearishly. Mabel can never understand how he can sleep there. In such an uncomfortable position. A tender relief comes to her at nine o'clock. Her favorite show commences. Wealthy women in smart clothes. Tall, sinfully handsome men. Elegantly appointed rooms. Swimming pools. Expensive cars. Children who don't talk back. Sex. Romance. Mabel knows it's only fantasy. But such fun. The good are clearly good. The bad baldly bad. Both good and bad always nice to look at. Secretly, it is more than fun and fantasy to Mabel. Deep down. She truly longs to step out of her life. Into the television world. But so secretly even she doesn't know.

Tonight: the evil woman is attempting to sabotage the catering business of the good, hard-working, nice-looking heroine. Mabel is that heroine. Patricia the evil saboteur. Though in age and position it is clearly the other way round. That doesn't matter to Mabel. Mabel's heart goes out to the heroine. Mabel roots for her. Mabel alone with her family. Mabel silently cheering. Mabel left hanging. Mabel waiting for another week. Mabel dreaming of caviar and diamonds. Mabel. Mabel. Mabel.

Mabel lies awake many a night. Waiting for Allen to come to bed. After he has dozed on the recliner. As late as one or two in the morning. Finally she drifts off. To awaken at five-thirty. Untouched. Allen thick with slumber. On his side of the bed. A quarantine box. It has been over a year since they last did it. Before that maybe six months. This is the dead giveaway. How she knows something is seriously wrong. The way she knows that Patricia has stolen her man. At first she reprimanded herself. Thinking: It's crazy, Mabel. He hasn't been sleeping with that no-good tart. She had pushed it from her mind.

But things would happen. Here a clue. There a hint. She noticed more and more the strange way Patricia regarded her when Mabel spoke. If not Patricia then who? She noted how Allen would react when she questioned him. When he was inexplicably absent or late. With anger. Unwarranted anger if he had done nothing. A wife has a right to ask. Allen, I just asked. Don't start yelling at me just because you take an hour to go pick up something that should take only fifteen minutes.

Then the baby. Of course the baby. Yes, the baby. He had Allen's eyes and Allen's smile. And if you put Patricia's and Allen's tones together you'd get that damn baby's color and why did she have to go and name it Alexander if it wasn't Allen's? Nobody in her family named Alexander and.

Mabel in bed. Mabel at night. Mabel can't sleep. Mabel's mind slips away from her. So many rabbits out of a broken hutch door. Mabel can't catch them. They scamper. They hop. They flee. Mabel in the dark. Mabel in an empty bed. Mabel watching the star in her mind. Mabel. Mabel. Mabel.

I almost left college because of him. He was the first one. He was the last one. Mama told me I didn't have to marry him. Daddy said I didn't have a choice. If I wanted to live. I wouldn't know how to be with another man. Wouldn't know how to feel. Allen taught me everything I know about being with a man. I knew it was a sin then. But I wanted to please Allen. Allen. Allen. When I came home the summer before my senior year. To work in tobacco. He paid attention to me. Nobody else ever really did. He looked so good. All sweaty. So good even with dirt all over him and his hands caked with tar. Allen would take me out on Saturday nights that summer. Allen gave me my first drink of beer. And Allen—I knew it was a sin, Lord, but I was a little drunk and after we did it once I didn't see any harm in it and it made Allen so happy. He needed me to make him happy. It didn't make any difference to me and, Allen, why don't you come to bed? Allen, why Patricia? It was that Christmas. It had to have been then. That night. Christmas Eve. It was cold in that car. It was in the backseat. An old Ford Fairlane. His hands smelled of grease. But good. He was already working as a mechanic down at the base. I didn't know for sure until February. I was showing at graduation. We were married right after. Allen. You ain't got to marry him. But I can't teach, Mama, if I don't. I love him. My voice cracked when I said that. I don't know if I loved him or not. But I wanted him. I wanted him. And the baby died. After all that. Can you believe that? Is that why, Allen? Cause the baby died? Cause Perry came along two years later and he turned out sorry? And Anne came along three years later and she turned out sorry? Allen? Is that why? Cause I can't have another, or so that doctor keeps saying? Is that why? Allen? Mabel finally falls asleep. Looking at the light on the television screen of her mind.

Mabel at church. Mabel in a white dress. Mabel smiling for all the world. Mabel good. Mabel true. Mabel washed in the Blood of the Lamb. But the Lamb won't save Mabel. Yet Mabel won't give up on the Lamb. So Mabel smiles. Mabel prays. Mabel pays her dues. Mabel. Mabel. Mabel.

Look who's here. Mabel cranes her neck. Mabel sees the bright and the good of Tims Creek. Dr. Streeter. Such a good catch for Clarissa. Mrs. Maggie Williams. Looking so fine and well-to-do. All good, upstanding Christian people. Not like Patricia. An unwed mother. Seducer of other people's husbands. Oh hello, Reverend. How are you? Just fine. Of course I'll chair the committee. My pleasure.

After the service Mabel moves through the crowd on the church lawn. She's well respected. A model Christian. A faithful servant. A good and faithful servant.

She talks to Gloria Brown about new robes for the choir. She notes Allen talking with Patricia Jones. Over by the sycamore tree.

". . . ton blend will be easier to clean . . . Mabel? Mabel? What's wrong, honey? You don't look so good. You look kinda faint."

"No, Gloria. I'm fine. I'm fine. Just fine. What were you saying?"

"That the cotton and nylon blend would look better but the rayon is just more practical and . . ."

The nerve, Mabel thinks. The gall. To talk to him here. In public. In my presence. Among good *Christian* folk. To flaunt her sin. With my own husband. How dare the little strumpet. How dare the.

"Mabel, honey? You sure you're all right?"

"Oh. Oh, yes, Gloria. Yes. I'm sorry. You know the preacher is coming to the house for dinner and I'm just a little distracted, you know. Why don't we talk later. I'm going to collect Allen and the children and get on home."

Mabel walks over to Allen. Now talking to Fred Jordan.

"Allen, honey, we better get on to the house. I got to finish dinner for Reverend Barden."

"Oh, okay now. Talk to you later, Fred."

Mabel in the car. Mabel thinking. Mabel wishing. Mabel hoping.

"What did Patricia Jones want with you?"

"Hgh?"

Mabel interprets his shock—is it really shock, Mabel?—as confirmation of guilt.

"Patricia Jones."

"Oh, that Jones girl. Her car. She needs a tuneup. Wants me to do it. Wanted to know when she can bring it around."

"Oh really?"

"Really. Why?"

Why. Why. Why. Why. Why? *Why?*

"Why you want to know?"

"Just curious."

Mabel at the dinner table. Mabel in the kitchen. Mabel talking to the Reverend. Mabel reminding the children to mind their manners. Mabel serving greens and beets. Mabel serving ham and rice. Mabel trying not to think about Patricia. Mabel trying to stay calm. To not be peculiar. Mabel so blue beneath her smile. Mabel. Mabel. Mabel.

They wave good-bye to the pastor. As he backs out of the driveway. The phone rings. Anne answers: "Ma, it's for you."

Who could it be? Gloria I bet. "Hello. Yes, honey. How are you? Good sermon today, wasn't it. Pastor just left. What can I do for you? Uh-huh. Why of course I will, Patricia. No problem at all. What time you leaving? Okay, fine. Don't think nothing of it, child. My pleasure."

Mabel wants to slam the receiver down. But she replaces it gently. Like a living thing. Not wanting to harm it. The hussy. The brazen little whore. The gall. To ask me to babysit my husband's baby. The hateful little bitch. I should have told her to.

"Who was that, Mabel?"

"Patricia Jones."

"What she want?"

"Me to babysit. Again."

"Oh."

Oh. Oh. Oh. Oh. The star in Mabel's mind gives a little flicker. Just a little flare. Allen didn't even—couldn't even—say a word. Of course he couldn't. I'm sure he gets a kick out of me babysitting his own child.

"Ma, can I go play with Timmy Phillips?"

"No!"

Everyone just stops. Everyone. Allen. Perry. Anne. All stop what they are doing. And stare at Mabel. Eyes wide with dismay. Mouths open in astonishment. She feels her hands clenched into tight balls. Her shoulders trembling.

"Honey, you okay?"

"I'm fine. Just fine." Mabel leaves the room. Goes into the bathroom. She wishes she could do the laundry. But it is Sunday. No work on the Lord's Day. Mabel the good Christian. Mabel obedient to the Law. Mabel faithful. Mabel forlorn. Mabel on a Sunday. Mabel. Mabel. Mabel.

Mabel at three o'clock. Mabel at Patricia's door. Mabel with a magazine in one hand. A purse on her shoulder. Mabel knocking on the door. Mabel ignoring the light. In her head. Mabel thinking how good she is to have come. How Christian of Mabel. Washed in the Blood of the Lamb.

"Miss Mabel. Thank you so much for keeping Alex. You know where everything is. I should be back before nine."

"No problem. Don't worry now. Everything will be fine. Just fine."

The mobile home smells of fish and onions. Doesn't the little homewrecker know to heat a little vinegar. In a dish. To take the scent away. And look at the furniture. Naugahyde. Peeling. Disgusting. Dust an inch thick behind the chair. Hasn't swept under the sofa.

Mabel looks in on Alex. Such a little cute thing. Sleeping quietly. With Allen's eyes. But are they Allen's eyes, Mabel, really? Of course they're Allen's eyes. Just look. Just look. If you've got eyes to see you'll see they're Allen's eyes.

Mabel paces. Mabel looks at her magazine. Mabel looks out the window. The baby cries. Mabel feeds him. Mabel thinks how good she must be to feed her husband's bastard child. How many women are as good as Mabel? How many? Mabel is good. Mabel is strong. Mabel rocks the child to sleep. Mabel sings:

> Go to sleepy, little baby,
> Go to sleepy, little baby,
> Mama and Papa both gone away,
> Left nobody but the baaabeee.

Mabel thinks: Mama. Papa. Who is your papa, little bastard

child? Will you ever know? Will you ever know it's my husband? The star in Mabel's mind begins to *krrkt* like a match being lit. The baby sleeps. Mabel puts it back in its bassinet. Mabel is a good woman. Mabel is strong.

Mabel turns on the television. A good TV movie is on. Mabel has seen it before. A nice family. A nice husband. A nice wife. A nice home. Nice car. Nice children. Nice. Nice. Mabel sees nice and nice sees Mabel and Mabel begins to wonder when she will be nice. Nice like the people on the screen. Oh just stop it, Mabel. It's just television. No one anywhere lives like this. No one. Maybe some. Maybe Miss Maggie. Certainly Gloria Brown and Clarissa Streeter. Their husbands are nice. Their hands are always clean. Not caked eternally with grease.

The baby begins to cry. Mabel picks it up. A bit annoyed. She wants to watch her program. She paces the floor. The baby stops. Mabel places it down. Gently.

Mabel tries to calm herself. To watch the television movie. The light now the size of a quarter. It pulses. She feels a slight thud in the back of her head. She watches television. The nice man has an affair with a good friend of the nice wife. A nice affair. No babies. Not like real life, Mabel thinks. Not like. The baby begins to cry. The pain. In her skull. Mabel's right eye twitches.

Mabel checks the diaper. Nothing. Mabel rocks the cradle. Coos. Looks on the baby's quiet. Envies the baby's innocence. Was I ever so innocent? Mabel thinks of her childhood. Of her mother. Fussing. Complaining. Talking about her. In front of others. As though Mabel were not there. Saying: "She's gonna be a big one. Fat I spect. Just hope she marries off before she runs to fat. Don't eat so much, girl. Put that cake right back." No innocence for Mabel.

Mabel goes back to her show. The climax. The nice wife confronts the nice-though-philandering husband and the nice-but-wicked friend is in peril and the nice man must help and the nice wife must choose. The baby cries.

Mabel tries to ignore the baby. Sits. But the wail the wail. Mabel goes to the cradle and looks down on the baby. The baby with Allen's lips. But are they Allen's lips, Mabel? Of course they are. And she rocks the cradle. Yet the baby only yells more. Loud. What's the matter, child? So loud. Demanding. Just like all of them.

Demanding. Hush hush hush. But the baby just cries. The light in Mabel's head like on the first day. Brighter. Harsher. And Mabel cannot see. Cannot see for the light. Bright bright bright. Mabel frantic. The baby's wail high-pitched. Piercing. Piercing her head. Or is it the light? She tries to pick up the baby. But cannot see cannot see cannot see. The light stabs the back of her eyes. Courses through her limbs. Shoots through her fingers. She finds the child. Good. But the wailing the wailing. It slices to the quick of her. She flinches and drops the babe. It hits the ground. Gives a breathy *uummph*. Begins to scream afresh. Mabel manages to pick it up but the blaze in her head and the baby's cries hurt. Oh blessed Lord blessed Lord it hurts so much why so much? Too much. In Mabel's head the wail becomes a choir of voices. Images. The deer. Mr. Todd. Patricia. Anne. Perry. Allen. Allen. Allen. Screeches of hate. Accusation. She wants to go away. Into the television forever. She wants to be nice forever. Oh shut up, Mabel yells. Shut up shut up shut up all of you just leave me alone.

Mabel puts the baby back in the bassinet. Mabel trembles. Mabel thinks: Calm yourself. Mabel steels herself against the wall of sound. Mabel picks up the baby. Baby baby screaming baby. *Sssshuuusssh. Sssshusssh. Ssshusssh.* But the baby keeps screaming. Oh it hurts. It hurts so much.

Mabel throws Alexander. She does not think. She does not see. Her eyes are closed. She throws Alex hard. As though he were a wild creature. Tearing at her brain. Up. Away. Go. She hears the sound. The thud. She hears silence. She smiles. At last. And Mabel's whole mind is flooded with God's Holy Light. Just as in the Garden. Him treading the Earth in the First Morning Dew. Silently. Such peace. She can see. So clearly. The light makes no sound. Mabel walks over to the baby. He makes no sound. He is still. His black eyes gaze heavenward. Mouth agape. Sweet little baby. Allen's little baby. Allen's and my little baby. I'll adopt it. Yes. I'll make everything all right. All right. Yes. I can. I will. We will name it Elroy. After my father. Yes.

Mabel picks up the baby. Gently now. Mabel sits before the television. Seeing only the Holy Light. Bathed in the electric-blue glow. Rocking rocking rocking. Singing:

Hush, little baby, don't you cry,
Papa's gonna buy

Mabel in an ambulance. Mabel in handcuffs. Mabel calling for her baby. Calling for the Lamb. The ambulance flashes red. The patrol car flashes blue. Quietly. Like the light in Mabel's mind. People stand all around. Staring. An inky sky above them. The stars wink down upon them. But can they hear the chorus below them? Singing:

Get sixteen pretty maidens to carry my coffin.
Sixteen pretty maidens to sing me a song.
Put branches of roses over my coffin,
So I'll look pretty as I ride along.

Mabel's mind a field of lilies. Not a sound in Mabel's mind. Only sweet light in Mabel's mind. Sing a song for Mabel. Washed in the Light of the Lamb. Sing a song for Mabel. Mabel. Mabel. Mabel. †

Interview

I met Randall Kenan on a cool, bright April morning in Chapel Hill, North Carolina. The sharp shadows and warm sunlight, azaleas and dogwoods blooming along the walkways, and the natural gray wood, cedar shakes, and wooden stairwells of his apartment building gave everything the open, radiant air of a Key West beach house.

Inside, Kenan greeted me with coffee and sweet rolls. As we sat down at the kitchen table, he filled me in on what he had been doing since publication that month of his new collection of short stories, *Let the Dead Bury Their Dead.* He was in town to visit a friend and see his younger sister who is studying at a secondary school nearby before making his way across the country to interview "black folk," as he put it, for a new nonfiction book about contemporary African-American culture.

Kenan's manner is at once unassuming and arresting in an utterly engaging way. Like the country preachers among his kinfolk, he is gregarious with an air of formality that is both impressive and comforting. You know where you stand with Randall Kenan and you clearly are welcome. On this Saturday morning, he was wearing a pair of pleated slacks and a starched oxford shirt; at a bookstore reading later that day he would have on a gray three-piece suit.

The qualities of sophistication, self-deprecating humor, and imaginativeness that characterize his fiction show also in his manner and voice. At twenty-eight, he is teaching fiction writing at Sarah Lawrence, and there are those who consider him to be something of a wunderkind. He has published two volumes of fiction in which the complexity of language and theme demonstrates an extraordinary achievement and promise. Terry McMillan has praised Kenan as "a genius; our 'black' Marquez." That day he laughed merrily and easily, taking great delight in performing "southernisms," using ritual phrases of greeting, asking about kinfolk, calling up memories of mama's cooking and how sorely missed it is, and so on, while at the same time talking with passion about his work. On the wall hung a stunning black and white photographic print of an athlete's torso, with a quotation from Rainer Maria Rilke: "For there is no place that does not see you. You must change your life." I asked Kenan about it. "It's amazing, isn't it? I liked this quote so much I put it as an epigraph to 'Run, Mourner, Run.' In that story, the main character betrays his friend out of a lethal combination of naivete and greed. I think one of the things Rilke was saying is that we are held, I mean impaled, you might say, by what shames us, and that what shames us becomes what compels us to the passionate life; we must transform it into creativity or flee from it forever in terror, leaving horrific destruction in our wake.

We talked together at the table for two hours or more, Kenan getting up occasionally to pour us more coffee. The phone rang every half hour or so; his publicist was calling from New York, once to ask Kenan's birthplace [was it Brooklyn or Chinquapin?], then calling back to ask how to spell "Chinquapin"; then, Was he teaching at Sarah Lawrence or Columbia? He politely answered each query, then returned to our talk, apologizing for the interruptions. "She's new. She is getting publicity packets together for my tour for the book. I'm thrilled to be doing this. It's all so exciting— exhausting but exciting." I asked him a long, involved question, something about his fiction and Calvinism, the origins of a tragic view of life in his beloved homeplace, the clarity and mythic nature of his fiction. He rested his hand at the nape of his neck, grinned, and reflected, "By all rights I should be totally crazy from all these spirits talking to me, the physics and metaphysics of it all. But . . . I *am*—and I love to write about it."

You're travelling around the country these days working on a new book.

Yes, I'm interviewing black folk across the nation about what it means to be black in the latter part of the twentieth century.

How would you respond to that question for yourself—especially since you have lived most of your life in the South?

I was born in Brooklyn but after six weeks I was brought back home to live with my paternal grandfather's family in Chinquapin, in Duplin County, North Carolina. Both my mother and my father were from Duplin County. My great-aunt took me home one weekend and apparently we had a grand old time. She did this more than once and one weekend she just didn't bring me back. I stayed on her farm until I went away to school.

You'd found your home. What did you all raise on the farm?

Hogs, chickens, corn and soybeans. My great-uncle, who farmed the place, died when I was three. My great-aunt then became a schoolteacher. But at least I was able to grow up in the midst of it.

Then you went off to school at strange Chapel Hill?

Strange. Strange. Very strange Chapel Hill.

When did you graduate?

I left in December of '84 and got my degree in '85. I studied with Max Steele and Doris Betts and Daphne Athas and Louis Rubin. And I slipped in Bland Simpson, too.

Did the University of North Carolina have a creative writing major?

No. You had to major in English, but they gave you honors in writing, sometimes. I was lucky enough.

Let's go back to growing up in Duplin County. Do you have any brothers and sisters?

It's all so complicated. My mother has two children, a boy and a girl, and my father has two children, a boy and a girl.

How did your family come by the land? How did they get to Chinquapin?

They were owned by the Kenans in Kenansville and I'm not quite certain of the details, but the Kenan family did participate in the "forty acres and a mule" policy. My great-great-great grandfather and my great-great grandfather who was a boy in 1863 were emancipated, along with his five brothers and sisters, and took over a huge portion of land in and around Chinquapin. Much of which is still in the family—the extended family, of course.

What do you remember about growing up in Chinquapin, especially your early experiences?

I've been back home for the last two months now and it has struck me how singular that growing up was. My grandfather recently pointed out how many churches there are in Maple Hill, a tiny neighboring community, poorer than ours and closer to the ocean. There are about fourteen. But in Chinquapin we only have two big churches for black folk and they're painfully similar to one another.

The community was polarized—they're both Baptist churches. And I never realized how much power those two churches had within our community. Most other black communities do have at least an A.M.E. [African Methodist Episcopal] church, a Baptist church, and perhaps a well-established Pentecostal place, a good storefront place.

One is more evangelical than the other, perhaps?

Not really. As happened with many churches in American Protestantism, there was a schism around the turn of the century.

I wonder what happened.

I never have been able to get that straightened out. It's really strange. So many people who would know are not talking. The closest one was my great-great-aunt Erie, and she has passed away. My great-great-grandfather had six children and she was the youngest. Erie Catherine Sharpless was born in 1897, so she was pushing a hundred when she died. Her funeral reminded me very much of Garcia Marquez's "Big Mama's Funeral." She had born twenty children in her life and of course they had in turn gone forth and multiplied. The town was overwhelmed.

The schism has stayed that way for ninety-two years?
Yes, the bifurcated church.
Which one did you go to?
I went to First Baptist, or as my friend in Raleigh says, "A-first-a Baptist." The other one was Saint Louis Baptist Church. I don't know where they got that odd name from.
What was your church like?
In retrospect, it was staid and stiff. It was as though the folks at my church were aspiring to higher social status. There were poor communities around Chinquapin, but a number of people in the community itself were doing fairly well. Many of them had owned their own land and had worked up from there. So they wanted to be "high Baptist." They were always getting it wrong, of course, but they kept aspiring.
At that time, did the service include the altar call, a time to be saved?
Yes. The big time to get saved was during revival. In most Baptist churches in North Carolina, that comes in September, around harvest time because the tobacco would have just been put in—you know, it's bad to be putting tobacco in past September, you might lose the crop, it might frost early, then what you gonna do? Our revival always coincided with the beginning of school and we would invite some outside person who would come and raise—what does a minister raise?
They can't raise hell. That would be a mistake. [Laughter]
Raise the spirit! Raise the Holy Ghost! And everyone would feel moved, certainly by Friday of revival week. The guest preacher preached every night. And we had some good ministers in my youth. I remember this one minister in particular who had been very active in the civil rights movement. He had some amazing anecdotes about threats on his life, and so on. You could tell that he had sort of metastasized all of that fear and commitment into a really vibrant ministry. I was lucky because Uncle Norman (he was an older cousin, really) was the chairman of the deacon board, so I got the chance to meet the guest ministers when they came to town.
Did you have them to supper?
Yes. You see my mother cooked for Uncle Norman because we were literally right across the road from him. His wife, Aunt Alice, died in the early seventies when I was nine. So for much of my

growing up, he would just come across the road for his meals—breakfast, dinner and supper. He was my first father figure. You see, when I was three, my great-uncle died.

It's significant, that early experience with death in your family.

I always think it's an amazing story—when I was three, the day that he died, they were grading tobacco in what they called the "pack house"; that is, they straighten it out and pick up the trash and put it in different piles for market. This was in September, of course. I remember it was early in the morning. My mother had this blanket, which I think she still has, and she spread it out on the porch of the pack house to put me down so I could take my nap and play while they worked. I remember seeing my great-uncle walking around. He didn't feel well, you could tell, and he lay down next to me and died there. And I didn't know what was going on. There was all this commotion.

You remember?

Yes. I remember touching him, asking what's wrong, and they said he doesn't feel well.

What a powerful experience.

Well, it's really strange at that age.

And you were only three?

I was only three but I remember it quite vividly. And I remember it now as sort of embarrassing because my mother (I call my great-aunt my mother) and everybody was crying. She was crying and they had gone to the house next door. I remember asking, what's wrong, why is she upset? How do you explain death to a three-year-old?

You must have been terrified.

I was terrified of ghosts afterward for a long time, but at the time I really didn't know what was going on.

Did you go to the funeral?

Yes.

Was that your first funeral?

Actually, I had probably been to a great many by then.

What was involved with the funeral usually? Did you have a wake?

When I was growing up it was at the house and they called it "the setting up." I didn't go to many of those. They stopped doing that by the time I became acutely aware of things. That had to be really morbid because it was like the Irish wakes where the coffin is in the living room and everybody is sitting around or in the kitchen eating and having a good time. Nowadays, they go to the funeral home, then they come back and they continue the tradition of "setting-up"—sans the body.

Clyde Edgerton's grandparents were farmers in rural Durham County. Edgerton's mother, who is now eighty-eight, and her older sisters have told me of times when somebody died, the women put the body on the kitchen table and washed and dressed it and got it into the homemade coffin. Then the body was laid out in the parlor for viewing.

And they would sit up all night watching over the body until the sun rose.

Sometimes they'd get a couple of young boys to watch while people were asleep, so that they'd be sure somebody stayed awake. These guys would be up all night, waiting to see if the corpse was going to sit up or anything.

Which invariably they had to do back then, I mean before proper embalming techniques.

Mrs. Edgerton was saying that preparing the corpse was just something the women did just like you strangle chickens for supper or have babies or whatever—you just did it. I think talking about funerals is an interesting way to approach this old-time spirituality.

It obviously preoccupies me.

Oh, yes. That's one thing that makes your fiction so exciting—the world beyond the concrete world that we know here seems to be very real for you. You evoke these very real spirits. I wondered what you thought about that. What are the origins of that ability to evoke the invisible world?

Well, I took the whole thing very seriously in those days—all that hell-fire preaching. For me this was just a very simple formulation: if God exists and if the Bible—especially if it is inerrant and is to be taken on any level as the literal truth—then you have this profound spiritual tension between good and evil. I've always wondered about spirits. Going back to the death of my great-uncle—some of the older children would tease me about his ghost coming back to haunt me.

You can count on those older kids to do that sort of thing, can't you?

I was the most peaceful child until I was three. I had no trouble going to sleep, but after his death I never took a nap.

Well, I guess not. When you did, somebody might lie down beside you and die. [Laughter]

The ghosts did seem to be present everywhere. The house I grew up in burned down in 1987. It was the old homestead, a place that my great-great-grandfather built. I think it had replaced a house that my great-great-great-grandfather had built. We would sit around and talk about the family, and my mother would say, "Well, in that room back there my mother died," (and she'd tell you about the day her mother died); then she'd say, "Then my brother, he died back in this room . . . and then up in this room Papa died," and so on. Every room for me was significant not so much for its function (bedroom, pantry) but for who died there. So I always had this palpable sense of these presences.

And then she would spin these yarns of being visited by departed relatives, particularly when she was ill. These stories were wonderful dovetailing blends of medical science, out-of-body experiences, and other unexplained phenomena—and these things would heal her, strangely enough.

She would be healed by the visitations?

For example, she has this one story which she tells with such convincing power, you don't doubt her one bit. She says she was sick, sick, sick, and her mother, her brother, and her father—who were all dead—came to visit her. She remembers them talking to her, then wiping her head with a cool cloth. Her mother doted on her and then looked at her father and said, "It's time to go," and they joined hands and flew away. When my mother woke up, the fever had gone. You could say, "Oh, it's all delirium, a dementia," but then it makes you wonder. When you're five years old and this huge authority figure tells you these things, it certainly affects the way you think.

It is a palpable thing. I think it's a great gift, although it must be terrifying. Not many people are able to see or hear or experience worlds other than this one.

And that authority was underpinned by a larger authority in the church and the Bible. They also condoned a concrete spiritual world. Most churches don't think of faith in terms of a world of spirits but rather in terms of "love" and other abstractions.

A friend once told me that "religion" is for people who are try-ing to figure out how to keep from going to hell and "spirituality" is for those people who have been to hell.

I like that.

The palpable spirituality that you heard and saw was undergirded by the authority of preaching which affirmed and amplified it.

And it was all in stratification. There was my great-aunt, and right across the road, there was the chairman of the deacon board and all these other deacons, and then the minister, all in hierarchy that marched on up to heaven. Not to mention the dead who hov-ered around; God knows where you put them. Most likely they put themselves wherever they wanted to be.

Horace [in A Visitation of Spirits] *was visited by both demons and ghosts. He was a tormented soul. Where did the demons come from?*

Well, of course, the negative pole. Going down, the bottom being hell . . . On one level I'm playing with very literary techniques. I'm taking from Dickens a great deal, but as opposed to having three spirits as Scrooge did, Horace has one. I was playing with the thought that in true madness, when somebody is losing their grip, there's something terrifying about the uncanny, like seeing some-thing terrifying in a clown's face.

It was very convincing. He was tortured by those horrible, scathing voices.

The sort of questions Horace was asking himself seemed to me at the time to be unprecedented. But now I see they're not, really. People like to think of themselves, particularly their own genera-tion, as being the first to ask difficult questions, to challenge scien-tific or religious notions. But in Horace's case, he was introducing these notions about science, about race relations and, most painfully, about sexuality in this very stultified community of Tim's Creek.

One thing I found that was so exciting about your work was the exploration of sexuality and spirituality at war in one person, par-ticularly in the story about the preacher, "Ragnorok: The Day the Gods Die."

I was hoping that I could actually take a stereotypical notion and find some sort of painful truths in it. That sort of hypocrisy is very present and it has always intrigued me. I'm not saying that I'm clean of any sort of hypocrisy or mendacity, myself. But certainly the idea of hypocrisy has always interested me in these people who are outwardly morally upright and stiff.

And self-righteous.

Yeah. People I knew who in front of other people were engaging in exactly polar opposite sorts of behavior. It's not a judgmental interest that I had, not a "How dare you, you wicked, wicked person?" interest, but an interest in what that kind of judgment does to you. As Paul said, "The spirit is willing but the flesh is weak."

I enjoyed it in part because of its irony. There was some humor, some fun—

Oh, yes, of course. I made him such a windbag. He was set up to be shot down; it was inevitable.

Let's talk about these stories for a little while. Your novel, as you suggested, is somewhat autobiographical.

I won't deny it.

Of course I don't want to diminish the art, the imagination that's involved because it's a silly question to ask: Is this really you? And who is this? There are no one-to-one correlations.

Depressing actually.

And all your friends and family say, "Randall that did not happen that way, I raised you right and I know that Uncle So-and-So really didn't so-and-so." Let the Dead Bury Their Dead *seems to me to be a great imaginative leap into the world of Tim's Creek on a deeper level. Was that intentional? Did you set about saying to yourself, "Now I have written about my past, I have come to terms with that in fiction, and now I'm ready to create an imaginative past, present and future?*

Not so much consciously, but it was necessary. Developing a history for Tim's Creek became a deliberate goal and it worked itself out. One of the things these stories are doing is pulling the history along. What I'm really doing is creating a story line; this book is particularly linked to a novel I'm interested in. It involves the McElwaine family and some issues that I really want to deal with, and the only way I can do that is to till this soil, the soil of Tim's

Creek. And the soil is so rich that I'm just finding it thoroughly inexhaustible.

You and Faulkner?

I'm afraid of being accused of "following" him, but I don't know if I'm really doing that. It looks that way right now.

The comparison's too facile.

Yes, if I were to say this is Chinquapin, to be very literal about it, I'd have to be dealing with the change of time. But to say Tim's Creek, my own creation, I can snap my fingers and it's still 1979. I don't really have to deal with the complex changes time has wrought. However, I am having to deal now with the ravages of time in my nonfiction—how people have gone away, how things like cable television have driven people off their porches back into the air-conditioning, and so on.

And what is lost when you do that.

Exactly. How you don't cook anymore, you put things into the microwave.

It's interesting to explore the relationship between storytelling and air-conditioning or between microwaves and storytelling. In one of these stories, "Angels Unaware," you do talk about cooking and storytelling.

Mr. John Edgar when he's cooking for Chi?

You know it made me hungry — his putting out all this really good food to nourish this poor angel.

And then Essie in "Origin of Whales" tells a story about collard greens.

They do upset your stomach.

If you eat that many.

So cooking and storytelling, all these things get explored in "tilling that particular soil" of Tim's Creek. That was spoken like a true farmer, somebody who understands what it means to be brought up on the land. Can you talk to me about your family, the community in which you grew up, the hierarchy of living and dead — and music. Recently, I heard the Badgette Sisters sing gospel music. They're now in their sixties and they grew up on a farm much like you did north of Rocky Mount. They sing these old, old gospel and spiritual tunes. And it's just the richest, softest, most meditative sound. They go around to different churches and that's part of their ministry; they just do it. If anybody calls them, they go.

Oh yes. There was good music but I'm always bemused when I hear people talk about how wonderful the music in black churches is and I noticed it particularly while I was going to a lot of churches around the country. I honestly believe that there is a directly proportional relationship between the poor churches where the actual music is really horrible, but spiritual and powerful in a visceral way; and the rich ones where there is less spirit, where they sing this soul-entrancing music with perfect notes, but where there is a hollowness and lack of conviction behind the music. I remember growing up, I didn't really listen. Once I came here to Chapel Hill and I joined the BSM gospel choir, I began to think about gospel music as a thing you can study formally, as opposed to simply a participatory activity, which is how I viewed it as a child.

So, the music itself was never really that good back at First Baptist. It was really the sense of everybody singing, everybody participating, the climbing that stair toward that particular form of ecstasy that you can only get in a fellowship service in which you are all rhythmically climbing and getting out of yourselves in that fashion. And the music as an objectification, as psalm, as ceremony in the sense of being something you watch and listen to was never really that important. In fact the ministers would get upset at the people and say, "Y'all ain't singing," when folks got too pretty. "We're here to worship the Lord." When my niece was in North Carolina School of Science and Math and her choir came to our church, I noticed that people weren't clapping and people weren't standing up and participating and singing along with the choir. To me that's a death knell because even though they were pretending to be high Baptist back when I was a child, it wasn't a matter of sound, it was a matter of participation and exalting; making a joyful noise. I remember most stirringly the most powerful prayer meetings were the ones during revival week. I remember Uncle Norman sat in the same chair every Sunday, every time we went to church. You had the altar in the middle, and to the left and right the pews that faced each other on either side of the altar and to the left sat the mothers of the church and on the right sat the deacons. So, Uncle Norman, chairman of the deacon board, would sit at the

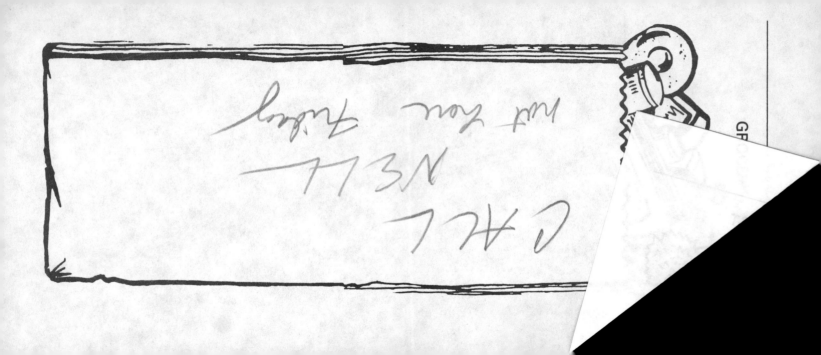

farthermost right at the front, closest to the minister. He would sit there and his song was "At the Cross." You didn't really lead; the prayer meeting had its own form, a wonderful shapeless, self-shaping, self-forming program. And often Uncle Norman started out if things were slow and he'd sing "At the cross, at the cross where my Saviour died" and, you know, he had his own rhythm. I just remember the sound of him singing, "At the cross, at the cross . . ." and everyone would chime in. Somebody would stand up and testify and then they'd sit down and then somebody would start up another song and then somebody would stand up and testify, and then somebody else might get the spirit and testify and then somebody'd start up singing. Each person had a song. But I haven't been to a prayer meeting in so long.

How are the "mothers of the church" determined?

Most of them are, as they call them, "deaconesses"—you know, the wives of deacons.

And are deacons and deaconesses elected?

Deacons are elected by the other deacons so it's sort of a self-perpetuating board. And they in turn elect the board of trustees, which takes care of the church's physical and financial needs; deacons take care of the spiritual side. The deacon board is higher than the board of trustees, which has always interested me. But for the women, it's not a formal thing—it's a matter of informally knowing when this woman has sort of "arrived." Actually they probably work harder than men keeping things together.

So the sense of community and the ecstasy would happen mostly during the prayer meetings?

Yes, but also during the regular services.

What was the regular service usually like?

There was a very strict order. You began with the invocation, "The Lord is in His holy temple. Let all the earth keep silent before Him. I was glad when they said let us go into the house of the Lord." Every Sunday morning I would hear that. Prior to that was Sunday school, which I was obliged to attend every Sunday.

Even if I missed church I didn't miss Sunday school, which was actually good. I was talking to my friend yesterday—sorry, another tangent—who I actually had this interesting debate with about God and whether or not He does bad things. And he was actually sort of marvelling because I was pulling (as a good literary scholar does) all of these things out of the Bible to back up my claim. And this man went to Duke Divinity School and he was just saying, "Boy, you know you're right, you know your Bible." But it's really because I didn't miss a Sunday at Sunday school. That's basically what it's all about.

Did you all have sword drills and memorizing Bible verses for each Sunday?

Yes, but that was more during vacation Bible school. I remember vacation Bible school started with blueberry season. We had this huge blueberry farm in Rose Hill, and I always remember that the bus would get back—they'd send this bus around to all the black communities to pick them up to go blueberry picking—and I remember that the bus would drop you off just in time to run in, take a bath real quick, put on your school clothes and get on the church bus to go to Sunday school.

You were well-organized.

And for my mother, vacation Bible school was her thing. She was always in charge of it and I remember that she'd always leave early and I'd be home alone for a brief time while getting ready for the church bus.

One thing that I'm afraid is getting lost as younger generations are coming up is a knowledge of biblical language. Your students may not know what you mean, or understand that you're quoting the Bible when you say, "I was glad when they said unto me let us go into the house of the Lord."

New Englanders, Congregationalists, tend still to have a good underpinning. But in New York I get to my wit's end because I might drop an allusion here or there and then have to backtrack to explain it because they didn't get it. What really bothers me is that they're sometimes proud of their ignorance: "I've never read the Bible," they say. "Who would waste their time? I'd rather be reading Edith Wharton."

Did you have an altar call after the regular church services?

It came just before the benediction, after the sermon.

I'm still caught up in this idea of the music.

Well you see, we had this little mimeographed program which sort of laid down what was supposed to happen. Everything was punctuated by music. The sermon was bracketed by a spiritual.

There's a big difference to me between "spiritual" and "gospel." A spiritual is really a classical form and gospel has its roots in blues and swing to an extent. Gospel's a much later form of spiritual music and it takes its message straight from the Greek translation which is "good news"—that is, it's generally happy. Spirituals can be very depressing.

Such as "Sometimes I Feel Like a Motherless Child," or "Were You There When They Crucified My Lord?"

This is part of what I studied here at Chapel Hill with that saintly woman, Sonia Stone, a professor in the African-American studies department. She died last year. She had gone through all sorts of battles to get tenure and so it was really doubly sad. She was only fifty. I even put together a little play about the difference between gospel and spirituals. Spirituals date back to before antebellum times. Slaves would use the spirituals as code messages and they were particularly useful in the underground railroad. There were restrictions on more than two blacks gathering together, blacks congregating at certain times in certain places—but in a field you can sing and the sound carries, so you could send messages way across distances. And just like in Africa, they beat the drum there and the song could leapfrog across the fields. Spirituals range in symbolic language from an obvious one like "Swing Low Sweet Chariot" to "Follow the Drinking Gourd" which, it was said, was how Harriet Tubman congregated people together.

You have written other plays, as well?

I wrote several. But that play was only performed once in Gerard Hall, in the tiny theater.

Do you still have it?

No. The only play I have from that time is one I wrote after that. There was a fire at my grandfather's house—the upstairs where I had stored all of my things while I lived in New York was gone, and practically two-thirds of all my school notes were burned.

That's a shame.

I call it a play but it was really one of those "docu-plays." We dramatized scenes in different uses of music, gospels, spirituals.

I'm sorry it is gone. I think my truest experiences in religious worship seem to come when music is involved. I wonder if you could talk to me about any of your stories, in Let the Dead Bury

Their Dead *especially, the stories that are dearest to you.*

That's like asking a mother, "Which child do you like best?" I'm always afraid that if I say "A" or "B," the other one will go bad or something. I'm fond of all of them for different reasons. I'll put it to you this way, the ones I think are the most crafted are "Cornsilk" and "Foundations of the Earth" because they are the oldest and I worked on them the hardest. I also like "Clarence and the Dead" and "Things of this World" because they were like gifts from somewhere, particularly "Clarence."

Not that I didn't labor over them all at some point, but none of them as much as I did over "Cornsilk" and "Foundations of the Earth." And because of the labor, I love them more. I'm sort of astonished at how biblical I have been or have become—each of them does have a sort of nugget of religious belief or concern. "Foundation" is obviously referring to Job. I've always wanted to deal with that moment—that's one of my favorite stories in the Bible. I studied it intensely for a long time. But there's something irreducible about that moment when Job confronts God. It always angers me when people think of Job as being very patient. That means they haven't read the book. Job rants and raves; I mean, the man summons God. But that moment when God says, "I have one question to ask of you," (as they say in the New Standard Revised version, as opposed to "Gird up your loins like a man," which I like much better. All my current theological friends, they hate it because I'm always quoting the King James version; of course they hate it because they all use the Revised Standard so it's always a matter of my having to translate from King James English to modern-day English so they'll know what I'm saying), but when God says, "Where were you when I laid the foundations of the earth?" What do you say to that sort of question? And then of course in the book He goes on and He tells Job all these other things but that alone, "Where were you when I laid the foundations of the earth?" "Cornsilk" is the one that I'm really going to get in trouble for.

Yes?

Yes, you will get in trouble for that story, Randall. I mean it's really a cautionary tale, and certainly sinners are much more interesting to read about than saints—we all know that and we all prefer to read about sinners. But in the end it's really a cautionary tale.

I think it's also a psychologically true tale.
Thank you.
It deals with the shadows within souls. But it made me see in new ways the relationship between the son and the father — the young man keeps protesting too much: "I'm not talking about my father," he says.

That story took me seven years to write and that's one of the reasons why. I wanted to write this story about incest and I'd been trying to do it very prissily. I kept failing. I've read all these stories about incest but I'd never read any that really convinced me in a way that I needed to be convinced, that left me feeling that I understood something about it. I'd been toying with it and toying with it and a friend of mine read it and said you obviously don't want to write this, Randall, because you're playing around. I was using very Jean Toomer-like language, which is really repressive 1920s talk, and that language really didn't work, didn't jibe with my understanding. And one day Bucchi Emechita, the great Nigerian writer and author of *The Joys of Womanhood*, came to Sarah Lawrence. The students were having lunch with her and I was invited. I got there late in the middle of lunch, and she was decked out in this amazing African garb. She had brought an entourage—an African woman who taught school, and a librarian, who is Chinese. So here I was, one black man. They were talking about rape and about men and how much of a problem that can be in African culture. And she was saying how rape is "a sin against the earth and when you sin against the earth, the earth will bring you back to it." She had such power. And that's where I got my impetus for redeveloping "Cornsilk."

You wrote of the earth and the taboos against violating it. You don't underestimate or sentimentalize this incest taboo and say evil is just a question of improper or a neglectful upbringing. In this story you grapple with a deep depravity on its own terms. In this sense it clearly makes a moral statement.

Yes, and transgressing in such a way that almost *cannot* be forgiven. It may sound like a horrible thing to say, but there are so many different varieties of incest, and they all have different pathologies attached to them. I mean it's very specific and yet it's sort of an infinite arrangement. It boggles the mind to think about what motivates this person to have done this particular act. I hope people realize the abhorrence I felt in the subject of this story; that it is very much a "cautionary tale." But I've already been called a "demented Negro" by a publisher in New York who publishes some of the most demented people around. At least I'm being noticed.

The taboo about it brings up very Calvinistic precepts that I've been taught, that are a part of the way that I think. You know the five tenets of Calvin: "The world is a wicked place and there ain't nothing you can do about it," "God's grace is all and sufficient," and so on. More to the point, are there sins you are willing to forgive in certain people but that they can never forgive in themselves?

I also didn't know the derivation of the word "chi" from the story "Things of This World" until I had talked with her. In Nigeria and in other languages such as Chinese and Korean, "chi" means "angel," but it's also your personal spirit; it's a multipurpose word. And it means the same thing in each language, one of those linguistic fascinations.

Tell me more about the Calvinistic teachings you were exposed to.

I bet you know more about it than I do.

I'm pretty rusty. I remember studying the Westminster Shorter Catechism. The longer catechism was actually the easier one. The shorter catechism set forth the tenets of Presbyterianism and you memorized these things straight from John Calvin. They are important underpinnings to southern religion.

God's grace is sufficient and irresistible, the world is a wicked place . . .

And original sin . . . the soul is depraved . . .

The only way you can attain salvation is through the grace of God—you don't know whether you're going to be saved or not, so it's better to behave as if you were.

That's the doctrine of the elect.

It's so predestined, it's frightening. Of course in the Baptist and Pentecostal faiths, being saved, being born again is very central. It goes back to the story of Nicodemus: "How do I obtain salvation?" "Ye must be born again." "What do you mean, do I have to go back and reenter my mother's womb?" Nicodemus asks. But predestination really throws me. I mean, I've heard Jehovah's Witnesses talk about all these strange numbers, like there are only going to be 144,000 saved. Why didn't God just take out one or the other—salvation by grace only or by free will? That always puzzled me.

I think that Calvinism undergirds much of the way southerners viewed the world. It's a pervasive world view that is quite distinctive.

Particularly different from Catholicism, the way the Catholic Church views the world. There's an innocence about Catholicism, a belief in ritual and mystery that's really different from the hard-nosed Southern Baptist view. These southern farmers who get out and work and sow every day—their preoccupation is about whether the crops are going to rise. It's a totally different kind of mystery, based on the natural rhythms of the land and weather, not dependent so much on the keeping of rites in an institution. Also some natural disruptions and interruptions occur which interestingly enough find a form of expression in the southern Protestant ceremony, but they take them in stride—your car might break down, your tractor might break down, floods might happen, your wife might go into labor—it's built into the southern service and attitudes toward ritual.

Yes, life is flawed, unpredictable.

Tell it like it is, John Calvin. Don't sugarcoat it. Catholicism doesn't seem to go in to that so harshly. It's much more wonderfully innocent in an odd sense; there seems to be more hopefulness. The doctrine of atonement seems to be more pervasive and important in the Catholic Church. I never did understand the plays of Samuel Beckett, for example, until I moved to New York. Existentialism as a world view just went over my head. But after a few months in New York, it all made sense—the absurdity of the world. Coming from a place like Chinquapin, North Carolina, and being steeped in this Calvinist worldview—seeing the world and my place in it as this celestial hierarchy among all these spirits—where all things were a matter of the soul's salvation or loss to eternity, there was no room for an absurdist vision of the world.

But after having gone to college, having an extended period of apostasy, and then going to New York, and seeing the absurd in extremis, the homelessness, rampant greed where there is no correlation between who's successful and who's not—it's a matter of "no clockmaker and the clock is broken." Suddenly all this existentialist stuff made sense.

Then it was wonderful that I had been given this rich literary background, had been force-fed all these books, even ones I didn't like, so I could know which ones to go back to and reread. I had this itching at the base of my neck, saying, "Yes, this is what Beckett was driving at. Oh yes." I'd go back and read *Godot* or see a production of it. And I saw all those things that I had heard in lectures in school and written down so dutifully, suddenly make sense in the context of New York—existentialism, secular humorism, I mean humanism—

I like "secular humorism."

Secular humorism-humanism, impressed itself upon me. I wanted to blend in my own way, the southern gothic (which is how people describe my sensibility but I don't really see it that way) and my Down East spirituality with this understanding of the world. And it occurred to me, existentialism actually dovetails with Calvinism— how bleak the world is.

Calvin was right?

How right Calvin was, oh my God, yes. Mind you, I'm still an agnostic. I haven't gotten back with Christendom since I had my schism and made my little congregation of one. Originally the story "Run, Mourner, Run" was going to be titled "The Wicked, the Wretched, and the Born Again," but everyone said that was too heavy-handed. And then, I started listening to Sweet Honey in the Rock singing "Run, Mourner, Run," a song that is attributed to Harriet Tubman. She would sing it while leading the slaves in the underground railroad to freedom. One line, "If I just had two wings," and the song's title were very important. Also the epigraph from a poem by Rilke (". . . for there is no place that does not see you. You must change your life") captured my imagination. It seemed a wonderful enigmatic line; to me these spoke to Dean Williams in the story more than anything else, in his particularly *southern* existential dilemma—being out of touch with salvation.

Tell me more about innocence being a sin.

That's really what Christianity teaches in a way. Your way to salvation is through knowledge. You can't be saved unless you know about Jesus and how to be saved. Which also led me also to apostasy. I kept wondering, what about those people who haven't heard about Christianity, haven't heard the Reverend Lassiter preach? It seems you have to know what to do in order to lead yourself or to be led to salvation.

You have to be very smart in this world to get by. You have to be very competent to live to a ripe old age, well-off, and healthy. There are so many things out there that can get you. So many ways you can hurt yourself.

Yes, I'm good at that, at shooting myself in the foot. Like the Barney Fife character on the Andy Griffith show.

Well, there's something always very endearing about him. I'm not the smartest person in the world either. But it does seem to be a responsibility. And it was something to do with how I was brought up. My mother would get very impatient with me when I would do something stupid, or ask silly questions or ask questions about things I could figure out on my own. I realize now she was very worried that I must be able to do all right on my own, if something happened to her and she were not there for me, as a young black man, alone.

When did you first experience what you term your apostasy?

I was having a lot of trouble in college about faith and what not. Because I had loved the notion of being pious. My doubt arose when I realized that my religion came from a cultural happenstance, when, where, and to whom I was born. Most of us inherit our religion. That really bothered me and I could never get over that.

Yes, what if you had been born in India?

Exactly, I would have been a Hindu, or if I were born in Japan, Shinto, or in Latin America, I would have been a Catholic. It bothered me that I had inherited my religion. It was tied in, too, with a sort of rebelliousness. Knowing the Bible, I could personally eviscerate it in such a way that only I could put it back together. And I began searching. Ironically, I've held onto most of my good friends, who were always very spiritual, very Christian. They're all now ministers or theologians. We continue to have very good conversations, because they know it's not just out of capriciousness or love of debauchery that I broke with Christendom. It's genuine. One minister friend said, "Be angry with God, don't be angry with the institution, or the people, because that will just engender hurt which will take much energy." Be angry with God about your confusions and the problems you have. It's much easier to sort out in the end than if you take it out on pastors and your family. And I always thought that was very wise.

It's also very frustrating because God you can't see.

So She and I have been fussing a lot the last ten years. My best friend went to Union in New York; he's at Vanderbilt now getting his Ph. D. in church history. And then there's my friend in Raleigh who went to Duke. So it's really strange to be becoming this notorious, infamous, nasty writer. All his friends are ministers.

But it makes all kinds of sense. You're still very much a spiritual person. You haven't renounced a spiritual quest, you are just coming to terms with your own doubts, and quarreling with things you were brought up with. You had a powerful cultural infusion that would be in stark contrast to somebody who grew up in New York in a highrise who barely hears the traffic in the street, much less is in touch with the land and has an extended family. You probably spent many nights at your uncle's house.

Many times, on the porch, listening to all these stories, not unlike *Let the Dead Bury Their Dead*, except he never got quite that wild.

Was there a Tyrell family in Chinquapin?

Yes, but they're really quite passive. I sort of animated them for my purposes but, yeah, they were there.

What were they involved in?

Sharecropping and land. I've sort of updated Mr. Tyrell as they have now updated themselves.

Do you think you'll go back there to live in Chinquapin?

It would be hard to imagine. The community is eroded, almost gone. It has a lot to do with something I think Toni Morrison said, that if any black person wants to succeed in this country they have to go away. I don't know what it was about that particular part of Duplin County. There were a lot of ambitious people and their children were sent away and a lot of them are doing well but they're not doing well in Duplin County, in Chinquapin. With their exodus and the attrition of being in a place with older people who were ultimately not having children, there won't be much in the future.

I'm just waiting for the day it will be a ghost town. And my connection there is really with the people. Even though I adore the land so much, one has to question, "Am I going to become this sort of hermit on the land?" And after this recent trip now I've just become so in love with the entire continent.

Where all have you been? You've still got to go to Alaska you said.

I actually started in New England and went around North America in a counterclockwise fashion.

What have you discovered?

Well, and I don't mean to be snide about it, but I don't know because I haven't written it yet, and I don't think I will really find out until I've written it down. I did confirm some of the things I was hoping to find, i.e., that African-American culture, which is really a variation of African culture, is so diverse it's mind-boggling. I was actually afraid that I wouldn't find that, so I'm relieved in a sense that I have. I'm relieved that I found black people prospering in every state that I went to. It was amazing—uncharacteristic places, when you think about there being black folks there, like North Dakota or Idaho or Minnesota—I found not only a history but a thriving presence. My real focus was to sit down with these people and ask them what they thought about race and culture.

My understanding of "race" was destroyed and replaced with the notion of race as a myth. When you think of the dialogue between black and white, race is always there, the word is there, and therefore it's part of our understanding, literally part of the way you think of people, the way you group people. So as I commenced on this journey, this sojourn in my own land, I was teasing with the idea, the ramifications of starting to think anew about being black, not as a race but solely as a culture, and the ramifications of this culture eroding the way it is in Chinquapin and the ways it's eroding around the nation. And what's replacing it? Some of the messages are very sobering. The young people in particular seem more often to be without hope. Ironically, it's the older people who are the most inspiring, hopeful. I don't really know what that means but it really should be the other way around, I should think, and that really surprised me more than anything else. I found the most buoyant, joyous, wise messages from the old folk but the young folk don't really connect with anything, they feel alienated. It's very difficult for them to find something to hold on to. And the great black churches we spoke of earlier have fallen apart and that puzzles me. What happened? Why was that allowed to crumble? Why has it been allowed to lose its potency? And you hear tales of women just like the ones I spoke of earlier in all these church communities, and not just the women but the men. And in the end the black community is not just a matriarchy, there have been strong black women but it's very patriarchical really. There has always been, I believe, a very real, strong male presence in black culture and it's really annoying when I hear the myth of the black matriarchy. So throughout I would hear about these histories of these powerful black men and women together in partnership up until the early sixties and then something happened. I'm asking more questions, trying to find out the right questions to ask.

I know what you mean. That's been part of my process of discovery, as an interviewer, too. Today I wasn't really sure what questions to ask you and they unfold from reading the fiction and from hearing you speak your heart. I'm so grateful to you for doing so. So I can't wait to read this book when it comes out. I know you'll be relieved to get it out there.

Actually I'm dying to go back to fiction because I've been scribbling on this novel and it wants to take over.

Tell me about that.

Actually I'm not afraid to talk about this novel—I can talk about it as long as it's far in the future. It's about Elihu McElwaine and his family (they keep popping up in *Let the Dead*). The last footnote in the title story mentions that McElwaine kills a white man while he's going to Chapel Hill in the sixties and he sort of disappears. The novel is the story of how he kidnaps the wealthiest white child and the wealthiest black child in Chapel Hill. He commits the perfect crime because he gets away with 3.3 million dollars, too. Twenty years later, he comes back into their lives wanting something. The white man is now a gay divinity student at Union Theological Seminary. The black student is a Wall Street "buppy," a lawyer. They're very opposite people now and they're forced together again. They don't even know each other; they don't even talk to each other anymore, and they're living in New York. For me it's sort of an opportunity to bring together the dichotomy of South and North.

You're in a unique position to be able to do that. You have the gifts to be able to do it, too, thank goodness.

Thank you.

That dichotomy between North and South is much debated and much touted. Does it really exist and if so, does the dichotomy exist along spiritual lines, along the lines of the different worldviews that we've been talking about between Calvinism and existentialism?

That's truly a fascination with me. And, in fact, the thing that's really tugging at me is this one character who's the black man's mother and she's from Tim's Creek. She's this poor girl who married well and has been living this doll's life. Something happens when her son is kidnapped in 1970. It takes her twenty years, but on the eve of the return of Elihu McElwaine, she just goes off, takes all of her husband's money, and goes to New York. She begins to work for the homeless. I'm really excited about her because I've never conceived of a character quite like her—and there's something about black women that I've always been sort of entranced and amazed by—but she represents the ultimate challenge to—it's exactly what you say—to bring together two worlds; because she's bringing this painful Calvinist upbringing that comes from Tim's Creek and it clashes with this empty middle class existence she sees. She's like a whirlwind, like a ball of fire that's descending on New York, this broken clock without a clockmaker.

And she's generous in a strong way. Have you seen the book I Dream a World *by Brian Lanker?*

Oh yes.

It's a great book. It suggests what you were saying about older people. It is inspiring and hopeful with messages of joy and hope, with adversity and suffering endured gracefully and triumphantly. Does she have a name, this woman in your new novel?

Clara DeBaptiste.

As in clarity.

Yes, though I didn't think about it like that.

We've been talking about the future a little bit—where do you see you're heading with your own spirituality?

I don't know. That's the big question. I have no idea where it's leading. There are a lot of problems which I'm avoiding anyway, probably by writing. J. Lee Greene, one of my mentors, a professor in the English department at Chapel Hill, always said that one of the things that people hate and fear most is solitude. And people think that writing is a very solitary activity, but it's not. I love to be alone, but not for solitude, rather so that I can be with these people, these characters. And in a sense the "problems of faith" I will have to deal with in solitude. My editor, a wonderful woman, is going to a convent next week to be alone, to get away from it all, literally. I think that on the one hand it's wonderful and on the other hand it's really terrifying. I had hoped in the writing of fiction, I might work out some of those things I'm avoiding in my personal life but no, I'm having fun. †

9

MARY WARD BROWN

Celebrating the True and Lively Word

"To do good work takes the concentration of a lifetime," maintains Mary Ward Brown, author of *Tongues of Flame*, a collection of short stories she began writing when she was in her sixties, and which was awarded the Ernest Hemingway Foundation Award for best first fiction in 1987. Brown spent her childhood on her parents' three thousand-acre plantation, complete with sawmill, store, and cotton gin, and she earned a bachelor's degree from Judson College, a small Baptist institution, nearby. In 1939 she married Charles Kirtley Brown and moved to Auburn, Alabama, for a few years while her husband worked as publicity director for the college. In 1943 the couple moved back to the land the author had by then inherited from her father. After spending a good part of her life raising a family, and having written for a brief time in the early 1950s, Brown decided in 1970 that she wished to write again. In 1978, when she was sixty-one, she published a short story in *McCall's*. She subsequently published eight of the eleven stories collected in *Tongues of Flame* in literary magazines such as *Grand Street*, *Ploughshares*, and *Prairie Schooner*. Her work has been represented in anthologies including *The Human Experience: Contemporary American and Soviet Fiction and Poetry*, *New Stories from the South: The Year's Best*, edited by Shannon Ravenel, and *Stories*, edited by Donald Hays. She is a 1993 recipient of Alabama's Governor's Award, given every two years for outstanding contributions to the arts in Alabama.

The characters in *Tongues of Flame* are everyday farmers, widows, and preachers of the Deep South caught in the dilemmas faced by folks who though rooted in the past, must face the change and disruption caused by the passing of time and the coming of the new, modern South. Facing a world that seems to reject many of the former customary ways of doing things, these characters often undergo a gradual but profound change in attitude, a transformed way of seeing things that brings about compassion, acceptance, or wry relief. In "Goodbye, Cliff," when an aged widow discovers fifteen years after her abusive husband's death that he was also unfaithful to her in life, she is devastated; yet she finds peace, secure in the knowledge that she will not be meeting him in heaven when she dies.

Mary Ward Brown was once asked why she wrote about race and religion so often in her fiction. She answered, "These are the overriding preoccupations of the South, of where I've lived all my life." Brown's vision comes not only from being an observer of her culture but from being a believer—in her region's future as well as in the value of its tormented past and in a Christian faith that is deeply rooted in her homeplace, where the frontier values of independence and rugged individualism are applied to belief as well as to politics. "I was raised in a Christian culture," Brown told me in a telephone conversation. "If I had been raised in Saudi Arabia, I would have been a Muslim. Christianity does not have the full claim to God. In fact, it's a real turn-off to me to be presented with a prepackaged notion of Christianity and of Christ as the 'only way.' I write about that turn-off in 'New Life.'"

Brown writes in a clear, sure, and caring voice, from a religious perspective about a people and a world she loves: "Creation is surpassingly wonderful, and God is greater than anyone can possibly imagine. I write about the things I do because I can't help it. I think flowers bloom to the glory of God. I write stories to the glory of God, to celebrate the privilege and miracle of being alive." †

A New Life

They meet by chance in front of the bank. Elizabeth is a recent widow, pale and dry-eyed, unable to cry. Paul, an old friend, old boyfriend, starts smiling the moment he sees her. She's never seen him look so happy, she thinks. Under one arm he carries a wide farm checkbook, a rubber band around it so things won't fall out.

"Well. This is providential." He grips her hand and holds on, beaming, ignoring the distance he's long kept between them. Everything about him seems animated. Even his hair, thick, dark, shot with early gray, stands up slightly from his head instead of lying down flat. In the sunlight the gray looks electric. "We've been thinking about you," he says, still smiling. "Should have been to see you."

"But you *did* come." Something is different about him, she thinks, something major. It's not just the weight he's put on.

"We came when everyone else was there and you didn't need us," he says. "We should have been back long ago. How are you?"

"Fine," she says, to end it. "Thank you."

He studies her face, frowns. "You don't look fine," he says. "You're still grieving, when John is with God now. He's well again. Happy!"

So that's it, she thinks. She's heard that Paul and his wife, Louise, are in a new religious group in town, something that has sprung up outside the church. They call themselves Keepers of the Vineyard. Like a rock band, someone said.

She turns to the bank as if she hasn't heard what he said. Behind them, small-town traffic moves up and down the street, a variety of mid-size cars and pickup trucks, plus an occasional big car or van. In front, the newly remodeled bank updates a street of old red-brick buildings. Some are painted white, green, gray. Around the corner the beauty shop is pink.

This is the southern Bible Belt, where people talk about God the way they talk about the weather, about His will and His blessings, about why He lets things happen. The Vineyard people claim that God also talks to them. Their meeting place is a small house on Green Street, where they meet, the neighbors say, "all the time."

Their leader is the new young pastor of the Presbyterian church, called by his first name, Steve. Regular church members look on the group with suspicion. They're crazy, they say. They go too far.

When told, Steve had simply shrugged. "Some thought Jesus was a little crazy, too," he'd countered, with a smile.

He is a spellbinding preacher and no one moves or dozes while he speaks, but his church is split in two. Some are for him and some against him, but none are neutral. He is defined by extremes.

Paul opens the door to the bank for Elizabeth. "What are you doing tonight?" he asks, over her shoulder.

When she looks back, surprised, he winks.

"Louise and I could come over after supper," he says. "How about it?"

She understands his winks and jokes. They're coverup devices, she'd decided years ago, for all he meant to hide. New hurts, old wounds, the real Paul Dudley. Only once had she ever seen him show pain. When his favorite dog, always with him, had been hit by a truck, he'd covered his face with his hands when he told her. But the minute she'd touched him, ready to cry too, he'd stiffened. "I'll have to get another one," he'd said, more to himself than to her. And right away he had. Another liver-spotted pointer.

"You're turning down a good way of life, though," her mother had said, a little sadly, when she didn't take the ring. It had been his mother's diamond. He'd also inherited a large tract of land and a home in the country.

She'd never confessed one of their problems, for fear that it might sound trivial. He had simply made her nervous. Wherever they'd gone, to concerts, plays, movies, he hadn't been able to sit still and listen, but had had to look around and whisper, start conversations, pick up dropped programs. Go for more popcorn. He had rummaged through his hair, fiddled with his tie, jiggled keys in his pocket, until it had been all she could do not to say, "Stop that, or I'll scream!"

He hadn't seemed surprised when she told him. Subdued at first, he had rallied and joked as he went out the door. But he'd cut her out of his life from then on, and ignored all her efforts to be friendly. Not until both were married to other people had he even stopped on the street to say hello.

Back home now in her clean, orderly kitchen, Elizabeth has put away groceries and stored the empty bags. Without putting it off, she has subtracted the checks she'd just written downtown. Attention to detail has become compulsive with her. It is all that holds her together, she thinks.

Just before daylight-savings dark, Paul and Louise drive up in a white station wagon. Paul is wearing a fresh short-sleeved shirt, the top of its sleeves still pressed together like uncut pages in a book. In one hand he carries a Bible as worn as a wallet.

Louise, in her late forties like Elizabeth, is small and blonde. Abandoned first by a father who had simply left home, then by a mother his leaving had destroyed, she'd been brought up by sad, tired grandparents. Her eyes are like those of an unspoiled pet, waiting for a sign to be friendly.

When Elizabeth asks if they'd like something to drink now or later, they laugh. It's a long-standing joke around Wakefield. "Mr. Paul don't drink nothing but sweetmilk," a worker on his place had said years ago.

"Now would be nice," he says, with a happy new smile.

Elizabeth leads the way to a table in her kitchen, a large light room with one end for dining. The table, of white wood with an airy glass top, overlooks her back lawn. While she fills goblets with tea and ice, Paul gazes out the window, humming to himself, drumming on the glass top. Louise admires the marigolds, snapdragons, and petunias in bloom. Her own flowers have been neglected this year, she says. Elizabeth brings out a pound cake still warm from the oven.

"Let's bless it," Paul says, when they're seated.

He holds out one hand to her and the other to Louise. His hand is trembling and so warm it feels feverish. Because of her? Elizabeth can't help thinking. No. Everyone knows he's been happy with his wife. Louise's hand is cool and steady.

He bows his head. "Lord, we thank you for this opportunity to witness in your name. We know that You alone can comfort our friend in her sorrow. Bring her, we pray, to the knowledge of Your saving grace and give her Your peace, which passes understanding. We ask it for Your sake and in Your name."

He smiles a benediction, and Elizabeth cuts the cake.

"The reason we're here, Elizabeth"—he ignores the tea and cake before him—"is that my heart went out to you this morning at the bank. You can't give John up, and it's tearing you apart."

What can she say? He's right. She can't give John up and she *is* torn apart, after almost a year.

"We have the cure for broken hearts," he says, as if stating a fact.

Louise takes a bite of cake, but when Paul doesn't she puts down her fork. On her left hand, guarded by her wedding band, is a ring that Elizabeth remembers.

"I have something to ask you, Elizabeth." He looks away tactfully. "Are you saved?"

She turns her tea glass slowly clockwise, wipes up the circle beneath it with her napkin. "I don't know how to answer that, Paul," she says. "What happened to John did something to my faith. John didn't deserve all that suffering, or to die in his prime. I can't seem to accept it."

"Well, that's natural. Understandable." He looks at her as through the bottom of bifocals. "In my heart I was rebellious myself at one time."

He hadn't been religious at all when she'd known him, she keeps thinking. On the contrary, he'd worked on a tractor all day Sunday while everyone else went to church, had joked about people who were overly religious.

"But I had an encounter with Jesus Christ that changed my life," he says, like a testimonial. "I kept praying, with all my heart, and He finally came to me. His presence was as real as yours is now." He pauses, shakes his head. "You have to really want Him, though. Most people have to hit rock bottom, the way I did, before they do. You have to be down so low you say, 'Lord, I can't make it on my own. You'll have to help me. *You* take over!'"

When was that? She tries to think. Things had gone so well for him, it seemed. He'd had all he said he wanted out of life when they were dating—a big family, and to live on his land. He'd been an only child whose parents had died young. Louise had been orphaned too, in a way. So they'd had a child every year or two before they quit, a station wagon full of healthy, suntanned children. All driving themselves by now, Elizabeth had noticed.

As for her, rock bottom had been back in that hospital room with John, sitting in a chair by his bed. Six months maybe, a year at the most, they'd just told her in the hall. She'd held his hand until the Demerol took effect and his hand had gone limp in hers. Then she'd leaned her head on the bed beside him and prayed, with all her heart. From hospital room to hospital room she had prayed, and at home in between.

"I've said that too, Paul, many times," she says. "I prayed, and nothing happened. Why would He come to you and not me?"

"Because you were letting something stand in your way, my dear." His smile is back, full force. "For Him to come in, you have to get rid of self—first of all your self-*will!* 'Not my will but Thine be done,' He said on the cross."

He breaks off, turns to the tea and cake before him. With the first bite of cake, he shuts his eyes tight. A blissful smile melts over his face.

"Umh, umh!" He winks at Louise. "How about this pound cake, Mama!"

Late the next afternoon, Elizabeth is watering flowers in her back yard. Before, she grew flowers to bring in the house, zinnias for pottery pitchers, bulbs for clear glass vases. Now she grows them for themselves, and seldom cuts them. She has a new irrational notion that scissors hurt the stems. After what she's seen of pain, she wants to hurt nothing that lives.

From where she stands with the hose, she sees a small red car turn into her driveway. In front of the house, two young girls in sundresses get out.

"Mrs. North?" the first girl says, when Elizabeth comes up to meet them. "You probably don't remember me, but I'm Beth Woodall and this is Cindy Lewis. We're from the Vineyard."

Beth is blonde and pretty. A young Louise, Elizabeth thinks. But Cindy has a limp and something is wrong with one arm. Elizabeth doesn't look at it directly.

"What can I do for you girls?"

"Oh, we just came to see you," Beth says. "Paul and Louise thought we might cheer you up."

In the living room, Beth is the speaker. "We all knew your husband from the paper, Mrs. North. He was wonderful! My dad read every line he ever wrote, and says this town is lost without him." She pushes back her hair, anchors it behind one ear. Her nails, overlong, pale as seashells, seem to lag behind her fingers. "We've all been praying for you."

Elizabeth rubs a wet spot the hose has made on her skirt. "Thank you," she says, looking down.

"I know how you feel, though," Beth says quickly. "My boyfriend, Billy Moseley, was killed in a wreck last year. He'd been my boyfriend since grammar school, and we'd have gotten married someday, if he'd lived." Her eyes fill up with tears. "We were just always . . . together."

Elizabeth remembers Billy. Handsome, polite. A star athlete killed by a drunk driver. She feels a quick stir of sympathy but, like everything painful since John died, it freezes before it can surface. Now it all seems packed in her chest, as in the top of a refrigerator so full the door will hardly shut. She looks back at Beth with dry guilty eyes.

"Well, I'm all right now," Beth says. "But I thought for a while it would kill me. I didn't want to live without Billy, until I met the people at The Vineyard. They made me see it was God's will for Billy to die and me to live and serve the Lord. Now I know he's waiting for me, and it's not as bad as it was." She shrugs. "I try to help Billy's mother, but she won't turn it over to the Lord."

The room is growing dark. Elizabeth gets up to turn on more lights, which cast a roseate glow on their faces, pale hands.

"Would you girls like a Coke?" she asks.

Beth blinks to dry her eyes. "Yes, ma'am," she says. "Thank you. A Coke would be nice."

They follow Elizabeth to the kitchen, where she pours Coca-Cola into glasses filled with ice cubes.

"You must get lonesome here by yourself," Cindy says, looking around. "Are your children away from home or something?"

Elizabeth hands her a glass and paper napkin. "I don't have children, Cindy," she says. "My husband and I wanted a family, but couldn't have one. All we had was each other."

"Ah!" Beth says quickly. "*We'll* be your children, then. Won't we, Cindy?"

It is seven o'clock in the morning and Elizabeth is drinking instant coffee from an old, stained mug, staring dejectedly out the kitchen window. During the night, she'd had a dream about John. He'd been alive, not dead.

John had been editor-publisher of the Wakefield SUN, the town's weekly paper, had written most of the copy himself. In the dream, he and Elizabeth had been in bed for the night.

John had liked to work in bed, and she had liked to read beside him, so they'd gone to bed early as a rule. Propped up on pillows, he had worked on editorials, for which he'd been known throughout the state. At times, though, he had put aside his clipboard and taken off his glasses. When he turned her way, his eyes—blue-gray and rugged like the tweed jacket he'd worn so many winters—could take on a look that made the book fall from her hand. Later, sometimes, on to the floor.

In the dream, as he looked at her, the phone by their bed had rung. He'd forgotten a meeting, he said, throwing off covers. He had to get down there. It had already started, a meeting he couldn't afford to miss. Putting on a jacket, he had stopped at the bedroom door.

"I'll be right back," he'd said happily.

But he wasn't back and never would be, she'd been reminded, wide awake. In the dark, she had checked the space beside her to be sure, and her loss had seemed new again, more cruel than ever, made worse by time. If only she could cry, she'd thought, like other widows! Cry, everyone told her. Let the grief out! But she couldn't. It was frozen and locked up inside her, a mass that wouldn't move.

She had waked from the dream at two in the morning, and hasn't been back to sleep since. Now she's glad to be up with something to do, if it's only an appointment with her lawyer. She has sold John's business but kept the building, and the legalities are not yet over. She wants to be on time, is always on time. It is part of her fixation on detail, as if each thing attended to were somehow on a list that if completed could bring back meaning to her life.

In the fall she will go back to teaching school, but her heart is not in it as before. For twenty years she had been, first of all, John's wife—from deadline to deadline, through praise, blame, long stretches of indifference. He couldn't have done it without her, he'd said, with each award and honor he'd been given.

Now no other role seems right for her, which is her problem, she's thinking as the front door bell rings.

Louise is there in a fresh summer dress, her clean hair shining in the sun. She smells of something faintly floral.

"May I come in?"

Still in a rumpled nightgown and robe, aware of the glazed-over look in her eyes, Elizabeth opens the door wider, steps back. "I have an appointment," she says, forcing herself to smile. "But come in. There's time for a cup of coffee."

At the white table, Louise takes the place she'd had before. "I won't stay long," she says.

Elizabeth puts on a pot of real coffee, gets out cups and saucers, sits down across from Louise. Outside, all is quiet. Stores and offices won't open until nine. So why is Louise in town at this hour?

"I was praying for you," she says, as if in answer. "But the Lord told me to come and see you instead."

Elizabeth looks at her, staring. "God told you?" she asks, in a moment.

Their eyes meet. Louise nods. "He wanted you to know that He loves you," she says. "He wanted me to bring you His love." Her face turns a sudden bright pink that deepens and spreads.

At a loss, Elizabeth looks away. She doesn't know what to say. A car starts up and drives off next door. A dog barks. When the coffee is ready, she pours it. She has learned to drink hers black, but Louise adds milk and sugar.

"Come to The Vineyard with us next time, Elizabeth," Louise says, all at once.

This is what she came for, Elizabeth thinks, and it's more than an invitation. It's a plea, as from someone on the bank to a swimmer having trouble in the water.

"It could save your life!" Louise says.

The Vineyard is a narrow, shotgun-style house of the 1890's, last used as a dentist's office. It has one large front room, with two small rooms and a makeshift kitchen behind it. Having been welcomed and shown around, Elizabeth stands against the wall of the front room with Paul and Louise. The group is smaller than she'd expected, and not all Presbyterian. Some are from other churches as well, all smiling and excited.

Everything revolves around Steve, a young man in jeans who looks like a slight blonde Jesus. When Elizabeth is introduced, he looks deep into her eyes.

"Elizabeth," he says, as if her knows her already. "We were hoping you'd come. Welcome to The Vineyard!"

He says no more and moves on, but she has felt his power like the heat from a stove. She finds herself following him around the room with her eyes, wishing she could hear what he says to other people.

The night is hot and windows are open, but no breeze comes through. Rotary fans sweep away the heat in front of them monotonously, in vain. Someone brings in a pitcher of Kool-Aid, which is passed around in paper cups.

"Okay, people." Steve holds up his cup and raises his voice for attention. "Let's have a song."

Everyone takes a seat on the floor, in a ring shaped by the long narrow room. A masculine girl with short dark hair stands up. She tests one key then another low in her throat, and leads off. "We are one in the Spirit, we are one in the Lord . . ."

Most of the singers are young, in shorts or jeans, but some are middle-aged or older. Of the latter, the majority are single women and widows like Elizabeth. The young people sit with folded legs, leaning comfortably forward, and the men draw up one leg or the other. But the women, in pastel pant suits or sleeveless dresses, sit up straight, like paper dolls bent in the middle.

The song gains momentum for the chorus, which ends, "Yes, they'll know-oh we are Christians by our love!"

"All *right*," Steve says. "Time to come to our Lord in prayer."

Someone clambers up to turn off the light switch and someone else lights a candle on the Kool-Aid table. In the dim light Steve reaches out to his neighbor on each side, and a chain of hands is quickly formed.

Elizabeth, without a hand to hold in her new single life, is glad to link in. She could be joining the human race again, she thinks, smiling quickly at the young woman on her left and Paul on her right. Paul's hand no longer trembles but feels as it had in high school—not thrilling but dependable, something to count on.

The room is suddenly hushed. "For the benefit of our visitor," Steve says, "we begin with sentence prayers around the circle, opening our hearts and minds to God."

Elizabeth feels a rush of misgiving. *Oh, no!* she thinks. *I can't do this!* She's never prayed out loud in her life except in unison, much less ad-libbed before other people.

But Steve has already started. "We thank you, Heavenly Father, for the privilege of being here. Guide us, we pray, in all we say and do, that it may be for the extension of Your kingdom. We thank you again for each other, but above all for your blessed son Jesus, who is with us tonight, here in this circle."

On Steve's right, a young man with shoulder-length hair takes up at once. "I thank you, Lord, for turning me around. Until I found you, all I lived for was that bottle. I didn't think about nobody but myself. But you have living water to satisfy my soul."

Eagerly, one after the other, they testify, confess, ask help in bringing others to Jesus as Lord and Savior. They speak of the devil as if he's someone in town, someone they meet every day.

In her turn, a checkout girl from the supermarket starts to cry and can't stop. From around the circle come murmurs of "God bless you" and "We love you" until her weeping begins to subside.

"My heart's too full tonight," the girl says at last. "I have to pass."

On each side, Elizabeth's hands are gripped tighter. The back of her blouse is wet with sweat. The room begins to feel crowded and close.

"Praise God!" a man cries out in the middle of someone's prayer.

"Help me, Lord," a woman whispers.

A teenage boy starts to pray, his words eerily unintelligible. Tongues?, Elizabeth wonders, electrified. They do it here, she's heard. But something nasal in his voice gives the clue, and she has a wild impulse to laugh. He's not speaking in tongues but is tongue-tied from a cleft palate.

Too soon, Elizabeth hears Paul's voice beside her, charged with emotion. He's praying about the sin of pride in his life, but she can't pay attention because she will be next. Heavy galloping hoof-beats seem to have taken the place of her heart.

When Paul is through, she says nothing. *I pass* flashes through her mind, but she doesn't say it. She is unable to decide on, much less utter, a word. Her hands are wet with cold perspiration. She tries to withdraw them, but Paul on one side and the young woman on the other hold on tight. Fans hum back and forth as her silence stretches out.

At last someone starts to pray out of turn, and the circle is mended. As the prayers move back toward Steve, she gives a sigh of relief and tries, without being obvious, to ease her position on the floor.

Steve gives a new directive. "We'll now lift up to God those with special needs tonight."

He allows them a moment to think, then leads off. "I lift up Jane, in the medical center for diagnosis," he says. "Her tests begin in the morning."

They pray in silence for Jane, for someone in the midst of divorce, for a man who's lost his job. An unnamed friend with an unidentified problem is lifted up.

Louise clears her throat for attention, then hesitates before speaking out. When she does, her voice is girlish and sweet as usual.

"I lift up Elizabeth," she says.

Elizabeth has avoided the telephone all day, though she's heard it ring many times. The weather is cloudy and cool, so she's spent the morning outside, weeding, hoeing, raking, and has come to one decision. She will not see the soul savers today.

Tomorrow, it may be, she can face them. Today, she will do anything not to. They were holding her up, she thinks, not for her sake but for theirs. They refuse to look on the dark side of things, and they want her to blink it away too. If she can smile in the face of loss, grief, and death, so can they. They're like children in a fairy tale, singing songs, holding hands. Never mind the dark wood, the wolves and witches. Or birds that eat up the breadcrumbs.

During lunch she takes the phone off the hook, eats in a hurry, and goes back out with magazines and a book. For supper she will go to Breck's for a barbecue and visit with whoever's there. When she comes back, the day will be over. "One day at a time," is the new widow's motto.

She is drying off from a shower when the front door bell rings. She doesn't hurry, even when it rings again and someone's fingers stays on the buzzer. The third time, she closes the bathroom door, little by little, so as not to be heard. Gingerly, as if it might shock her, she flips off the light switch.

Soon there is knocking on her back door, repeated several times. She can hear voices but not words. When she continues to be still, hardly breathing for fear they will somehow know or divine that she's there, the knocking stops and the voices, jarred by retreating footsteps, fade away. At last, through a sneaked-back window curtain, she can see the small red car moving off.

Suddenly, in her mind's eye, she can also see herself as from a distance, towel clutched like a fig leaf, hiding from a band of Christians out to save her soul!

For the first time in her widowhood, she laughs when she's alone. It happens before she knows it, like a hiccough or a sneeze. Shocked, she laughs more, with an ease she'd thought lost to her forever.

Smiling still, she dresses in a hurry, is about to walk out the back door when the front door bell rings.

This time she goes at once, car keys in hand, to open the door. Beth and Cindy, plus Steve and two policemen, stare back at her. The policemen are in uniform, dark blue pants and lighter blue shirts, with badges, insignia, and guns on their belts. Obviously, they've been deciding how to get in the house without a key.

For a moment no one speaks. Then Beth, wide-eyed, bursts out, "You scared us to death, Mrs. North! We thought you had passed out or something. We knew you were in there because of your car."

"I didn't feel like seeing anyone today." Elizabeth's voice is calm and level. Where did it come from, she thinks, that unruffled voice? She should be mad or upset, and she's not.

"Sorry we bothered you, Mrs. North," the older policeman says. "Your friends here were worried."

And suddenly, out of the blue, Elizabeth is suffused with what seems like pure benevolence. For a split-second, and for no reason, she is sure that everything is overall right in the world, no matter what. And not just for her but for everyone, including the dead. The air seems rarified, the light incandescent.

"It was no bother," she says, half-dazed, to the policeman. "I thank you."

Steve has said nothing. His eyes are as calm as ever, the eyes of a true believer, blessed or cursed with certainty. His focus has been steadily on her, but now it breaks away.

"Let's go, people," he says lightly. "God bless you, Elizabeth. Glad you're okay."

Elizabeth has slept all night, for once. As she sits down to cereal and coffee, she is sure of one thing. She has to start what everyone tells her must be "a whole new life" without John, and she has to do it now. Though frozen and numb inside still, she can laugh. And she has experienced, however fleetingly, what must have been grace.

When a car door slams out front, not once but twice, she gets up without waiting for anyone to ring or knock. It is Paul and Louise, for the first time not smiling. Paul has on khaki work clothes. Louise has brushed her hair on top, but underneath sleep tangles show.

On the living room sofa, they sit leaning forward. Paul rocks one knee nervously from side to side, making his whole body shake from the tension locked inside him.

"They should have come to us instead of going to the police," he says at once. "They just weren't thinking."

"No. It was my fault," Elizabeth says. "I should have gone to the door."

"Why *didn't* you?" Louise asks.

"Well . . ." She falls silent.

"Our meeting upset you?" Paul asks, in a moment.

Elizabeth's housecoat is old and too short. They catch her like this every time, she thinks. Why can't they call before they come, like everyone else? She begins to check snaps down her front.

"Level with us, honey," Paul says. "We're your friends. What upset you so much?"

Except for the faint click of a snap being snapped, the room is utterly quiet.

"We need to pray about this," Paul says. "Let's pray . . ."

"No!" Elizabeth is on her feet without thinking. "No, Paul. I can't, I'm sorry." She's out of breath as from running. "This has

got to stop! I can't be in your Vineyard. You'll have to find somebody else . . ."

He's silent for so long a countdown seems to start. Then he stands
up slowly, Louise at his side as if joined. At the door, with his hand
on the knob, he turns.

"Well, Elizabeth," he says. "I guess it's time to say goodbye."

Her heart slows down as if brakes had been applied. The beats
become heavy, far apart. She can feel them in her ears, close to
her brain.

"I'm sorry, Paul!" she says quickly. Before his accusing eyes, she
says it again, like holding out a gift she knows to be inadequate.
"I'm *sorry!*"

But this time he has no joke or smile. Without a word, he takes
Louise by the arm, and they turn to go.

Elizabeth watches them walk to the car, side by side, not touching. Paul opens the door for Louise, shuts her quickly in, and gets
behind the wheel himself. The station wagon moves out of sight
down the driveway.

Elizabeth's cereal is soggy, her coffee cold. She pushes it all away,
props her elbows on the table, and buries her face in her hands.
Suddenly, as from a thaw long overdue, she's crying. Sobs shake
her shoulders. Tears seep through her fingers and run down her
wrists. One drop falls on the glass top, where it sparkles like a jewel
in the morning sunlight. †

Interview

Mary Ward Brown has a rare ability to inspire trust and delight simply by talking to you. Over a period of two years, through much talking on the telephone, we established a friendship based on news of family and church, ideas about writing and editing, and a passion for all kinds of music, especially jazz. One conversation might be about "ailments" and grandchildren, the next about a fascination with Anton Chekov and Cormac McCarthy. Brown gives the impression of being completely comfortable, at home in her own skin. Without apparent effort she can bridge any gap in distance, acquaintanceship, or age with shared confidences, a genuine interest in the doings of others, and an understanding of the subtle complexities of being a southerner and a woman living near the place of her birth, Marion Junction, Alabama—twenty-one miles from Browns, the nearest town, home of Bob and Bonnie's Cafe and one grocery store.

She describes herself as a "country woman" who usually wears jeans or jeans skirts around the house, not the sort of ruffled blouse she has on in a photograph for *People* magazine. "I don't know why I chose that blouse to wear. I think I wanted to hide some of my wrinkles and it turned out all right. That photographer, Will McIntyre, is very talented." The photograph shows a face that is open, bright, and smiling with warm intelligence and good humor. With a slender build, hair pulled back, and arms folded across her chest, she looks as if she is capable of serving you a full farm breakfast accompanied by a raucous account of her trip to Birmingham to see a specialist or of her trip to Russia she and other writers took three years ago as guests of the Soviet Writers' Union.

Her voice is at once clear, wry, soft, and emphatic. She talks in a rural Alabama accent flavored with the no-nonsense inflection of a newspaper editor. Her syntax and phrasing are just slightly out of the ordinary; her sentences often take on the quality of found poems. Of Larry Brown, she says, "He can ever more write fiction"; of growing old (she is seventy-five): "Old age is scary territory. Everybody feels for you, but nobody can reach you."

She is passionate about her fiction and intensely interested in the short story form. Although enthusiastic about being interviewed, she asked me to give her the interview questions in writing, so that she could respond thoughtfully and fully to them in a letter. To Brown, each word is a live thing, of both flesh and spirit, and she tends to each one with care.

It isn't surprising that someone who is so in tune with the nuance and cadence of language loves listening to jazz, to "the blue note, the improvisation, the beat—I'm crazy about Charlie Parker, Billie Holliday." To her, they share the genius that great fiction writers have for eliciting emotion, capturing the timelessness of human feelings in the lyrical line. My conversations with her over many months led me to realize that Mary Ward Brown has that same genius for the "true and lively" word, the rhythm and the import, in fiction and in life.

Would you begin by telling me a little about where you grew up and how you began to write?

I grew up where I live now, in the Black Belt of Alabama, twenty-one miles from Selma. I write only short stories, most of them collected in *Tongues of Flame*, published by Seymour Lawrence/Dutton in 1986.

I always wanted to write, to put everything into sentences on paper, but I came late to fiction. In the fifties I wrote a few stories, took a class in creative writing at the University of Alabama, then another by correspondence from the University of North Carolina. But writing was always obsessive with me, so I gave it up until I was a widow, twenty-five years later.

What is your personal religious history, your experience with religion as a child?

My parents were Baptist, but the only church in our rural community was Methodist, so we went there. We went every Sunday, but religion was a Sunday kind of thing. The Bible was around, but no one read it except on Sunday morning before Sunday school, maybe. No one seemed to question any of it, at least not aloud. It was all mixed up with morality.

Faulkner has said of his own exposure to religion as a child, "It's not so much what I believe or don't believe; it's just there."

Faulkner was right.

How have your religious views changed over the years? What has been instrumental in changing them? If you aren't an "orthodox" or "churched" Christian now, how do you see yourself, your beliefs, in relation to institutional religion?

I went to church with my parents until I went to college. I didn't go far, to nearby Judson College in Marion, but I went as a boarding student. Once away from home, I avoided church as much as possible. Religion simply wasn't attractive to me. I wasn't attracted to the religious people that I knew. I didn't really think much about religion until I began to have panic attacks as a young wife, and came face to face with my own mortality. Eventually I joined the Episcopal Church and have considered myself "churched" for forty years, but I'm probably not orthodox. I'm Christian because I live in a Christian culture, but I think I could be anything. If I lived in the Far East, I would get down on the ground and bow to whatever they bow to. I think God is greater than any form of religion.

Why do you think that religion (or some form of religious expression) seems to play such a significant part in so much of the South's literature? Does it do so in yours? Why?

I can't generalize about religion in southern literature, but it seems to get into my work all the time. Someone once asked me, "Why do you always write about race and religion?" If I do, it's because they're the main preoccupations of the region where I live. In *A Turn in the South*, V. S. Naipaul says, "Religion was like something in the air, a store of emotion on which people could draw according to their need. . . . In no other part of the world had I found the people so driven by the idea of good behavior and the good religious life. And that was true for black and white."

I think what I do is create characters, then let them come to grips with my deepest concerns. Or maybe it's the other way around—concerns, then characters. It's mostly subconscious, like dreams, and a mystery. It's like play, in a way, except that it's dead serious. My hope is simply to connect with the reader, but there's nothing specific that I want the reader to gain—except maybe another view of our common humanity.

Is there such a thing as moral fiction?

Yes, I think there is moral fiction. It has nothing to do with

didacticism, but with a writer's commitment to telling the truth—
after first asking himself if it's truth worth telling. Faulkner talks
about "the old verities" and about writing of the heart, not the glands.
John Gardner in his book, *On Moral Fiction*, says that true art "seeks
to improve life, not debase it."

*Who are some of the influential figures who have inspired you in
your writing? Who are some you admire?*

I think perhaps all the writers I've read and loved have been some
kind of influence, but no influence is sustained once I start to work.
The aesthetic problems and solutions are then up to me. No one can
lead the way, unfortunately.

The writers I most admire continue to be Tolstoy and Chekov,
Faulkner and Flannery O'Connor. Flaubert has always been there
because of *Madame Bovary* and "A Simple Heart," and recently I
added Gogol because of *Dead Souls*. Cormac McCarthy is someone
whose work I am discovering now. I could go on and on. When I
was young, I was under the spell of Katherine Mansfield, and later
Katherine Anne Porter. I still think Katherine Anne Porter is a
great short story writer. If I've actually been influenced by anyone,
I suppose it would be those two women.

*What are some of your reactions to the religious perspectives and
works of Flannery O'Connor and Walker Percy?*

I thought Flannery O'Connor was a great writer before I ever
knew that she wrote from a viewpoint of Roman Catholic orthodoxy.
I'm sorry to say that I've only read one book by Walker Percy, *The
Last Gentleman*.

*Do you view yourself as a Christian writer? Or is this term inher-
ently misleading or too limiting? Are your fictional works and your
religious views intentionally (perhaps inescapably) intertwined or
are you able to regard them as separate entities?*

I don't view myself as a Christian writer, but my impulse to write
at all is probably religious. I'm profoundly grateful for a chance to
be alive on this earth and I think I write out of that feeling. I think
that what I write is some kind of offering to whoever or whatever
brought the universe into being and keeps it going. I don't feel personally in touch with the power in control, but I do feel impelled to
put something on the altar as I go by, so to speak. I want my stories

to be as true as I can make them for this reason. I want my stories to be good and true, that's all.

I'm curious to know if you are a "Christian reader," that is, if you read fiction from a Christian perspective, as Cleanth Brooks said of himself in his book, The Hidden God: Hemingway, Faulkner, Yeats, Eliot, and Warren.

No, I'm not a Christian reader. When I read I'm looking for art, not religion. I'm intensely interested in—I love—the short story form. Chekov's work is timeless. He wrote about nineteenth-century Russia, but the emotions are the same as the people we know.

Are there any specific characters in your works who seem to voice in some way your own views or conflicts concerning faith?

I don't think so. They voice their own views, I hope. When I'm formulating a story, I don't intend to be drawing on my own experiences or ambivalences. But later, after the stories are out on their own, I'm sometimes embarrassed to see how revealing they are.

Do you draw directly or indirectly from the Bible as a source in your writing?

I don't draw on the Bible, because I don't know much about it, I'm ashamed to say. I know the four Gospels and that's about all.

Several of the main characters in Tongues of Flame *are middle-aged women who are confronted through pain, disillusionment, or loss with having to see their lives in new ways, often ways that strike at the roots of the old order of things that defined their lives up to now. Can you talk about Elizabeth ("A New Life") and Dovey ("Tongues of Flame") in this light?*

Dovey is about good intentions and good works that backfire in ways that are totally unexpected, also about the subconscious elements in our motives. Elizabeth, I suppose, is Everywoman trying to cope with radical grief. In the story, she's a foil for the soul savers, Paul and Louise.

In your stories you have created spellbinding characters, such as Steve, the charismatic leader of the Vineyard people in "A New Life," and the Reverend Benefield—men of God who seem to be genuinely impassioned preachers, yet seem also to embody or suggest something that is untrustworthy (perhaps they are merely cagey, perhaps worse than that). What are your thoughts about these characters? About real preachers such as these that you've known?

Steve is the true believer, absolutely sincere, convinced that he has the key to salvation, driven to pass it on.

The Reverend Benefield is a professional evangelist, whose success is measured by the number of souls he saves. He feels free to use whatever means seem to work. His very fervor is a part of his technique, in a way. He uses ingenuity, even tricks, that Steve would never stoop to use. He also has humor, in contrast to Steve's high seriousness. I've known real preachers more or less like both of them.

In "A New Life," the narrator tells the reader, "This is the southern Bible Belt, where people talk about God the way they talk about the weather, about His will and His blessing, about why He lets things happen." This sentence alone captures the pervasive intensity of religion in the not-very-distant past in the South. Do you think that this way of seeing and talking about God is as pervasive as it used to be? Is it dying out in the modern South? Is it intensifying?

I think that it's as pervasive as it ever was among people who are relatively unsophisticated, and some who are not. Especially during times of illness, death, tragedy, any kind of disaster. Also the opposite—good fortune is viewed as a blessing from God.

Would you speak about the ambiguity of the ending of "A New Life"? Does the little band of Christians save Elizabeth indirectly, or is it just the opposite, i.e., that she truly resisted their efforts, and saved herself by learning to grieve for her husband by herself? Was she touched by grace in spite of events leading up to her tears?

Elizabeth is definitely not saved by the Keepers of the Vineyard. They wind up turning her off completely. She's saved by the natural renewal of the life force within her, plus a reminder from outside— a hit of grace—that life is good in spite of suffering. Yes, all the events of the story combine to bring about her tears of release.

In "Tongues of Flame," "Dovey" is a wonderful name. It evokes the image of the dove descending from heaven in the New Testament, and the words of the old country song, "On the wings of a snow-white dove." It also suggests the pet name "lovey dovey."

I wish I could claim all those marvelous reasons for Dovey's name, but I can't. I don't know why I chose it. It just seemed a good sweet country name.

An interesting theme you explore in "Tongues of Flame" is the mysterious and potent interrelationship between religious fervor, the impulse to nurture, and sexual passion. Dovey's dream in which E. L. is lying beside her and touches her, flushing her with pleasure, while her husband, Floyd, sleeps on her other side is testimony to that confusion/symmetry. Would you comment on that dream, what it means to Dovey, and to the story?

Dovey wouldn't want me to talk about her dream! But that's a good question. I'll let those preachers and choir directors who became involved, to their embarrassment and sometimes sorrow, explain it. †

10

HARRY CREWS

The Writer as Shaman

"In Bacon County, Georgia where I come from, you don't curse the land, the sun, the wind, rain, and you don't curse God. All are the same blasphemy," says Harry Crews in an interview with filmmaker Gary Hawkins. Crews is the author of thirteen novels, two collections of nonfiction, and an autobiography, *A Childhood: A Biography of a Place*, a penetrating memoir of the significant events of his early life in rural south Georgia during the Great Depression. "The world was full of mystery and awesome power," he says in *A Childhood*. "It was only right ways of doing things, ritual ways of doing things, that kept any of us safe."

The world of Harry Crews's childhood was one of profound poverty and explosive violence, but also of strong ties to family and place. Crews was born in 1935 in Alma, Georgia. After high school, he served in the United States Marine Corps from 1953 to 1956, attaining the rank of sergeant. Having earned a B.A. in English from the University of Florida in 1960 and an M.S. Ed. in 1962, Crews taught English at Broward Junior College from 1962 to 1968. He began teaching creative writing and English at the University of Florida in 1968, the same year he published his first novel, *The Gospel Singer*. With numerous articles and essays in *Esquire, The Sewanee Review, The Georgia Review*, and *Playboy*, as well as longer works of fiction and nonfiction, Crews has established himself as a respected yet controversial writer whose vision is both comic and tragic, nostalgic and grotesque, and whose characters are often physically deformed or strangely obsessed.

Throughout his work, he has been unafraid to explore the primal elements of human nature.

According to Crews, the stories his people told about themselves and the natural world they lived in formed a bedrock of meaning and shared understanding that enabled them to withstand the onslaughts of weather, disease, famine, and time. In the interview with Hawkins, he explains, "Making stories was not so that we could understand . . . but so that we could live. . . . The stories help you to deal with the world, to live with it and stand it. If you have that . . . the ritual, the stories, the understanding, even if it's dead wrong (it may be) of the world around you, what you have in fact, and it cannot be denied, is a core of confidence that everything's gonna be all right. "Yet, along with this core of confidence, Harry Crews held to a deeply ingrained conviction of man's basic "no-goodness" in the sight of God, and an utter dependence upon Divine Grace, which is the heart of what Robert Coles has called the "hard, hard religion" of Calvinist Protestantism. Feeling keenly our loss of "connectedness" to the world around us, to community, to the extended family, and to all living things, Crews wrestles again and again in his fiction with, as he puts it, "the nature of belief" in an appallingly secular world.

Beginning with his first novel, *The Gospel Singer* (1968), Crews's fiction has been characterized by a preoccupation with violence and the grotesque and a bleakness of vision tempered with compassion. *The Gospel Singer* deals with the desperate need for instant salvation in the fictional town of Enigma, Georgia. In *Car* (1972), Crews creates a comically absurd metaphor of modern secular life by having a character set about to eat a car, piece by piece. Of *The Knockout Artist* (1989), Jerry Leath Mills, literary critic and professor of English at the University of North Carolina, writes that Eugene Talmadge Biggs pursues a "vision of lost innocence within a context of known and constant peril" in the brutal, "value-inverted" world of boxing where "love is weakness and cold self-interest is power." Mills describes the world of bodybuilding developed by Crews in *Body* as a "constantly unfolding metaphor for the self-alteration that life in the New South seems to require."

The recent novel *Scar Lover* explores the power of guilt, with its paradoxically destructive and transforming nature (the epigraph is a phrase from James Dickey, "Guilt is magic"), but it is love without reservation that redeems this novel's lost souls. "If I have a home to come to, I am there," Pete says, lying in Sarah's arms. Love redeems in this novel through natural, unself-conscious acts of total acceptance.

In Crews's novel-in-progress, he returns to his obsession with the nature of "outsidedness." Set in an old age home, the novel will explore the boundaries of what it means to be "normal," and what it means to be a "freak,"—invisible and powerless, yet all-too-conspicuous in ways that only serve to obscure the humanity within.

This obsession has its roots in the writer's early childhood. By the time he was six years old, just as he had begun to recover from infantile paralysis, Crews suffered third-degree burns over three-quarters of his body from falling into a vat of scalding water. As he said to Hawkins, "I felt, at that moment, when I was pulled out [of the cauldron] and stood on the ground, abandoned by God. . . . Because I had been introduced thoroughly to God and religion and heaven and angels and robes and harps and streets of gold by then. And it was quite obvious that living right, being good, brings good things—that's what I'd been taught—we all know it's a lie; it might, it might not. And so, in my mind's eye, I was forsaken." It was seared into his consciousness that, as he put it, "I was guilty of something neither man nor God can forgive."

Crews links the controlling forces of violence and suffering in his life, the haunting sense of abandonment and outsidedness, his anguished search for redemptive meaning, and his drive to create fiction as art in one powerfully compelling metaphor—the writer as shaman. A shaman heals the afflictions of body and soul through mythmaking and storytelling to give understanding and solace, meaning and identity to individual souls in community. In hearing these stories, the listeners participate in their own healing by identifying with, judging, and then forgiving the characters they read about. As the shaman must take on the demons of the afflicted community, the writer inhabits the deeper mysteries that ordinary folks are unwilling to contemplate. To Crews, being a fiction writer "means you spend most of your time thinking about, meditating upon, trying to dissect and understand just those aspects of the human animal that other human beings try their damndest never to think about."

In this excerpt from *Scar Lover*, Pete's mother-in-law-to-be (Mrs. Leemer) and the mysterious Linga, a neighborhood Rastafarian, are in the Leemers' kitchen preparing the deceased Mr. Leemer for cremation that will be held later that day in the back yard of the Leemers' home. George and Mr. Winecoff, Pete's coworkers, are helping out. Meanwhile, Sarah Leemer, Pete's beloved, is waiting for him in the upstairs bedroom. †

From

Scar Lover

Pete, who was breathing again normally after nearly smothering in astonishment, said: "If you don't mind my asking, what is it you're doing?"

"I do mind."

"Preparing the corpse," said Linga.

"Satisfied?" Mrs. Leemer asked.

Pete was not. He'd always wondered why the women where he came from insisted on doing this. He wanted to know what Henry was being prepared for. Dead was as prepared as anybody could get. But he thought it best to leave it alone.

"Where's Sarah?" Pete said.

"I think she said she was going to her room," said Mr. Winekoff.

In a voice harder than a man's, Linga said, "We will not ask you again to be gone from here." She said it without looking up from Henry Leemer's feet, where she was having a particularly difficult time with one of his big toes.

George almost ran over Mr. Winekoff getting out of the room, with Pete following closely.

In the little hallway leading to the front door, Mr. Winekoff said, "I'll be on the front porch of the boardinghouse when you need me."

"I tink I rest in me Hudson fo some more while," said George. "Rest me in de Hudson and tink bout de straight razor Linga care in her shoe. Linga lak dat razor, lak ta care it in her shoe an dat make some more shit for me ta tink bout. Linga some more good wit dat straight razor."

"Razor?" said Pete.

"In de shoe."

"In her goddam shoe?"

"It de nigger in her. She tink it mus be some law dat all niggers got ta care de razor in dere shoe."

"Probably a useful thing to know," said Pete.

"Fo sho now, mon. Dat a sho an certain ting. But restin up in me Hudson gon take me down. I come loose dis way, me Hudson tighten me up. Come on, Pete-Pete, mon, an res up wit me and de ganja in de Hudson."

"I don't think so, George. I had the most god-awful dream—I guess it was a dream, but it didn't feel like it—I had it when we were on the way back with Henry. It was about . . . well, it wouldn't do any good to tell you about it. It's complicated and doesn't seem to make a lot of sense."

"Don tink on de sense, mon, an put de ear on de ganja. Wha de ganja say bring it true. It bring de spirits an de spirits dey don lie ta ya, mon. But ya kin nebber know ta hear les ya leartn ta trus. Ya nuh trus anyting some much, I am tinkin."

"I trust you, George, you know I do."

"Don tink bout me, mon. Ya trus de spirits." He turned to go but Pete put a hand on his shoulder and stopped him.

"Do you know what they're doing back in there?" He pointed toward the dining room they had just left.

"Fixin up de dead mon. Ya know dat good as I know dat."

"I know that. Mrs. Leemer told me. Fixing him for what?"

"Fo de fire. Fo de burnin."

"Damn, George. Burning? Where in the hell do they think they can burn him?"

"Linga an me hab de camp—many Rastas an much land—way out dere in da Cedar Creek. Dey may be gon do it dere. Linga tell Henry's woman no need ta worry on it."

Pete knew right where he meant. Cedar Creek was just north of Jacksonville and the name Cedar Creek made it sound like a beautiful place. But there was not a creek, Cedar or otherwise, anywhere near it. Or if there was Pete had never seen it. It was a fucking swamp, was what it was.

"It's not enough dry wood out there for a wienie roast, George. I've been out that way more than once, and I know."

"I hab stack an stack o dry oak lef ober from when it be cold. But I be tinkin ta bring more dan some from de mon's own woodpile here fo him luck on de journey home."

It seemed to Pete that Mr. Leemer had run out of luck some time back. Seeing hin lying naked on a shelf in a room filled with other dead people, a room cold enough to keep hamburger in, made Pete feel that the luck had pretty much run out.

"Well," said Pete, "I hope to hell they know what they are doing."

George became very serious. "Linga know all time wha she am doin. Eben when Linga don know wha she am doin, she know wha she am doin. I hab me whole life cause I know dis."

"I'm obliged to you for telling me." Pete did not doubt for a moment that what George had said was true.

"Linga say cause o de big mistake ya born who ya born, cause she tink ya a Rasta."

"I don't believe we had one in the whole state of Georgia," Pete said.

"Ya hab leas one till ya lef, I am tinkin. I go now ta join wit de smoke in me fine car. Dere is some more goin on now here in dis house I nuh lak."

"There is none of this that I like," Pete said.

George touched Pete's hand briefly before leaving, saying, "Ya wrong dere. But ya gone fine wha ya fine if ya look o ya don look."

Pete stood where he was for a moment, marveling at the truth of what George had said. He was now going in search of Sarah. And with all that had happened, would she be waiting for him? Wanting him? And he her? A miracle. And a tingling in his loins reminded him that the greatest miracle was yet to come.

He knew where her room was and also knew that she would not be in it. She would be in his room. He took the steps to the top of the house two at a time and when he reached the top landing, just as he had known it would, a thin line of light showed under his door. And his loins quieted but his heart pounded.

Pete opened the door. A dim lamp she had found somewhere was burning on a table in one corner of the small room. She was lying on his bed, long and lean, her beautiful hair fanned around her head and a folded washcloth over her eyes. He had opened the door very quietly and she did not move. Her mounded breasts rose and fell smoothly, regularly, and at first he thought she was asleep. But she was not.

"Pete?" she said, even though he would have thought she could not possibly have heard him enter.

"Yes," he said.

"Did you do what you said you were going to do?"

"Yes," he said.

"Sit on the bed," she said. He did. "Take my hand." Her hand was long and thin and chilled. She grasped his hand and closed on it with surprising strength.

"Is he downstairs now?"

"Yes. In the dining room."

She took the cloth from her eyes. She had been crying but her eyes were dry now and shot with a web of veins, with deep circles of a bruised color, not black but a light purple.

"The dining room?"

The only way to tell her was to tell her. "They brought his sawhorses in from the woodlot and took down a door to place on the sawhorses."

"And he's on . . ."

"The door."

"Who else is there now?"

"Your mother and Linga."

"What are they doing?"

"Preparing your father to be cremated." He had almost said burned but at the last moment realized what a brutal word *burned* was. "It was the way he wanted it. They are only doing what he asked to have done."

"You know where?"

"Where?"

"Where will they do it?"

"George and Linga have a place out at Cedar Creek. There's nothing there for miles around but marsh and swamp."

"I know the place. And it's dreadful. Ugly. They're going to burn up my daddy in the middle of the night in the ugliest place I can think of."

Pete thought: *One place is as good and as bad as another.* But he said: "I think your daddy would have wanted it that way. I don't mean it being ugly and a swamp. He was just a man that wanted a job done when he wanted it done. He didn't strike me as a man concerned with appearances."

"It doesn't have to be done this way."

"Maybe," said Pete. It was the only thing he could think of to say.

"Do you know how much life insurance he left?"

"No."

"A lot. There could be a preacher and music and flowers and a church. Nothing about what they're doing seems right."

That fucking insurance. He wondered if he ought to talk to her about it. About it and the illustrated buzzard circling over it. But this was the wrong time, the wrong place.

"Except that was the way he wanted it," he said.

"Hold me."

He bent over her and put his arms under her, felt her shoulder blades, as thin and delicate as a bird's, and felt her heart beating against his chest.

"Could we kiss?" she asked.

He put his lips softly on hers and felt a passion that was hot and desperate rise to meet him. Her mouth opened and their tongues touched and touched again. Her breath, the whole inside of her mouth, tasted sweet beyond saying. And her mouth was hotter still. And her breasts seemed to grow fuller under him and one of her hands, which had been buried in his hair, slipped out of it and slid down his spine to the small of his back and he stretched full beside her and her hand, long fingers splayed, pressed hard into his back before she slid it under his belt and he felt her fingers touch his flesh and they were no longer cold. They were hot and restless there on the muscles of his back under his shirt.

Her mouth was no longer frantic against his and her breasts no longer full and rising. Though she made no move, he could feel her open like a flower. With the hand that was not on his back she did something with her blouse and when it opened she was not wearing anything under it. Her hand moved from under his shirt to the back of his head and she moved his face between her breasts and he thought: If I have a home to come to, I am there.

"Tell me," she said, "what they are doing."

He knew she meant what they were doing with her father and he did not want to tell her, but he did. "He must be bathed."

"Bathed?"

"Yes. And his nails clipped and cleaned and his hair and eyebrows trimmed, and—"

"I ought to be down there," she said.

"No. Daughters do not prepare their fathers."

"Never?"

"Never."

"Then I ought not to be down there?"

"No."

"I ought to be here?"

"Yes."

"Then I am in the right place?"

"Yes."

"I have passed from him to you."

"That is for you to say."

"I have passed from him to you."

Where had their clothes gone? There must have been much movement, hurried movement, but he remembered none of it. In the dim, shadowed light from the lamp on the table, they were naked on his bed and everywhere he moved she was there to receive him and everywhere she moved he was there to receive her.

"And this is the right time?" she said.

"This is the right time," he said on no authority but the language of his heart. His head had nothing to do with this.

She made a sound in her throat like a mourning dove and they were joined, and for a moment the whole world seemed to be very still and they were no longer kissing but their eyes were joined as their flesh was joined and he felt something hot and immediate start behind his eyelids and he knew they were tears. Both her hands came up and brushed his cheeks.

"I can't help it," he said.

"It's all right. It is a good thing. This is a good thing." And the tips of her fingers touched his cheeks again.

"And we are one blood now," he said.

"Yes," she said, smiling widely and happily and holding him to her, "we are one blood."

He wanted to tell her how he had lost all blood in the world but had now found it again when he had given up all hope of ever doing so. But he did not know how to say it, and the world that had gone very still was moving again, great rhythmic waves of movement that he did not even know had started until it was beyond stopping and with wonder, awe, surprise, and love he suddenly understood that it was her, his Sarah, and it was him, and they were not separate in the moving but together as water is together as it washes in upon the shore and back out again and in again, and finally in the mingling salty water pulsing in and out upon the shore—a pulsing that had become an image in his head—he heard the mourning dove cry again, more urgent now, and she was quiet under him, her mouth on his, and her own cheeks wet with tears. †

Interview

Harry Crews stood on a busy sidewalk in downtown Raleigh, North Carolina, leaning against a brick wall outside Harry's Bar and Grill, a popular student hangout near North Carolina State University. He was talking to a group of students, filmmakers, reporters, the novelists Lee Smith and Tim McLaurin, my assistant, Hannah Byrum, and me. Crews was waiting for a ride to the university library where he would see a preview for students and faculty of a Gary Hawkins documentary film about his life. Though it isn't far to walk, Crews welcomed the lift; his knees, injured a while back in a motorcycle accident, buckled slightly as he leaned against the building. It was clear that he had lived life hard—his face showed a nose broken in nine places, a deeply creased forehead, a chiselled jaw, and uneven cheekbones (one, it is said, was flattened by a pool cue). Beneath craggy brows, his light blue eyes seemed to have a cast of sadness about them, even when he laughed. Once a middleweight boxer and brown belt in karate, Crews was heavier now, but still fearsome-looking. A single, pierced earring—a skull-and-crossbones—was barely visible against his earlobe; his graying hair was cut in a Mohawk, with a few tendrils falling over the collar line in back. A line from e. e. cummings, "How Do You Like Your Blue-eyed Boy, Mr. Death?", was tatooed in calligraphy beneath a gaping skull on his upper right arm.

A recovering alcoholic, Crews does not drink or smoke today, though his hoarse voice still holds the effects of years of hard use. As he spoke, his words fired out in rapid succession, in a tone that was sometimes sober, sometimes uproariously funny, his eyebrows alternately scowled and rose to punctuate his thoughts. As Lee Smith told Crews about this book and my hopes to interview him, he turned, focused intensely on my face for an instant and gave me a bear hug. "It's great to be here. Look at all these pretty girls," he said, laughing, releasing me and letting his eyes and huge, open arms embrace the crowd around him. "I'll be glad to let you ask me questions. I don't know if I have any answers, but I'll try." Then we were off to the preview in the small library theater where he would take questions from the audience after the showing.

As the lights went up after the film preview, Crews rose from his seat in the front row of the theater and made his way up three steps to the stage, talking to the audience of students and professors as he went. Though it was clearly painful for him to walk, he moved surprisingly quickly. When he reached the stage, he grabbed a molded plastic chair and sat down gingerly to face the audience in front of the blank screen. A portion of the question-and-answer session follows:

I could, of course, give some sort of a lecture—but I'm not going to do it now and I'm not going to do it tonight—some sort of lecture about literature, or writing nonfiction or writing autobiography— autobiography, or what this is really, is a memoir of my childhood, but I would much rather talk with you than at you. I would much rather you ask whatever question you may have brought here and have you know that I know that the question is important. For God in heaven's sakes don't not ask it because you think it's, well, it's too obvious, it's too simpleminded, it's too unanswerable, or whatever. If you've got a question, it's important, and it's a good question. I make no claims that I can answer those questions, but I can respond to them. Writing's the only thing that I've ever worked at consistently and as hard as I could work. I only teach four months out of the year now at the university, but since I started doing that, I work harder, harder than I ever worked when I was teaching full time. So. Take a minute.

What kept you from giving up during the ten years you were trying to publish and weren't getting anywhere?

As I said, questions one can't answer but only react to, or talk around. [Laughter] For whatever reason, I realized how unlettered I was—I'm not going to say dumb, but how unlettered I was, how much I did not know. How much I had to master before I could write something of value that somebody could pay money for and feel like they got something back for what they paid. And, I simply could not think of myself then, nor can I think of myself now, as anything else but a writer. All the years I was at the university, I worked with young men and women who wanted to be fiction writers. Usually, I'd have two or three or four a year who really had the fire in their belly, who had already caught the disease for which there is no cure, and who were a great joy to work with. But I always told them, I told the institution, I told anybody that wanted to hear it, that I was a writer who taught, not a teacher who wrote. And there's nothing wrong with teaching, God knows, and we need a hell of a lot more, and a hell of a lot better than we have, and we always will need that, but the thing about writing is, and to this day I can get close to it but I can't say it: When I get through writing something and it's done and I look at it and I think before me this was not, and because of me, this is. Nobody's got a piece of this. All mine. I get the heat, the criticism, the slanderous, dumbass remarks that people make to you, but once in a while I get something else. But even if I got nothing from anybody else—the writing gives me—gives back to me—something that I can't get anywhere else. I can't get it from a woman who loves me, I can't get it from a great meal, I can't get it from a great drunk—I don't drink anymore, I haven't had a drink in three years, won't say I won't get drunk tonight but I ain't drunk now. But I was a bad drinker. A real, real, real bad drinker, like drunk for nine years, day and night—*but* I wrote, nonetheless. I couldn't get it from drinking, from anything else. But I could get it—I think it's about the closest a man can get to knowing what it feels like to have a baby, I mean you carry this thing so long, this gestation period with a baby, okay, nine months or a little shorter or a little more, but a book it could be three years, it could be three months, it could be, you know, I wrote a book in six weeks, *Car*, and it's been translated into French; it did well. I think it's a good book. It'd be a better book—this is an important thing for those of you who want to be writers—it would be a better book if I had not hated my subject so passionately. You cannot write well out of hatred. You have to, well, hey, it's a machine, a machine. You certainly can't write about people or somebody well, out of hatred. And the reason I hate cars? I can give you one sentence: How much sense does it make for a one-hundred-and-fourteen pound housewife to get into four thousand pounds of machinery and drive two blocks for a thirteen-ounce loaf of bread? And the little town that I live in is hardly big as this damn room. Little town. I could take you to the intersection where all four corners got a gas station on it. The combustion and the madness of the thing. Changing everything about it every damn year. But much of the time, much of the time, unfortunately, when I'm writing, whatever I'm writing about, I have started it, I'm into it, and I want to get inside it and do something to it because it's on my back like a junkie's needle is on his back. Heroin's riding him, well, that subject's riding me. And I don't think that's probably the best way, but I can't be what I'm not. Larry Brown, he's a helluva writer, stayed with me for a week not long ago at my house, we had a helluva time, talking and stuff. When Larry Brown was talking about me staying there at the typewriter for three hours every day—I do that. I been at a typewriter and I don't know what comes next. And what I say to myself is, I say okay, you don't have to write, just sit here three hours and you can leave, but you can't write letters, and you can't clean your fingernails, and you can't, obviously, look out a window. I always look at a wall when I write. And you know three hours is a long time to sit there like that, you can't read anything, and you'll eventually do something, even if it's wrong.

I really got that from something that Flannery O'Connor said which I think is just damn beautiful. You see, she said it much more elegantly than I just said it, and hers has got that element of mystery in it that I love, because where's all this stuff come from? You think I know? If I did I'd give it to you because some of you want it, you'd like to have it, and I'd give it to you. Share it. There's enough for everybody. I don't know where it comes from. She said, "I go to the typewriter everyday for three hours so that if anything comes, I am prepared to receive it." To receive it, dig it? To receive it is the blossoming mystery. Receive it? Flannery O'Connor has an essay that begins "I am no vague believer." She was hard into Catholicism, God bless her heart, hey that's cool, I'm not a Catholic, but she was and, but, *receive* it.

It is—I know I'm rambling here, but let me, just for a second, take this a little farther, and dangerously so. I'm getting out of my depth here saying this, but I'm going to say it, anyway. Anthropologists and others separate societies that are primitive from societies that are not primitive on the basis of whether or not they can leave a written record. If a society can leave a written record, it is not primitive. It can't leave a written record, it's primitive. But if it can't leave a written record, the history of the tribe and the people and their gods and how their gods interact with one another and with man and how the seeds and animals came to flourish over the earth, they've got all that—who carries those stories? Who carries the oral tradition? Without exception: the shamans. The medicine men. The, what we would call, preachers. I mean, the guy that goes up on the butte somewhere and fasts for four days, and has no water, and stares into the sun, and he finally has a vision, and I'm going to tell that guy that he didn't have a vision? I couldn't do what he did, it would scare me. I'd go blind, I'd die, you know, and a lot of other things. But he didn't. I saw a documentary not long ago on television about an Indian, seventy years old, who wanted to go to the sweat lodge, or whatever kind of lodge it is where you sweat, a guy seventy years old and they show him running down this road towards this other ritual that he was going to, and he looked like a young man. And he had all the world joined together. Everything was a part of everything else. And when you write, what you are trying to do is to create a world that has integrity, and has coherence. It is all of a piece, every image or every action, or every line of dialogue resonates against some other line of dialogue or image or metaphor, or whatever, and a lot of this resonates against a bunch of them. And of course it's all language, isn't it? It's so easy to see that with poetry and so damn hard to see it with fiction. But it works for fiction, too.

What motivated you to write your autobiography?

Thank you for asking; that's a good one. I had a reason and I can give it to you. I thought that if I wrote it all down, if I relived it again, remembered it again, as vividly as I possibly could, the stink and the blood and the hurt (and some joy and happiness) of it, if I did that, and I am either blessed or cursed, depending on your point of view with the kind of memory that if I can get one little thing and I just hang onto that, I can gradually get it all. I can bring back whole conversations that I had ten years ago, thirty years ago when I was in the Marine Corps, but anyway, I thought if I wrote it all down—you already know the answer, don't you? I would be purged of it. It would be cathartic. I would no longer wake up with a bed sweated through with nightmares.

You mentioned Flannery O'Connor's religious belief and the certainty that she had, and on the screen you talk about something like the same kind of certainty in sports. I noticed that every one of your books is organized around an activity like bodybuilding, or football or karate, and I wonder if you think in terms of that analogy — are the people in those books looking for a kind of secular equivalent for what people used to get out of religion?

I don't know if they're looking for it or not, but I am, and that's the way I think. That's the thing that fascinates me the most. I'm thinking about the life of the greatest wire walker in the world now, his last name is D-e-t-i-t-e. It's French and I don't speak French. He's the guy that walked between the trade towers. He did it without anybody knowing it, until he was already up there and then they couldn't get him off the wire; he was fifty stories in the air. Never works with a net. He's alive. On one of my books I quote—I guess it's *The Knockout Artist*—I quote Karl Wallenda. About six weeks before he died in a conversation he said—'cause he never worked with a net, never worked with a net, and he fell sixty feet to a concrete floor to his death in his seventies—and what I quote there is, "Walking the wire is living. Everything else is just waiting." And if you care about fiction, or poetry, or music, or any of the arts—if you care about it enough, doing it is like walking the wire. Doing it is as dangerous in its own way. You either disappear into a bottle, or you stick your head in the oven, or cut your wrists. I mean look at the lives of artists and their ends, or whatever. Dylan Thomas drank himself to death. My God, in the meantime while he was taking the very few years it took him to drink himself to death, his life was such a madhouse scramble. I don't know what people do. I believe it was his art that drove him to that kind of thing—I guess anything could drive him to that kind of thing. I'm just thinking out loud. Yes.

Have you ever sat at the typewriter and nothing looks right, or do you think of something and write it out, or do you get an idea and decide to go out and do it, to live the experience and then write about it?

I have to be honest and tell you just flat out "no." No, that's one of the things I've not done because, very early on, I was impressed by a number of writers, one of them is Robert Penn Warren, talking about that kind of thing. I had a book called *Karate Is a Thing of the Spirit,* and I never would have written *Karate Is a Thing of the Spirit* if I hadn't just stumbled by a place and saw—I'd never seen any karate—and it turned out there was a guy in there named Durk Mosey, a German, raised in Argentina, and he was an eighth-degree black belt, and did all those things eighth-degree black belts do. Madness, madness, madness. And I wanted inside that madness. And I went inside. I had no notion of writing a book about karate. But if I hadn't studied with him for almost three years, I never would've written the book. I couldn't have written the book. Let me just say this one last thing about that right there. There's a bunch of guys, men and women, seems like there's more men than women, who disappear into the library, and every six years or so they come out with a great big book. I'll give you two titles, both of them written by the same guy: *The Agony and the Ecstasy* and *Passions of the Mind,* the first about Michelangelo, the second about Freud. They're about that damn thick, and they make excellent doorstops.

What was the cost to you to create a space for yourself, for your writing?

Oh, God. Let me just answer you this day, this way. On most days, at my age, on most days, if I let myself think about it, I think the cost was much, *much* too heavy, too great, too great. I had to give up too many things. May have hurt too many people, maybe deny myself things that I shouldn't have denied myself. I'm not sure that I did any of those things, but I sometimes—if I get into one of those things, I think about it. Because that space you're talking about, if you really are sucessful about creating it, it does cost. Strangely enough, Sean Penn—my last book was dedicated to him; he's become a great friend of mine 'cause we're making, he's not in an acting role, he's going to direct, and we're going to do *The Knockout Artist*—he talks about building that box for himself when it's time for the cameras to roll. And he's got to do it, he's got to have his space made already, before he moves, and really in a sense, you've either been there and know what a guy's talking about when he says "My space, I've got to have it to do it," or it makes no sense. You can't explain it, somehow.

I'd like to know what authors you read when you were in the Marines.

Ho, my God. Well . . .

Not the ones that you didn't like. The ones that really made an impression.

Okay, that turns out to be a very easy thing to talk about. I discovered Graham Greene when I was in the Marine Corps, and I proceeded to read everything that he had done. I went to considerable trouble to get inter-library loans, in effect—try that on a Marine base, but it can be done—and got everything he's done, his plays, his novels, travelogues, letters, all, everything, and continued to read him until he died. He never learned how to type. I don't know if you know that. He wrote it all in longhand, some of it dictated, but much of it, he did not type, couldn't—in his phrase, "I never mastered the machine." And the reason I read him, see, I owe a great debt to Graham Greene, because whatever else Graham Greene does, he tells you a story, Jack. He's got a strong narrative line, the line of the action. It used to be called, you know, a *narrative art*. And narration is defined as a sequence of events in some chronology, so I like fiction where it's a story—I want a story. That's all I am, screwed up, all those people with those names, I don't want to know about it. Who, what am I? I'm just a story-teller. I tell stories. My strong suit, and I think it's Greene's—first the narrative line, second the dialogue. The dialogue and or dialect—that is, dialogue turned into dialect. Writing effective dialect is damn difficult unless you really know the dialect. You can't fake it. You can fake it to everybody who doesn't know it, but the guy who knows the dialect, he reads one line of it, he knows you're faking.

After the preview, Harry Crews and I arranged to meet in the lobby at the Crowne Park Hotel. When I arrived there, I called his room from the house phone near the front desk. The phone rang half a ring—

"Harry Crews."

"Hello, Harry, this is the religion lady. Can you come down to the lobby?"

"Would you mind coming up here to my room to talk?" he asked. "I mean, I'm bushed. Don't worry. You've got the girl with you. If I get you into any trouble, you can both beat me up." With that, he hung up. Hannah ("the girl") and I grabbed Cokes and snacks from a vending machine downstairs and rode the elevator to Crews's room, not knowing quite what to expect. In fact, we encountered a polite and engaging man who addressed each query with a searing intensity as if it were the most important question on earth.

Okay, here's what I'm fascinated by that I wanted you to react to: In his book, Flannery O'Connor's South, *Robert Coles writes about fundamentalism in the South and he quoted Flannery O'Connor. Flannery O'Connor said—*

Curious that she should be from Milledgeville and a Roman Catholic. That strikes me as just—but, but, go ahead.

She wrote to John Hawkes, "I don't think you should write something as long as a novel around anything that is not of the greatest concern to you and everybody else, and for me this is always a conflict between an attraction for the holy and the dis-belief in it that we breathe in with the air of the times."

All right. I will tell you this, that people find, I don't know as I've ever said it for publication, but I don't mind saying it for publica-tion—people I've said it to, other writers and audiences as we had

today—I don't think anybody in my house believes it much, but I
have now for a long time, say, after about my seventh novel, I
thought that everything I'd written up to that time was a search for
faith, and everything I've written since that time, fiction anyway,
was a search for faith. Or to say it another way, because search for
faith doesn't exactly please me, because search for faith doesn't
exactly say what I'm trying to say, it's a search for the nature of
belief. I am a believer and I don't think a day passes that I don't
think about it, dwell upon it. My brother, who is a very devout
Baptist is terribly displeased with the work I do (he's been in my
house once in the last twenty years) because he finds it, as he says,
pornographic, but then he took one look at one of Flannery
O'Connor's books and found it pornographic, too, but that's all
right, he's a good man. I am a believer, but not a—I don't consider
myself affiliated with, or part of, or belonging to any institutionalized religion that I know of. That is to say—"You're a Methodist,
right?" Or "You go to the Baptist church, right?" or—no, I'm not a
Methodist, and I don't go to the Baptist church, although I've been
to the Baptist church, I've been to the Methodist church, I've been
to the Catholic church. I spent a very long time going to church
after church after church trying to find one I could go to because
the thing I thought was, it came to me, that going to church, if it's
nothing else, even if you can't believe that there's an everlasting
life, that you have a soul that transcends the flesh, whatever—even
if you don't believe that, you could go to a church one day a week,
or more for that matter, you probably ought to go, most of us, certainly I should go more, and do this: meditate upon how we have
failed ourselves, and failed our fellow man. I—now don't get me
wrong, I don't think I'm the worst guy in the world. I think I'm
immodest and bad enough to think I'm a pretty good guy. I try
to—guy's in a ditch, I try to give him a hand. And I hope he'll pass
it along if he can do it. But you can go there and think about your
actions and how they are made manifest in the world that you happen to live in—I happen to live in the South—all right. Because
God is dead. He was dead a long time before Nietzsche said God is
dead. God is dead because this is a secular world we live in. I mean,
like it or not, deny it as you will, it is a secular world. That somehow offends me, really deeply offends me that it's a secular world.

When I wrote *Karate Is a Thing of the Spirit*—that year—you can check me on this—that year, Buick, their advertising slogan that year was, "Buick: Something to Believe In." That was the slogan they had. Okay, I'm going to believe in a car. Well, wonderful. You'll pardon me if I find that obscene. I don't want to believe in a car. I would rather it run and not break down but that's about as far as it goes. Now that we have made religions of—we have made something that is very close to the framework of what religion used to be, once opon a time was, and belief in "a God" was. We've made it out of all things material, this materialistic world. The guy who dies with the highest score wins, the most toys, money in his bank account, you know. All sports that people—I'm a sports fan, and I love boxing, and I recognize at the same time that it is totally indefensible. You can't defend boxing as anything but a brutal, terrible, barbaric act that is uncivilized, and if you happen to be a believer, unholy. That we would give millions of dollars to the these two individuals, to hire this menagerie of trainers and dietitians, and lawyers, everything else, to make them as mean as they can make them and then put them in the ring, with the sole purpose of seeing which one can knock the other one senseless. And many, more than most people think, many, many men have died in the ring. Buoniconti, one of the best linebackers that ever lived. His son was playing linebacker about four years ago in college, paralyzed from the neck down, forever. Nick Buoniconti who's now a lawyer, used to be an NFL linebacker, one of the great ones. So we've made a secular thing out of that and a whole bunch of other things we've named, like cars, and as we've already said, the material things. But then, I say well, I apparently can't make that leap of faith. I can reason myself along for a certain distance towards something that's other than human, bigger than human, more mysterious than human, and the rest of it. But then I can't reason any farther. I can reason towards it, but I can't make that leap of faith. What I can do is, I can contemplate the natural laws of the universe. I mean, rocks do not fall sideways if you turn them loose, they fall down, always. The mystery of a peanut putting the blossom on top of the ground and its fruit under the ground, the mystery of sap rising in pine trees at a certain time of the year, and those are just things everybody notices, it gets much more mysterious than that—I refuse to believe that I, or you, or any of my fellow beings, are an accident, or that we are some kind of a spark of electricity that happened back, whenever. And so, the characters in my books—in *The Gospel Singer,*in the karate book, in *The Knockout Artist*, certainly in the car book—my characters, not surprisingly, are doing essentially what I do much of. I writhe, and "suffer" is not too strong a word. I writhe and suffer in my unknowing. I don't know, and I want to know. On the other hand, if I read the Koran, the Bhagavad Gita, the Old Testament, the New Testament, it isn't about knowing, it's about faith. And it may be that mankind has developed the physical world to such an incredible degree that it has simply overwhelmed his ability to have any faith. I mean we got machines, Jack, that can do, I mean *they're* almost godlike. I mean I know that's blasphemous, but, at least I said "almost." I mean, I don't know if you've ever seen on television, or documentaries, or maybe in person, some factories that have, the automobile business has got it up for electronics. And it's all done by robotic maneuvers, these robots, they go zzzt-zzzt-zzzt, it's things moving down, and they've even got machines now that can reproduce themselves. Now think about that for a minute. Now that's like being a human being reproducing another human being. The machine tears up, the machine knows it's torn up. If the part to fix it is available and the right program has been placed into the machine, then it takes out the broken part, gets the new part, puts it back in, and then works just like it ever did. We've got machines now that we can talk to and the machine will type. It will transcribe; well, it doesn't type the way we normally think of it, but it does in fact transcribe the human voice. You just talk to it and it will put it on paper, and that can be taken off by another machine into regular English, and if you speak to it in French, it'll take it off in that, if it's got the right program built into it.

And most people save themselves a lot of pain or a lot of frustration by just refusing to think about the things that I've been talking about. I'd give you this: that to be a fiction writer means you spend most of your time thinking about, meditating upon, trying to dissect and understand just those aspects of the human animal that other human beings try their damndest never to think about. They don't want to think about that. I mean after all there is, in *Oedipus the King,* if you ask—if you had a big auditorium full of men, and you looked out at them and you said, "Where is the man who has not dreamt of sleeping with his mother?" They would all say, "Not me." The line is in *Oedipus,* and it's as common as field peas, and it doesn't make anybody bad and it doesn't make anybody incestuous, it makes somebody human. There are mysteries we don't understand, and we are not going to understand them, I don't think. I know I won't, I don't believe anybody will.

Now down there where I come from, those good folks have reduced—reduced is a bad choice of words—they have compressed and boiled down the religious experience to something that is hard and fast and simple in the best sense of the word. Simple doesn't mean simpleminded, an atom is simple. It doesn't mean it's easy or simplistic. They boil it down to something very, very simple. I leave to minds better than mine to judge them. If you're a snake handler and you pick up the snakes in a religious ecstasy and the snakes do not bite you because you are a believer, or nine of them bite you and you do not die because you are a believer, who am I, Harry Crews, to say that that is some kind of a charlatan, false, phony, accidental happenstance. I'm not prepared to say that and never will be. And if you look at religions around the world, you see that all over the face of this earth, there are people whose religious experience and the way they worship things are every bit as, if you want to use the word "bizarre," as handling snakes or drinking a cup of arsenic. I can drink it and I won't die because I believe. And they drink it and they don't die. Well, in India there are holy men who live at the top of a mountain of solid ice, utterly naked, and why don't they die? They stick nails through their cheeks and they do not bleed because they can control the capillaries in their body. That's the only possible explanation for why they are not bleeding; the capillaries do not rupture. Well, they say there's got to be some trick to it. Well, maybe so, maybe so. But you go take care of that. I don't know about those things. And I personally in my . . . but if I ever come to the place where *I* ought to be, and I don't think I'm there yet, I think I'll come there through fiction because that's my work and that's my search. But if I don't, I don't. Human beings are manifestly too hard on one another. Everybody wants everybody else to be better than they are. Hey, we're all flawed and faulted, and I mean, we're all—maybe none of you've done it and maybe the next fifty people we've seen haven't done it, but good men and women have just slapped the hell out of a three-year-old baby—didn't, not on the ear or something, but—well, think: slapping a three-year-old baby? I mean, that's despicable and cruel and—yes it is, yes it is. It's also human. You're tired, your nerves are bad, money's short, you don't know what you're going to do with this, you're worried about that, and it happens. And what I, I'm sometimes talking to students outside of the classroom, at my house or something, and what I have been known to say is that I think the kindest and best thing you can do for yourself is to forgive yourself. There's no reason to continue to beat on yourself and hate yourself for a moment of fallibility, and let it turn into a cancer that you carry thirty years later. That's just a loser's way that accomplishes nothing. You admit you did it, you admit the wrongness of it, you try to make amends for it. Most times it's impossible to make amends for it. It's been done. It's like you say something to your wife, something really ugly, and then you didn't mean it, and then you say, "I'm not—let me take that back." Well, you know, I'm sorry. You can't take that back. The words have been said. And you may live together for, you know, fifty years happily after that, but those words are between you. It might conceivably make your marriage stronger. So you can see that in my writing and in my life and belief (the things that make that writing), it's a very dicey situation. Sometimes it comes up seven, and sometimes it comes up snake eyes, and sometimes it comes up and there's nothing on it—it's a blank face, and all I know to do until somebody somehow convinces me otherwise, is to continue to wrestle with it as best I can. I think young people have it so hard because if you do manage to stay alive long enough, you begin to see more and more how much of the bad stuff that you do or have done—yeah, you shouldn't have done it but it doesn't make you Satan, and it doesn't make you irrevocably horrible, in anybody's eyes—shouldn't. Shouldn't and whatever gods may be that look down, up or wherever, I don't for a minute believe, by the very nature of being God, it would be impossible for it Him/Her, to condemn a man. We're too frail, we would be too frail no matter how many bombs we have, we make enough bombs—we already have—to blow the whole place up and we're still very, very frail. I mean, little tiny micro-organisms that you can't even see without an electronic microscope can enter the pores of your skin and you'll be dead tomorrow. That isn't a very strong fortress for walking around in. If you went to church, if anybody went to church once a week and got on his knees and simply thought about that, I don't think it would hurt him a hell of a lot. I think it'd make him probably sleep a little better.

The epigraph in Scar Lover *is "Guilt is magic."*

It's the last line of a poem by James Dickey. He, as best I can understand it (Jim's been my friend for many years but I wouldn't ask him to explain a line to me), as best I can make out, having heard him really talk about it in all kinds of contexts, guilt is magic because we can't forgive or heal ourselves, so it can make us do just anything. It can make us do anything. All those Japanese in the Second World War that were kamikaze pilots and they didn't even have wheels once they took off in a plane loaded full of dynamite, they didn't even have wheels to land. They had to go down in a smokestack or a ship out there somewhere, and to do otherwise would dishonor them, not just them but their entire blood line, mama, daddy and everybody else, and their ancestors, and being ancestor worshippers, they would be guilty of that, so *guilt* sends them down the smokestack. It's a powerful magic to send a man down a smokestack with a plane loaded with dynamite, I should think.

In Scar Lover, *Pete and Sarah fall in love with each other and it seems that guilt becomes transformed into redemption.*

I hope so. I hope so. I wrote it out of the conviction that unqualified love, unqualified love can heal anything. It can heal emotional scars, physical scars, it can heal the crippled, it can—speaking here in metaphor—but it can make the crippled man walk and the blind man see. It occurred to me one day, like when I wrote that book or shortly before I wrote it, that you probably know that you really, really, really love—let's talk about a man and a woman—you really know, if you're a man, you really know that you love a woman when you love her imperfections. She might have a—I don't know—a little funny twist to her nose or a little lobe of her ear, or whatever, odd-shaped chin that maybe six years ago when you first met her you thought she was a great person, she made you feel good, and you liked her company and she made you feel comfortable and safe, but you thought the chin was, well, you wished it was. . . . But then one day you found that that was the very thing that you loved, you loved that little chin. Little chin's fine, and she's fine, and I'm hers and she's mine, and we're one flesh and that's where you are. That is, of course, right out of the Bible, but most people get away from having to embarrass themselves in front of other people, embarrass themselves to themselves, by simply refusing to think about those things. Let's just not think about it, for God's sake. Let's not talk about it, certainly not in the family where you know mama and daddy and little brother, and everybody's present.

You talked at one time about writers who do go to the line, who do embarrass themselves and talk about these things, do probe when others look away, as being the shamans, the medicine men, of the community.

Yes.

Can you talk about that, about how that works?

Well, they are the keepers of the oral tradition of the society since they can't write. Since they can't write, primitive societies have to keep their stories. But it's not just primitive societies. Galileo was driven to prove that Copernicus was wrong about the way the heavenly bodies moved about. He certainly could write. He was certainly not a part of a primitive society. He was part of a very sophisticated society. He searched nonetheless. And people who can't write, so-called primitive, backwards societies, whatever, third-world peoples. Hey man, they've got to somehow come to some kind of understanding, some kind of grips with the fact that it rains, that lightning comes down and sets fire to those woods over there, and burns it off on the bottom and chars the trees, but then in about a month all these little green things start growing out, and it's this wonderful green grass comes where before it was black. Well, they got to—and the sun coming up, and the sun going down and all those things, the moon waxing and waning, all of those things they've got to understand—and they usually do it by making it into stories, giving those things personalities, even names. And they do what the rest of us do, they do the best they can. I often say that all the best fiction is about the same thing. It's somebody doing the best he can with what he's got to do it with, sometimes nobly, sometimes ignobly. And we are not all equally strong, equally talented, equally destined to live out a very long life. And, you know what I'm going to do is I'm going to soak myself in a hot tub. I am so tired. I was all over the country before I came here.

Oh, yes. For your book?

Oh, yes ma'am, I sure was. I've been travelling for so long, and did I bring my magic Afrin? Isn't this obscene? I can't believe I left it at home. Thank you for letting me go on.

This was wonderful. I could listen to you all day.

Got to rest, sometime. Don't want to, but got to, if I want to survive.

And as you wrote one time, "Surviving is triumph enough."
Thank you. †

11

CLYDE EDGERTON

A Garden of Paradoxes

Clyde Edgerton was born in the rural community of Bethesda, North Carolina, in 1944. He attended the University of North Carolina at Chapel Hill, earning his Ph.D. in English Education there in 1975. From 1966 to 1971, he was a pilot in the United States Air Force, serving one year in Southeast Asia. He has published five novels: *Raney* (1985), *Walking Across Egypt* (1987), *The Floatplane Notebooks* (1988), *Killer Diller* (1991), and *In Memory of Junior* (1992); his short stories have appeared in *Southern Review, Southern Exposure, Chattahoochee Review*, and elsewhere. His work has appeared in anthologies such as *Family Portraits: Remembrances by Twenty Distinguished Writers*, edited by Carolyn Anthony, and *New Stories From the South: The Year's Best, 1990*, edited by Shannon Ravenel. Awarded a John Simon Guggenheim Foundation Fellowship in 1989, Edgerton is a 1991 recipient of the Lyndhurst Prize. He and his family live in Durham, North Carolina.

Edgerton's popular and critically acclaimed novels cut through to the essentials of what it means to be human, and in so doing touch the reader's heart and tickle the funny bone. With wit and gentle satire, Edgerton explores the timeless verities that prevail in the midst of tumultuous change both in family life and in the larger culture in the late twentieth century. Each novel takes place in a fictitious small town in rural North Carolina. These towns, like the South as a whole, are in the midst of cultural transformation. As do many novelists from the region, Edgerton writes about the sense of shared history and beliefs, the long tradition of storytelling, the obsessive debate over race, and the strong ties of family and religion that still characterize the southern experience. Also like many of his contemporaries, he is keenly aware of the waning of these traditional values, and of the often irreconcilable conflicts inherent in them. The replacing of old values by new, urban, ones solves little, Edgerton shows us. The clear and arresting voices of his characters tell us that gentle faith and courage transcend the forces of loss and change.

Edgerton's novels are incisive social satires that may seem at first to be deceptively lighthearted. His first novel, *Raney*, is about change itself. Set in Listre, North Carolina, in the mid-seventies, it concerns the delicate balance in the marriage of urban-reared Charles and rural-born, dyed-in-the-wool country girl Raney, two people whose backgrounds, though both southern, are markedly different. Edgerton's second novel, *Walking Across Egypt*, depicts the life of Mattie Rigsbee, an elderly, genuinely Christian lady who triumphs, despite age and loneliness, by taking in one juvenile delinquent, Wesley Benfield, to love and cook for. *The Floatplane Notebooks* is more complex, ambitious, and darkly tragic in its overtones than the first two novels. It is a book about "what wars do to people, and about persistence, the lingering of a family through generations," Edgerton says (*Contemporary Authors*, Volume 134).

The meaning of being a good Christian is one of the serious issues explored in *Killer Diller*. Wesley Benfield is now grown and living in the B.O.T.A. (Back on Track Again), a halfway house for young adult offenders. Wesley's hilarious attempts to justify his carnal desire for his dieting girlfriend, Phoebe Trent, with his desire to be a good, Bible-centered Christian are set against the more sinister machinations of the Sears twins, Ned and Ted, who are president and provost of the local Baptist college. Edgerton's latest novel, *In Memory of Junior*, may be his most complex work. As Mark Winegardner has written, the novel captures the "unadorned insanity of The Way We Live Now. . . . Edgerton's South is neither the Confederacy-haunted Old nor the Atlanta-faceless New. The only war that rages here is the one between life and death: between, among, and within ourselves."

Edgerton's origins in a small North Carolina town and in a fundamentalist Baptist church were at once both sustaining and vexing forces in his life. He articulates the connection, as he sees it, between religion and the human relationships he loves to write about: "My general topic is relationships among human beings, especially in families. Sometimes religion is a fertile area in which to examine these relationships. Of course, some people could argue that in writing about human beings, you are always writing about religion, about theological issues. That makes sense, I think."

In the following passage from *Raney*, Millie Shepherd, Raney's mother-in-law, persuades Raney, a Free-Will Baptist, to accompany her and her son Charles to an Episcopal church service. †

From

Raney

I was just beginning to relax when Millie asks, "Is there an Episcopal church nearby?" I had forgot about her changing over to the Episcopals.

"There's one in White Level," says Charles. "Sara—at the library—goes there."

"You're more than welcome to come to our church," I said. "And since we're going to eat at Mama's, we'll be close by."

"I really like the formality of the Episcopal service," says Millie. "I've gotten used to it. Charles, give them a call this week and if they're celebrating Eucharist Sunday morning at around ten or eleven, I could slip over for that."

I didn't know what a Eucharist was. Likely as not they'd be celebrating something.

"Or," she says, "if you two like, you could come along with me."

"I don't think I could go to an Episcopal church," I said.

"Why not?" they both said.

"They're against some of the things we believe in most."

"What do you mean by that?" said Charles.

"Well, they serve real wine at the Lord's supper. And they have priests, don't they?"

"Yes," said Millie.

"Well, I don't especially approve of the way priests drink."

"Jesus drank—if that's what you mean—as I understand it," she says.

"I don't think so."

"Well, he turned the water into wine at the wedding feast."

"Yes, but that was grape juice."

"Grape juice?"

"If Jesus turned water into wine on the spot," I said, "it had to be grape juice because it didn't have time to ferment."

There was a pause.

"If Jesus could make wine," says *Charles* (you could tell whose side he was on), "he could just as easily make it fermented as not, couldn't he? Why mess around with half a miracle?"

"I've been going to Bethel Free Will Baptist Church for twenty-four years now," I said, "and Mr. Brooks, Mr. Tolley, Mr. Honney-cutt, and all these other men have been studying the Bible for all their lives and they say it's grape juice. All added together they've probably studied the Bible over a hundred years. I'm not going to sit in my own kitchen and go against that."

"But there are Buddhist monks," says Charles, "who have studied religion for an accumulation of millions of years and they say Jesus was only a holy man and not the son of God. You can find anybody who's studied something for X number of years. I'm not sure what that proves."

"These Buddhist monks were not studying the Bible," I said. "They were studying the *Koran*. We talked about that in Sunday School."

"I don't think they were studying the *Koran*," says Mrs. Shepherd. "You're talking about Islam."

"Well, the point is: I'm not talking about the Bible. If it's not in the Bible I'm not interested in it because if I have to stop believing in the Bible I might as well stop living on earth."

"Here, let's get the dishes washed up," says Mrs. Shepherd. "I appreciate your faith—I guess it's a small matter anyway. Sometimes I think we spend too much time on relatively picky religious matters."

It won't no *picky* matter to me.

While we were cleaning up I saw where Charles got his habit of taking the strainer out of the sink and leaving it out, and turning on the faucet and leaving it on. But I didn't say anything. She was nice to help.

Before we finished cleaning up, somebody knocked on the front door. That durn TEA Club meeting. I felt like I hadn't had time to get my bearings.

The meeting was something, and Millie joined in just like she knew everybody.

There was this woman dressed in rags who brought her baby in a sack on her back. Looked like she'd just walked away from a plane crash with her baby all tangled up in her clothes. What's more, she was cock-eyed. Looked like she was looking in two directions at once. Like those pictures of John Kennedy.

There were more unusual people there. But listen to what the meeting was about: they all, including Charles, and his mama, just flown in from Atlanta, are dead set against the Ferris-Jones nuclear power plant being built north of here.

That takes a lot a gall. These scientists have been working for years to get this plant built and Charles and these, well . . . a couple of them looked like hippies to me, and there was a doctor and two college teachers who looked like they don't eat right and the one with the baby—they all get together and in about fifteen minutes decide that the nuclear power plant has got to go. Has got to *go*, mind you.

They haven't hurt anything at the power plant. And electricity certainly has to come from somewhere.

I was in Pope's the other day and the mayor, Mr. Crenshaw, was talking to Mrs. Moss. He said the power plant was the best thing that ever happened to Listre—that it would bring new jobs and make taxes lower.

Now he's the mayor. He's somebody I can listen to. Somebody with a respectable position in the community who *has* to know what he's talking about, else he wouldn't be mayor.

Sometimes I believe these hippies and college professors sit around and frown and complain about what's helping a community most.

Look at the war. These hippies and such were telling the people who knew the most about it how to run it. So we lost. Now they're doing the same thing with this power plant. Do you see the people from the power plant telling the hippies how to be hippies? No, because they don't know anything about it. So they keep their mouths shut.

Charles told me I could come up front to the meeting but I stayed back in the kitchen. After about thirty minutes, Millie did come back and talk to me about how nice Charles and me had fixed up the house. She had a glass of wine, but that's the only one she drunk as far as I know. I never thought I'd see wine under a roof I lived under. Live and learn. I won't be a prude; but I do have principles and I will certainly keep close guard on what goes on. We're not going to have any alcohol under this roof for more than twelve hours, and otherwise only on some special occasions of Charles's. And when we have a child we'll have to discuss the whole thing very seriously. I never saw a drop of alcohol at home except in a bottle Uncle Nate brought in.

I told Millie about Charles painting the living room and she thought it was funny about not being able to find any drapes to go with the old paint. She said Charles just had a good "role model" for fixing up around the house because Bill, Dr. Shepherd, had always helped her. I thought about Daddy. He's never done anything, as far as I can remember inside the house. He works outside, but not inside. I don't think Mama wants him working in the house. She certainly never lets anybody do anything in the kitchen.

Charles won't do a thing outside but pull up crabgrass out of the sidewalk cracks once in a while. I don't know why he gets such a kick out of that. I think it's connected somehow to his strange ideas about germs. He buys these big jars of alcohol to clean the bathroom sink with. I've seen him through the bathroom door— through the crack. He'll scrub around the hole in the bottom of the sink with a ball of cotton soaked in alcohol. Lord knows where else he scrubs. I'll bet he goes through a bottle of alcohol every two weeks. I go in there some mornings and it smells like County Hospital. I started to ask Millie about that but I didn't. Maybe he got it from her. (It's funny what all you find out about your husband after you get married.)

When they finished the meeting, Charles came back to the kitchen and showed me this letter they wrote with Charles's name signed. Charles asked me what I thought. I said if they all wrote it, why didn't they all sign it? This is the letter. Millie told him a couple of words to change.

A state geologist has recently claimed that an area near the proposed Ferris-Jones nuclear power plant is ideal for a hazardous waste disposal site. One of the reasons given is the low population of the area. I suppose the reasoning is that if there are problems, then fewer people will suffer.

It occurs to me that any reason to NOT put something in a highly populated area should also be a good reason NOT to put it in an area of low population.

The sad fact is that problems of nuclear waste disposal are not solved. This generation should not be making decisions that will cause future generations to suffer horrible consequences.

Charles Shepherd

Charles took off work Tuesday afternoon; we took his mama to the airport; and when we got back home we had a little talk which turned into a argument.

I merely asked Charles why he has to be friends with these college professors and such—why he can't be friends with my friends. He went with me *once* to see Madora and her husband, Larry. And Sandra and Billy Ferrell have asked us over for supper twice and he wouldn't go either time. I know they won't ask us again.

"*These* people *think*," he says.

"Think?" I said. "Who *don't* think? Everybody thinks."

"I mean think about something important, something beyond the confines of their own lives."

"What is that supposed to mean?"

"It means getting beyond Listre and Bethel. That's what it means. Raney, the way it works is this: small people talk about themselves; mediocre people talk about other people; and thinking people talk about ideas."

"What does that have to do with anything?" I said. See, what happens is: Charles spouts out this stuff he's read in the library and expects the words to be formed in gold in my head. But I'm sorry.

"It has to do with who I want to be friends with," says Charles. "Madora and—what's his name?—Larry are not interested in anything outside their kitchen, living room, and bedroom."

"I'll have you know," I said, "that Madora and Larry go to Bethel

Free Will Baptist Church. Don't tell me that Jesus Christ is only in their kitchen, living room, and bedroom."

"The problem," says Charles, "the whole problem is just that: Jesus wouldn't have a kitchen, living room, and bedroom."

"He would if he lived in Bethel." I tried to let that sink in. "No matter what your mama thinks."

"Why are you bringing her into this?" (I wasn't sure.) "Raney. Jesus Christ was a radical. If the people at Bethel Free Will Baptist Church met Jesus they'd laugh at him . . . or lynch him."

"A radical? Charles, I had a personal experience with Jesus Christ when I was twelve years old. He wasn't a radical then. And I did not laugh. As a matter of fact, I cried."

"Were you saved, Raney? Is that it? Were you saved and now you're going to heaven and nothing else matters?"

"Charles," I said, and I was mad, "you can run down whoever and whatever you want to, but when you run down my experience with Jesus Christ you are putting yourself below the belly of a hog." I was tore up. I had to cry. I walked out of the kitchen, into the bedroom and slammed the door with both hands as hard as I could; and Charles goes out the front door and drives off. And didn't come back for thirty minutes.

We didn't speak Wednesday or Thursday, but had started warming up some on Friday. Then Friday night we went to see a movie— some awful thing Charles wanted to see—and then Saturday morning the Sneeds business was all over *The Hansen County Pilot*. As I said, Sneeds runs Daddy's store. Sneeds Perry. I don't know him except from when I go in the store. He's always seemed nice.

What he did was get arrested in Raleigh at two A.M. Friday night for trying to pick up this woman he *thought* was a you-know-what but instead was a policewoman. They caught him red-handed. And then the whole subject had to come up at Sunday dinner with Mrs. —, with Millie, there visiting.

She came back Saturday night on the airplane, which was late, and I could of sworn I smelled liquor on her breath. Then we had to wait for all those suitcases, which we loaded into the trunk and carted home and into the guest room again.

Charles had found out that the Episcopal service started at 10:30 A.M. Sunday and that they were having that Eucharist, so they decided they'd go for sure and Millie wanted to know if I was going with them. They seemed like they wanted me to, so I said yes. I wanted to see what the service was like, if nothing else.

The service was the most unusual church service you've ever seen. First of all, I didn't know any of the hymns, and *neither did the regular people there.* You'd expect the regular people there to know their own hymns. They wandered all around on notes that didn't have anything to do with the melody and, all in all, didn't sing with any spunk. And they kept kneeling on these teenie-tiny benches. It was up and down, up and down. I got right nervous looking out the corner of my eye to see when it was up and when it was down.

The priest had a yellow robe with a butterfly on the back. Now that is plum sacrilegious if you ask me. A house of worship is no place to play Halloween.

One of the most surprising things of all was that the very thing you come to church to hear wasn't there. A sermon. There was no sermon. The priest talked about three minutes on hope and people in the ghettos, which may have been a sermon to him, but not to me.

They had the Lord's supper, but they didn't pass it around. You had to go up front, kneel down (of course), and get it.

I was a little nervous about drinking real wine in church. But when I thought about it I ended up figuring maybe that was the best place to do it and God would forgive me. It was red wine and about knocked my socks off. It was stronger somehow than Madora's white wine and that expensive stuff that I tried in the kitchen at Charles's TEA party. (That bottle had the price tag on it. Six dollars and something. It seemed like to me it should have cost less because it kind of disappeared once you got it in your mouth.) I want you to know the priest gulped down every bit that was left over at the end. That was an education to me.

All in all, it just wasn't *set up* like a church service. I must admit, several people were nice after the service, but most of them had Yankee accents. They were probably people who've come down to work at the new G.E. plant outside White Level.

Charles said he liked it—that it was "formal." I didn't see anything formal about it. It was confusing to me. †

Interview

Often when he is being interviewed, Clyde Edgerton will describe himself
as having been raised by twenty-two aunts and uncles (who all lived in the
same community where he was born) and three "mothers"—Truma, his
actual mother, who at eighty-nine still lives in Bethesda; her younger sister, Lila, who lives in nearby Durham; and her older sister, Oma Crutch-
field, who died two years ago at the age of ninety-one. The only child
among the three families, Clyde received a rich store of family stories,
jokes, and legends, along with "more than enough attention" and an
unshakable sense of belonging and identity. When he was asked to speak
about his heroes, Edgerton read an essay about his beloved Uncle Bob
(brother to the three "mothers"), a carnival worker, truck driver/moon-
shine hauler, general store and trailer park owner, husband of four wives,
hunter/poacher, inveterate storyteller, and family man who wrote his
nephew, Clyde, shortly before his death: "Of all the nephews, you was
my favorite."

Edgerton and his family are expected at five different family reunions a
year and at the annual grave-cleaning held every Saturday before
Mother's Day in the old family graveyard. Located in what is now
Umstead State Park, near Bethesda, this little graveyard, the wisteria vine
that now covers an acre around it, and the tall pine trees are all that is left
of what was once a small farming community and millsite on Crabtree
Creek. It was here that Clyde's grandparents and great-grandparents lived
and were buried. Since the 1940s family and friends have gathered on
Mother's Day Saturday each year to tend the graves and have a picnic.
This is when the oldest, funniest, most apocryphal stories are told. Clyde
points out the almost-obscured landmarks to the young cousins and his

daughter—the old abandoned well where his Uncle Bob's chicken, named "Piddle Diddle," fell and was rescued, the millstones that are now partially buried in the ground near the creek, the barest ruins of the homeplace where Aunt "Sarah" (whose chickens were said to have roosted on her bed) used to live. It's out of this rich heritage that Edgerton lives and writes his fiction, producing stories that are alive with richly drawn characters, humor, and an intermingling of comedy and tragedy that is as true and timeless as the place he comes from.

For me it is in some ways difficult and in others easy to write about Clyde Edgerton. We met twenty years ago in a graduate class in education when we both were schoolteachers; two years later we were married. Soon we will move to a place in the country outside Chapel Hill, but for this interview, we sat in the living room of our home in downtown Durham. The spacious room is shaped in a hexagon, with tall windows set in three sides, and high, coffered ceilings.

Though it was early May, the day was surprisingly warm and humid. We'd sent a gaggle of young children—our daughter (then eight) and her friends—to play outside on the wide porch that spanned the entire front and one side of the house. Shrieks and thumps from the wooden glider glancing off a stone pillar supporting the porch came through the front window from time to time. Inside, we pushed stacks of books, manuscripts, toys, magazines, and newspapers aside on the glass coffee table to make room for the tape recorder, and settled down with tall glasses of iced tea.

What do you see as the relationship between your own religious beliefs and those of your characters? I'm thinking now in particular of those in the novel Raney.

My personal religious beliefs are perhaps more slippery, less certain than those of some of the characters in *Raney*. I'd be uneasy in making any theological position statements. However, I have spent many hours in organized religious activities. I guess you'd say I've got a plenitude of experience and a paucity of religious "positions," beyond those which have to do with behavior among and between people. I have convictions about how to treat people. These intersect, or overlap, with the positions of most major religions, I suppose. Fundamentalists of most sects and religions are quite clear as to the moral consequences of certain physical behaviors—drinking, and so on, but now I'm not so clear about these. For example, rather than saying to the world, "God said this to Adam and Eve and God said this to Moses," now I'm less sure than I was about the facts of the matter and the importance to my life of these facts. I guess more than ever, though, I'm clear about the stories in the Bible— for example the made-up stories that Jesus kept telling. Stories live on, don't they? Stories and death are always racing neck and neck to the finish line.

And the characters in Raney?

Oh, yes. Well, I was raised in the Southern Baptist church. It was in a small, rural community. Later, I went away to college in Chapel Hill and then served in the air force in Southeast Asia. The combination of a liberal arts education and fighting in a war had a great impact on me. Conflicts arose between what I'd been taught at home and what I came to see and believe. In my fiction, I try to present some of these conflicts as occurring between my characters acted out in dramatic scenes.

Because my bent is fiction rather than history, philosophy, or theology, I choose to play out conflicts on a stage with made-up characters. The effect of all this on the reader depends a lot on what the reader believes about the subject. For example, I like to think that some dramatic scenes I portray are played out in a funny way, with a humorous tone. But to some, the conflicts I portray are not humorous at all.

In religion, since there is such a diversity, a divergence of views about what happened, what's "true," you can find yourself popular or unpopular because you've been perceived as turning fiction into some kind of statement of belief, which it's *not*. I enjoy putting two positions in conflict in front of the reader.

In general, how closely, do you think, do your characters' conflicts resemble your own?

My general topic is relationships among human beings, especially in families. Sometimes religion is a fertile area in which to examine these relationships. Of course, some people could argue that in writing about human beings, you are always writing about religion, about theological issues. That makes sense, I think.

That doesn't answer your question. The answer is they—the characters—are made up, and some I probably resemble and some

I'm sure I don't. Rather, my beliefs may resemble the beliefs of some of my characters.

You mentioned that some people do not find your portrayal of these conflicts as humorous. What role do you see your humor playing in your fiction?

When I think of a person having religious beliefs, I think of those beliefs as being "carved in stone." It's a touchy topic. Questioning someone's beliefs, even—or especially—in fiction, can cause much ill feeling, much stopping of listening. What I'd like is for my fiction to bring pleasure to readers. That pleasure might include thinking beyond the immediate surface of the story. If I have disarmed a reader with humor, then the chances of the reader thinking more deeply about his or her life or behavior may increase. May decrease, come to think of it. Anyway, that's kind of a technical reason. Another important reason is my own natural inclination— humor helps keep me from being depressed about my doubts when they're strongest. It can be a distancing technique and an endearing technique at the same time. I must continually warn myself, or remind myself, that I'm writing about relationships between characters. In doing so, it's not necessary for me to state or even understand "theological" positions technically.

Along these lines, how do you see being raised a Southern Baptist has influenced you as an artist? How has it shaped or hindered your "bent" to write?

It's a paradox—something like a paradox pushes me to write fiction. In my church, the same older people who loved me like aunts and uncles also refused to consider letting black human beings, created in the image of God, have entry into our place of worship. While I can clearly understand the cultural conditioning which would lead to this paradox—I experienced it myself—my sense of, my beliefs about, what the historical Jesus would do in the church I was raised in at the time I was growing up creates a kind of excitement, drama, conflict, tension. There is a need to write it out, to understand it, and in the process, to entertain myself and my reader.

Do you think this kind of paradox might be more indigenous to, or more pronounced, in the South than in the rest of the country?

The paradox is just easier to spot in the South. Sometimes it can be seen as a "reverse" hypocrisy. Instead of saying one thing and doing another, they, the members of the church, did exactly as they said they would. You ask yourself, under what conditions would people who voted out blacks be willing to sacrifice for those same black people, out of love, like Good Samaritans? I know some of these folks would sacrifice a lot. It's like, they're speaking bad things, but doing good.

In other regions of the country, class prejudice, ageism, sexism may be less apparent. The Protestant religion is a prominent feature throughout all of our southern culture. There is a lot of talk, many statements of belief, and there are behaviors that support these statements, and behaviors that negate them—it's all part of the picture. At the heart of everything are the big questions of good and evil. What is good? What is evil? Why? How?

In the South religion is a serious matter. Questions of good and evil, eternity, and hell fire, are on every street corner, everywhere. In a funny way, religion goes beyond life and death, beyond everyday commerce, architecture, living. The southern artist *must* come to terms with it. It—southern Protestantism—stamps a lasting imprint on those who witness it. It seems to evoke extreme behaviors, extreme people—like televangelists and writers.

If your job is to write about relationships between people, religion in the South is a fruitful topic, regardless of your personal beliefs.

Doris Betts traces some of the origins of this southern seriousness about religion to the Civil War. She says with the South's defeat in the war, and with Reconstruction, southerners experienced both personally and culturally what it meant to be broken and disgraced, to be cast out of mainstream society, to be "standing in the need of prayer." A southerner was likely to feel an irreconcilable sense of both pride and guilt in having fought for the cause of family and states rights, yet at the same time for the right to own slaves. This sense of humiliation and ambivalence would not be felt by the rest of the country until the Vietnam War, a century later.

But as a young person, I had little awareness of guilt about slavery. What my elders felt and taught me—though not directly—was a kind of pride in being a southerner, a distrust of Yankees, Catholics, and blacks. This is a form of, a reaction to, guilt, I suppose.

What most influences my writing that I'm aware of are probably my childhood experiences. The guilt I felt was related to the inevitability of heaven and hell. If I masturbated, I'd go to hell. If I lied, or stole, I'd go to hell—unless I repented. Then I'd go to heaven. All of this was not always taught directly to me in words, but this is what I absorbed somehow—some of what I absorbed. This awareness came at an early age, too. I accepted Jesus as my personal saviour when I was seven. It was a norm as early as I could stand up, to think very seriously about good and evil and my soul's destination.

Poverty had a strong influence, too. Although we were not poor, we knew we could not waste anything. That was a sin. The experiences of previous generations taught us to live frugally.

Poverty and religion are at once both vexing and fertile areas for fiction, aren't they?

There seem to be connections between racial hatred, southern religion, and poverty. A child can come up with some fairly odd beliefs. I've had to cast off some of these early beliefs firmly. We seemed to believe we had the one true answer to any theological question. An outcome of this was a kind of self-righteousness that in my view now as an adult is sinful. The danger for the artist is to let his ethical stances change his fiction from being about relationships between people to being statements of what you believe. Sometimes I come close to the edge.

It's another paradox. The more you believe in certain positions, the more you're tempted to state them outright. And the more exciting it is to write with religion as a backdrop to relationships among characters.

Robert Penn Warren has said that all fiction writing has to do with the saving or loss of the immortal soul to good or evil. With such a strong sense of the absolute, and of the high stakes involved, how could such a writer as Warren avoid the pitfalls of didacticism, of making theological statements about what one believes thinly disguised as fiction?

Robert Penn Warren also said, "Verisimilitude is all." By that I think he meant the artist's characters and situations must above all remain true to experience. No forced manipulations. The outcome must seem to grow naturally out of the situation.

I choose not to wrestle with those ultimate issues in absolute terms—whether or not the soul is going toward salvation or an evil end. I think most writers set up, are engaged in, a process of coming to terms all their lives with the paradoxes in religion. Grappling with the questions is what excites the artist, if he or she is to be successful as an artist. Being a Protestant, straight-down-the-line conservative believer requires a diminishing of curiosity about the physical and metaphysical world, the world of the soul. And in art those curiosities are required. The kind of religious teaching I grew up with was based on certainty, a lack of curiosity. No examination.

It reminds me of a bumper sticker I once saw: "The Bible says it, I believe it, and that's the end of it."

Yes, that's it. End of discussion. At the extreme it ends in something like religious-government fusion. All Americans should read our Constitution while thinking about our reluctance to talk back to dictatorial religious bullies.

In light of all this, if you do not choose to wrestle with ultimate issues in absolute terms, what would you say does compel you to write?

A continuous awe of how people—how people live together. That something like a person, a human being, can talk to another one is just an amazing fact, not to speak of *doing* something with another one of these human being creatures. Also, I suppose that through writing I get a sense of control in a chaotic, open-ended universe of the imagination. I'm sure there are some unconscious reasons, too. The need to put contradictions, conflicts, in front of myself, to make them be played out in dramatic situations. Other people have the desire, the predisposition, I guess, to play out such conflicts in sociology, philosophy, math, or even, say, computer science.

I was hungry to put questions that weren't asked before myself in fiction as a movement toward resolution. If all were resolved, there would be no fun in life—that's why some religious know-it-alls, conservative or liberal, are so dull. Sometimes I'm re-creating the paradox of very loving people who may have "anti-Christian" ideas. I created them in fiction, so if fiction works, then maybe readers will see and like the humanness of a character such as Raney, for example, while disagreeing with some of her positions. If the story works, the paradox remains. If the story doesn't work, the reader

says, "I hate her positions, so I hate her. I love her positions, therefore I love her." This, anyway, is a plausible conjecture, a good
guess about some of what compels me to write.

*How do you see your religion, your southern heritage, and your
art are all tied up together?*

Well. First, you have the distinction between religion as pronounced to me by an organized church and then you have the religion that was practiced by church members— bringing food to the
sick, etc. Because in the South, Protestant religion is such a powerful factor, it's likely that someone would be exposed to it. Once
exposed to and then going on to an intellectual kind of life, a sort of
pondering, you have a growing garden of paradoxes and conflicts.
My being influenced by the transcendentalists in high school and
college added to the conflict early on. Emerson said that there is too
much emphasis on the personality of Jesus—that the soul knows
no persons. I remember being struck by that way back yonder. I
remember wondering how much Jesus would want us to be worrying
about him, and how much he'd want us to worry about what we were
doing in the world. That's kind of fun to think about. Maybe they
have to go together. That's the kind of thing that would be interesting
to have a couple of characters talk about. See what they said.

*In talking of the relationship of his art to his life and his beliefs,
Reynolds Price has expressed what he is about in terms of a conscious search for and a fascination with the mysteries of life and of
faith. Can you describe your writing as a kind of search? A delving
into the mysteries?*

An artist, most artists, I suppose, are consciously trying to create
that which has never existed before. It's a gift from God, or Nature,
or wherever—being able to create something good which will last a
while. To my way of thinking, religion is a set of assumptions and
beliefs. A spiritual quest is a search for meaning, for truths, for the
mysterious. I realize I am more concerned with behaviors, how ethical precepts are lived out in everyday life—but that is a direct
reflection of the religious spirit, it seems to me. I try not to intel-
lectualize or make abstractions, which seems to be what I'm doing now.

*How do you see the relationship of Flannery O'Connor's theology
to her art, her fiction?*

My response to her fiction may not be what she intended. My reaction is less along theological lines than perhaps she would hope for. But on the other hand I suppose she would like my response, since my response takes me back to her fiction with new rewards each time. I like what Louis Rubin had to say about her work in his essay in *A Gallery of Southerners* called "Flannery O'Connor's Company of Southerners Or, 'The Artificial Nigger' Read as Fiction Rather Than Theology." There he regards her as a fiction writer more than as a theologian. I don't pull from her writing straight theological meanings as some people do. I see delightful, funny, sad, elegantly written stories about relationships between people.

What do you think ultimately compelled Flannery O'Connor to write?

I think a delight in the habit of writing fiction. If I had written the first two-thirds of "Good Country People," I'd be ecstatic about what was going to happen, regardless of the presence or absence of Grace in the lives of the characters. I think great fun impelled her to write. However, I think that Flannery O'Connor was more deeply aware of why she was writing fiction than I am aware of why she did—or why I do. We could be writing for the same reasons, but she had a better hold on her reasons. Her sense of story and character was so powerful that it made some of her "messages" less obvious than she might have thought. For me—as a reader—that's a good outcome.

Some theologians have made a useful distinction between religion and theology, saying that religion can be thought of as regulative function, telling the tribe what to do, how to survive, in a hostile world. Theology, on the other hand, is a speculative function, answering questions like what is the meaning of life? What is our relationship to God? What's going wrong? All religions contain a theology and most theologies imply religions, but they are different in function. Both religion and art give us a world of order to inhabit. How do you see your fiction in light of this notion, this suggestion of an analogous relationship between religion and art?

Well, your distinction between religion and theology is interesting. I'd never thought about it that way. But I don't think about these matters very much. Maybe I should, but I don't. I think some other people should. It's all I can do to write made-up stories about made-up characters. To do this job well, with clarity and simplicity and depth, takes more time than I often have. And I do believe that all the while that I'm trying to do it right, I'm working toward meaning and order, toward making something out of chaos, something that makes sense, something that helps me understand human beings, behavior, good, and evil. I guess that sounds like I'm engaged in a religious enterprise, doesn't it? †

12

ALLAN GURGANUS

When I'm Fog on a Coffin Lid

Allan Gurganus was born in Rocky Mount, North Carolina, in 1947, the eldest of four sons. His first novel, *Oldest Living Confederate Widow Tells All*, was published in 1989. A *New York Times* bestseller for eight months, it was awarded the Sue Kaufman Prize for the Best First Work of Fiction and has been translated into Italian, Spanish, French, and German.

Since 1974, Gurganus's short fiction has appeared in *Harper's*, *The Atlantic*, *GRANTA*, *Antaeus*, *The Paris Review*, and *The New Yorker*. He has won two grants from the National Endowment for the Arts, a Danforth Fellowship, an Ingram Merrill Grant, and many other awards. *White People*, a collection of novellas and stories, was published in 1990. A finalist for the PEN-Faulkner Prize, it was given the Southern Book Award and the 1991 *Los Angeles Times* Book Prize for the Best Work of American Fiction published that year. Gurganus has taught fiction writing at Stanford, Duke and the Iowa Writers' Workshop; he is permanently affiliated with Sarah Lawrence College. His award-winning paintings are represented in many private and public collections, and he has illustrated two chapbooks of his own fiction.

Gurganus's political and artistic lives are inseparable. He writes for the *New York Times* op-ed page and cofounded Writers for Harvey Gantt, which sponsors a series of nationwide readings in an effort to defeat Senator Jesse Helms. He has raised tens of thousands of dollars for AIDS research and was recently honored for his work by Episcopal Caring Response to AIDS.

Gurganus currently lives in Chapel Hill and New York. He is at work on a book of essays, *You Meet All Kinds,* and a new novel, scheduled to appear in 1994, entitled *The Erotic History of a Southern Baptist Church.* Citing "the possibilities of friendship, gardening, and narrative" as his religious affiliation (*Contemporary Authors,* Volume 135), Gurganus describes his fiction writing as constituting "less a career, more a mission. Hailing from a long line of preachers—genteel evangelical—tea-drinkers and pulpit pounders—I continue that rich narrative tradition." †

It Had Wings

Find a little yellow side street house. Put an older woman in it. Dress her in that tatty favorite robe, pull her slippers up before the sink, have her doing dishes, gazing nowhere—at her own backyard. Gazing everywhere. Something falls outside, loud. One damp thwunk into new grass. A meteor? She herself (retired from selling formal clothes at Wanamaker's, she herself—a widow and the mother of three scattered sons, she herself alone at home a lot these days) goes onto tiptoe, leans across a sinkful of suds, sees—out near her picnic table, something nude, white, overly-long. It keeps shivering. Both wings seem damaged.

"No way," she says. It appears human. Yes, it is a male one. It's face up and, you can tell, it is extremely male (uncircumcised). This old woman, pushing eighty, a history of aches, uses, fun—now presses one damp hand across her eyes. Blaming strain, the luster of new cataracts, she looks again. Still, it rests there on a bright air mattress of its own wings. Outer feathers are tough quills, broad at bottom as rowboat oars. The whole left wing bends far under. It looks hurt.

The widow, sighing, takes up her blue willow mug of heated milk. Shaking her head, muttering, she carries it out back. She moves so slow because: arthritis. It criticizes every step. It asks about the mug she holds. Do you really need this?

She stoops, creaky, beside what can only be a young angel, unconscious. Quick, she checks overhead, ready for what?—some TV news crew in a helicopter? She sees only a sky of the usual size, a Tuesday sky stretched between weekends. She allows herself to touch this thing's white forehead. She gets a mild electric shock. Then, odd, her tickled finger joints stop aching. They've hurt so long. A practical person, she quickly cures her other hand. The angel grunts but sounds pleased. His temperature's a hundred and fifty, easy—but for him, this seems somehow normal. "Poor thing," she says, and—careful—pulls his heavy curly head into her lap. The head hums like a phone knocked off its cradle. She scans for neighbors, hoping they'll come out, wishing they wouldn't, both.

"Look, will warm milk help?" She pours some down him. Her wrist brushes angel skin. Which pulls the way an ice tray begs whatever touches it. A thirty-year pain leaves her, enters him. Even her liver spots are lightening. He grunts with pleasure, soaking up all of it. Bold, she presses her worst hip deep into crackling feathers. The hip has been half numb since a silly fall last February. All stiffness leaves her. He goes, "Unhh." Her griefs seem to fatten him like vitamins. Bolder, she whispers private woes: the Medicare cuts, the sons too casual by half, the daughters-in-law not bad but not so great. Those woes seem ended. "Nobody'll believe. Still, tell me some of it." She tilts nearer. Both his eyes stay shut but his voice, like clicks from a million crickets pooled, goes, "We're just another army. We all look alike—we didn't, before. It's not what you expect. We miss this other. Don't count on the next. Notice things here. We are just another army."

"Oh," she says.

Nodding, she feels limber now, sure as any girl of twenty. Admiring her unspeckled hands, she helps him rise. Wings serve as handles. Kneeling on damp ground, she watches him go staggering toward her barbecue pit. Awkward for an athlete, really awkward for an angel, the poor thing climbs up there, wobbly. Standing, he is handsome, but as a vase is handsome. When he turns this way, she sees his eyes. They're silver, each reflects her: a speck, pink, on green green grass.

She now fears he plans to take her up, as thanks. She presses both palms flat to dirt, says, "The house is finally paid off.—Not just yet," and smiles.

Suddenly he's infinitely infinitely more so. Silvery. Raw. Gleaming like a sunny monument, a clock. Each wing puffs, independent. Feathers sort and shuffle like three hundred packs of playing cards. Out flings either arm; knees dip low. Then up and off he shoves, one solemn grunt. Machete swipes cross her backyard, breezes cool her upturned face. Six feet overhead, he falters, whips in makeshift circles, manages to hold aloft, then go shrub-high, gutter-high. He avoids a messy tangle of phone lines now rocking from the wind of him. "Go, go," the widow, grinning, points the way. "Do. Yeah, good." He signals back at her, open-mouthed and left down here. First a glinting man-shaped kite, next an oblong of aluminum in sun. Now a new moon shrunk to decent star, one fleck, fleck's memory: usual Tuesday sky.

She kneels, panting, happier and frisky. She is hungry but must first rush over and tell Lydia next door. Then she pictures Lydia's worry lines bunching. Lydia will maybe phone the missing sons: "Come right home. Your Mom's inventing . . . company."

Maybe other angels have dropped into other Elm Street back-yards? Behind fences, did neighbors help earlier hurt ones? Folks keep so much of the best stuff quiet, don't they.

Palms on knees, she stands, wirier. This retired saleswoman was the formal-gowns adviser to ten mayors' wives. She spent sixty years of nine-to-five on her feet. Scuffing indoors, now staring down at terry slippers, she decides, "Got to wash these next week." Can a person who's just sighted her first angel already be mulling about laundry? Yes. The world is like that.

From her sink, she sees her own blue willow mug out there in the grass. It rests in muddy ruts where the falling body struck so hard. A neighbor's collie keeps barking. (It saw!) Okay. This happened. "So," she says.

And plunges hands into dishwater, still warm. Heat usually helps her achy joints feel agile. But fingers don't even hurt now. Her bad hip doesn't pinch one bit. And yet, sad, they all will. By supper-time, they will again remind her what usual suffering means. To her nimble underwater hands, the widow, staring straight ahead, announces, "I helped. He flew off stronger. I really egged him on. Like *any*body would've, really. Still, it was me. I'm not just somebody in a house. I'm not just somebody alone in a house. I'm not just somebody else alone in a house."

Feeling more herself, she finishes the breakfast dishes. In time for lunch. This old woman should be famous for all she has been through—today's angel, her years in sales, the sons and friends— she should be famous for her life. She knows things, she has seen so much. She's not famous.

Still, the lady keeps gazing past her kitchen café curtains, she keeps studying her own small tidy yard. An anchor fence, the picnic table, a barbecue pit, new Bermuda grass. Hands braced on her sink's cool edge, she tips nearer a bright window.

She seems to be expecting something, expecting something decent. Her kitchen clock is ticking. That dog still barks to calm itself. And she keeps staring out: nowhere, everywhere. Spots on her hands are darkening again. And yet, she whispers, "I'm right here, ready. Ready for more."

Can you guess why this old woman's chin is lifted? Why does she breathe as if to show exactly how it's done? Why should both her shoulders, usually quite bent, brace so square just now?

She is guarding the world.

Only, nobody knows. †

Interview

I met with Allan Gurganus at his home, a yellow frame cottage surrounded by lush herb and flower gardens at the end of a quiet lane in Chapel Hill, North Carolina, in early September 1991. Though he lives in New York City for part of each year, Gurganus had come home to North Carolina to recuperate from a nationwide tour for his collection of short stories, *White People,* and to see family and friends. An easygoing and gracious host, he greeted me at the front door with a hug, his ear to a portable telephone. On the other end of the line his father was talking about the health and doings of his mother and three brothers in Rocky Mount, North Carolina, his hometown. Having said good-bye, he offered iced tea, and we sat on the sofa under the picture window looking out on chrysanthemums, asters, and camellias blooming in the early fall air outside.

Tall and slim, Gurganus was dressed in tan slacks and pin-striped shirt. He is usually a sharp dresser; a bow tie, three-piece suit, and long, camel hair overcoat are signature staples. In his mid-forties, he is boyishly handsome, with an urbane, witty manner that puts one completely at ease. His blond hair is not styled at all, falling back and around his collarline in "mad genius" fashion.

We were surrounded by books, papers, magazines, and manuscripts of all description lying scattered about the floor and over end tables and chair. Gurganus pulled a faded scrapbook from a pile of papers on the sidetable. It had been made by a little boy sometime during the mid-to-late-fifties. Author Josephine Humphreys had found it in a flea market in Charleston and sent it as a gift. Gurganus took great delight in showing the bits of Americana it held and describing the insights into the heart of a ten-year-old boy it offered. As he talked about the "campy" memorabilia and about his own boyhood in the fifties, he revealed the keen and loving sensibility of a storyteller, what Phoebe-Lou Adams of *The Atlantic* called a "quiet conviction and a nice appreciation of how decent citizens get on with life and each other." She pointed out his "exceptional ability to make the ordinary interesting"; I would like to add, that he makes the common-place quietly, comically, heroic.

Where would you like to start, Allan? The forgiveness of sin, or the resurrection of the body?

Best to begin with my childhood, and slouch forward from there. Like so many southerners, I "came to" in a church. My mother's church was the Edgemont Presbyterian Church in Rocky Mount, North Carolina. I had three younger brothers; we practically comprised the entire Sunday school ourselves. When I was fairly young, my father had a "conversion experience," and joined a fundamentalist church called the People's Missionary Baptist Church.

The Presbyterian church meant white-collar workers: Buicks and a couple of Cadillacs. The Baptist church was Fords with mud-flaps, pick-up trucks, and Chevrolets, tops. My father would have preferred that we quit the Presbyterian church and convert with him. But my mother held to her beliefs, and I'm enormously grateful that she did. What if I had grown up in a fundamentalist Baptist church as well as a fundamentalist Baptist home? (My father was a strong disciplinarian and a firm Bible believer who opened every meal with prayer, and read the Bible at the table before we ate.) I think if I had attended a "dunker's" church, and had to put up first-hand with the strictures that insisted on no dancing, no extraordinarily fast movements on Sundays, no cards, no movies, no fun, I would probably be in jail now. This sounds like a joke. It is not.

That kind of joyless, middle-aged attitude toward experience, watching the neighbors, judging everyone harshly, that Baptist sense that the world is a duty and not a pleasure—it seemed so alien to me as a child, and it grows increasingly ugly and disturbing to me as a grownup. Sexuality has to be repressed, reined in, denied. Food is mere fuel. You work as hard as you possibly can; you give a lot of your earnings to the church. Those were the precepts practiced by the Missionary Baptists. The Presbyterian church seemed more euphemistic, far blander. We Presbyterians, for instance, really were terrible at singing. The choir featured six earnest people who'd been in college glee clubs. They sang about as well as the average person would if you held them up at gunpoint in the mall and said, "Sing."

Sounds like Episcopalians.

True. That contrast between Mother's religion and Daddy's to me stakes out the twin poles of American Protestant faith: sugar and salt. Imagine the change from our Presbyterian service, which was terribly muffled, and genteel, and discreet to the point of being narcotic; imagine encountering the Baptist service which despite my thirteen-year-old snobbism, I enjoyed. I was struck by the seeming disparity between the gloomy, gory beliefs they professed and the joy that they took in their music—the music in the down-at-the-heels Baptist church was terribly upbeat. It 'swung' and had a millworker's bluesiness to it. A Presbyterian hymn had to drag in order to be successful. Penitent, hobbled, Scottish, certainly not spontaneous.

"This is my Father's world . . ."

That's right. Over and over again. Whereas in the Baptist church there always seemed to be an organist and a pianist providing a bebop, a rhythm and music with real singing, real emotion.

It sounds very similar to black gospel.

It was much closer to black gospel than anybody in the People's Missionary Baptist Church would willingly admit. The hardship of life was much more apparent to Baptist people working at the cotton mill or enduring menial, mechanics' jobs than to the Presbyterian bankers and desk clerks.

I had a blessedly schizophrenic childhood (blessed for any novelist, that is). On the one hand, I felt—class-wise—most at home as a Presbyterian, but in my gut I felt drawn to the erotic undercurrent reverberating whenever I stepped into the cinderblock Baptist church. People were physically involved; people shouted "amen" from the congregation. My Presbyterian component assumed that we were all about spirit, not about the body at all, except as an embarrassing shelf for the spirit.

Another comical differentiation: vacation Bible school. At the Presbyterian church, refreshments were Pepsi, Coca-Cola, Sundrop, Mountain Dew, Orange-Ade or Nu-Grape sodas, drunk out of bottles cooled in big zinc vats filled with crushed ice. These were served with those thin lemon cookies, or Toll House cookies. Then came the party favors with some sort of religious significance; they were part of the curriculum. Plus all the school paste you could eat. I used to love that school paste.

Yeah, that's good stuff.

The Baptist refreshments, on the other hand, consisted of Premium saltines and Kool-Aid. Period. One too salty, one too sweet. So, I feel as a writer, as an erotic creature, as a spiritual being, that I fell somewhere between Scottish Presbyterian refinement and the down-home red-clay, red-blood-of-the-Lamb, Bible-pounding fundamentalist Baptist religion which meant (and still means) my father's crowd.

What pyschological or spiritual effects, what toll, did this intensity and double-identity have on you, do you think?

The paradox is well known among southern kids: because of this enforced, policed religion, my belief in a conscious and patrolling God never really took hold. I remember in some ways thinking of church as primarily a social institution. Its class extremes were so painfully visible in a small town.

When I was about five years old, a little girl who spoke whole sentences at an early age and was considered something of a prodigy, pointed to a pine tree, ninety-five feet tall and said to me, "Do you think God is bigger than that?" I remember thinking at the time, "That is the stupidest thing I ever heard in my life!" And in some ways my relation to God, the concept (sounds like a movie, doesn't it? *God the Concept, Part II*) has stayed right there. I still question. These days I'm likelier to view God as Time, a surface that allows us each to decorate It briefly.

But it's clear from talking with you and reading your works that you are not completely alienated from your old-time religion. What have you held onto, or perhaps, what still holds onto you?

What held me from childhood was the sermon itself as a possibility. As I listened to a thousand dull sermons and several dozen good ones, I began to understand that while I seemed to be a skeptical, detached, twelve-year-old just passing the time in church, the lessons of the gospel spoke to me, changed and moved me.

I was born in '47. I came of age in the late fifties to mid-sixties when social change, namely desegregation, kept crackling all around us. I got to watch resistance to change, the incredible hypocrisy of white people sitting in church meetings and discussing how black folks would naturally be turned away from our church, should blacks ever arrive (they would certainly not come for our singing). So, if you don't believe that God is much bigger than a pine tree, and if the behaviors you see around you are weekly racism, weekly sexism, hatred in His name, you grow aware of contradictions. The church's most recent lapse in a long series of lapses is its attitude toward gay people. "Do unto others as you would have them do unto you"—a radical idea, rarely practiced.

It goes even deeper than hypocrisy or complacency.

Yes, into the perpetuation of evil. But the sermons interested me, the rise and fall, the chance for examples. I also found fascinating and erotic the idea of being a preacher myself. I somehow wanted to offer consolation to the people of my church, ones who had suffered real tragedy. When I was young, a little boy named Jakie Sharp had leukemia and we all watched him die in a very slow and horrible way. But it gave everybody a chance to act kindly toward his parents and toward him, to participate in the mystical, unsettling experience of seeing a four-year-old disappear. I kept thinking myself into the role of the person who sits there at the hospital offering comfort at his moment of death. The answers are not easy, or apparent, then or now. The answers I came up with were the answers I would offer anybody outside the religious context: everybody dies; the world is mysterious; you've done terrifically well through this whole ordeal; let's hope we learn something from it; go home and rest; it will take a long time to get over this. Now, recovery begins.

And we're sitting with you on the mourner's bench.

Yes, that's exactly right. This is a communal experience; you're not alone. Which is in some ways both "civilian" advice and Christian advice—it is the comfort of art, too, of course. I was not much interested in explicating joy. I was most involved in treating the tragic circumstances, in comforting people. That's the part of the figure of Christ that appealed to me the strongest, and first. That, and the music. The music has always seemed organized religion's one greatest justification. And I listen to it now, as an unchurched, "unwashed" adult, and draw such comfort from it.

You haven't rededicated recently?

Not lately. Maybe I'm due for a three thousand-mile checkup, a spiritual oil change.

Tell me more about the music.

I listen to the Mozart Requiem, the Faure Requiem, the Verdi Requiem. I listen to the Bach B-minor Mass. I listen to black gospel music quite often. And I find it enormously consoling, renewing. In Jessye Norman's collection of black spirituals, I find the message of reconciliation and reward, promise, and an acknowledgement of pain as moving as anything I know. And if I can separate the church from dogma, I can also do a clean separation between the stilted social institution and a ferocious personal expression of spiritual feeling in music.

You seem to have a deeply passionate concern with things religious. Did you have any relatives who preached or who influenced you in these ways?

My father is a lay preacher now and belongs to that organization that puts Bibles in the drawers of motel rooms worldwide. My father's Uncle Bill, my great uncle, owned a circus tent. He'd experienced "the call," and being also the owner of a Cadillac car, he claimed quite a farflung congregation. But Great-uncle Bill got fired by his parishoners. They really pulled the rug out from under poor Bill; they took back his tent. See, Bill had gone and bought himself a very expensive pinkie ring out of the church coffers. He was much too cocky not to wear the thing while he preached and gestured; they noticed. Like the oldest living confederate widow, I feel closest to these itinerant outlaws in my family. In my own life, I hope I can wear the emerald pinkie ring and keep my tent.

Can you tell me about how those issues that you cherish and struggle with in your religious upbringing may have made themselves manifest in your work?

With the first novel, *Oldest Living Confederate Widow Tells All*, we're residing in the voice of a woman who grew up in the church and who has in some ways remained there. She says, "Forgiveness interests me."

You don't do it on a small canvas.

No, no, it's not a miniature. And the role of the church in Lucy's life could first be characterized via Lucy Marsden's comic affection for her church. There's a scene in the novel where all the teetotaling Baptists at a picnic drink kegs of Christmas cider. The cider has been in a general store basement for much too long. And since Luke Lucas, the storeowner, is a notorious tightwad and a deacon, he sees an opportunity to get credit for offering these kegs and at the same time clear a corner of his store room. And, of course, the inevitable happens. Everybody in the church (some for the first time ever) becomes—you should forgive the expression—"zoo-faced drunk" on church property. [Laughter] In the cemetery and all around the churchyard, folks begin to evince long-repressed behaviors. People are making passes at other people's spouses; the children are stealing things from each other; Christians are insulting fellow Christians. Lucy as a child sees the Baptist stiffness and pretense undercut by the animal that we all are. Hyprocrisy is exposed in a very forthright and comical way, a loving way.

It sounds like you had a great time with that.

I had great fun writing it. So much of the book meant laughing aloud alone. And there's another scene: Lucy is sitting in church with her girlfriend, Shirley. These girls are sitting in church holding hands, listening to a particularly ferocious revivalist preacher tell everybody in the congregation that they have sinned and that they are infinitely corrupt and wicked. And Lucy looks at Shirley and thinks: "Everybody is always telling me that I have sinned and I don't know what that means. I've never done anything wrong in my life. Sure, I've told a teeny lie here and there, and I stole one piece of horehound candy from the general store once, but those aren't really sins. I don't know what it means to be a sinner." At that moment she is speaking, I think, for me. It's a very basic insight that continues to hold me; I see in someone like Jesse Helms an endless willingness to detach from yourself those qualities in yourself you find most disturbing. First, you isolate sexuality, which is inherently anarchic and difficult to contain. Then you farm out your erotic energy into closing down a porn store; you blame the gay man who must be publicly humiliated. All the cruelty that's meted out so that we can feel better about ourselves. What an utter lack of self-knowledge that reveals. And yet, such suppression is the very stock-in-trade of fiction writing. And it's certainly a favorite device of us southerners who grew up in the church. As storytellers, we've had to become a different kind of self-defending preachers. I mean, we must specialize in tales that don't necessarily end in an easy moral. Because, oddly, morality *has* no moral.

As southerners growing up immersed in old-time religion and at the same time legally sanctioned racism, we learned at the very least that honor and "right and wrong" are an ambiguous, complicated business.

And yet to be utterly perverse and contradictory, "Do unto others as you would have them do unto you" might be the novelist's own motto. That might be a fitting description of artful storytelling. The greatest storytellers are the ones who treat their subjects with equal justice under the law and who provide, as novels and stories do, a zone of perfect justice where the world can be recast. A garden spot for our familiar failures, endlessly and richly replayed.

We yearn for that perfect justice.

Where good can be rewarded and bad can be punished. But not necessarily the good or bad that we grew up with in the Baptist cosmology. So that the morality of a thinking person and a writing person is inherently "cranky," probably at odds with the majority view, and complicated.

How is that? It must be that you have required yourself to develop and use a more thoughtful, compassionate lens?

It's the writer's responsibility to take care of everybody just as it is the preacher's responsibility to look after all his flock. Every ragged, errant little lamb. And so the beauty of the imagination, the beauty of the "call," as it were, is precisely that it doesn't say "Run!" when you spy someone like Jesse Helms. It's my born duty to try and understand this man. To understand his story is to understand his origins and to understand his origins is to understand his community and to understand his community is to understand its ethos and to understand the ethos is to understand the church. Which means again facing what's wrong and right with institutionalized religion.

Which eventually must bring us to another important aspect of the southern church, and that is the role and contribution of the black church in southern history and culture. Is that something you're talking about in White People?

Yes. I named my book of stories *White People* because I wanted to suggest that we are one people among many. I look at you and I see tans and peach tones, but I don't see white. I look at black people and I see brown and umber and blue, not black. So we're calling each other by only partial truths. Black is the presence of all color and white is the absence of it. I think that's a fitting starting point to talk about black and white religion.

As a kid, I attended black services. And I heard preachers who were not playing it safe by being blank and uncontroversial. In the black church I heard acceptance and resilience and joy (such a rare commodity under any circumstance). And I used to bike to tent revivals. The fairgrounds were five blocks from us. This was always in the warm months. Some guy would be coming through, black or white, with a loudspeaker and an organ and a piano. In 1959, I saw buckets being passed on the ends of long handles filled with money out of the pockets of migrant workers and farmers and people who had ridden to town on flatbed trucks, people who had clearly given from their souls. In the Presbyterian church it was seventy-five cents a week or the five-dollar bill discreetly folded.

Or you'd put it in an envelope.

Utter comedy. In my work, I try to make that contrast between black and white outlook manifest since writing about the South in the last thirty years means writing about race relations. There is an interesting loadedness in how frequently the servants are actually the masters.

Right. It's an irony that is not lost on many of us here in the South, especially black southerners, I would think.

Put in narrative, it is profoundly pertinent and charged. It's also profoundly Christian. Christ in the iconography is both the Shepherd with the crook and He is the sheep. He is both the person who will lead us and He is the sacrificial lamb. He is the Master and the Servant. And I think part of the schizophrenia of Christianity is precisely this kind of split role. We each feel both and neither. So writing about black and white people in the same story is a way, as it were, to quadruple the doubleness.

It seems to me that the little novella, Blessed Assurance, *explores that paradox most fully.*

In that novella, I consider a white man who at the age of fifty-nine is finally a millionaire. Yet he finds that he is endlessly remembering and reimagining the period of his impoverished life as a child of millworkers when he sold funeral insurance to black people. These black folks believed that, though they've had a rough time in this world, if they just threw a splashy enough funeral, they would be regarded as kings and queens rolling into the next world. And the young Jerry found himself in this terrible position, "carrying" his favorite clients who couldn't afford the insurance. If they don't pay, they will forfeit the thousands of dollars they have shelled out over many, many years.

They have paid for ten funerals ten times over.

That's right. So he, like all of us, is caught up in a cycle of exploitation that he recognizes but can't break free of. Jerry is caught up in the classic Christian dilemma—for whom am I responsible? What does it benefit a man to gain the world if he loses his soul? And yet at the same time, here's this eighteen-year-old-boy whose parents have brown lung disease, no health insurance, and are totally dependent on him. He is having to choose how many people he can carry for how far.

Which makes for a long, painful list.

That's right. I wanted to express through comedy (which is what I feel most drawn to and I feel is, in some ways, my own best chance at telling the truth) these darker, larger facts about what it means to be white and what it means to be black. And how necessary it is to keep trying and at the same time how necessary it is to conceive the difference between our two perspectives. Jerry finally says, I can't live at the emotional pitch of black religion. And I think what he missed is precisely that the black people in the congregation can't either. They don't live in the state of ecstasy when they are scrubbing toilets, or washing your car. It seems to me they need this Sunday state of exaltation and release precisely because their daily reality is so much grimmer than ours and the dangers are so much more present. It's not so much about transcendence as it is about breaking even. I believe you have to have that kind of velocity and jolt to repay yourself for everything that's been taken away from you.

It's a kind of recompense.

Absolutely, absolutely.

With Blessed Assurance, *with "Condolences to Every One of Us," and others, I have noticed that you are able to express such a complexity of moral issues. It's almost as if you set a problem for yourself, as philosophers do, and then try to explore all different angles of it. Are you consciously aware of doing that?*

Well, I am becoming conscious, as you asked the question, and my fiction is the means. The story as divining rod. One of the many things that I got from growing up in a Bible-believing, professing household—is this notion of accountability for other people. I am also the eldest of four children which is, in itself, a lesson in ethics and responsibility.

Oh, yes.

My brothers attended schools all over town, and when it was six o'clock and time to sit down to dinner, my father would say, "Where is your brother? Your brother is late. Why is your brother not here?" And I was like the sergeant who is responsible for the privates and corporals beneath me. It's a huge, early lesson in accountability as my brothers' keeper. And I think all writers are people who inherently feel accountable for other people. They are trying endlessly to answer, not only for themselves, but for others. It's a very egocentric occupation, in that sense, to presume to speak for anyone else. But it helps if your attitude is an ethical one.

Do you see yourself as an "ethical writer"?

I try to not only write my fiction with an eye to the ethical but to live my life that way. I mean, I have enemies but they are not people that I have alienated intentionally. I have been very fortunate and there are people who resent that. But there is no one that I have spurned or made fun of. I'm not a practicing Christian in the sense that I believe that when I take the Holy Eucharist, the Premium saltine in my mouth or the Welch's grape juice becomes the body and blood of Christ. I think it's a symbol. But on the ethical level, I am a "born-again" Christian in this sense: every day of my life, I devote to doing my work well, which is very Calvinistic and very baseline Ten Commandments. I honor my parents, or try. I feel closer to my parents now than ever before; I'm so grateful we've all lived long enough with our professed Christian forgiveness that we got around to truly forgiving each other! I honor my friends and I try to honor my fictional characters. And I try to conceive of complex characters who are in difficult ethical situations. Putting a character in a difficult position and seeing what she or he does and how that makes him or her feel afterwards is relentlessly fascinating to me.

For example, Lucy Marsden.

Lucy is in a terrible dilemma because she has, out of her desire to take care of people, committed a crime. She has been accustomed to thinking that her veteran husband was a criminal because he was so cruel to her and her nine children. But she has wound up participating in that same kind of destruction herself, unintentionally. So she has a crime to confess, and she brings the weight of that crime to bear, which is really why she is telling the long, long story. It's an act of contrition as well as an act of celebration. And I always ask myself this question when I've come up with the idea for a story or a novel: What's at stake here? And if what's at stake is one ruined dinner party or bad feelings from one of the neighbors, then that's not a story that interests me. I'm only interested in stories in which the stakes are literally life and death.

Otherwise, it would seem hardly worth the time or effort.

Yes, and I think a lot of contemporary fiction is not. We are living in an ethically bankrupt culture. And it's only to be expected that the art of the culture will reflect that. The people whose work I respond to and honor are those writers who ask the really hard questions. We then inevitably come back to this question of how responsible we are—not just for ourselves and not just for our own family and for the posterity of our grandchildren, to the people in the charity ward, the people in the mental institutions, the people who were born in trouble and have lived in trouble and will die in trouble.

Yes, indeed.

And working well and honestly and daily is another way that I try to live my ethics. I have too much respect for books to publish things that I don't believe in absolutely, that I don't think are built for eternity. It may sound a little presumptuous, but I grew up in the church, so I'm allowed to use a word like "eternity."

You have earned a right to feel at home with that kind of language.

It's said that one gains access to and is able to invoke a sense of the sacred only with such language.

I'm grateful to the church for allowing me to use such cosmic poetry. The fundamental text of Western Civilization is, along with Shakespeare, the Bible. And you can't imagine, as a novelist writing a book, not using the Bible consciously or unconsciously as the ultimate pattern. One reason I used epigraphs to begin every chapter of *Oldest Living* is precisely to pay homage to a much greater book, but one whose diversity of experience and richness of prose and moral example in narratives I aspire to re-create in my own fallen, minor heroic way. And the scale of my book never embarrassed me because I felt there are precedents for this kind of exhaustive attempt to say how much a single human life can mean. And biblical language is not sentimentalized language either. You are "washed in the blood," and so on.

They don't sugarcoat it, do they?

I mean it's rough. Those nails in those hands. And ultimately, the validity of Christianity for me is precisely that the center of the religion is a response to suffering.

Yes.

And that's what fiction is about, as I understand it—a response to suffering. Even comedy is famously a response to despair; the last resort in encountering dastardly deeds is making a joke. And frequently it's that kind of tension release that averts deeper pain. Humor has a kind of ethical value for me and it's a kind of salvation that I depend on.

You and Flannery O'Connor intersect at that point.

Well, I love to intersect with Flannery O'Connor whenever I can. If martyrdom must come, I would like to be nailed to a cross near Miss O'Connor's. And when I think of her dying at thirty-nine, when I think of how much she wrote, I recall Christ dying at thirty-three and how much he managed in that brief lifetime. They both understood from early on that they had a terribly limited amount of time. And I add Stephen Crane to that list and Keats and any number of people who perished early. There's an absolute urgency in O'Connor and a willingness to comically face up to the darkest questions about responsibility and salvation that hold you, that grip your soul. And I respect her as I respect Faulkner, the greatest American novelist of the twentieth century including anybody living now. I've just been rereading *Light in August* which is such an incredibly important book in the sense of these ethical questions that we are talking about. Who is responsible for the deformities in Joe Christmas's character and to whom is Joe Christmas, thus deformed, answerable? Is there only one solution to that dark center in him, the one devoted to violence and short-term solutions? Is the only solution to annihilate him in order to stop him? Joe Christmas is a way of talking about every page of every newspaper we pick up and the eternal dilemma of the presence of evil in our lives.

The evil we see among us is within our own souls.

Exactly. How inured we are to it and how jaded we've become to cruelty and how unprepared we are for public goodness.

I think some of the fundamentalist churches have laid the seeds for that embarrassment because they stress private behavior as being the quintessential thing that matters when it comes to living a pious, "saved" life.

Right.

So the church thrived on preachments against drinking and smoking and playing cards yet never faced the monumental ethical issue of slavery in which it was directly implicated. Some preachers went so far as to find citations from the Bible to justify slavery, doing their part to keep it an institution in the South for over three hundred years. Chapter and verse.

Yes. Antebellum pastors stood up and preached God's blessing on slavery with the black people outside the church building, straining to listen through its open windows. And that's why being a novelist at this moment is so freighted with meaning. Who else is or can be the moral arbiter, in an age when "the bottom line" is god. The role that the novelist assumes is that of a kind of moral timekeeper, almost a referee of ethics, which is a very dangerous role. It is one that nobody with much sense would seek. When you are writing about characters who are living in ethical dilemmas and making decisions, you inevitably suggest solutions. Or at least you suggest that an ethical outlook is not utterly outmoded in this age of cynicism and commercialism.

As I read about your characters and their dilemmas, a couple of things strike me: first is, the fallen nature of humankind—that try as you might, you can't avoid hurting someone nor can you avoid cowardice — there's a center of cowardice in each person's nature. But it also struck me that these people are trying, they are "squaring their shoulders," like the old woman in "It Had Wings," to receive an inkling of the transcendent, to be heroic. They are trying. So it is at once a very sad and a very hopeful view of human nature.

Yes. For me, the heroes are the people who get up every day and try. We are all going to be dead in fifty or sixty years, anyway. And what we leave behind is the legacy of struggling and the legacy of good and honest work. And also the legacy of love. I'm imagining our living our own lives from our funerals backward. I'm imagining a funeral which is an enormous traffic jam and a joyful occasion because everybody is jockeying to tell wonderful stories about you, about charitable acts, and about lessons well taught.

That is a kind of quiet heroism.

Absolutely. The first story I ever published was called "Minor Heroism," and I think that phrase is a kind of leitmotif of my work. I mean heroism is partial, by nature of our compromised state. It may be minor compared to what needs to be done. And it's minor because we are all the victims of our own histories and cultures.

If you are going to live at the end of the Roman Empire, you want to be in downtown Rome. You don't want to be out in some dusty outskirt. You want to be there when the torches come through town. And I'm glad to be aware in the middle of it. And I want to tell the story of it. And inevitably, telling the story of it is colored by having grown up in the church. Which means trying to emulate, not the wrathful, short-tempered Father/God of the Old Testament, but the image of Christ, a god-man of unearthly sweetness. He says that by honoring our own humanity and by treating each other ethically, we can achieve whatever aspects of heaven can be found in this fallen, suffering world. And it's as valid a way of proceeding as any way I've seen. It certainly beats the Wharton School of Business graduates who claim the more money you make, and the faster you make it, the more important and powerful you are.

The one who dies with the most toys wins.

Exactly. That's why I've opted for teaching—and teaching part-time—so I could write. Teaching is a kind of discipleship, it's a kind of mission. And the wonderful thing about being overtaken by notoriety and finally by some money at the ripe old age of forty-two is I have a new Ford station wagon which I love.

It has a great stereo.

For gospel, honey. But I've kept my expectations roughly where they were. Which means that I can go on writing for as long as I like, and in a manner I approve of. Amen. There may be one more residual benefit of having sat through all those sermons and that is precisely the belief in the possibility of a soul. And by that I don't mean a dove-shaped, membranous figure of . . .

Casper, the Friendly Ghost?

That's right [laughter] . . . that will fly up when your blood ceases to flow and your heart ceases to beat. But I mean that all of us are potentially more than the sum of our parts—we are more than our smartness, more than our emotions, more than our social conditioning, more than our class attitudes and racial outlook. We are all capable of becoming a story that's larger than ourselves if we can find a way to include more people than ourselves. And the paradox is that for a serious novelist or short story writer, this means finding more people within yourself.

Yes, I've heard writers speak of that phenomenon, sometimes as a village of people within.

And my village is called Falls because I understand that the Fall actually happened. That we are all sinners in some way. I mean, that we are separated from a kind of completion. So we must complete each other. That, and love, and the subject of time really constitute the basic message of all imaginative poetry and prose. Freud's concepts of Love and Work. Auden's "Love each other and die."

The Fall and the subject of time. T. S. Eliot, William Faulkner . . .

Yeah, good company. The fact of mortality and the fact of community. And that's in some ways, very simply stated, Christ's message. We know that He is an actual historical figure because His name is on the records. And the reason people are drawn to His message after two thousand years is because that message has a kind of personal validity when it's practiced in its pure form. It can give people a tremendous sense of power and control over their lives, a tremendous gratitude about the presence of other people in their lives.

An acceptance of suffering, a gratitude for community.

Absolutely. And so, for that reason, I am glad to have been "churched." Every novelist wants to experience every institution—I've been to Kiwanis Club meetings, Rotary meetings, fortune tellers, you know, dermatologists . . .

Psychiatrists.

Pyschiatrists. I've even done psychiatrists [laughter] . . . porn theaters, turkey farms . . . I want to experience everything that anybody can experience by going someplace. And seeing something. And, if only for that reason, I'm thankful I grew up in the church.

Your experiences being "churched" must be quite useful in your next novel.

The book I am working on, and will be for some years, is called *The Erotic History of a Southern Baptist Church.* It derives in part from the recognition that erotic transcendence and spiritual transcendence frequently come from the same place.

Sex and spirit, erotic passion and spiritual passion, are rooted in the same psychic territory.

That's right. The similarity first struck me when I was about ten or eleven years old. I had pedaled my green Schwinn to a tent meeting. This was a white evangelical revival, directed by a very sexy guy named T. L. Lowery. He looked like Elvis's youngish father. He was a big guy with big arms and big shoulders and a big jaw and a lot of hair, greaser hair—which he would always sweep back over his right ear. And the women and men were literally rolling around in the sawdust to the upbeat tempo of the organ and bebop piano, and I noticed they were wet around their mid-sections. It was my first indication that the overflowing spirit overflowed in strange and mysterious places. And then slowly, in my own incredibly salacious eleven-year-old imagination, I began to conceive a whole new reality. You could say I learned the facts of life by looking at people in tent revivals. So that the visitation of the spirit and the welling up of a sort of sensual overload came together for me at that moment. Then the next week, our very handsome young Presbyterian preacher named the Reverend Brooks preached a sermon. It was very warm and there was no air conditioning. He took off his jacket and, still preaching, began rolling up his sleeves. I

could feel a kind of new level of attention spiral from the congregation—from the men and the women—as he folded back his
starched white sleeves and showed us his beautiful pale arm with
his powder blue veins and an inch or two of magnificant pure white
biceps. And later, I heard an old lady in the churchyard saying,
"You know, didn't the Lord give the young Reverend Brooks a
beautiful voice with which to address us? And didn't the Lord give
the young Reverend Brooks a beautiful appearance? And, oh, didn't
the Lord give the Reverend Brooks beautiful, beautiful, pale arms?"
And I thought, uh-hum, something's going on here. So what I'm
trying to do is use this as a kind of crux, a cross, if you will.

How will that work?

I'm trying to use this as the center of a history of a very small
congregation outside Falls, North Carolina, and trace the history of
the church from the 1880s to the 1970s by following this crosscurrent—this erotic crosscurrent—and by following the history of
the American experiment or the American psyche as it is reflected
in the attitudes toward race, money, success, and community that
are evinced over almost a hundred years by this one little church.

This will be good.

Here's hoping. One way of looking at this is to imagine that at
every moment in history, there's a search committee looking for a
preacher. And what they want in a preacher is everything they
want for themselves at this moment. I mean, Christ gave Himself
to be an endless example of what we want and what we aspire to.
He is traditionally portrayed as handsome, yet rough-hewn, and
possessed of a tremendous tenderness that we all long for and find
so seldom in our lives. But by tracing the history of what this
church wants in its preacher decade after decade and conversely
showing what they get instead, I have an opportunity to play
expectation against reality. That is a wonderful canvas. Also, the
church in this novel ends as a television ministry. So our chronicle
goes from the church's first preacher who is a naturalist (he presses
ferns, knows all the birds, and leads expeditions of children from
the church through the woodlands which are spectacular and pris-
teen and beautiful in the 1880s) to a television station striding the
parking lot on the same location. And, at the end, a businessman is
in control of the church, just as businessmen, alas for our ethics and

aesthetics, now control this country. It's a comedy of foiled expectations, of vanity and overreaching. But I do not want it to be simply
a send-up of religion or of the church. I want a poem to the spirit of
religion's best: "In the beginning was the Word, and the Word was
with God, and the Word was God."

You use every kind of lyrical, extravagant language in Confederate Widow *to such powerful effect. It's like an opera on a grand
scale.*

I'm all for experiencing as much music in the service of a story as
one can concoct, naturally. But music must be bent to the service of
the story. But when people tell me they have memorized passages
from my books, I'm thrilled.

*That is a wonderful tribute to your achievement and to the
potentialities of language itself.*

That richness of language remembers and resonates, recalls
greater works, like the King James Bible. And not only does it recall
for us, it makes the writer's work lasting and memorable as a work
of art. And we want—all writers want—to be remembered, because
if you're remembered, then you are useful.

Bless your heart, Allan. You are useful.

But to have written a book that people are holding on to and perhaps to have written two books like that—I hope I've already justified my lifetime. And now the rest is pure bonus for me. Pure grace.

*Reynolds Price has suggested that the novel (more so than
tragedy, or the epic poem), comes closer than anything else to
being a truly Judeo-Christian form. He proposes that, in its
attempt to elicit understanding of and mercy for all creation, the
novel ultimately evokes and teaches mercy in us, even forgiveness
for all creation. Is there, to you, a particular form—perhaps the
"epic novel"—that seems to be able to hold and reveal reality to
you most completely or truthfully?*

There are those who believe that the sermon is the primary literary form of American life. The offhand welcoming joke, the quick
escalating to the statement of a brimstone problem, a cry about
what must be done to avert pure-tee damnation, a suggestion of
redemption and its necessary three steps, a rising of steam leading
toward a final hymn that offers "the call" to publicly admit your
guilt and the buoyant send-off that pushes you out into the world,

if not renewed, then rescared and revivified. From Cotton Mather's surreal visions of hell to Hawthorne's allegories of American guilt, to Whitman's promissory hymns, to Twain's biting moralizing satires, to Dreiser's Ashcan School of Social Darwinism, to Faulkner's postlapsarian South, to Flannery O'Connor's godless modernity vs. ancient mysteries, to Marilynne Robinson's watery, postmodern version of heaven and of hell in *Housekeeping*, we feel the sermon's lash and balm in every great American book.

And now for you?

The sermon remains the form I hold up to experience—the Sermon hidden in the Story. And when *The New Republic* compared chapters of my novel to Christ's open-ended, life-soaked parables, some still small voice in me went, "Me? Me, with my own tent and pulpit? Yeah! Now we're cooking!" My pulpit stands wedged between the covers of each book. As the heirs of those persecuted for religious beliefs, we Americans continually seek not just freedom of religion, but freedom from religion. Freedom from religious persecution.

Which one is better off, in the end, do you think—the writer or the preacher—in carving some sense of meaning or justification for his or her work, in being remembered?

I just received an opinion survey that asked: "Do you believe in an afterlife?" I was all set to check "no" when I changed my mind. Instead, I wrote, "Yes, I believe in the afterlife called literature." Literature, rolling on forever in its Eden, constitutes my own ideal kind of perpetual tent-preacher's route; and you get to keep the circus tent. To welcome others into your stories years after you're just so much fog on a coffin lid, that surely constitutes as sweet a state of grace as I can imagine. The moral of all my stories? The moral weight and transforming joy of the Story itself. To the holiness of "Once upon a time," yes, I say daily, "Amen, amen." †

Selected References

INTRODUCTION

Brinkmeyer, Robert H. *The Art and Vision of Flannery O'Connor.* Baton Rouge: Louisiana State University Press, 1989.

———. *Three Catholic Writers of the Modern South.* Jackson: University Press of Mississippi, 1985.

Hobson, Fred. *The Southern Writer in the Postmodern World.* Athens: The University of Georgia Press, 1991.

Kazin, Alfred. "William Faulkner and Religion: Determinism, Compassion, and the God of Defeat." In *Faulkner and Religion.* Faulkner and Yoknapatawpha Conference, no. 14, edited by Doreen Fowler and Ann J. Abadie, 3–20. Jackson: University Press of Mississippi, 1991.

Moore, Robert R. "Literature and Religion." In *Encyclopedia of Southern Culture,* edited by Charles Reagan Wilson and William Ferris, 1291. Chapel Hill: University of North Carolina Press, 1989.

O'Connor, Flannery. *The Habit of Being.* Edited by Sally Fitzgerald. New York: Farrar, Straus, Giroux, 1979.

———. *Mystery and Manners: Occasional Prose.* Selected and edited by Sally and Robert Fitzgerald. New York: Farrar, Straus and Giroux, 1961.

———. *Wise Blood.* New York: Farrar, Straus and Giroux, 1962.

Rubin, Jr., Louis D. *A Gallery of Southerners.* Baton Rouge: Louisiana State University Press, 1982.

Wilson, Charles Reagan. "Faulkner and the Southern Religious Culture." In *Faulkner and Religion.* Faulkner and Yoknapatawpha Conference, no. 14, edited by Doreen Fowler and Ann J. Abadie, 21–42. Jackson: University Press of Mississippi, 1991.

Wyatt-Brown, Bertram. *The House of Percy: Honor, Mind, and Melancholy in a Southern Family.* Forthcoming from Oxford University Press.

TEXT

Alderson, Laura. "Doris Betts: An Interview." *Poets and Writers Magazine* 20 (January/February 1992): 36–44.

Adams, Phoebe-Lou. "White People." Review of *White People* by Allan Gurganus. *The Atlantic Monthly*, February, 1991, 92.

Betts, Doris. "The Fingerprint of Style." In *Voicelust: Eight Contemporary Fiction Writers on Style*, edited by Allen Wier and Don Hendrie, Jr., 7–23. Lincoln: University of Nebraska Press, 1985.

Brooks, Cleanth. *The Hidden God: Studies in Hemingway, Faulkner, Yeats, Eliot, and Warren.* New Haven: Yale University Press, 1963.

Coles, Robert. *Flannery O'Connor's South.* Baton Rouge: Louisiana State University Press, 1980.

Corn, Alfred, ed. *Incarnation: Contemporary Writers on the New Testament.* New York: Penguin Books, 1990.

Crews, Harry. *A Childhood: The Biography of a Place.* New York: Quill, 1983.

———. Interview by Gary Hawkins, March 1990. Unpublished.

Davis, Thulani. "Southern Women Stake Their Claim." *Voice Literary Supplement* (February 1986): 11.

Hill, Dorothy Combs. *Lee Smith.* Twayne State Author Series. Edited by Frank Day. New York: Twayne Publishers, 1992.

Hooks, Bell and Cornell West. *Breaking Bread: Insurgent Black Intellectual Life.* Boston: South End Press, 1991.

Kimball, Sue Laslie. "The 'Gentle Insurrections' of Doris Betts's Short Fiction." In *The Home Truths of Doris Betts with a Bibliography*, edited by Sue Laslie Kimball and Lynn Veach Sadler, 58–65. Fayetteville, North Carolina: Methodist College Press, 1992.

Lanker, Brian. *I Dream A World: Portraits of Black Women Who Changed America. Photographs and Interviews.* Edited by Barbara Summers. New York: Stewart, Tabori, and Chang, 1989.

McMillan, Terry, ed. *Breaking Ice: An Anthology of Contemporary African-American Fiction.* New York: Penguin Books, 1990.

Mills, Jerry Leath. "Down and Out." Review of *The Knockout Artist*, by Harry Crews. *The Independent*, April 27, 1989, 35.

———. "Harry Crews Is Back—and Bleak." Review of *Body* by Harry Crews. *Book World: The News and Observer*, October 7, 1990, 4J.

Minor, Valerie. "Carolina Dreamin.'" Review of *Let the Dead Bury Their Dead and Other Stories* by Randall Kenan. *The Nation*, July 6, 1992, 28–29.

Pearson, Michael. "Stories to Ease the Tension: Clyde Edgerton's Fiction." *The Hollins Critic* 27 (October 1990): 2–8.

Price, Reynolds. *A Palpable God: Thirty Stories Translated from the Bible With an Essay on the Origins and Life of Narrative.* San Francisco: North Point Press, 1985.

———. "Dodging Apples." *South Atlantic Quarterly* 71 (Winter 1972): 1–15.

Smith, Lee. Personal communication to Dorothy Hill, July 1989.

Winegardner, Mark. "Dead People Down South." Review of *In Memory of Junior,* by Clyde Edgerton. *Cleveland Free Times.* November 18, 1992, 20.

Index

408   LIBRARY OF CONGRESS CATALOGING-IN-PUBLICATION DATA

The Christ-haunted landscape : faith and doubt in southern fiction / by Susan Ketchin.
    p.   cm.
Includes bibliographical references.
ISBN 0-87805-669-6.—ISBN 0-87805-670-X (pbk.)
    1. American fiction—Southern States—History and criticism.   2. American fiction—
Christian authors—History and criticism.   3. American fiction—20th century—History
and criticism.   4. Christianity—Southern States—History—20th century.   5. Christian
fiction, American—History and criticism.   6. Belief and doubt in literature.   7. Religion
and literature.   8. Faith in literature.   I. Ketchin, Susan.
PS261.C47   1994
813'.5409382—dc20
                                                                                        93-30875
                                                                                        CIP